Science fiction's favourite creation, the monster from outer space, is presented here in ten of the best modern SF classics by a range of fine authors. One of mankind's oldest wishes – to communicate with beings other than fellow humans – has found a new refinement in science fiction, and this collection explores that fascinating concept with insight, imagination and originality.

D1425989

edited by Anthony Cheetham

Bug-Eyed Monsters

Ten SF Stories

Panther

Granada Publishing Limited
Published in 1974 by Panther Books Ltd
Frogmore, St Albans, Herts AL2 2NF

First published in Great Britain by Sidgwick & Jackson 1972
The stories in this collection are reprinted by
arrangement with the authors and the authors'
representatives. The year of first publication
is given in the Contents list.
Made and printed in Great Britain by
Richard Clay (The Chaucer Press) Ltd
Bungay, Suffolk
Set in Linotype Times

Contents

Introduction
What is a Vug?

'Help! We are surrounded by Vugs!' This deathless line, from a slightly below par novel by one of science fiction's most talented writers, reveals clearly the weakest chink in the Bug-Eyed Monster's armour. However sinister, malevolent and talented he may be, he is more liable to provoke in the reader a snigger of derision than a shiver of fear.

In one respect this is the fault of H. G. Wells. His octopoid martians in THE WAR OF THE WORLDS spawned the archetype, for later generations, of the overgrown nasties equipped with tentacles, carapaces, beaks, antennae, multi-faceted eyes, misanthropy, and halitosis, whose colonial ambitions centred on Sol III.

Capitalizing on our inherited dislike of bugs and reptiles, their creators generally failed to take advantage of the truly fascinating avenues of speculation opened up by the realization that alien life forms must exist somewhere in the universe.

Given the same chain of chemical accidents that created life on earth, it is possible, even likely, that these forms would resemble man. But given a different chain of accidents, it is almost inconceivable that the native species would bear any resemblance at all to any creature living on earth, from homo sapiens to a cockroach. This collection is therefore devoted to some of the stories that have most successfully cast off their imaginative links with mundane creatures and come up with something truly alien.

The range of the selections is as diverse as possible. A natural starting point is Howard Koch's radio adaptation of Wells's WAR OF THE WORLDS, which was so realistically done that thousands of listeners were convinced a real invasion was underway. The alien in Frederic Brown's ARENA is also cast as man's natural enemy, but a galactic police force is luckily on hand to prevent an outbreak of total war. William Tenn's DESERTER again looks at the man/alien conflict, but adds a new twist to remind us that appearances aren't everything.

In Bertram Chandler's novella it is man who is cast as the alien – by monsters he has himself unwittingly created. James

Blish's SURFACE TENSION predicates a monster invisible to the naked eye in a world where man has adapted to his environment, rather than vice-versa.

The possibilities of symbiotic cooperation as an alternative to conflict are explored lightheartedly in Philip José Farmer's MOTHER and with serious ecological intent in Frank Herbert's GREENSLAVES. Damon Knight's STRANGER STATION warns that the Monster may be so alien that cooperation with man may be impossible, despite goodwill on both sides.

The last word is reserved for Terry Carr's DANCE OF THE CHANGER AND THREE which describes a world so totally alien that no communication with man would be possible or meaningful.

Finally, a word of apology to the hard core of s.f. fans who may have been beguiled by the title of this anthology into supposing that it is a nostalgic tribute to the vugs and other grotesques of the space-westerns published in magazines during the thirties and forties, rather than a cross-section of more recent classics, some of which they are already familiar with. Nevertheless I hope the present selection will go some way to updating and restoring the image of the Bug-Eyed Monster.

October 1972

Anthony Cheetham

Invasion From Mars
by Howard Koch

NARRATOR: We know now that in the early years of the twentieth century this world was being watched closely by intelligences greater than man's and yet as mortal as his own. We know now that as human beings busied themselves about their various concerns they were scrutinized and studied, perhaps almost as narrowly as a man with a microscope might scrutinize the transient creatures that swarm and multiply in a drop of water. With infinite complacence people went to and fro over the earth about their little affairs, serene in the assurance of their dominion over this small spinning fragment of solar driftwood which by chance or design man has inherited out of the dark mystery of Time and Space. Yet across an immense ethereal gulf, minds that are to our minds as ours are to the beasts in the jungle, intellects vast, cool, and unsympathetic, regarded this earth with envious eyes and slowly and surely drew their plans against us. In the thirty-ninth year of the twentieth century came the great disillusionment.

It was near the end of October. Business was better. The war scare was over. More men were back at work. Sales were picking up. On this particular evening, October 30, the Crossley service estimated that thirty-two million people were listening in on radios.

ANNOUNCER CUE: ... for the next twenty-four hours not much change in temperature. A slight atmospheric disturbance of undetermined origin is reported over Nova Scotia, causing a low-pressure area to move down rather rapidly over the northeastern states, bringing a forecast of rain, accompanied by winds of light gale force. Maximum temperature 66; minimum 48. This weather report comes to you from the Government Weather Bureau.

ANNOUNCER TWO: We now take you to the Meridian Room in the Hotel Park Plaza in downtown New York, where you will be entertained by the music of Ramon Raquello and his orchestra.

(*Spanish theme song . . . Fades*)

ANNOUNCER THREE: Good evening, ladies and gentlemen. From the Meridian Room in the Park Plaza in New York City, we bring you the music of Ramon Raquello and his orchestra. With a touch of the Spanish, Ramon Raquello leads off with 'La Cumparsita.'

(*Piece starts playing*)

ANNOUNCER TWO: Ladies and gentlemen, we interrupt our program of dance music to bring you a special bulletin from the Intercontinental Radio News. At twenty minutes before eight, central time, Professor Farrell of the Mount Jennings Observatory, Chicago, Illinois, reports observing several explosions of incandescent gas, occurring at regular intervals on the planet Mars.

The spectroscope indicates the gas to be hydrogen and moving toward the earth with enormous velocity. Professor Pierson of the Observatory at Princeton confirms Farrell's observation, and describes the phenomenon as (quote) like a jet of blue flame shot from a gun (unquote). We now return you to the music of Ramon Raquello, playing for you in the Meridian Room of the Park Plaza Hotel, situated in downtown New York.

(*Music plays for a few moments until piece ends . . . Sound of applause*)

Now a tune that never loses favor, the ever-popular 'Star Dust.' Ramon Raquello and his orchestra . . .

(*Music*)

ANNOUNCER TWO: Ladies and gentlemen, following on the news given in our bulletin a moment ago, the Government Meteorological Bureau has requested the large observatories of the country to keep an astronomical watch on any other disturbances occurring on the planet Mars. Due to the unusual nature of this occurrence, we have arranged an interview with the noted astronomer, Professor Pierson, who will give us his views on this event. In a few moments we will take you to the Princeton Observatory at Princeton, New Jersey. We return you until then to the music of Ramon Raquello and his orchestra.

(*Music*)

ANNOUNCER TWO: We are ready now to take you to the Princeton Observatory at Princeton, where Carl Phillips, our commentator, will interview Professor Richard Pierson, famous astronomer. We take you now to Princeton, New Jersey.

(*Echo chamber*)

PHILLIPS: Good evening, ladies and gentlemen. This is Carl Phillips, speaking to you from the observatory at Princeton. I am standing in a large semicircular room, pitch-black except for an oblong split in the ceiling. Through this opening I can see a sprinkling of stars that cast a kind of frosty glow over the intricate mechanism of the huge telescope. The ticking sound you hear is the vibration of the clockwork. Professor Pierson stands directly above me on a small platform, peering through the giant lens. I ask you to be patient, ladies and gentlemen, during any delay that may arise during our interview. Beside his ceaseless watch of the heavens, Professor Pierson may be interrupted by telephone or other communications. During this period he is in constant touch with the astronomical centers of the world – Professor, may I begin our questions?

PIERSON: At any time, Mr. Phillips.

PHILLIPS: Professor, would you please tell our radio audience exactly what you see as you observe the planet Mars through your telescope?

PIERSON: Nothing unusual at the moment, Mr. Phillips. A red disk swimming in a blue sea. Transverse stripes across the disk. Quite distinct now because Mars happens to be at the point nearest the earth – in opposition, as we call it.

PHILLIPS: In your opinion, what do these transverse stripes signify, Professor Pierson?

PIERSON: Not canals, I can assure you, Mr. Phillips, although that's the popular conjecture of those who imagine Mars to be inhabited. From a scientific viewpoint the stripes are merely the result of atmospheric conditions peculiar to the planet.

11

PHILLIPS: Then you're quite convinced as a scientist that living intelligence as we know it does not exist on Mars?

PIERSON: I should say the chances against it are a thousand to one.

PHILLIPS: And yet how do you account for these gas eruptions occurring on the surface of the planet at regular intervals?

PIERSON: Mr. Phillips, I cannot account for it.

PHILLIPS: By the way, Professor, for the benefit of our listeners, how far is Mars from the earth?

PIERSON: Approximately forty million miles.

PHILLIPS: Well, that seems a safe enough distance – Just a moment, ladies and gentlemen, someone has just handed Professor Pierson a message. While he reads it, let me remind you we are speaking to you from the observatory in Princeton, New Jersey, where we are interviewing the world-famous astronomer, Professor Pierson. ... One moment, please. Professor Pierson has passed me a message which he had just received. Professor, may I read the message to the listening audience?

PIERSON: Certainly, Mr. Phillips.

PHILLIPS: Ladies and gentlemen, I shall read you a wire addressed to Professor Pierson from Dr. Gray of the National History Museum, New York. '9:15 p.m. eastern standard time. Seismograph registered shock of almost earthquake intensity within a radius of twenty miles of Princeton. Please investigate. Signed, Lloyd Gray, Chief of Astronomical Division.' Professor Pierson, could this occurrence possibly have something to do with the disturbances observed on the planet Mars?

PIERSON: Hardly, Mr. Phillips. This is probably a meteorite of unusual size and its arrival at this particular time is merely a coincidence. However, we shall conduct a search, as soon as daylight permits.

PHILLIPS: Thank you, Professor. Ladies and gentlemen, for the past ten minutes we've been speaking to you from the observatory at Princeton, bringing you a special interview with Professor Pierson, noted astronomer. This is Carl Phillips speaking. We now return you to our New York studio.

(Fade in piano playing)

ANNOUNCER TWO: Ladies and gentlemen, here is the latest bulletin from the Intercontinental Radio News, Toronto, Canada: Professor Morse of Macmillan University reports observing a total of three explosions on the planet Mars, between the hours of 7:45 p.m. and 9:20 p.m., eastern standard time. This confirms earlier reports received from American observatories. Now, nearer home, comes a special announcement from Trenton, New Jersey. It is reported that at 8:50 p.m. a huge, flaming object, believed to be a meteorite, fell on a farm in the neighborhood of Grovers Mill, New Jersey, twenty-two miles from Trenton. The flash in the sky was visible within a radius of several hundred miles and the noise of the impact was heard as far north as Elizabeth.

We have dispatched a special mobile unit to the scene, and will have our commentator, Mr. Phillips, give you a word description as soon as he can reach there from Princeton. In the meantime, we take you to the Hotel Martinet in Brooklyn, where Bobby Millette and his orchestra are offering a program of dance music.

(Swing band for 20 seconds ... Then cut)

ANNOUNCER TWO: We take you now to Grovers Mill, New Jersey.

(Crowd noises ... Police sirens)

PHILLIPS: Ladies and gentlemen, this is Carl Phillips again, at the Wilmuth farm, Grovers Mill, New Jersey. Professor Pierson and myself made the 11 miles from Princeton in ten minutes. Well, I – I hardly know where to begin, to paint for you a word picture of the strange scene before my eyes, like something out of a modern Arabian Nights. Well, I just got here. I haven't had a chance to look around yet. I guess that's it. Yes, I guess that's the – thing, directly in front of me, half buried in a vast pit. Must have struck with terrific force. The ground is covered with splinters of a tree it must have struck on its way down. What I can see of the – object itself doesn't look very much like a meteor, at least not the meteors I've seen. It looks more like a huge cylinder. It has a diameter of – what would you say, Professor Pierson?

13

PIERSON (*off*): About thirty yards.

PHILLIPS: About thirty yards – The metal on the sheath is – well, I've never seen anything like it. The color is sort of yellowish-white. Curious spectators now are pressing close to the object in spite of the efforts of the police to keep them back. They're getting in front of my line of vision. Would you mind standing on one side, please?

POLICEMAN: One side, there, one side.

PHILLIPS: While the policemen are pushing the crowd back, here's Mr. Wilmuth, owner of the farm here. He may have some interesting facts to add. Mr. Wilmuth, would you please tell the radio audience as much as you remember of this rather unusual visitor that dropped in your backyard? Step closer please. Ladies and gentlemen, this is Mr. Wilmuth.

WILMUTH: I was listenin' to the radio —

PHILLIPS: Closer and louder, please.

WILMUTH: Pardon me!

PHILLIPS: Louder, please, and closer.

WILMUTH: Yes, sir – while I was listening to the radio and kinda drowsin', that Professor fellow was talkin' about Mars, so I was half dozin' and half —

PHILLIPS: Yes, yes, Mr. Wilmuth. And then what happened?

WILMUTH: As I was sayin', I was listenin' to the radio kinda halfways —

PHILLIPS: Yes, Mr. Wilmuth, and then you saw something?

WILMUTH: Not first off. I heard something.

PHILLIPS: And what did you hear?

WILMUTH: A hissing sound. Like this: sssssssss – kinda like a fourt' of July rocket.

PHILLIPS: Then what?

WILMUTH: Turned my head out the window and would have swore I was to sleep and dreamin'.

PHILLIPS: Yes?

WILMUTH: I seen a kinda greenish streak and then zingo! Somethin' smacked the ground. Knocked me clear out of my chair!

PHILLIPS: Well, were you frightened, Mr. Wilmuth?

WILMUTH: Well, I – I ain't quite sure. I reckon I – I was kinda riled.

PHILLIPS: Thank you, Mr. Wilmuth. Thank you.

WILMUTH: Want me to tell you some more?

PHILLIPS: No – that's quite all right, that's plenty – Ladies and gentlemen, you've just heard Mr. Wilmuth, owner of the farm where this thing has fallen. I wish I could convey the atmosphere – the background of this – fantastic scene. Hundreds of cars are parked in a field in back of us. Police are trying to rope off the roadway leading into the farm. But it's no use. They're breaking right through. Their headlights throw an enormous spot on the pit where the object's half-buried. Some of the more daring souls are venturing near the edge. Their silhouettes stand out against the metal sheen.

(*Faint humming sound*)

One man wants to touch the thing – he's having an argument with a policeman. The policeman wins — Now, ladies and gentlemen, there's something I haven't mentioned in all this excitement, but it's becoming more distinct. Perhaps you've caught it already on your radio. Listen (*Long pause*) ... Do you hear it? It's a curious humming sound that seems to come from inside the object. I'll move the microphone nearer. Here. (*Pause*) Now we're not more than twenty-five feet away. Can you hear it now? Oh, Professor Pierson!

PIERSON: Yes, Mr. Phillips?

PHILLIPS: Can you tell us the meaning of that scraping noise inside the thing?

PIERSON: Possibly the unequal cooling of its surface.

PHILLIPS: Do you still think it's a meteor, Professor?

PIERSON: I don't know what to think. The metal casing is definitely extra-terrestrial – not found on this earth. Friction with the earth's atmosphere usually tears holes in a meteorite. This thing is smooth and, as you can see, of cylindrical shape.

PHILLIPS: Just a minute! Something's happening! Ladies and gentlemen, this is terrific! This end of the thing is beginning to flake off! The top is beginning to rotate like a screw! The thing must be hollow!

VOICES: She's a movin'!

Look, the darn thing's unscrewing!

Keep back, there! Keep back, I tell you.

Maybe there's men in it trying to escape!

It's red-hot, they'll burn to a cinder!

Keep back there! Keep those idiots back!

(Suddenly the clanking sound of a huge piece of falling metal)

VOICES: She's off! The top's loose!

Look out there! Stand back!

PHILLIPS: Ladies and gentlemen, this is the most terrifying thing I have ever witnessed — Wait a minute! Someone's crawling out of the hollow top. Someone or – something. I can see peering out of that black hole two luminous disks – are they eyes? It might be a face. It might be —

(Shout of awe from the crowd)

Good heavens, something's wriggling out of the shadow like a gray snake. Now it's another one, and another. They look like tentacles to me. There, I can see the thing's body. It's large as a bear and glistens like wet leather. But that face. It – it's indescribable. I can hardly force myself to keep looking at it. The eyes are black and gleam like a serpent. The mouth is V-shaped with saliva dripping from its rimless lips that seem to quiver and pulsate. The monster or whatever it is can hardly move. It seems weighed down by – possibly gravity or something. The thing's raising up. The crowd falls back. They've seen enough. This is the most extraordinary experience. I can't find words – I'm pulling this microphone with me as I talk. I'll have to stop the description until I've taken a new position. Hold on, will you please, I'll be back in a minute.

(Fade into piano)

ANNOUNCER TWO: We are bringing you an eyewitness account of what's happening on the Wilmuth farm, Grovers Mill, New Jersey.

(More piano)

We now return you to Carl Phillips at Grovers Mill.

PHILLIPS: Ladies and gentlemen (Am I on?) – ladies and gentlemen, here I am, back of a stone wall that adjoins Mr. Wilmuth's garden. From here I get a sweep of the whole scene. I'll give you every detail as long as I can talk. As long as I can see. More state police have arrived. They're drawing up a cordon in front of the pit, about thirty of them. No need to push the crowd back now. They're willing to keep their distance. The captain is conferring with someone. We can't quite see who. Oh, yes, I believe it's Professor Pierson. Yes, it is. Now they've parted. The professor moves around one side, studying the object, while the captain and two policemen advance with something in their hands. I can see it now. It's a white handkerchief tied to a pole – a flag of truce. If those creatures know what that means – what anything means! ... *Wait!* Something's happening!

(*Hissing sound followed by a humming that increases in intensity*)

A humped shape is rising out of the pit. I can make out a small beam of light against a mirror. What's that? There's a jet of flame springing from that mirror, and it leaps right at the advancing men. It strikes them head on! Good Lord, they're turning into flame!

(*Screams and unearthly shrieks*)

Now the whole field's caught fire. (*Explosion*) The woods – the barns – the gas tanks of automobiles – it's spreading everywhere. It's coming this way. About twenty yards to my right —

(*Crash of microphone ... Then dead silence ...*)

ANNOUNCER TWO: Ladies and gentlemen, due to circumstances beyond our control, we are unable to continue the broadcast from Grovers Mill. Evidently there's some difficulty with our field transmission. However, we will return to that point at the earliest opportunity. In the meantime, we have a late bulletin from San Diego, California. Professor Indellkoffer, speaking at a dinner of the California Astronomical Society, expressed the opinion that the explosions on Mars are undoubtedly nothing more than severe volcanic disturbances on the surface of the planet. We continue now with our piano interlude.

(*Piano ... Then cut*)

Ladies and gentlemen, I have just been handed a message that came in from Grovers Mill by telephone. Just a moment. At least forty people, including six state troopers, lie dead in a field east of the village of Grovers Mill, their bodies burned and distorted beyond all possible recognition. The next voice you hear will be that of Brigadier General Montgomery Smith, commander of the State Militia at Trenton, New Jersey.

SMITH: I have been requested by the governor of New Jersey to place the counties of Mercer and Middlesex as far west as Princeton, and east to Jamesburg, under martial law. No one will be permitted to enter this area except by special pass issued by state or military authorities. Four companies of State Militia are proceeding from Trenton to Grovers Mill, and will aid in the evacuation of homes within the range of military operations. Thank you.

ANNOUNCER: You have just been listening to General Montgomery Smith commanding the State Militia at Trenton. In the meantime, further details of the catastrophe at Grovers Mill are coming in. The strange creatures, after unleashing their deadly assault, crawled back in their pit and made no attempt to prevent the efforts of the firemen to recover the bodies and extinguish the fire. Combined fire departments of Mercer County are fighting the flames which menace the entire countryside.

We have been unable to establish any contact with our mobile unit at Grovers Mill, but we hope to be able to return you there at the earliest possible moment. In the meantime we take you – uh, just one moment please.

(*Long pause ... Whisper*)

Ladies and gentlemen, I have just been informed that we have finally established communication with an eyewitness of the tragedy. Professor Pierson has been located at a farmhouse near Grovers Mill where he has established an emergency observation post. As a scientist, he will give you his explanation of the calamity. The next voice you hear will be that of Professor Pierson, brought to you by direct wire. Professor Pierson.

PIERSON: Of the creatures in the rocket cylinder at Grovers Mill, I can give you no authoritative information – either as to their nature, their origin, or their purposes here on earth. Of their destructive instruments I might venture some conjectural explanation. For want of a better term, I shall refer to the mysterious weapon as a heat-ray. It's all too evident that these creatures have scientific knowledge far in advance of our own. It is my guess that in some way they are able to generate an intense heat in a chamber of practically absolute nonconductivity. This intense heat they project in a parallel beam against any object they choose, by means of a polished parabolic mirror of unknown composition, much as the mirror of a lighthouse projects a beam of light. That is my conjecture of the origin of the heat-ray.

ANNOUNCER TWO: Thank you, Professor Pierson. Ladies and gentlemen, here is a bulletin from Trenton. It is a brief statement informing us that the charred body of Carl Phillips, the radio commentator, has been identified in a Trenton hospital. Now here's another bulletin from Washington, D.C.

Office of the director of the National Red Cross reports ten units of Red Cross emergency workers have been assigned to the headquarters of the State Militia stationed outside of Grovers Mill, New Jersey. Here's a bulletin from State Police, Princeton Junction: The fires at Grovers Mill and vicinity now under control. Scouts report all quiet in the pit, and no sign of life appearing from the mouth of the cylinder. And now, ladies and gentlemen, we have a special statement from Mr. Harry McDonald, vice-president in charge of operations.

McDONALD: We have received a request from the militia at Trenton to place at their disposal our entire broadcasting facilities. In view of the gravity of the situation, and believing that radio has a definite responsibility to serve in the public interest at all times, we are turning over our facilities to the State Militia at Trenton.

ANNOUNCER: We take you now to the field headquarters of the State Militia near Grovers Mill, New Jersey.

CAPTAIN: This is Captain Lansing of the Signal Corps, attached to the State Militia now engaged in military operations in the vicinity of Grovers Mill. Situation arising from the reported presence of certain individuals of unidentified nature is now under complete control.

The cylindrical object which lies in a pit directly below our position is surrounded on all sides by eight battalions of infantry, without heavy fieldpieces, but adequately armed with rifles and machine guns. All cause for alarm, if such cause ever existed, is now entirely unjustified. The things, whatever they are, do not even venture to poke their heads above the pit. I can see their hiding-place plainly in the glare of the searchlights here. With all their reported resources, these creatures can scarcely stand up against heavy machine-gun fire. Anyway, it's an interesting outing for the troops. I can make out their khaki uniforms, crossing back and forth in front of the lights. It looks almost like a real war. There appears to be some slight smoke in the woods bordering the Millstone River. Probably first started by campers. Well, we ought to see some action soon. One of the companies is deploying on the left flank. A quick thrust and it will all be over. Now wait a minute! I see something on top of the cylinder. No, it's nothing but a shadow. Now the troops are on the edge of the Wilmuth farm. Seven thousand armed men closing in on an old metal tube. Wait, that wasn't a shadow! It's something moving – solid metal – kind of a shieldlike affair rising up out of the cylinder – It's going higher and higher. Why, it's standing on legs – actually rearing up on a sort of metal framework. Now it's reaching above the trees and the searchlights are on it! Hold on!

(*Silence*)

ANNOUNCER TWO: Ladies and gentlemen, I have a grave announcement to make. Incredible as it may seem, both the observations of science and the evidence of our eyes lead to the inescapable assumption that those strange beings who landed in the Jersey farmlands tonight are the vanguard of an invading army from the planet Mars. The battle which took place tonight at Grovers Mill has ended in one of the most startling defeats ever suffered by an army in modern times; seven thousand men armed with rifles and machine guns pitted against a single fighting machine of the invaders from Mars. One hundred and twenty known survivors. The rest strewn over the battle area from Grovers Mill to Plainsboro crushed and trampled to death under the metal feet of the monster, or burned to cinders by its heat-ray. The monster is now in control of the middle section of New Jersey and has effectively cut the state through its center. Communication lines are down from Pennsylvania to the Atlantic Ocean. Railroad tracks are torn and service from New York to Philadelphia discontinued except routing some of the trains through Allentown and Phoenixville. Highways to the north, south, and west are clogged with frantic human traffic. Police and army reserves are unable to control the mad flight. By morning the fugitives will have swelled Philadelphia, Camden, and Trenton, it is estimated, to twice their normal population.

At this time martial law prevails throughout New Jersey and eastern Pennsylvania. We take you now to Washington for a special broadcast on the National Emergency ... The Secretary of the Interior —

SECRETARY: Citizens of the nation: I shall not try to conceal the gravity of the situation that confronts the country, nor the concern of your government in protecting the lives and property of its people. However, I wish to impress upon you – private citizens and public officials, all of you – the urgent need of calm and resourceful action. Fortunately, this formidable enemy is still confined to a comparatively small area, and we may place our faith in the military forces to keep them there. In the meantime placing our faith in God we must continue the performance of our duties each and every one of us, so that we may confront this destructive adversary with a nation united, courageous, and consecrated to the preservation of human supremacy on this earth. I thank you.

ANNOUNCER: You have just heard the Secretary of the Interior speaking from Washington. Bulletins too numerous to read are piling up in the studio here. We are informed that the central portion of New Jersey is blacked out from radio communication due to the effect of the heat-ray upon power lines and electrical equipment. Here is a special bulletin from New York. Cables received from English, French, German scientific bodies offering assistance. Astronomers report continued gas outbursts at regular intervals on planet Mars. Majority voice opinion that enemy will be reinforced by additional rocket machines. Attempts made to locate Professor Pierson of Princeton, who has observed Martians at close range. It is feared he was lost in recent battle. Langham Field, Virginia: Scouting planes report three Martian machines visible above treetops, moving north toward Somerville with population fleeing ahead of them. Heat-ray not in use; although advancing at express-train speed, invaders pick their way carefully. They seem to be making conscious effort to avoid destruction of cities and countryside. However, they stop to uproot power lines, bridges, and railroad tracks. Their apparent objective is to crush resistance, paralyze communication, and disorganize human society.

Here is a bulletin from Basking Ridge, New Jersey: Coon hunters have stumbled on a second cylinder similar to the first embedded in the great swamp twenty miles south of Morristown. U.S. Army fieldpieces are proceeding from Newark to blow up second invading unit before cylinder can be opened and the fighting machine rigged. They are taking up position in the foothills of Watchung Mountains. Another bulletin from Langham Field, Virginia: Scouting planes report enemy machines, now three in number, increasing speed northward kicking over houses and trees in their evident haste to form a conjunction with their allies south of Morristown. Machines also sighted by telephone operator east of Middlesex within ten miles of Plainfield. Here's a bulletin from Winston Field, Long Island: Fleet of army bombers carrying heavy explosives flying north in pursuit of enemy. Scouting planes act as guides. They keep speeding enemy in sight. Just a moment, please. Ladies and gentlemen, we've run special wires to the artillery line in adjacent villages to give you direct reports in the zone of the advancing enemy. First we take you to the battery of the 22nd Field Artillery, located in the Watchung Mountains.

OFFICER: Range thirty-two meters.
GUNNER: Thirty-two meters.
OFFICER: Projection, thirty-nine degrees.
GUNNER: Thirty-nine degrees.
OFFICER: Fire!

(*Boom of heavy gun ... Pause*)
OBSERVER: One hundred and forty yards to the right, sir.
OFFICER: Shift range – thirty-one meters.
GUNNER: Thirty-one meters.
OFFICER: Projection – thirty-seven degrees.
GUNNER: Thirty-seven degrees.
OFFICER: Fire!

(*Boom of heavy gun ... Pause*)
OBSERVER: A hit, sir! We got the tripod of one of them.

22

They've stopped. The others are trying to repair it.

OFFICER: Quick, get the range! Shift thirty meters.

GUNNER: Thirty meters.

OFFICER: Projection – twenty-seven degrees.

GUNNER: Twenty-seven degrees.

OFFICER: Fire!

(*Boom of heavy gun ... Pause*)

OBSERVER: Can't see the shell land, sir. They're letting off a smoke.

OFFICER: What is it?

OBSERVER: A black smoke, sir. Moving this way. Lying close to the ground. It's moving fast.

OFFICER: Put on gas masks. (*Pause*) Get ready to fire. Shift to twenty-four meters.

GUNNER: Twenty-four meters.

OFFICER: Projection, twenty-four degrees.

GUNNER: Twenty-four degrees.

OFFICER: Fire! (*Boom*)

OBSERVER: I still can't see, sir. The smoke's coming nearer.

OFFICER: Get the range. (*Coughs*)

OBSERVER: Twenty-three meters (*Coughs*)

OFFICER: Twenty-three meters. (*Coughs*)

OBSERVER: Projection twenty-two degrees. (*Coughing*)

OFFICER: Twenty-two degrees. (*Fade in coughing*)

(*Fading in ... sound of airplane motor*)

COMMANDER: Army bombing plane, V-8-43 off Bayonne, New Jersey, Lieutenant Voght, commanding eight bombers. Reporting to Commander Fairfax, Langham Field – This is Voght, reporting to Commander Fairfax, Langham Field – Enemy tripod machines now in sight. Reinforced by three machines from the Morristown cylinder. Six altogether. One machine partially crippled. Believed hit by shell from army gun in Watchung Mountains. Guns now appear silent. A heavy black fog hanging close to the earth – of extreme density, nature unknown. No sign of heat-ray. Enemy now turns east, crossing Passaic River into Jersey marshes. Another straddles the Pulaski Skyway. Evident objective is New York City. They're pushing down a high-tension power station. The machines are close together now, and we're ready to attack. Planes circling, ready to strike. A thousand yards and we'll be over the first – eight hundred yards ... six hundred ... four hundred ... two hundred ... There they go! The giant arm raised – Green flash! They're spraying us with flame! Two thousand feet. Engines are giving out. No chance to release bombs. Only one thing left – drop on them, plane and all. We're diving on the first one. Now the engine's gone! Eight —

OPERATOR ONE: This is Bayonne, New Jersey, calling Langham Field – This is Bayonne, New Jersey, calling Langham Field – Come in, please – Come in, please —

OPERATOR TWO: This is Langham Field – go ahead —

OPERATOR ONE: Eight army bombers in engagement with enemy tripod machines over Jersey flats. Engines incapacitated by heat-ray. All crashed. One enemy machine destroyed. Enemy now discharging heavy black smoke in direction of —

OPERATOR THREE: This is Newark, New Jersey – This is Newark, New Jersey – Warning! Poisonous black smoke pouring in from Jersey marshes. Reaches South Street. Gas masks useless. Urge population to move into open spaces – automobiles use routes 7, 23, 24 – avoid congested areas. Smoke now spreading over Raymond Boulevard —

OPERATOR FOUR: 2X2L – calling CQ – 2X2L – calling CQ – 2X2L – calling 8X3R —

OPERATOR FIVE: This is 8X3R – coming back at 2X2L.

OPERATOR FOUR: How's reception? How's reception? K, please. Where are you, 8X3R? What's the matter? Where are you?

(Bells ringing over city gradually diminishing)

ANNOUNCER: I'm speaking from the roof of Broadcasting Building, New York City. The bells you hear me ringing to warn the people to evacuate the city as the Martians approach. Estimated in last two hours three million people have moved out along the roads to the north, Hutchison River Parkway still kept open for motor traffic. Avoid bridges to Long Island – hopelessly jammed. All communication with Jersey shore closed ten minutes ago. No more defenses. Our army wiped out – artillery, air force, everything wiped out. This may be the last broadcast. We'll stay here to the end. People are holding service below us – in the cathedral.

(*Voices singing hymn*)

Now I look down the harbor. All manner of boats, over-loaded with fleeing population, pulling out from docks.

(*Sound of boat whistles*)

Streets are all jammed. Noise in crowds like New Year's Eve in city. Wait a minute – Enemy now in sight above the Palisades. Five great machines. First one is crossing river. I can see it from here, wading the Hudson like a man wading through a brook – A bulletin's handed me – Martian cylinders are falling all over the country. One outside Buffalo, one in Chicago, St. Louis – seem to be timed and spaced – Now the first machine reaches the shore. He stands watching, looking over the city. His steel, cowlish head is even with the skyscrapers. He waits for the others. They rise like a line of new towers on the city's west side – Now they're lifting their metal hands. This is the end now. Smoke comes out – black smoke, drifting over the city. People in the streets see it now. They're running toward the East River – thousands of them, dropping in like rats. Now the smoke's spreading faster. It's reached Times Square. People trying to run away from it, but it's no use. They're falling like flies. Now the smoke's crossing Sixth Avenue – Fifth Avenue – a hundred yards away – it's fifty feet—

OPERATOR FOUR: 2X2L calling CQ – 2X2L calling CQ – 2X2L calling CQ – New York – Isn't there anyone on the air? Isn't there anyone – 2X2L—

II

PIERSON: As I set down these notes on paper, I'm obsessed by the thought that I may be the last living man on earth. I have been hiding in this empty house near Grovers Mill – a small island of daylight cut off by the black smoke from the rest of the world. All that happened before the arrival of these monstrous creatures in the world now seems part of another life – a life that has no continuity with the present, furtive existence of the lonely derelict who pencils these words on the back of some astronomical notes bearing the signature of Richard Pierson. I look down at my blackened hands, my torn shoes, my tattered clothes, and I try to connect them with a professor who lives at Princeton, and who on the night of October 30 glimpsed through his telescope an orange splash of light on a distant planet. My wife, my colleagues, my students, my books, my observatory, my – my world – where are they? Did they ever exist? Am I Richard Pierson? What day is it? Do days exist without calendars? Does time pass when there are no human hands left to wind the clocks? In writing down my daily life I tell myself I shall preserve human history between the dark covers of this little book that was meant to record the movements of the stars. But to write I must live, and to live I must eat – I find moldy bread in the kitchen, and an orange not too spoiled to swallow. I keep watch at the window. From time to time I catch sight of a Martian above the black smoke.

The smoke still holds the house in its black coil – But at length there is a hissing sound and suddenly I see a Martian mounted on his machine, spraying the air with a jet of steam, as if to dissipate the smoke. I watch in a corner as his huge metal legs nearly brush against the house. Exhausted by terror, I fall asleep.

It's morning. Sun streams in the window. The black cloud of gas has lifted, and the scorched meadows to the north look as though a black snowstorm had passed over them. I venture from the house. I make my way to a road. No traffic. Here and there a wrecked car, baggage overturned, a blackened skeleton. I push on north. For some reason I feel safer trailing these monsters than running away from them. And I keep a careful watch. I have seen the Martians feed. Should one of their machines appear over the top of trees, I am ready to fling myself flat on the earth. I come to a chestnut tree. October, chestnuts are ripe. I fill my pockets. I must keep alive. Two days I wander in a vague northerly direction through a desolate world. Finally I notice a living creature – a small red squirrel in a beech tree. I stare at him and wonder. He stares back at me. I believe at that moment the animal and I shared the same emotion – the joy of finding another living being – I push on north. I find dead cows in a brackish field. Beyond, the charred ruins of a dairy. The silo remains standing guard over the wasteland like a lighthouse deserted by the sea. Astride the silo perches a weathercock. The arrow points north.

Next day I came to a city vaguely familiar in its contours, yet its buildings strangely dwarfed and leveled off as if a giant had sliced off its highest towers with a capricious sweep of his hand. I reached the outskirts. I found Newark, undemolished,

but humbled by some whim of the advancing Martians. Presently, with an odd feeling of being watched, I caught sight of
something crouching in a doorway. I made a step toward it,
and it rose up and became a man – a man, armed with a large
knife.

STRANGER: Stop – Where did you come from?

PIERSON: I come from – many places. A long time ago from
Princeton.

STRANGER: Princeton, huh? That's near Grovers Mill!

PIERSON: Yes.

STRANGER: Grovers Mill – (*Laughs as at a great joke*)
There's no food here. This is my country – all this end of town
down to the river. There's only food for one – Which way are
you going?

PIERSON: I don't know. I guess I'm looking for – for people.

STRANGER: (*nervously*) What was that? Did you hear something just then?

PIERSON: Only a bird – a live bird!

STRANGER: You get to know that birds have shadows these
days – Say, we're in the open here. Let's crawl into this doorway and talk.

PIERSON: Have you seen any Martians?

STRANGER: They've gone over to New York. At night the
sky is alive with their lights. Just as if people were still living in
it. By daylight you can't see them. Five days ago a couple of
them carried something big across the flats from the airport. I
believe they're learning how to fly.

PIERSON: Fly!

STRANGER: Yeah, fly.

PIERSON: Then it's all over with humanity. Stranger, there's
still you and I. Two of us left.

STRANGER: They got themselves in solid; they wrecked
the greatest country in the world. Those green stars, they're
probably falling somewhere every night. They've only lost
one machine. There isn't anything to do. We're done. We're
licked.

PIERSON: Where were you? You're in a uniform.

STRANGER: What's left of it. I was in the militia – National
Guard. That's good! Wasn't any war any more than there's
war between men and ants.

PIERSON: And we're eatable ants. I found that out. What
will they do to us?

27

STRANGER: I've thought it all out. Right now we're caught as we're wanted. The Martian only has to go a few miles to get a crowd on the run. But they won't keep doing that. They'll begin catching us systematic like – keeping the best and storing us in cages and things. They haven't begun on us yet!

PIERSON: Not begun!

STRANGER: Not begun. All that's happened so far is because we don't have sense enough to keep quiet – bothering them with guns and such stuff and losing our heads and rushing off in crowds. Now instead of our rushing around blind we've got to fix ourselves up according to the way things are now. Cities, nations, civilization, progress —

PIERSON: But if that's so, what is there to live for?

STRANGER: There won't be any more concerts for a million years or so, and no nice little dinners at restaurants. If it's amusement you're after, I guess the game's up.

PIERSON: And what is there left?

STRANGER: Life – that's what! I want to live. And so do you! We're not going to be exterminated. And I don't mean to be caught, either, and tamed, and fattened, and bred like an ox.

PIERSON: What are you going to do?

STRANGER: I'm going on – right under their feet. I gotta plan. We men, as men, are finished. We don't know enough. We gotta learn plenty before we've got a chance. And we've got to live and keep free while we learn. I've thought it all out, see.

PIERSON: Tell me the rest.

STRANGER: Well, it isn't all of us that are made for wild beasts, and that's what it's got to be. That's why I watched you. All these little office workers that used to live in these houses – they'd be no good. They haven't any stuff to 'em. They just used to run off to work. I've seen hundreds of 'em, running wild to catch their commuters' train in the morning for fear that they'd get canned if they didn't; running back at night afraid they won't be in time for dinner. Lives insured and a little invested in case of accidents. And on Sundays, worried about the hereafter. The Martians will be a godsend for those guys. Nice roomy cages, good food, careful breeding, no worries. After a week or so chasing about the fields on empty stomachs they'll come and be glad to be caught.

PIERSON: You've thought it all out, haven't you?

STRANGER: You bet I have! And that isn't all. These Martians will make pets of some of them, train 'em to do tricks. Who knows? Get sentimental over the pet boy who grew up and and had to be killed. And some, maybe, they'll train to hunt us.

PIERSON: No, that's impossible. No human being —

STRANGER: Yes they will. There's men who'll do it gladly. If one of them ever comes after me —

PIERSON: In the meantime, you and I and others like us – where are we to live when the Martians own the earth?

STRANGER: I've got it all figured out. We'll live underground. I've been thinking about the sewers. Under New York are miles and miles of 'em. The main ones are big enough for anybody. Then there's cellars, vaults, underground storerooms, railway tunnels, subways. You begin to see, eh? And we'll get a bunch of strong men together. No weak ones, that rubbish, out.

PIERSON: And you meant me to go?

STRANGER: Well, I gave you a chance, didn't I?

PIERSON: We won't quarrel about that. Go on.

STRANGER: And we've got to make safe places for us to stay in, see, and get all the books we can – science books. That's where men like you come in, see? We'll raid the museums, we'll even spy on the Martians. It may not be so much we have to learn before – just imagine this: Four or five of their own fighting machines suddenly start off – heat-rays right and left and not a Martian in 'em. Not a Martian in 'em! But men – men who have learned the way how. It may even be in our time. Gee! Imagine having one of them lovely things with its heat-ray wide and free! We'd turn it on Martians, we'd turn it on men. We'd bring everybody down to their knees.

PIERSON: That's your plan?

STRANGER: You and me and a few more of us, we'd own the world.

PIERSON: I see.

STRANGER: Say, what's the matter? Where are you going?

PIERSON: Not to *your* world. Good-bye, stranger....

PIERSON: After parting with the artilleryman, I came at last to the Holland Tunnel. I entered that silent tube anxious to know the fate of the great city on the other side of the Hudson. Cautiously I came out of the tunnel and made my way up Canal Street.

I reached Fourteenth Street, and there again were black powder and several bodies, and an evil ominous smell from the gratings of the cellars of some of the houses. I wandered up through the Thirties and Forties; I stood alone on Times Square. I caught sight of a lean dog running down Seventh Avenue with a piece of dark brown meat in his jaws, and a pack of starving mongrels at his heels. He made a wide circle around me, as though he feared I might prove a fresh competitor. I walked up Broadway in the direction of that strange powder – past silent shop windows, displaying their mute wares to empty sidewalks – past the Capitol Theater, silent, dark – past a shooting-gallery, where a row of empty guns faced an arrested line of wooden ducks. Near Columbus Circle I noticed models of 1939 motor cars in the show rooms facing empty streets. From over the top of the General Motors Building I watched a flock of black birds circling in the sky. I hurried on. Suddenly I caught sight of the hood of a Martian machine, standing somewhere in Central Park, gleaming in the late afternoon sun. An insane idea! I rushed recklessly across Columbus Circle and into the Park. I climbed a small hill above the pond at Sixtieth Street. From there I could see, standing in a silent row along the Mall, nineteen of those great metal Titans, their cowls empty, their arms hanging listlessly by their sides. I looked in vain for the monsters that inhabit those machines.

Suddenly, my eyes were attracted to the immense flock of black birds that hovered directly below me. They circled to the ground, and there before my eyes, stark and silent, lay the Martians, with the hungry birds pecking and tearing brown shreds of flesh from their dead bodies. Later when their bodies were examined in laboratories, it was found that they were killed by the putrefactive and disease bacteria against which their systems were unprepared – slain after all man's defenses had failed, by the humblest thing that God in His wisdom put upon the earth.

Before the cylinder fell there was a general persuasion that through all the deep of space no life existed beyond the petty surface of our minute sphere. Now we see farther. Dim and wonderful is the vision I have conjured up in my mind of life spreading slowly from this little seed-bed of the solar system throughout the inanimate vastness of sidereal space. But that is a remote dream. It may be that the destruction of the Martians is only a reprieve. To them, and not to us, is the future ordained perhaps.

Strange it now seems to sit in my peaceful study at Princeton writing down this last chapter of the record begun at a deserted farm in Grovers Mill. Strange to see from my window the university spires dim and blue through an April haze. Strange to watch children playing in the streets. Strange to see young people strolling on the green, where the new spring grass heals the last black scars of a bruised earth. Strange to watch the sightseers enter the museum where the disassembled part of a Martian machine are kept on public view. Strange when I recall the time I first saw it, bright and cleancut, hard and silent, under the dawn of that last great day.

Not Only Dead Men
by A. E. van Voigt

June 29, 1942—Smashed in every timber, and, with no trace of
the crew, the whaleship *Albatross* was found today by an
American patrol ship in the Bering Straits. Naval authorities
are mystified by reports that the deck and sides of the schooner
were staved in as by gigantic blows, not caused 'by bombs,
torpedoes, shellfire, or other enemy action', according to the
word received. The galley stoves were said to be still warm,
and as there have been no storms in this region for three
weeks, no explanations has been forthcoming.

The *Albatros*s sailed from a West coast American port early
in March, with Captain Frank Wardell and a crew of eighteen,
all of whom are missing.

Captain Wardell of the whaleship, *Albatross*, was thinking
so darkly of the three long whaleless months that he had
started to edge the schooner through the narrows before he
saw the submarine lying near the shore in the sheltered waters
of that far-northern bay of Alaska.

His mind did a spinning dive into blankness. When he came
up for air his reflexes were already working. The engine-room
indicator stood at REVERSE FULL SPEED. And his immediate
plan was as clear as it was simple.

He parted his lips to shout at the wheelman; then closed
them again, made for the wheel, and, as the ship began to go
backward, guided her deftly behind the line of shoals and the
headland of trees. The anchor went down with a rattle and a
splash that echoed strangely on the windless morning.

Silence settled where the man-made sound had been; and
there was only the quiet ripple of that remote northern sea, the
restless waters lapping gently against the *Albatross*, washing
more sullenly over the shoals behind which she lay, and occasionally letting out a roar as a great wave smashed with a
white fury at a projecting rock.

Wardell, back on the small bridge, stood very still, letting his
mind absorb impressions and – listening.

But no alien sound came to disturb his straining ears, no

33

Diesel engines raging into life, no fainter hum of powerful electric motors. He began to breathe more steadily. He saw that his first mate, Preedy, had slipped softly up beside him.

Preedy said in a low voice:

'I don't think they saw us, sir. There was not a soul in sight. And, besides, they're obviously not fit to go to sea.'

'Why not?'

'Didn't you notice, sir – they haven't got a conning tower? It must have been shot away.'

Wardell was silent, shocked at himself for not having noticed. The vague admiration that had begun to show inside him at the cool way in which he handled the ship deflated a little.

Another thought came into his mind; and he scowled with a dark reluctance at the very idea of revealing a further deficiency in his observation. But he began grudgingly:

'Funny how your mind accepts the presence of things that aren't there.' He hesitated; then: 'I didn't even notice whether or not their deck gun was damaged.'

It was the mate who was silent now. Wardell gave a swift glance at the man's long face, realized that the mate was undergoing a private case of shock and annoyance, and said quickly:

'Mr. Preedy, call the men forward.'

Conscious again of superiority, Wardell went down to the deck. With a great deliberateness he began examining the anti-sub gun beside the whale gun. He could hear the men gathering behind him but he did not turn until feet began to shuffle restlessly.

He looked them over then, glancing from face to rough, tough, leather-beaten face. Fifteen men and a boy, not counting the engineer and his assistant – and every one of them looking revitalized, torn out of the glumness that had been the stock expression around the ship for three months.

Wardell's mind flashed back over the long years some of these men had been with him; he nodded, his heavy face dark with satisfaction, and began:

'Looks like we've got a disabled Jap sub cornered there, men. Our duty's clear. The navy gave us a three-inch gun and four machine guns before we sailed, and —'

He stopped, frowned at one of the older men. 'What's the

34

matter, Kenniston?'

'Begging your pardon, cap'n, that thing in there isn't a sub. I was in the service in '18, and I can tell one at a glance, conning tower bombed off or not.

'Why, that vessel in there has metal walls like dark scales – didn't you notice? We've got *something* cornered in there, sir, but it isn't a sub.'

From where he lay with his little expedition, behind the line of rock ledge, Wardell studied the strange vessel. The long, astoundingly hard walk to reach this vantage point had taken more than an hour. And now that he was here, what about it?

Through his binoculars, the – ship – showed as a streamlined, cigar shaped, dead metal that lay motionless in the tiny pattern of the waves that shimmered atop the waters of the bay. There was no other sign of life. Nevertheless —

Wardell stiffened suddenly with a sharp consciousness of his responsibilities – all these men, six here with him, carrying two of the precious machine guns, and the other men on the schooner.

The alienness of the vessel with its dark, scaly metal walls, its great length – struck him with a sudden chill. Behind him somebody said into the silence of that bleak, rocky landscape:

'If only we had a radio-sending set! What a bomber could do to that target! I —'

Wardell was only dimly aware of the way the man's voice sank queerly out of audibility. He was thinking heavily: Two machine guns against *that*. Or, rather – even the mental admission of greater strength came unwillingly – four machine guns and a three-incher. After all, the weapons back on the *Albatross* had to be included, even though the schooner seemed dangerously far away. He —

His mind went dead slow. With a start he saw that the flat, dark reach of deck below was showing movement: a large metal plate turning, then jerking open as if springs had snapped at it with irresistible strength. Through the hatchway thus created a figure was coming.

A figure – *a beast. The* thing reared up on horny, gleaming legs, and its scales shone in the late-morning sun. Of its four arms, one was clutching a flat, crystalline structure, a second held a small, blunt object that showed faintly crimson in the dazzling sunbeams. The other two arms were at ease.

The monster stood there under the Earth's warm sun, silhouetted against the background of limpid, blue-green sea, stood there arrogantly, its beast head flung back on its short neck with such a pride and confidence that Wardell felt a tingle at the nape of his neck.

'For Heaven's sake,' a man whispered hoarsely, 'put some bullets in it.'

The sound more than the words reached into the region of Wardell's brain that controlled his muscles.

'Shoot!' he rasped. 'Frost! Withers!'

Chat-chat-chat! The two machine guns yammered into life, wakening a thousand echoes in the virgin silence of the cove.

The figure, which had started striding briskly along the curving deck in the direction away from shore, its webbed feet showing plainly at each step, stopped short, turned – and looked up.

Eyes as green and fiery as a cat's at night blazed at, seemingly straight at, Wardell's face. The captain felt the muscles of his body constrict; his impulse was to jerk back behind the ledge, out of sight, but he couldn't have moved to save his life.

The mind-twisting emotion must have been evoked in every man present. For the machine guns ceased their stammering; and there was unnatural silence.

The yellow-green reptile moved first. It started to run, back toward the hatch. Reaching the opening, it stooped and seemed about to leap down headfirst, as if it couldn't get in too fast.

Instead of going down, however, it handed the crystalline object that it had held in one hand to somebody below; then it straightened.

There was a clang as the hatch banged shut – and the reptile stood alone on the deck, cut off from escape.

The scene froze like that for a fraction of a second, a tableau of rigid figures against a framework of quiet sea and dark, almost barren land. The beast stood absolutely still, its head flung back, its blazing eyes fixed on the men behind the ledge.

Wardell had not thought of its posture as a crouching one, but abruptly it straightened visibly and bounced upward and sideways like a frog leaping, or a diver jack-knifing. Water and beast met with a faint splash. When the shimmering veil of agitated water subsided, the beast was gone.

They waited.

'What goes down,' Wardell said finally in a voice that had in it the faintest shiver, 'must come up. Heaven only knows what it is, but hold your guns ready.'

The minutes dragged. The shadow of a breeze that had been titillating the surface of the bay died completely; and the water took on a flat, glassy sheen that was only broken far out near the narrow outlet to the rougher sea beyond.

After ten minutes, Wardell was twisting uneasily, dissatisfied with his position. At the end of twenty minutes he stood up.

'We've got to get back to the ship,' he said tensely. 'This thing is too big for us.'

They were edging along the shore five minutes later when the clamor started: a distant shouting, then a long, sharp rattle of machine-gun fire, then – silence.

It had come from where the schooner lay out of their line of vision behind the bank of trees half a mile across the bay.

Wardell grunted as he ran. It had been hard enough walking – earlier. Now, he was in an agony of jolts and half stumbles. Twice, during the first few minutes, he fell heavily.

The second time he got up very slowly and waited for his panting men to catch up with him. There was no more running because – it struck him with piercing sharpness – what had happened on the ship *had* happened.

Gingerly, Wardell led the way over the rock-strewn shore with its wilderness of chasms. He kept cursing in a sweat of fury with himself for having left the *Albatross*. And there was a special rage at the very idea that he had automatically set his fragile wooden ship against an armored sub.

Even though, as it had turned out, it wasn't a sub.

His brain stalled before the bare contemplation of what it might be.

For a moment he tried, mentally tried, to picture himself here, struggling over the barren shore of this rocky inlet in order to see what a – lizard – had done to his ship. And he couldn't. The picture wouldn't piece together. It was not even remotely woven of the same cloth as all that life of quiet days and evenings that he had spent on the bridges of ships, just sitting, or smoking his pipe, mindlessly contemplating the sea.

Even more dim and unconnectable was the civilization of

back-room poker games and loud laughing, bold-eyed women who made up his life during those brief months when he was in harbor, that curious, aimless life that he always gave up so willingly when the time came to put to sea again.

Wardell pushed the gray, futile memory from him, said:

'Frost, take Blakeman and McCann and pick up one drum of water. Danny ought to have them all filled by now. No, keep your machine gun. I want you to stay with the remaining drums till I send some more men. We're going to get that water and then get out of here.'

Wardell felt the better for his definite decision. He would head south for the naval base; and then others, better equipped and trained, would tackle the alien ship.

If only his ship was still there, intact – just what he feared he wasn't certain – he was conscious of the queasiest thrill of relief as he topped the final and steepest hill – and there she was. Through his glasses he made out the figures of men on the deck. And the last sodden weight of anxiety in him yielded to the fact that, barring accidents to individuals, everything was all right.

Something had happened, of course. In minutes he would know —

For a time it seemed as if he would never get the story. The men crowded around him as he clambered aboard, more weary than he cared to admit. The babble of voices that raged at him, the blazing excitement of everyone, did not help.

Words came through about a beast 'like a man-sized frog' that had come aboard. There was something about the engine room, and incomprehensibility about the engineer and his assistant waking up, and —

Wardell's voice, stung into a bass blare by the confusion, brought an end to the madness. The captain said crisply:

'Mr. Preedy, any damage?'

'None,' the mate replied, 'though Rutherford and Cressy are still shaky.'

The reference to the engineer and his assistant was obscure, but Wardell ignored it. 'Mr. Preedy, dispatch six men ashore to help bring the water aboard. Then come to the bridge.'

A few minutes later, Preedy was giving Wardell a complete account of what had happened. At the sound of the machine-gun fire from Wardell's party, all the men had crowded to port side of the ship and had stayed there.

The watery tracks left by the creature showed that it had used the opportunity to climb aboard the starboard side and had gone below. It was first seen standing at the fo'c's'le hatchway, coolly looking over the forward deck where the guns were.

The thing actually started boldly forward under the full weight of nine pairs of eyes, apparently heading straight for the guns; abruptly, however, it turned and made a running dive overboard. Then the machine guns started.

'I don't think we hit him,' Preedy confessed.

Wardell was thoughtful. 'I'm not sure,' he said, 'that it's bothered by bullets. It —' He stopped himself. 'What the devil am I saying? It runs every time we fire. But go on.'

'We went through the ship and that's when we found Rutherford and Cressy. They were out cold and they don't remember a thing. There's no damage, though, engineer says; and, well, that's all.'

It was enough, Wardell thought, but he said nothing. He stood for a while, picturing the reality of a green-and-yellow lizard climbing aboard his ship. He shuddered. What could the damned thing have wanted?

The sun was high in the middle heavens to the south when the last drum of water was hoisted aboard, and the whaler began to move.

Up on the bridge, Wardell heaved a sigh of relief as the ship nosed well clear of the white-crested shoals and headed into deep water. He was pushing the engine-room indicator to FULL SPEED AHEAD when the thud of the Diesels below became a cough that – ended.

The *Albatross* coasted along from momentum, swishing softly from side to side. In the dimly lighted region that was the engine room, Wardell found Rutherford on the floor laboriously trying to light a little pool of oil with a match.

The action was so mad that the captain stopped, stared, and then stood there speechless and intent.

For the oil wouldn't take fire. Four matches joined the burned ends on the floor beside the golden puddle. Then:

'Hell's bells!' said Wardell, 'you mean that *thing* put something in our oil that —'

He couldn't go on; and there was no immediate answer. But finally, without looking up, the engineer said thickly:

'Skipper, I've been tryin' ta think. Wha' for would a bunch of lizards be wantin' us ta lay to here?'

Wardell went back on deck without replying. He was conscious of hunger. But he had no illusions about the empty feeling inside him. No craving for food had ever made him feel like that.

Wardell ate, scarcely noticing his food, and came out into the opening feeling logy and sleepy. The climb to the bridge took all strength and will. He stood for a moment looking out across the narrows that led into the bay.

He made a discovery. In the brief minutes that the Diesels had operated on the untainted oil in the pipes, the *Albatross* had moved to a point where the dark vessel in the distance was now visible across the bows.

Wardell studied the silent alien ship sleepily then gazed along the shore line through his glasses. Finally he turned his attention to the deck in front of him. And nearly jumped out of his skin.

The *thing* was there, calmly bending over the whale gun, its scaly body shining like the wet hide of a big lizard. Water formed in little dark pools at its feet, spread damply to where Gunner Art Zote lay face downward, looking very dead.

If the interloper had been a man, Wardell was sure he could have forced his paralyzed muscles to draw the revolver that hung from his belt. Or even if the thing had been as far away as when he had first seen it.

But he was standing there less than twenty-five feet from it, staring down at that glistening, reptilian monstrosity with its four arms and its scale-armored legs; and the knowledge in the back of his mind that machine-gun bullets hadn't hurt it before, and —

With a cool disregard for possible watching eyes, the reptile began to tug at the harpoon where it protruded from the snout of the whale gun. It gave up after a second and went around to the breech of the gun. It was fumbling there, the crimson thing it held flashing with spasmodic incarnadine brilliance, when a wave of laughter and voices shattered the silence of the afternoon.

The next second the galley door burst open and a dozen men debouched upon the deck. The solid wooden structure that was the entrance to the fo'c's'le hid the beast from the gaze.

They stood for a moment, their ribald laughter echoing to the skies above that perpetually cold sea. As from a vast distance, Wardell found himself listening to the rough jokes, the rougher cursing; and he was thinking: like children they were. Already the knowledge that the strangest creatures in all creation had marooned them here on a fuelless ship must seem a dim thing in their minds. Or they wouldn't be standing like mindless fools while —

Wardell stopped the thought, astounded that he had allowed it to distract him for a single second. With a gasp he snatched at his revolver and took aim at the exposed back of the lizard where it was now bending over the strong dark cable that attached the harpoon to the ship.

Curiously, the shot brought a moment of complete silence. The lizard straightened slowly and turned half in annoyance. And then —

Men shouted. The machine gun in the crow's-nest began to yelp with sort, excited bursts that missed the deck and the reptile, but made a white foam in the water beyond the ship's bows.

Wardell was conscious of a frantic irritation at the damned fool up there. In the fury of his annoyance he turned his head upward and yelled at the fellow to learn to aim properly. When he looked again at the deck the beast wasn't there.

The sound of a faint splash permeated through a dozen other noises; and, simultaneously, there was a stampede for the rails as the crew peered down into the water. Over their heads, Wardell thought he caught the yellow-green flash in the depths, but the color merged too swiftly, too easily, with the shifting blue-green-gray of the northern sea.

Wardell stood very still; there was a coldness in the region of his heart, an empty sense of unnormal things. His gun hadn't wavered. The bullet couldn't have missed. Yet nothing had happened.

The clammy tightness inside him eased as he saw Art Zote getting shakily up from the deck, not dead, not dead after all. Abruptly, Wardell was trembling in every nerve. Good old Art. It took more than a scoundrelly lizard to kill a man like that.

'Art!' Wardell yelled in a blaze of his tremendous excitement, 'Art, turn the three-incher on that sub. Sink the damn thing. We'll teach those skunks to —'

The first shell was too short. It made a pretty spray a hundred yards from that distant metal hull. The second one was too far; it exploded futilely, stirring a hump of grayish rock on the shore into a brief, furious life.

The third smashed squarely on the target. And so did the next ten. It was beautiful shooting, but at the end of it Wardell called down uneasily:

'Better stop. The shells don't seem to be penetrating – I can't see any holes. We'd better save our ammunition for point-blank range, if it comes to that. Besides —'

He fell silent, reluctant to express the thought that had come to his mind, the fact that so far the creatures on that mysterious vessel had done them no harm, and that it was the *Albatross* and its crew that was doing all the shooting. There was, of course, that business of their oil being rendered useless and the curious affair just now, the thing coming aboard for the single purpose of studying the harpoon gun. But, nevertheless —

He and Preedy talked about it in low, baffled tones during the foggy afternoon and the cold evening, decided finally to padlock all the hatches from the inside and put a man with a gun in the crow's-nest.

Wardell wakened to the sound of excited yelling. The sun was just streaking over the horizon when he tumbled out onto the deck, half dressed. He noticed, as he went through the door, that the padlock had been neatly sliced out.

Grim, he joined the little group of men gathered around the guns. It was Art Zote, the gunner, who querulously pointed out the damage:

'Look, cap'n, the dirty beggars have cut our harpoon cable. And they've left us some measly copper wire or something in its place. Look at the junk.'

Wardell took the extended wire blankly. The whole affair seemed senseless. He was conscious of the gunner's voice continuing to beat at him:

'And the damn stuff's all over the place, too. There's two other harpoon sets, and each set is braced like a bloomin' masthead. They bored holes in the deck and ran the wires through, and lashed them to the backbone of the ship. It wouldn't be so bad if the stuff was any good, but that thin wire – hell!'

'Get me a wire cutter,' Wardell soothed. 'We'll start clearing it away, and —'

Amazingly, it wouldn't cut. He strained with his great strength, but the wire only looked vaguely shiny, and even that might have been a trick of light. Behind him, somebody said in a queer voice:

'I think maybe we got a bargain. But what kind of a whale are they getting us ready for?

Wardell stood very still, startled by the odd phrasing of the words: *What ... are they getting us ready for?*

He straightened, cold with decision. 'Men,' he said resonantly, 'get your breakfasts. We're going to get to the bottom of this if it's the last thing we ever do.'

The oarlocks creaked; the water whispered gently against the side of the rowboat – and every minute Wardell liked his position less.

It struck him after a moment that the boat was not heading directly at the vessel; and that their angle of approach was making for a side view of the object he had already noticed at the front of the stranger's metal deck.

He raised his glasses; and then he just sat there too amazed even to exclaim. It was a weapon all right – a *harpoon gun.*

There was no mistaking it. They hadn't even changed the design, the length of the harpoon, or — Wait a minute! What about the line?

He could make out a toy-sized roller beside the gun, and there was a coppery gleam coming from it that told a complete story.

'They've given us,' he thought, 'a cable as good as their own, something that will hold – anything.' Once again the chill struck through him, and the words that one of his crew had used: *What kind of a whale —*

'Closer!' he said hoarsely.

He was only dimly conscious that this kind of boldness was utterly rash. Careful, he thought, there were too many damn fools in hell already. Foolhardiness was —

'Closer!' he urged.

At fifty feet, the long, dark hull of the ship, even a part of what was under water, showed plainly; and there wasn't a scratch to indicate where the shells from the three-incher had exploded, not a sign of damage anywhere.

Wardell was parting his lips to speak again, his mind hard

on his determination to climb aboard under cover of the point-blank range of the machine gun – when there was a thunder of sound.

It was a cataclysmic sound, like whole series of monstrous guns firing one after the other. The roar echoed hugely from the barren hills and spat backward and forward across the natural hollow made by the almost completely landlocked bay.

The long, torpedo-shaped ship began to move. Faster, faster – it made a great half circle, a wave of fiery flashes pouring into the water from its rear; and then, having avoided the rowboat completely, headed for the narrows that led to the open sea.

Suddenly, a shell splashed beside it, then another and a third; Wardell could see the muzzle flame of the three-incher on the distant deck of the *Albatross*. There was no doubt that Art Zote and Preedy thought the hour of crisis was at hand.

But the stranger heeded not. Straight for the narrows it thundered along the gauntlet made by the shallows, and then out to deep water. It rumbled a full mile past the schooner, and then the fiery explosions ceased. The skies emptied of the rolling roar on roar of sound. The ship coasted on momentum, then stopped.

And lay there, silent, lifeless as before, a dark shape protruding out of the restless waters. Somewhere along its course, Art Zote had had the sense to stop his useless firing.

In the silence, Wardell could hear the heavy breathing of the men laboring at the oars. The rowboat shuddered at each thrust, and kept twisting as the still-turbulent waters of the bay churned against its sides.

Back on the whaler, Wardell called Preedy into his cabin. He poured out two stiff drinks, swallowed his own portion with a single, huge gulp, and said:

'My plan is this: We'll fit up the small boat with grub and water, and send three men down the coast for help. It's obvious we can't go on playing this game of hide and seek without even knowing what the game is about. It shouldn't take three good men more than a week to get to, say, the police station on the Tip, maybe sooner. What do you think?'

What Preedy thought was lost in the clattering boots. The door burst open. The man who unceremoniously pushed into the room held up two dark objects, and yelled:

'Look, cap'n, what one of them beasts just threw on board:

44

a flat, metal plate and a bag of something. He got away before we even saw him.'

It was the metal board that snatched Wardell's attention. Because it seemed to have no purpose. It was half an inch thick by ten inches long by eight wide. It was a silvery, metallic color on one side and black on the other.

That was all. He saw then that Preedy had picked up the bag and opened it. The mate gasped:

'Skipper, look! There's a photograph in here of the engine room, with a pointer pointing at a fuel tank – and some gray powder. *It must be to fix up the oil.*'

Wardell lowered the metal plate, started to grab for the bag, and stopped himself with a jerk as an abnormalness about the – black – of the metal board struck him with all the force of a blow.

It was – three-dimensional. It started at an incredible depth inside the plate, and reached to his eyes. Curious, needlesharp, intensely bright points of light peered out of the velvety, dead blackness.

As Wardell stared at it – it changed. Something floated onto the upper edge, came nearer, and showed itself against the blackness as a tiny animal.

Wardell thought: 'A photograph, by Heaven, a moving photograph of some kind.'

The thought shredded. A photograph of *what*?

The animal looked tiny, but it was the damnedest horror his eyes had ever gazed on, a monstrous, many-legged, long-bodied, long-snouted, hideous miniature, a very caricature of abnormal life, a mad creation of an insane imagination.

Wardell jumped – for the thing grew huge. It filled half that fantastic plate, and still it looked as if the picture was being taken from a distance.

'What is it?' he heard Preedy gasp over his shoulder.

Wardell did not answer – for the story was unfolding before their eyes:

The fight in space had begun in the only way a devil-Blal was ever contacted: unexpectedly. Violent energies flashed; the inertialess police ship spun desperately as the automatics flared with incandescent destruction – too late.

The monster showed high on the forward visiplate, a thin, orange radiance breaking out from its thick head. Commander

Ral Dorno groaned as he saw that orange radiance hold off the white fire of the patrol vessel – just long enough to ruin the ship.

'Space!' he yelled, 'we didn't get his Sensitives in time. We didn't...'

The small ship shuddered from stem to stern. Lights blinked and went out; the communicator huzzaed with alien noise, then went dead. The atomic motors stuttered from their, soundless, potent jiving to a hoarse, throbbing ratchetting. And stopped.

The spaceship began to fall.

Somewhere behind Dorno, a voice – Senna's – yelled in relief: 'Its Sensitives are turning back. We did get it. It's falling, too.'

Dorno made no reply. Four scaly arms held out in front of him, he fumbled his way from the useless visiplate, and peered through the nearest porthole grimly.

It was hard to see against the strong light of the sun of this planetary system, but finally he made out the hundred-foot-long, bullet-shaped monstrosity. The vicious ten-foot snout of the thing was opening and closing like the steel traps of a steam shovel. The armored legs pawed and clawed at the empty space; the long, heavy body writhed in a stupendous working of muscles.

Dorno grew aware of somebody slipping up beside him. Without turning, he said tautly:

'We've knocked out its Sensitives, all right. But it's still alive. The pressure of the atmosphere of that planet below will slow it down sufficiently, so that the fall will only stun it. We've got to try to use our rockets, so that we don't land within five hundred *negs* of that thing. We'll need at least a hundred *lan*-periods for repair, and —'

'Commander ... what is it?'

The words were almost a gasp, so faint were they. Dorno recognized the whisper as coming from the novitiate, Carliss, his ship wife.

It was still a little strange to him, having a wife other than Yarosan. And it took a moment in this crisis to realize that that veteran of many voyages was not with him. But Yarosan had exercised the privilege of patrol women.

'I'm getting to the age where I want some children,' she had said, 'and as, legally, only one of them can be yours, I want

46

you, Ral, to find yourself a pretty trainee and marry her for two voyages —'

Dorno turned slowly, vaguely irritated at the idea that there was somebody aboard who didn't automatically know everything. He said curtly:

'It's a devil-Blal, a wild beast with an I.Q. of ten that haunts these outer-unexplored systems, where it hasn't yet been exterminated. It's abnormally ferocious; it has in its head what is called a sensitive area, where it organically manufactures enormous energies.

'The natural purpose of those energies is to provide it with a means of transportation. Unfortunately, when that thing is on the move, any machine in the vicinity that operates on forces below the molecular level are saturated with that – organic – force. It's a long, slow job draining it off, but it has to be done before a single atomic or electronic machine will function again.

'Our automatics managed to destroy the Blal's Sensitives at the same time as it got us. We have now to destroy its body, but we can't do that till we get our energy weapons into operation again. Everything clear?'

Beside him, Carliss, the female Sahfid, nodded hesitantly. She said finally:

'Suppose it lives on the planet below? And there are others there? What then?'

Dorno sighed. 'My dear,' he said, 'there is a regulation that every crew member should familiarize himself or herself with data about any system which their ship happens to be approaching, passing, or —'

'But we only saw this sun half a *lan* ago.'

'It's been registering on the multiboard for three *lans* – but never mind that. The planet below is the only one in this system that is inhabited. Its land area being one twentieth or more of the whole, it was colonized by the warm-blooded human beings of Wodesk. It is called Earth by its people, and has yet to develop space travel.

'I could give you some astrogeographical technical information, including the fact that the devil-Blal wouldn't willingly go near such a planet because it most violently doesn't like an eight-*der* gravity or the oxygen in the atmosphere. Unfortunately, it will live in spite of this physical and chemical irreconcilability, and that is the enormous, indeed the absolutely mortal danger.

'It has a one-track hate mind. We have destroyed its main organic energy source, but actually its entire nervous system is a reservoir of sensitive forces. In its hunting, it has to project itself through space in pursuit of meteorites traveling many miles per second; to enable it to keep track of them, it ages ago developed an ability to attune itself to any material body.

'Because of the pain we have caused it, it has been attuned to us from the first energy exchange; therefore, as soon as it lands it will start for us, no matter how far away we are. We must make sure that it doesn't get to us before we have a disintegrator ready. Otherwise —'

'Surely, it can't damage a metalite spaceship.'

'Not only can, but will. Its teeth are not just teeth. They project thin beams of energy that will dissolve any metal, however hard. And, when it's through with us, just imagine the incalculable damage it will do on Earth before the patrol discovers what has happened – all this not counting the fact that it is considered an absolute catastrophe by Galactic psychologists when a planet learns before it should that there is an enormously superior Galactic civilization.'

'I know.' Carliss nodded vigorously. 'The regulation is that if any inhabitant of such a planet so much as glimpses us, we must kill him or her forthwith.'

Dorno made a somber sound of agreement, summarized grimly:

'Our problem accordingly is to land far enough from the beast to protect ourselves, destroy it before it can do any harm, and finally make certain that no human being sees us.'

He finished: 'And now, I suggest that you observe how Senna uses the rocket tubes to bring us down safely in this emergency landing. He —'

A gas light flickered outside the door of the control room. The Sahfid who came in was bigger even than the powerful Dorno. He carried a globe that burned mistily, and shed a strong white light.

'I have bad news,' said Senna. 'You will recall we used rocket fuel chasing the Kjev outlaws, and have not yet had the opportunity of replacing it. We shall have to land with a minimum of maneuvering.'

'W-what!' Dorno exclaimed, and exchanged a startled

glance with the female.

Even after Senna went out, he had nothing to say. There *was* nothing to say – for here was disaster.

They labored – Dorno and Carliss, Senna and Degel his wife – with a quiet, restless fury. After four *lans*, all the drainers were in position; and there was nothing to do but wait drearily while the electronic structures normalized in their agonizingly slow way. Dorno said:

'Some of the smaller motors, and the useless hand weapons and the power tools in the machine shop will be in operation before the devil-Blal arrives. But nothing of value. It will require four day-and-night periods of this planet before the drive motors and the disintegrators are working again – and that makes it rather hopeless.

'I suppose we could fashion some kind of reaction gun, using the remnants of our rocket fuel as a propellant. But they would only enrage the beast.'

He shrugged. 'I'm afraid it's useless. According to our final observations, the monster will have landed about a hundred *negs* north of us, and so it will be here sometime tomorrow. We —'

There was a clang as the molecular alarms went off. A few moments later, they watched the schooner creep through the narrows, then hastily back out again. Dorno's unwinking lidless eyes watched thoughtfully until the whaler was out of sight.

He did not speak immediately, but spent some time examining the automatic photographs, which were entirely chemical in their operation, and therefore unaffected by the catastrophe that had struck the rest of the ship. He said finally, slowly:

'I'm not sure, but I think we're in luck. The enlargers show that that ship has got two guns aboard, and one of those guns has a hooked thing protruding from it – that gives me an idea. We must, if necessary, use our remaining rocket fuel to stay near the vessel until I have been aboard and investigated.'

'Be careful!' said Carliss anxiously.

'My transparent armor,' Dorno told her, 'will protect me from all except the most sustained gunfire —'

A warm sun blazed down on the bay, and that made utterly surprising the bitter cold of the water. The icy feel of it in his gills was purest agony – but even the brief examination of the harpoon gun from the fo'c's'le hatchway told him that here

49

was the answer.

'A most remarkable weapon,' he told his companions when he returned to the patrol ship. 'It will require a stronger explosive to drive it into the Blal, and, of course, better metal in every phase of its construction. I shall have to go back for measurements and later to install the new equipment. But that will be simple. I succeeded in negating their fuel.'

He ended: 'That will have to be rectified at the proper time. They must be able to maneuver when the Blal arrives.'

'But will they fight?' asked Carliss.

Dorno smiled mirthlessly. 'My dear,' he said, 'that is something which we shall not leave to chance. A scopeograph film will tell them the rather appalling story. As for the rest, we shall simply keep their ship between ourselves and the devil-Blal; the beast will sense life-force aboard their vessel and, in its stupid way, connect them with us. Yes, I can guarantee that they'll fight.'

Carliss said: 'The Blal might even save us the trouble of having to kill them later.'

Dorno looked at her thoughtfully. 'Oh, yes,' he said, 'the regulations! I assure you that we shall carry them out to the letter.'

He smiled. 'Some day, Carliss, you must read them all. The great ones who prepared them for us to administer made them comprehensive. Very comprehensive.'

Wardell's fingers whitened on his binoculars, as he studied the great, bulging back that glinted darkly in the swell half a mile to the north, bearing straight down on the ship. The monster left a gleaming trail in the sea as it swam with enormous power.

In a way, the part of it that was visible looked like nothing else than a large whale. Wardell clutched at the wild hope, and then —

A spume of water sprayed the sea; and his illusion smashed like a bullet-proof jacket before a cannon ball.

Because no whale on God's wide oceans had ever retched water in such a formidable fashion. Wardell had a brief, vivid mental picture of ten-foot jaws convulsively working under the waves, and spreading water like a bellows.

For a moment, he felt violent anger at himself that he should have, even for a second, imagined it was a whale. Rage died, as it struck him that the thought was not really a wasted one. For it was a reminder that he had all his years played a game where fear was not a factor.

Very slowly, very carefully, he straightened. He called in a calm, resonant voice:

'Men, we're in this whether we like it or not. So let's take it in our stride like the damnedest best whalers in the business —'

All the damage to the *Albatross* was done in the first two minutes after the harpoon belched forth from Art Zore's gun.

At that cruel blow, a nightmare, eyeless head, champing tons of water, reared up; and the attack was a flailing thing of armored legs that stamped as madly at the sea as at the frantically backing schooner.

She was clear at last; and Wardell, clambering shakily out of the ruins of the bridge, grew aware for the first time of the thunderous engines of the lizard's ship, and of a second harpoon sticking in the side of the monster – the harpoon's gleaming coppery tail extending tenuous and taut back to the scale-armored vessel.

Four more harpoons lashed forth, two from each ship; and then they had the thing stretched between them.

For a solid hour. Art Zote pumped the remnants of their shells into a body that writhed with an agonized but unkillable ferocity.

And then, for three long days and nights, they hung on, while a beast that wouldn't die twisted and fought with a senseless and endless fury —

It was the fourth morning.

From the shattered deck of his ship, Wardell watched the scene on the other vessel. Two lizards were setting up a curious glittering structure, that began to glow with a gray, misty light.

The almost palpable mist poured onto the beast in the sea; and where it struck was – change – that – became-nothingness.

There was not a sound now, not a movement, aboard the *Albatross*. Men stood where they were, and stared in a semi-paralyzed fascination, as a one-hundred-ton monster yielded its elements before the transcendental force that was tearing at it.

A long half-hour passed before the hard and terrible body was dissolved —

The glittering disintegrator was withdrawn then, and for a

while there was – deadness. A thin fog appeared on the horizon to the north, and blew over the two ships. Wardell waited with his men, tense and cold and – wondering.

'Let's get out of here,' somebody said. 'I don't trust those scoundrels even after we helped them.'

Wardell shrugged helplessly. 'What can we do? That bag of chemical powder they threw aboard along with the motion-picture machine, released only one fuel tank, and that the half-empty one. We've used all except a few gallons in maneuvering. We —'

'Damn those scum!' another man moaned. 'It's the mysterious way they did it all that I don't like. Why, if they wanted our help, didn't they come and ask us?'

Wardell hadn't realized how great his own tension was. The sailor's words brought a wave of rage.

'Oh, sure,' he scathed at the fellow. 'I can just picture it. I can just see us rolling out the welcome mat – with a blast from our three-incher.

'And if they ever did get to tell us that they wanted to take the measurements of our harpoon gun, so they could build one of their own, and would we let them fix ours so that it would hold twenty whales at once, and would we please hang around here until that hellish thing arrived — Oh, yes, we should have stayed. Like hell we would!

'But they weren't as big saps as all that. It's the damnedest, cold-blooded thing I ever saw pulled off, but we stayed because we had to, and no please or thank you about it. The thing that worries me is the fact that we've never seen their kind before, or heard of them. That might only prove that dead men have told no tales, but—'

His voice faded, for there was life again on the lizard ship, another structure being set up, smaller, duller in appearance than the first and equipped with odd, gunlike projectors.

Wardell went rigid, then his bellow echoed across the deck:

'That can only be for us. Art, you've still got three shells. Stand by, ready to fire —'

A puff of silver-shining smoke cut off his words, his thoughts his consciousness – instantaneously.

Dorno's soft, hissing voice made a quiet design of sound against the silence of the spaceship cabin:

'The regulations are designed to protect the moral continuity of civilization, and to prevent a too literal interpretation of basic laws by time-calloused or thoughtless administrators. It is right that low-degree planets should be protected from contact, so vitally right that death is a justifiable measure against those who glimpse the truth, BUT —'

Dorno smiled, said: 'When important assistance has been rendered a Galactic citizen or official, no matter what the circumstances, it is morally necessary to the continuity of civilized conduct that other means be taken to prevent the tale from spreading —

'There are precedents, of course,' Dorno added quietly. 'Accordingly, I have been plotting our new course. It will take us past the distant sun of Wodesk, from whose green and wonderful planets Earth was originally colonized.

'It will not be necessary to keep our guests in a cataleptic state. As soon as they recover from the effects of the silver gas, let them ... experience the journey.'

Arena
by Fredric Brown

Carson opened his eyes, and found himself looking upward into a flickering blue dimness.

It was hot, and he was lying on sand, and a sharp rock embedded in the sand was hurting his back. He rolled over to his side, off the rock, and then pushed himself up to a sitting position.

'I'm crazy,' he thought. 'Crazy – or dead – or something.' The sand was blue, bright blue. And there wasn't any such thing as bright blue sand on Earth or any of the planets.

Blue sand.

Blue sand under a blue dome that wasn't the sky nor yet a room, but a circumscribed area – somehow he knew it was circumscribed and finite even though he couldn't see to the top of it.

He picked up some of the sand in his hand and let it run through his fingers. It trickled down onto his bare leg. *Bare?*

Naked. He was stark naked, and already his body was dripping perspiration from the enervating heat, coated blue with sand wherever sand had touched it.

But elsewhere his body was white.

He thought: Then this sand is really blue. If it seemed blue only because of the blue light, then I'd be blue also. But I'm white, so the sand *is* blue. *Blue sand.* There isn't any blue sand. There isn't any place like this place I'm in.

Sweat was running down in his eyes.

It was hot, hotter than hell. Only hell – the hell of the ancients – was supposed to be red and not blue.

But if this place wasn't hell, what was it? Only Mercury, among the planets, had heat like this and this wasn't Mercury. And Mercury was some four billion miles from —

It came back to him then, where he'd been. In the little one-man scouter, outside the orbit of Pluto, scouting a scant million miles to one side of the Earth Armada drawn up in battle array there to intercept the Outsiders.

That sudden strident nerve-shattering ringing of the alarm bell when the rival scouter – the Outsider ship – had come within range of his detectors —

No one knew who the Outsiders were, what they looked like, from what far away galaxy they came, other than that it was in the general direction of the Pleiades.

First, sporadic raids on Earth colonies and outposts. Isolated battles between Earth patrols and small groups of Outsider spaceships; battles sometimes won and sometimes lost, but never to date resulting in the capture of an alien vessel. Nor had any member of a raided colony ever survived to describe the Outsiders, who had left the ships if indeed they had left them.

Not a too-serious menace, at first, for the raids had not been too numerous or destructive. And individually, the ships had proved slightly inferior in armament to the best of Earth's fighters, although somewhat superior in speed and maneuverability. A sufficient edge in speed, in fact, to give the Outsiders their choice of running or fighting, unless surrounded.

Nevertheless, Earth had prepared for serious trouble, for a showdown, building the mightiest armada of all time. It had been waiting now, that armada, for a long time. But now the showdown was coming.

Scouts twenty billion miles out had detected the approach of a mighty fleet – a showdown fleet – of the Outsiders. Those scouts had never come back, but their radiotronic messages had. And now Earth's armada, all ten thousand ships and half-million fighting spacemen, was out there, outside Pluto's orbit, waiting to intercept and battle to the death.

And an even battle it was going to be, judging by the advance reports of the men of the far picket line who had given their lives to report – before they had died – on the size and strength of the alien fleet.

Anybody's battle, with the mastery of the solar system hanging in the balance, on an even chance. A last and *only* chance, for Earth and all her colonies lay at the utter mercy of the Outsiders if they ran that gauntlet —

Oh yes. Bob Carson remembered now.

Not that it explained blue sand and flickering blueness. But that strident alarming of the bell and his leap for the control panel. His frenzied fumbling as he strapped himself into the seat. The dot in the visiplate that grew larger.

The dryness of his mouth. The awful knowledge that this was *it*. For him, at least, although the main fleets were still out of range of one another.

This, his first taste of battle. Within three seconds or less he'd be victorious, or a charred cinder. Dead.

Three seconds – that's how long a space-battle lasted. Time enough to count to three, slowly, and then you'd won or you were dead. One hit completely took care of a lightly armed and armored little one-man craft like a scouter.

Frantically – as, unconsciously, his dry lips shaped the word 'One' – he worked at the controls to keep that growing dot centered on the crossed spiderwebs of the visiplate. His hands doing that, while his right foot hovered over the pedal that would fire the bolt. The single bolt of concentrated hell that had to hit – or else. There wouldn't be time for any second shot.

'Two.' He didn't know he'd said that, either. The dot in the visiplate wasn't a dot now. Only a few thousand miles away, it showed up in the magnification of the plate as though it were only a few hundred yards off. It was a sleek, fast little scouter, about the size of his.

And an alien ship, all right.

'Thr —' His foot touched the bolt-release pedal —

And then the Outsider had swerved suddenly and was off the crosshairs. Carson punched keys frantically, to follow.

For a tenth of a second, it was out of the visiplate entirely, and then as the nose of his scouter swung after it, he saw it again, diving straight toward the ground.

The ground?

It was an optical illusion of some sort. It *had* to be, that planet – or whatever it was – that now covered the visiplate. Whatever it was, it couldn't be there. Couldn't possibly. There *wasn't* any planet nearer than Neptune three billion miles away – with Pluto around on the opposite side of the distant pinpoint sun.

His *detectors*! *They* hadn't shown any object of planetary dimensions, even of asteroid dimensions. They still didn't.

So it couldn't be there, that whatever-it-was he was diving into, only a few hundred miles below him.

And in his sudden anxiety to keep from crashing, he forgot even the Outsider ship. He fired the front braking rockets, and even as the sudden change of speed slammed him forward against the seat straps, he fired full right for an emergency turn. Pushed them down and *held* them down, knowing that he needed everything the ship had to keep from crashing and that a turn that sudden would black him out for a moment.

It did black him out.

And that was all. Now he was sitting in hot blue sand, stark naked but otherwise unhurt. No sign of his spaceship and – for that matter – no sign of *space*. That curve overhead wasn't a sky, whatever else it was.

He scrambled to his feet.

Gravity seemed a little more than Earth-normal. Not much more.

Flat sand stretching away, a few scrawny bushes in clumps here and there. The bushes were blue, too, but in varying shades, some lighter than the blue of the sand, some darker.

Out from under the nearest bush ran a little thing that was like a lizard, except that it had more than four legs. It was blue, too. Bright blue. It saw him and ran back again under the bush.

He looked up again, trying to decide what was overhead. It wasn't exactly a roof, but it was dome-shaped. It flickered and was hard to look at. But definitely, it curved down to the ground, to the blue sand, all around him.

He wasn't far from being under the center of the dome. At a guess, it was a hundred yards to the nearest wall, if it was a wall. It was as though a blue hemisphere of *something*, about two hundred and fifty yards in circumference, was inverted over the flat expanse of the sand.

And everything blue, except one object. Over near a far curving wall there was a red object. Roughly spherical, it seemed to be about a yard in diameter. Too far for him to see clearly through the flickering blueness. But, unaccountably, he shuddered.

He wiped sweat from his forehead, or tried to, with the back of his hand.

Was this a dream, a nightmare? This heat, this sand, that vague feeling of horror he felt when he looked toward the red thing?

A dream? No, one didn't go to sleep and dream in the midst of a battle in space.

Death? No, never. If there were immortality, it wouldn't be a senseless thing like this, a thing of blue heat and blue sand and a red horror.

Then he heard the voice —

Inside his head he heard it, not with his ears. It came from nowhere or everywhere.

'Through spaces and dimensions wandering,' rang the words in his mind, *'and in this space and this time I find two people about to wage a war that would exterminate one and so weaken the other that it would retrogress and never fulfill its destiny, but decay and return to mindless dust whence it came. And I say this must not happen.'*

'Who . . . what are you?' Carson didn't say it aloud, but the question formed itself in his brain.

'You would not understand completely. I am —' There was a pause as though the voice sought – in Carson's brain – for a word that wasn't there, a word he didn't know. *'I am the end of evolution of a race so old the time can not be expressed in words that have meaning to your mind. A race fused into a single entity, eternal —*

'An entity such as your primitive race might become' – again the groping for a word – *'time from now. So might the race you call, in your mind, the Outsiders. So I intervene in the battle to come, the battle between fleets so evenly matched that destruction of both races will result. One must survive. One must progress and evolve.'*

'One?' thought Carson. 'Mine, or —?'

'It is in my power to stop the war, to send the Outsiders back to their galaxy. But they would return, or your race would sooner or later follow them there. Only by remaining in this space and time to intervene constantly could I prevent them from destroying one another, and I cannot remain.

'So I shall intervene now. I shall destroy one fleet completely without loss to the other. One civilization shall thus survive.'

Nightmare. This had to be nightmare, Carson thought. But he knew it wasn't.

It was too mad, too impossible, to be anything but real.

He didn't dare ask *the* question – *which?* But his thoughts asked it for him.

'The stronger shall survive.' said the voice. *'That I can not – and would not – change. I merely intervene to make it a complete victory, not'* – groping again – *'not Pyrrhic victory to a broken race.*

'From the outskirts of the not-yet battle I plucked two individuals, you and an Outsider. I see from your mind that in your early history of nationalisms battles between champions, to decide issues between races, were not unknown.

'*You and your opponent are here pitted against one another, naked and unarmed, under conditions equally unfamiliar to you both, equally unpleasant to you both. There is no time limit, for here there is no time. The survivor is the champion of his race. That race survives.*'

'But —' Carson's protest was too inarticulate for expression, but the voice answered it.

'*It is fair. The conditions are such that the accident of physical strength will not completely decide the issue. There is a barrier. You will understand. Brain-power and courage will be more important than strength. Most especially courage, which is the will to survive.*'

'But while this goes on, the fleets will —'

'*No, you are in another space, another time. For as long as you are here, time stands still in the universe you know. I see you wonder whether this place is real. It is, and it is not, As I – to your limited understanding – am and am not real. My existence is mental and not physical. You saw me as a planet; it could have been as a dustmote or a sun.*

'*But to you this place is now real. What you suffer here will be real. And if you die here, your death will be real. If you die, your failure will be the end of your race. That is enough for you to know.*'

And then the voice was gone.

And he was alone, but not alone. For as Carson looked up, he saw that the red thing, the red sphere of horror which he now knew was the Outsider, was rolling toward him.

Rolling.

It seemed to have no legs or arms that he could see, no features. It rolled across the blue sand with the fluid quickness a drop of mercury. And before it, in some manner he could not understand, came a paralyzing wave of nauseating, retching, horrid hatred.

Carson looked about him frantically. A stone, lying in the sand a few feet away, was the nearest thing to a weapon. It wasn't large, but it had sharp edges, like a slab of flint. It looked a bit like blue flint.

He picked it up, and crouched to receive the attack. It was coming fast, faster than he could run.

No time to think out how he was going to fight it, and how anyway could he plan to battle a creature whose strength, whose characteristics, whose method of fighting he did not know? Rolling so fast, it looked more than ever like a perfect sphere.

Ten yards away. Five. And then it stopped.

Rather, it *was stopped*. Abruptly the near side of it flattened as though it had run up against an invisible wall. It bounced, actually bounced back.

Then it rolled forward again, but more slowly, more cautiously. It stopped again, at the same place. It tried again, a few yards to one side.

There was a barrier there of some sort. It clicked, then, in Carson's mind. That thought projected into his mind by the Entity who had brought them there: '– accident of physical strength will not completely decide the issue. There is a barrier.'

A force-field, of course. Not the Netzian Field, known to Earth science, for that glowed and emitted a crackling sound. This one was invisible, silent.

It was a wall that ran from side to side of the inverted hemisphere; Carson didn't have to verify that himself. The Roller was doing that; rolling sideways along the barrier, seeking a break in it that wasn't there.

Carson took half a dozen steps forward, his left hand groping out before him, and then his hand touched the barrier. It felt smooth, yielding, like a sheet of rubber rather than like glass. Warm to his touch, but no warmer than the sand underfoot. And it was completely invisible, even at close range.

He dropped the stone and put both hands against it, pushing. It seemed to yield, just a trifle. But no farther than that trifle, even when he pushed with all his weight. It felt like a sheet of rubber backed up by steel. Limited resiliency, and then firm strength.

He stood on tiptoe and reached as high as he could and the barrier was still there.

He saw the Roller coming back, having reached one side of the arena. That feeling of nausea hit Carson again, and he stepped back from the barrier as it went by. It didn't stop.

But did the barrier stop at ground level? Carson knelt down and burrowed in the sand. It was soft, light, easy to dig in. At two feet down the barrier was still there.

The Roller was coming back again. Obviously, it couldn't find a way through at either side.

There must be a way through, Carson thought. *Some* way

we can get at each other, else this duel is meaningless.

But no hurry now, in finding that out. There was something to try first. The Roller was back now, and it stopped just across the barrier, only six feet away. It seemed to be studying him, although for the life of him, Carson couldn't find external evidence of sense organs on the thing. Nothing that looked like eyes or ears, or even a mouth. There was though, he saw now, a series of grooves – perhaps a dozen of them altogether, and he saw two tentacles suddenly push out from two of the grooves and dip into the sand as though testing its consistency. Tentacles about an inch in diameter and perhaps a foot and a half long.

But the tentacles were retractable into the grooves and were kept there except when in use. They were retracted when the thing rolled and seemed to have nothing to do with its method of locomotion. That, as far as Carson could judge, seemed to be accomplished by some shifting – just *how* he couldn't even imagine – of its center of gravity.

He shuddered as he looked at the thing. It was alien, utterly alien, horribly different from anything on Earth or any of the life forms found on the other solar planets. Instinctively, somehow, he knew its mind was as alien as its body.

But he had to try. If it had no telepathic powers at all, the attempt was foredoomed to failure, yet he thought it had such powers. There had, at any rate, been a projection of something that was not physical at the time a few minutes ago when it had first started for him. An almost tangible wave of hatred.

If it could project that, perhaps it could read his mind as well, sufficiently for his purpose.

Deliberately, Carson picked up the rock that had been his only weapon, then tossed it down again in a gesture of relinquishment and raised his empty hands, palms up, before him.

He spoke aloud, knowing that although the words would be meaningless to the creature before him, speaking them would focus his own thoughts more completely upon the message.

'Can we not have peace between us?' he said, his voice sounding strange in the utter stillness. 'The Entity who brought us here has told us what must happen if our races fight – extinction of one and weakening and retrogression of the other. The battle between them, said the Entity, depends upon what we do here. Why can not we agree to an external peace – your race to its galaxy, we to ours?'

Carson blanked out his mind to receive a reply.

It came, and it staggered him back, physically. He actually recoiled several steps in sheer horror at the depth and intensity of the hatred and lust-to-kill of the red images that had been projected at him. Not as articulate words – as had come to him the thoughts of the Entity – but as wave upon wave of fierce emotion.

For a moment that seemed an eternity he had to struggle against the mental impact of that hatred, fight to clear his mind of it and drive out the alien thoughts to which he had given admittance by blanking out his own thoughts. He wanted to retch.

Slowly his mind cleared as, slowly, the mind of a man wakening from nightmare clears away the fear-fabric of which the dream was woven. He was breathing hard and he felt weaker, but he could think.

He stood studying the Roller. It had been motionless during the mental duel it had so nearly won. Now it rolled a few feet to one side, to the nearest of the blue bushes. Three tentacles whipped out of their grooves and began to investigate the bush.

'O.K.,' Carson said, 'so it's war then.' He managed a wry grin. 'If I got your answer straight, peace doesn't appeal to you.' And, because he was, after all, a quiet young man and couldn't resist the impulse to be dramatic, he added. 'To the death!'

But his voice, in that utter silence, sounded very silly, even to himself. It came to him, then, that this *was* to the death. Not only his own death or that of the red spherical thing which he now thought of as the Roller, but death to the entire race of one or the other of them. The end of the human race, if he failed.

It made him suddenly very humble and very afraid to think that. More than to think it, to *know* it. Somehow, with a knowledge that was above even faith, he knew that the Entity who had arranged this duel had told the truth about its intentions and its powers. It wasn't kidding.

The future of humanity depended upon *him*. It was an awful thing to realize, and he wrenched his mind away from it. He had to concentrate on the situation at hand.

There had to be some way of getting through the barrier, or of killing through the barrier.

Mentally? He hoped that wasn't all, for the Roller obviously had stronger telepathic powers than the primitive, undeveloped ones of the human race. Or did it?

He had been able to drive the thoughts of the Roller out of his own mind; could it drive out his? If its ability to project were stronger, might not its receptivity mechanism be more vulnerable?

He stared at it and endeavored to concentrate and focus all his thoughts upon it.

'*Die*,' he thought. '*You are going to die. You are dying. You are —*'

He tried variations on it, and mental pictures. Sweat stood out on his forehead and he found himself trembling with the intensity of the effort. But the Roller went ahead with its investigation of the bush, as utterly unaffected as though Carson had been reciting the multiplication table.

So *that* was no good.

He felt a bit weak and dizzy from the heat and his strenuous effort at concentration. He sat down on the blue sand to rest and gave his full attention to watching and studying the Roller. By close study perhaps, he could judge its strength and detect its weaknesses, learn things that would be valuable to know when and if they should come to grips.

It was breaking off twigs. Carson watched carefully, trying to judge just how hard it worked to do that. Later, he thought, he could find a similar bush on his own side, break off twigs of equal thickness himself, and gain a comparison of physical strength between his own arms and hands and those tentacles.

The twigs broke off hard; the Roller was having to struggle with each one, he saw. Each tentacle, he saw, bifurcated at the tip into two fingers, each tipped by a nail or claw. The claws didn't seem to be particularly long or dangerous. No more so than his own fingernails, if they were let to grow a bit.

No, on the whole, it didn't look too tough to handle physically. Unless, of course, that bush was made of pretty tough stuff. Carson looked around him and, yes, right within reach was another bush of identical type.

He reached over and snapped off a twig. It was brittle, easy to break. Of course, the Roller might have been faking deliberately but he didn't think so.

On the other hand, where was it vulnerable? Just how would he go about killing it, if he got the chance? He went back to studying it. The outer hide looked pretty tough. He'd need a sharp weapon of some sort. He picked up the piece of rock again. It was about twelve inches long, narrow, and fairly sharp on one end. If it chipped like flint, he could make a serviceable knife out of it.

The Roller was continuing its investigations of the bushes. It rolled again, to the nearest one of another type. A little blue lizard, many-legged like the one Carson had seen on his side of the barrier, darted out from under the bush.

A tentacle of the Roller lashed out and caught it, picked it up. Another tentacle whipped over and began to pull legs off the lizard, as coldly and calmly as it had pulled twigs off the bush. The creature struggled frantically and emitted a shrill squealing sound that was the first sound Carson had heard here other than the sound of his own voice.

Carson shuddered and wanted to turn his eyes away. But he made himself continue to watch; anything he could learn about his opponent might prove valuable. Even this knowledge of its unnecessary cruelty. Particularly, he thought with a sudden vicious surge of emotion, this knowledge of its unnecessary cruelty. It would make it a pleasure to kill the thing, if and when the chance came.

He steeled himself to watch the dismembering of the lizard, for that very reason.

But he felt glad when, with half its legs gone, the lizard quit squealing and struggling and lay limp and dead in the Roller's grasp.

It didn't continue with the rest of the legs. Contemptuously it tossed the dead lizard away from it, in Carson's direction. It arced through the air between them and landed at his feet.

It had come through the barrier! The barrier wasn't there any more!

Carson was on his feet in a flash, the knife gripped tightly in his hand, and leaped forward. He'd settle this thing here and now! With the barrier gone —

But it wasn't gone. He found that out the hard way, running head on into it and nearly knocking himself silly. He bounced back, and fell.

And as he sat up, shaking his head to clear it, he saw something coming through the air toward him, and to duck it, he threw himself flat again on the sand, and to one side. He got his body out of the way, but there was a sudden sharp pain in the calf of his left leg.

He rolled backward, ignoring the pain, and scrambled to his feet. It was a rock, he saw now, that had struck him. And the Roller was picking up another one now, swinging it back gripped between two tentacles, getting ready to throw again.

It sailed through the air toward him, but he was easily able to step out of its way. The Roller, apparently, could throw straight, but not hard nor far. The first rock had struck him only because he had been sitting down and had not seen it coming until it was almost upon him.

Even as he stepped aside from that weak second throw, Carson drew back his right arm and let fly with the rock that was still in his hand. If missiles, he thought with sudden elation, can cross the barrier, then two can play at the game of throwing them. And the good right arm of an Earthman —

He couldn't miss a three-foot sphere at only four-yard range, and he didn't miss. The rock whizzed straight, and with a speed several times that of the missiles the Roller had thrown. It hit dead center, but it hit flat, unfortunately, instead of point first.

But it hit with a resounding thump, and obviously it hurt. The Roller had been reaching for another rock, but it changed its mind and got out of there instead. By the time Carson could pick up and throw another rock, the Roller was forty yards back from the barrier and going strong.

His second throw missed by feet, and his third throw was short. The Roller was back out of range – at least out of range of a missile heavy enough to be damaging.

Carson grinned. That round had been his. Except —

He quit grinning as he bent over to examine the calf of his leg. A jagged edge of the stone had made a pretty deep cut, several inches long. It was bleeding pretty freely, but he didn't think it had gone deep enough to hit an artery. If it stopped bleeding of its own accord, well and good. If not, he was in for trouble.

Finding out one thing, though, took precedence over that cut. The nature of the barrier.

He went forward to it again, this time groping with his hands before him. He found it; then holding one hand against it, he tossed a handful of sand at it with the other hand. The sand went right through. His hand didn't.

Organic matter versus inorganic? No, because the dead lizard had gone through it, and a lizard, alive or dead, was certainly organic. Plant life? He broke off a twig and poked it at the barrier. The twig went through, with no resistance, but when his fingers gripping the twig came to the barrier, they were stopped.

*H*e couldn't get through it, nor could the Roller. But rocks and sand and a dead lizard —

How about a live lizard? He went hunting, under bushes, until he found one, and caught it. He tossed it gently against the barrier and it bounced back and scurried away across the blue sand.

That gave him the answer, in so far as he could determine it now. The screen was a barrier to living things. Dead or inorganic matter could cross it.

That off his mind, Carson looked at his injured leg again. The bleeding was lessening, which meant he wouldn't need to worry about making a tourniquet. But he should find some water, if any was available, to clean the wound.

Water – the thought of it made him realize that he was getting awfully thirsty. He'd *have* to find water, in case this contest turned out to be a protracted one.

Limping slightly now, he started off to make a full circuit of his half of the arena. Guiding himself with one hand along the barrier, he walked to his right until he came to the curving sidewall. It was visible, a dull blue-gray at close range, and the surface of it felt just like the central barrier.

He experimented by tossing a handful of sand at it, and the sand reached the wall and disappeared as it went through. The hemispherical shell was a force-field, too. But an opaque one, instead of transparent like the barrier.

He followed it around until he came back to the barrier, and walked back along the barrier to the point from which he'd started.

No sign of water.

Worried now, he started a series of zigzags back and forth between the barrier and the wall, covering the intervening space thoroughly.

No water. Blue sand, blue bushes, and intolerable heat. Nothing else.

It must be his imagination, he told himself angrily, that he was suffering *that* much from thirst. How long had he been here? Of course, no time at all, according to his own space-time frame. The Entity had told him time stood still out there, while he was here. But his body processes went on here, just the same. And according to his body's reckoning, how long had he been here? Three or four hours, perhaps. Certainly not long enough to be suffering seriously from thirst.

But he was suffering from it; his throat dry and parched. Probably the intense heat was the cause. It was *hot*! A hundred and thirty Fahrenheit, at a guess. A dry, still heat without the slightest movement of air.

He was limping rather badly, and utterly fagged out when he'd finished the futile exploration of his domain.

He stared across at the motionless Roller and hoped it was as miserable as he was. And quite possibly it wasn't enjoying this, either. The Entity had said the conditions here were equally unfamiliar and equally uncomfortable for both of them. Maybe the Roller came from a planet where two-hundred degree heat was the norm. Maybe it was freezing while he was roasting.

Maybe the air was as much too thick for it as it was too thin for him. For the exertion of his explorations had left him panting. The atmosphere here, he realized now, was not much thicker than that on Mars.

No water.

That meant a deadline, for him at any rate. Unless he could find a way to cross that barrier or to kill his enemy from this side of it, thirst would kill him, eventually.

It gave him a feeling of desperate urgency. He *must* hurry. But he made himself sit down a moment to rest, to think.

What was there to do? Nothing, and yet so many things. The several varieties of bushes, for example. They didn't look promising, but he'd have to examine them for possibilities. And his leg – he'd have to do something about that, even without water to clean it. Gather ammunition in the form of rocks. Find a rock that would make a good knife.

His leg hurt rather badly now, and he decided that came first. One type of bush had leaves – or things rather similar to leaves. He pulled off a handful of them and decided, after examination, to take a chance on them. He used them to clean off the sand and dirt and caked blood, then made a pad of fresh leaves and tied it over the wound with tendrils from the same bush.

The tendrils proved unexpectedly tough and strong. They were slender, and soft and pliable, yet he couldn't break them at all. He had to saw them off the bush with the sharp edge of a piece of the blue flint. Some of the thicker ones were over a foot long, and he filed away in his memory, for future reference, the fact that a bunch of the thick ones, tied together, would make a pretty serviceable rope. Maybe he'd be able to think of a use for rope.

Next he made himself a knife. The blue flint *did* chip. From a footlong splinter of it, he fashioned himself a crude but lethal weapon. And of tendrils from the bush, he made himself a rope-belt through which he could thrust the flint knife, to keep it with him all the time and yet have his hands free.

He went back to studying the bushes. There were three other types. One was leafless, dry, brittle, rather like a dried tumbleweed. Another was of soft, crumbly wood, almost like punk. It looked and felt as though it would make excellent tinder for a fire. The third type was the most nearly woodlike. It had fragile leaves that wilted at a touch, but the stalks, although short, were straight and strong.

It was horribly, unbearably hot.

He limped up to the barrier, felt to make sure that it was still there. It was.

He stood watching the Roller for a while. It was keeping a safe distance back from the barrier, out of effective stone-throwing range. It was moving around back there, doing something. He couldn't tell what it was doing.

Once it stopped moving, came a little closer, and seemed to concentrate its attention on him. Again Carson had to fight off a wave of nausea. He threw a stone at it and the Roller retreated and went back to whatever it had been doing before.

At least he could make it keep its distance.

And, he thought bitterly, a devil of a lot of good *that* did him. Just the same, he spent the next hour or two gathering stones of suitable size for throwing, and making several neat piles of them, near his side of the barrier.

His throat burned now. It was difficult for him to think about anything except water.

But he *had* to think about other things. About getting through that barrier, under or over it, getting *at* that red sphere and killing it before this place of heat and thirst killed him first.

The barrier went to the wall upon either side, but how high and how far under the sand?

For just a moment, Carson's mind was too fuzzy to think out how he could find out either of those things. Idly, sitting there in the hot sand – and he didn't remember sitting down – he watched a blue lizard crawl from the shelter of one bush to the shelter of another.

From under the second bush, it looked out at him.

Carson grinned at it. Maybe he was getting a bit punch-drunk, because he remembered suddenly the old story of the desert-colonists on Mars, taken from an older desert story of Earth – 'Pretty soon you get so lonesome you find yourself talking to the lizards, and then not so long after that you find the lizards talking back to you —'

He should have been concentrating, of course, on how to kill the Roller, but instead he grinned at the lizard and said, 'Hello, there.'

The lizard took a few steps toward him. 'Hello,' it said.

Carson was stunned for a moment, and then he put back his head and roared with laughter. It didn't hurt his throat to do so, either; he hadn't been *that* thirsty.

Why not? Why should the Entity who thought up this nightmare of a place not have a sense of humor, along with the other powers he had? Talking lizards, equipped to talk back in my own language, if I talk to them—It's a nice touch.

He grinned at the lizard and said, 'Come on over.' But the lizard turned and ran away, scurrying from bush to bush until it was out of sight.

He was thirsty again.

And he had to *do* something. He couldn't win this contest by sitting here sweating and feeling miserable. He had to *do* something. But what?

Get through the barrier. But he couldn't get through it, or over it. But was he certain he couldn't get under it? And come to think of it, didn't one sometimes find water by digging? Two birds with one stone —

Painfully now, Carson limped up to the barrier and started digging, scooping up sand a double handful at a time. It was slow, hard work because the sand ran in at the edges and the deeper he got the bigger in diameter the hole had to be. How many hours it took him, he didn't know, but he hit bedrock four feet down. Dry bedrock; no sign of water.

And the force-field of the barrier went down clear to the bedrock. No dice. No water. Nothing.

He crawled out of the hole and lay there panting, and then raised his head to look across and see what the Roller was doing. It must be doing something back there.

It was. It was making something out of wood from the bushes, tied together with tendrils. A queerly shaped framework about four feet high and roughly square. To see it better, Carson climbed up onto the mound of sand he had excavated from the hole, and stood there staring.

There were two long levers sticking out of the back of it, one with a cup-shaped affair on the end of it. Seemed to be some sort of catapult, Carson thought.

Sure enough, the Roller was lifting a sizable rock into the cup-shaped outfit. One of his tentacles moved the other lever up and down for a while, and then he turned the machine slightly as though aiming it and the lever with the stone flew up and forward.

The stone raced several yards over Carson's head, so far away that he didn't have to duck, but he judged the distance it had traveled, and whistled softly. He couldn't throw a rock that weight more than half that distance. And even retreating to the rear of his domain wouldn't put him out of range of that machine, if the Roller shoved it forward almost to the barrier.

Another rock whizzed over. Not quite so far away this time.

That thing could be dangerous, he decided. Maybe he'd better do something about it.

Moving from side to side along the barrier, so the catapult couldn't bracket him, he whaled a dozen rocks at it. But that wasn't going to be any good, he saw. They had to be light rocks, or he couldn't throw them that far. If they hit the framework, they bounced off harmlessly. And the Roller had no difficulty, at that distance, in moving aside from those that came near it.

Besides, his arm was tiring badly. He ached all over from sheer weariness. If he could only rest awhile without having to duck rocks from that catapult at regular intervals of maybe thirty seconds each —

He stumbled back to the rear of the arena. Then he saw even that wasn't any good. The rocks reached back there, too, only there were longer intervals between them, as though it took longer to wind up the mechanism, whatever it was, of the catapult.

Wearily he dragged himself back to the barrier again. Several times he fell and could barely rise to his feet to go on. He was, he knew, near the limit of his endurance. Yet he didn't dare stop moving now, until and unless he could put that catapult out of action. If he fell asleep, he'd never wake up.

One of the stones from it gave him the first glimmer of an idea. It struck upon one of the piles of stones he'd gathered together near the barrier to use as ammunition, and it struck sparks.

Sparks. Fire. Primitive man had made fire by striking sparks, and with some of those dry crumbly bushes as tinder —

Luckily, a bush of that type was near him. He broke it off, took it over to a pile of stones, then patiently hit one stone against another until a spark touched the punklike wood of the bush. It went up in flames so fast that it singed his eyebrows and was burned to an ash within seconds.

But he had the idea now, and within minutes he had a little fire going in the lee of the mound of sand he'd made digging the hole an hour or two ago. Tinder bushes had started it, and other bushes which burned, but more slowly, kept it a steady flame.

The tough wirelike tendrils didn't burn readily; that made the firebombs easy to make and throw. A bundle of faggots tied about a small stone to give it weight and a loop of the tendril to swing it by.

He made half a dozen of them before he lighted and threw the first. It went wide, and the Roller started a quick retreat, pulling the catapult after him. But Carson had the others ready and threw them in rapid succession. The fourth wedged in the catapult's framework, and did the trick. The Roller tried desperately to put out the spreading blaze by throwing sand, but its clawed tentacles would take only a spoonful at a time and his efforts were ineffectual. The catapult burned.

The Roller moved safely away from the fire and seemed to concentrate its attention on Carson and again he felt that wave of hatred and nausea. But more weakly; either the Roller itself was weakening or Carson had learned how to protect himself against the mental attack.

He thumbed his nose at it and then sent it scuttling back to safety by throwing a stone. The Roller went clear to the back of its half of the arena and started pulling up bushes again. Probably it was going to make another catapult.

Carson verified – for the hundredth time – that the barrier

was still operating, and then found himself sitting in the sand beside it because he was suddenly too weak to stand up.

His leg throbbed steadily now and the pangs of thirst were severe. But those things paled beside the utter physical exhaustion that gripped his entire body.

And the heat.

Hell must be like this, he thought. The hell that the ancients had believed in. He fought to stay awake, and yet staying awake seemed futile, for there was nothing he could do. Nothing, while the barrier remained impregnable and the Roller stayed back out of range.

But there must be *something*. He tried to remember things he had read in books of archaeology about the methods of fighting used back in the days before metal and plastic. The stone missile, that had come first, he thought. Well, that he already had.

The only improvement on it would be a catapult, such as the Roller had made. But he'd never be able to make one, with the tiny bits of wood available from the bushes – no single piece longer than a foot or so. Certainly he could figure out a mechanism for one, but he didn't have the endurance left for a task that would take days.

Days? But the Roller had made one. Had they been here days already? Then he remembered that the Roller had many tentacles to work with and undoubtedly could do such work faster than he.

And besides, a catapult wouldn't decide the issue. He had to do better than that.

Bow and arrow? No; he had tried archery once and knew his own ineptness with a bow. Even with a modern sportsman's durasteel weapon, made for accuracy. With such a crude, pieced-together outfit as he could make here, he doubted if he could shoot as far as he could throw a rock, and knew he couldn't shoot as straight.

Spear? Well, he *could* make that. It would be useless as a throwing weapon at any distance, but would be a handy thing at close range, if he ever got to close range.

And making one would give him something to do. Help keep his mind from wandering, as it was beginning to do. Sometimes now, he had to concentrate awhile before he could remember why he was here, why he had to kill the Roller.

Luckily he was still beside one of the piles of stones. He

sorted through it until he found one shaped roughly like a spearhead. With a smaller stone he began to chip it into shape, fashioning sharp shoulders on the sides so that if it penetrated it would not pull out again.

Like a harpoon? There was something in that idea, he thought. A harpoon was better than a spear, maybe, for this crazy contest. If he could once get it into the Roller, and had a rope on it, he could pull the Roller up against the barrier and the stone blade of his knife would reach through that barrier, even if his hands wouldn't.

The shaft was harder to make than the head. But by splitting and joining the main stems of four of the bushes, and wrapping the joints with the tough but thin tendrils, he got a strong shaft about four feet long, and tied the stone head in a notch cut in the end.

It was crude, but strong.

And the rope. With the thin tough tendrils he made himself twenty feet of line. It was light and didn't look strong, but he knew it would hold his weight and to spare. He tied one end of it to the shaft of the harpoon and the other end about his right wrist.

At least, if he threw his harpoon across the barrier, he'd be able to pull it back if he missed.

Then when he had tied the last knot and there was nothing more he could do, the heat and the weariness and the pain in his leg and the dreadful thirst were suddenly a thousand times worse than they had been before.

He tried to stand up, to see what the Roller was doing now, and found he couldn't get to his feet. On the third try, he got as far as his knees and then fell flat again.

'I've got to sleep,' he thought. 'If a showdown came now, I'd be helpless. He'd come up here and kill me, if he knew. I've got to regain some strength.'

Slowly, painfully, he crawled back away from the barrier. Ten yards, twenty . . .

The jar of something thudding against the sand near him waked him from a confused and horrible dream to a more confused and more horrible reality, and he opened his eyes again to blue radiance over blue sand.

How long had he slept? A minute? A day?

Another stone thudded nearer and threw sand on him. He got his arms under him and sat up. He turned around and saw the Roller twenty yards away, at the barrier.

It rolled away hastily as he sat up, not stopping until it was as far away as it could get.

He'd fallen asleep too soon, he realized, while he was still in range of the Roller's throwing ability. Seeing him lying motionless, it had dared come up to the barrier to throw at him. Luckily, it didn't realize how weak he was, or it could have stayed there and kept on throwing stones.

Had he slept long? He didn't think so, because he felt just as he had before. Not rested at all, no thirstier, no different. Probably he'd been there only a few minutes.

He started crawling again, this time forcing himself to keep going until he was as far as he could go, until the colorless, opaque wall of the arena's outer shell was only a yard away.

Then things slipped away again . . .

When he awoke, nothing about him was changed, but this time he knew that he had slept a long time.

The first thing he became aware of was the inside of his mouth; it was dry, caked. His tongue was swollen.

Something was wrong, he knew, as he returned slowly to full awareness. He felt less tired, the stage of utter exhaustion had passed. The sleep had taken care of that.

But there was pain, agonizing pain. It wasn't until he tried to move that he knew that it came from his leg.

He raised his head and looked down at it. It was swollen terribly below the knee and the swelling showed even halfway up his thigh. The plant tendrils he had used to tie on the protective pad of leaves now cut deeply into the swollen flesh.

To get his knife under that imbedded lashing would have been impossible. Fortunately, the final knot was over the shin bone, in front, where the vine cut in less deeply than elsewhere. He was able, after an agonizing effort, to untie the knot.

A look under the pad of leaves told him the worst. Infection and blood poisoning, both pretty bad and getting worse.

And without drugs, without cloth, without even *water*, there wasn't a thing he could do about it.

Not a thing, except *die*, when the poison had spread through his system.

He knew it was hopeless, then, and that he'd lost.

And with him, humanity. When he died here, out there in the universe he knew, all his friends, everybody, would die too.

And Earth and the colonized planets would be the home of the red, rolling, alien Outsiders. Creatures out of nightmare, things without a human attribute, who picked lizards apart for the fun of it.

It was the thought of that which gave him courage to start crawling, almost blindly in pain, toward the barrier again. Not crawling on hands and knees this time, but pulling himself along only by his arms and hands.

A chance in a million, that maybe he'd have strength left, when he got there, to throw his harpoon-spear just *once*, and with deadly effect, if – on another chance in a million – the Roller would come up to the barrier. Or if the barrier was gone, now.

It took him years, it seemed, to get there.

The barrier wasn't gone. It was as impassable as when he'd first felt it.

And the Roller wasn't at the barrier. By raising up on his elbows, he could see it at the back of its part of the arena, working on a wooden framework that was a half-completed duplicate of the catapult he'd destroyed.

It was moving slowly now. Undoubtedly it had weakened, too.

But Carson doubted that it would ever need that second catapult. He'd be dead, he thought, before it was finished.

If he could attract it to the barrier, now, while he was still alive— He waved an arm and tried to shout, but his parched throat would make no sound.

Or if he could get through the barrier ...

His mind must have slipped for a moment, for he found himself beating his fists against the barrier in futile rage, and made himself stop.

He closed his eyes, tried to make himself calm.

'Hello,' said the voice.

It was a small, thin voice. It sounded like ...

He opened his eyes and turned his head. It *was* the lizard.

'Go away,' Carson wanted to say. 'Go away, you're not really there, or you're there but not really talking. I'm imagining things again.'

But he couldn't talk; his throat and tongue were past all speech with the dryness. He closed his eyes again.

'Hurt,' said the voice. 'Kill. Hurt – kill. Come.'

He opened his eyes again. The blue ten-legged lizard was still there. It ran a little way along the barrier, came back, started off again, and came back.

'Hurt,' it said. 'Kill. Come.'

Again it started off, and came back. Obviously it wanted Carson to follow it along the barrier.

He closed his eyes again. The voice kept on. The same three meaningless words. Each time he opened his eyes, it ran off and came back.

'Hurt. Kill. Come.'

Carson groaned. There would be no peace unless he followed the blasted thing. Like it wanted him to.

He followed it, crawling. Another sound, a high-pitched squealing, came to his ears and grew louder.

There was something lying in the sand, writhing, squealing. Something small, blue, that looked like a lizard and yet didn't . . .

Then he saw what it was – the lizard whose legs the Roller had pulled off, so long ago. But it wasn't dead; it had come back to life and was wriggling and screaming in agony.

'Hurt,' said the other lizard. 'Hurt. Kill. Kill.'

Carson understood. He took the flint knife from his belt and killed the tortured creature. The live lizard scurried off quickly.

Carson turned back to the barrier. He leaned his hands and head against it and watched the Roller, far back, working on the new catapult.

'I could get that far,' he thought, 'if I could get through. If I could get through, I might win yet. It looks weak, too. I might . . .'

And then there was another reaction of black hopelessness, when pain snapped his will and he wished that he were dead. He envied the lizard he'd just killed. It didn't have to live on and suffer. And he did. It would be hours, it might be days, before the blood poisoning killed him.

If only he could use that knife on himself . . .

But he knew he wouldn't. As long as he was alive, there was the millionth chance . . .

He was straining, pushing on the barrier with the flat of his hands, and he noticed his arms, how thin and scrawny they were now. He must really have been here a long time, for days, to get as thin as that.

How much longer now, before he died? How much more

heat and thirst and pain could flesh stand?

For a little while he was almost hysterical again, and then came a time of deep calm, and a thought that was startling.

The lizard he had just killed. *It had crossed the barrier, still alive.* It had come from the Roller's side; the Roller had pulled off its legs and then tossed it contemptuously at him and it had come through the barrier. He'd thought, because the lizard was dead.

But it hadn't been dead; it had been unconscious.

A live lizard couldn't go through the barrier, but an unconscious one could. The barrier was not a barrier, then, to living flesh, but to conscious flesh. It was a *mental* projection, a *mental* hazard.

And with that thought, Carson started crawling along the barrier to make his last desperate gamble. A hope so forlorn that only a dying man would have dared try it.

No use weighing the odds of success. Not when, if he didn't try it, those odds were infinitely to zero.

He crawled along the barrier to the dune of sand, about four feet high, which he'd scooped out in trying – how many days ago? – to dig under the barrier or to reach water.

That mound was right at the barrier, its farther slope half on one side of the barrier, half on the other.

Taking with him a rock from the pile nearby, he climbed up to the top of the dune and over the top, and lay there against the barrier, his weight leaning against it so that if the barrier were taken away he'd roll on down the short slope, into the enemy territory.

He checked to be sure that the knife was safely in his rope belt, that the harpoon was in the crook of his left arm and that the twenty-foot rope was fastened to it and to his wrist.

Then with his right hand he raised the rock with which he would hit himself on the head. Luck would have to be with him on that blow; it would have to be hard enough to knock him out, but not hard enough to knock him out for long.

He had a hunch that the Roller was watching him, and would see him roll down through the barrier, and come to investigate. It would think he was dead, he hoped – he thought it had probably drawn the same deduction about the nature of the barrier he had drawn. But it would come cautiously. He would have a little time . . .

He struck.

Pain brought him back to consciousness. A sudden, sharp pain in his hip that was different from the throbbing pain in his head and the throbbing pain in his leg.

But he had, thinking things out before he had struck himself, anticipated that very pain, even hoped for it, and had steeled himself against awakening with a sudden movement.

He lay still, but opened his eyes just a slit, and saw that he had guessed rightly. The Roller was coming closer. It was twenty feet away and the pain that had awakened him was the stone it had tossed to see whether he was alive or dead.

He lay still. It came closer, fifteen feet away, and stopped again. Carson scarcely breathed.

As nearly as possible, he was keeping his mind a blank, lest its telepathic ability detect consciousness in him. And with his mind blanked out that way, the impact of its thoughts upon his mind was nearly soul shattering.

He felt sheer horror at the utter *alienness*, the *differentness* of those thoughts. Things that he felt but could not understand and could never express, because no terrestrial language had words, no terrestrial mind had images to fit them. The mind of a spider, he thought, or the mind of a praying mantis or a Martian sand-serpent, raised to intelligence and put in telepathic rapport with human minds, would be a homely familiar thing, compared to this.

He understood now that the Entity had been right: Man or Roller, and the universe was not a place that could hold them both. Farther apart than god and devil, there could never be even a balance between them.

Closer. Carson waited until it was only feet away, until its clawed tentacles reached out ...

Oblivious to agony now, he sat up, raised and flung the harpoon with all the strength remained to him. Or he thought it was all; sudden final strength flooded through him, along with a sudden forgetfulness of pain as definite as a nerve block.

As the Roller, deeply stabbed by the harpoon, rolled away, Carson tried to get to his feet to run after it. He couldn't do that; he fell, but kept crawling.

It reached the end of the rope, and he was jerked forward by the pull of his wrist. It dragged him a few feet and then stopped. Carson kept on going, pulling himself toward it hand over hand along the rope.

It stopped there, writhing tentacles trying in vain to pull out the harpoon. It seemed to shudder and quiver, and then it must have realized that it couldn't get away, for it rolled back toward him, clawed tentacles reaching out.

Stone knife in hand, he met it. He stabbed, again and again, while those horrid claws ripped skin and flesh and muscle from his body.

He stabbed and slashed, and at last it was still.

A bell was ringing, and it took him a while after he'd opened his eyes to tell where he was and what it was. He was strapped into the seat of his scouter, and the visiplate before him showed only empty space. No Outsider ship and no impossible planet.

The bell was the communications plate signal; someone wanted him to switch power into the receiver. Purely reflex action enabled him to reach forward and throw the lever.

The face of Brander, captain to the *Magellan*, mother-ship of his group of scouters, flashed into the screen. His face was pale and his black eyes glowed with excitement.

'*Magellan* to Carson,' he snapped. 'Come on in. The fight's over. We've won!'

The screen went blank; Brander would be signaling the other scouters of his command.

Slowly, Carson set the controls for the return. Slowly, unbelievingly, he unstrapped himself from the seat and went back to get a drink at the cold-water tank. For some reason, he was unbelievably thirsty. He drank six glasses.

He leaned there against the wall, trying to think.

Had it happened? He was in good health, sound, uninjured. His thirst had been mental rather than physical; his throat hadn't been dry. His leg —

He pulled up his trouser leg and looked at the calf. There was a long white scar there, but a perfectly healed scar. It hadn't been there before. He zipped open the front of his shirt and saw that his chest and abdomen was criss-crossed with tiny, almost unnoticeable, perfectly healed scars.

It *had* happened.

The scouter, under automatic control, was already entering the hatch of the mother-ship. The grapples pulled it into its individual lock, and a moment later a buzzer indicated that the lock was air-filled. Carson opened the hatch and stepped outside, went through the double door of the lock.

He went right to Brander's office, went in, and saluted.

Brander still looked dizzily dazed. 'Hi, Carson,' he said. 'What you missed! What a show!'

'What happened, sir?'

'Don't know, exactly. We fired one salvo, and their whole fleet went up in dust! Whatever it was jumped from ship to ship in a flash, even the ones we hadn't aimed at and that were out of range! The whole fleet disintegrated before our eyes, and we didn't get the paint of a single ship scratched!

'We can't even claim credit for it. Must have been some unstable component in the metal they used, and our sighting shot just set it off. Man, oh man, too bad you missed all the excitement.'

Carson managed to grin. It was a sickly ghost of a grin, for it would be days before he'd be over the mental impact of his experience, but the captain wasn't watching, and didn't notice.

'Yes, sir,' he said. Common sense, more than modesty, told him he'd be branded forever as the worst liar in space if he ever said any more than that. 'Yes, sir, too bad I missed all the excitement.'

Surface Tension
by James Blish

Dr. Chatvieux took a long time over the microscope, leaving la Ventura with nothing to do but look out at the dead landscape of Hydrot. Waterscape, he thought, would be a better world. The new world had shown only one small, triangular continent, set amid endless ocean; and even the continent was mostly swamp.

The wreck of the seed-ship lay broken squarely across the one real spur of rock Hydrot seemed to possess, which reared a magnificent twenty-one feet above sea-level. From this eminence, la Ventura could see forty miles to the horizon across a flat bed of mud. The red light of the star Tau Ceti, glinting upon thousands of small lakes, pools, ponds, and puddles, made the watery plain look like a mosaic of onyx and ruby.

'If I were a religious man,' the pilot said suddenly, 'I'd call this a plain case of divine vengeance.'

Chatvieux said: 'Hmn?'

'It's as if we've been struck down for – is it *hubris*, arrogant pride?'

'Well, is it?' Chatvieux said, looking up at last. 'I don't feel exactly swollen with pride at the moment. Do you?'

'I'm not exactly proud of my piloting,' la Ventura admitted. 'But that isn't quite what I meant. I was thinking about why we came here in the first place. It takes arrogant pride to think that you can scatter men, or at least things like men, all over the face of the Galaxy. It takes even more pride to do the job – to pack up all the equipment and move from planet to planet and actually make men suitable for every place you touch.'

'I suppose it does,' Chatvieux said. 'But we're only one of several hundred seed-ships in this limb of the Galaxy, so I doubt that the gods picked us out as special sinners.' He smiled drily. 'If they had, maybe they'd have left us our ultraphone, so the Colonization Council could hear about our cropper. Besides, Paul, we try to produce men adapted to Earthlike planets, nothing more. We've sense enough – humility enough, if you like – to know that we can't adapt men to Jupiter or to Tau Ceti.'

'Anyhow, we're here,' la Ventura said grimly. 'And we

aren't going to get off. Phil tells me that we don't even have our germ-cell bank any more, so we can't seed this place in the usual way. We've been thrown onto a dead world and dared to adapt to it. What are the panatropes going to do – provide built-in water wings?'

'No,' Chatvieux said calmly. 'You and I and the rest of us are going to die, Paul. Panatropic techniques don't work on the body, only on the inheritance-carrying factors. We can't give you built-in waterwings, any more than we can give you a new set of brains. I think we'll be able to populate this world with men, but we won't live to see it.'

The pilot thought about it, a lump of cold collecting gradually in his stomach. 'How long do you give us?' he said at last.

'Who knows? A month, perhaps.'

The bulkhead leading to the wrecked section of the ship was pushed back, admitting salty, muggy air, heavy with carbon dioxide. Philip Strasvogel, the communications officer, came in, tracking mud. Like la Ventura, he was now a man without a function, but it did not appear to bother him. He unbuckled from around his waist a canvas belt into which plastic vials were stuffed like cartridges.

'More samples, Doc,' he said. 'All alike – water, very wet. I have some quicksand on one boot, too. Find anything?'

'A good deal, Phil. Thanks. Are the others around?'

Strasvogel poked his head out and hallooed. Other voices rang out over the mudflats. Minutes later, the rest of the survivors were crowding into the panatrope deck: Saltonstall, Chatvieux's senior assistant; Eunice Wagner, the only remaining ecologist; Eleftherios Venezuelos, the delegate from the Colonization Council; and Joan Heath, a midshipman whose duties, like la Ventura's and Strasvogel's, were now without meaning.

Five men and two women – to colonize a planet on which standing room meant treading water.

They came in quietly and found seats or resting places on the deck, on the edges of tables, in corners.

Venezuelos said: 'What's the verdict, Dr. Chatvieux?'

'This place isn't dead,' Chatvieux said. 'There's life in the sea and in the fresh water, both. On the animal side of the ledger, evolution seems to have stopped with the crustacea; the most advanced form I've found is a tiny crayfish, from one of the local rivulets. The ponds and puddles are well-stocked with protozoa and small metazoans, right up to a wonderfully variegated rotifer population – including a castle-building rotifer like Earth's *Floscularidae*. The plants run from simple algae to the thalluslike species.'

'The sea is about the same,' Eunice said, 'I've found some of the larger simple metazoans – jellyfish and so on – and some crayfish almost as big as lobsters. But it's normal to find salt-water species running larger than fresh-water.'

'In short,' Chatvieux said, 'We'll survive here – if we fight.'

'Wait a minute,' la Ventura said. 'You've just finished telling me that we wouldn't survive. And you were talking about us, not about the species, because we don't have our germ-cell banks any more. What's ...'

'I'll get to that again in a moment,' Chatvieux said. 'Salton-stall, what would you think of taking to sea? We came out of it once; maybe we could come out of it again.'

'No good,' Saltonstall said immediately. '*I* like the idea, but I don't think this planet ever heard of Swinburne, or Homer, either. Looking at it as a colonization problem, as if we weren't involved ourselves, I wouldn't give you a credit for *epi oinopa ponton*. The evolutionary pressure there is too high, the competition from other species is prohibitive; seeding the sea should be the last thing we attempt. The colonists wouldn't have a chance to learn a thing before they were destroyed.'

'Why?' la Ventura said. The death in his stomach was becoming hard to placate.

'Eunice, do your sea-going Coelenterates include anything like the Portuguese man-of-war?'

The ecologist nodded.

'There's your answer, Paul,' Saltonstall said. 'The sea is out. It's got to be fresh water, where the competing creatures are less formidable and there are more places to hide.'

'We can't compete with a jellyfish?' la Ventura asked, swallowing.

'No, Paul,' Chatvieux said. 'The panatropes make adaptations, not gods. They take human germ-cells – in this case, our own, since our bank was wiped out in the crash – and modify them toward creatures who can live in any reasonable environment. The result will be manlike and intelligent. It usually shows the donor's personality pattern, too.

'But we can't transmit memory. The adapted man is worse than a child in his new environment. He has no history, no techniques, no precedents, not even a language. Ordinarily the seeding teams more or less take him through elementary school before they leave the planet, but we won't survive long enough for that. We'll have to design our colonists with plenty of built-in protections and locate them in the most favorable environment possible, so that at least some of them will survive the learning process.'

The pilot thought about it, but nothing occurred to him which did not make the disaster seem realer and more intimate with each passing second. 'One of the new creatures can have my personality pattern, but it won't be able to remember being me. Is that right?'

'That's it. There may be just the faintest of residuums – panatropy's given us some data which seem to support the old Jungian notion of ancestral memory. But we're all going to die on Hydrot, Paul. There's no avoiding that. Somewhere we'll leave behind people who behave as we would, think and feel as we would, but who won't remember la Ventura, or Chatvieux, or Joan Heath – or Earth.'

The pilot said nothing more. There was a gray taste in his mouth.

'Saltonstall, what do you recommend as a form?'

The panatropist pulled reflectively at his nose. 'Webbed extremities, of course, with thumbs and big toes heavy and thorn-like for defense until the creature has had a chance to learn. Book-lungs, like the arachnids, working out of intercostal spiracles – they are gradually adaptable to atmosphere-breathing, if it ever decides to come out of the water. Also I'd suggest sporulation. As an aquatic, our colonist is going to have an indefinite lifespan, but we'll have to give it a breeding cycle of about six weeks to keep its numbers up during the learning period; so there'll have to be a definite break of some duration in its active year. Otherwise it'll hit the population problem before it's learned enough to cope with it.'

'Also, it'll be better if our colonists could winter inside a good hard shell,' Eunice Wagner added in agreement. 'So sporulation's the obvious answer. Most microscopic creatures have it.'

'Microscopic?' Phil said incredulously.

'Certainly,' Chatvieux said, amused. 'We can't very well

crowd a six-foot man into a two-foot puddle. But that raises a question. We'll have tough competition from the rotifers, and some of them aren't strictly microscopic. I don't think your average colonist should run under 25 microns, Saltonstall. Give them a chance to slug it out.'

'I was thinking of making them twice that big.'

'Then they'd be the biggest things in their environment,' Eunice Wagner pointed out, 'and won't ever develop any skills. Besides, if you make them about rotifer size, it'll give them an incentive for pushing out the castle-building rotifers.

'They'll be able to take over the castles as dwellings.'

Chatvieux nodded. 'All right, let's get started. While the panatropes are being calibrated, the rest of us can put our heads together on leaving a record for these people. We'll micro-engrave the record on a set of corrosion-proof metal leaves, of a size our colonists can handle conveniently. Some day they may puzzle it out.'

'Question,' Eunice Wagner said. 'Are we going to tell them they're microscopic? I'm opposed to it. It'll saddle their entire early history with a gods-and-demons mythology they'd be better off without.'

'Yes, we are,' Chatvieux said; and la Ventura could tell by the change in the tone of his voice that he was speaking now as their senior. 'These people will be of the race of men, Eunice. We want them to win their way back to the community of men. They are not toys, to be protected from the truth forever in a fresh-water womb.'

'I'll make that official,' Venezuelos said, and that was that.

And then, essentially, it was all over. They went through the motions. Already they were beginning to be hungry. After la Ventura had his personality pattern recorded, he was out of it. He sat by himself at the far end of the ledge, watching Tau Ceti go redly down, chucking pebbles into the nearest pond, wondering morosely which nameless puddle was to be his Lethe.

He never found out, of course. None of them did.

I

Old Shar set down the heavy metal plate at last, and gazed instead out the window of the castle, apparently resting his eyes on the glowing green-gold obscurity of the summer waters. In the soft fluorescence which played down upon him, from the Noc dozing impassively in the groined vault of the chamber, Lavon could see that he was in fact a young man. His face was so delicately formed as to suggest that it had not been many seasons since he had first emerged from his spore.

But of course there had been no real reason to expect an old man. All the Shars had been referred to traditionally as 'old' Shar. The reason, like the reasons for everything else, had been forgotten, but the custom had persisted; the adjective at least gave weight and dignity to the office.

The present Shar belonged to the generation XVI, and hence would have to be at least two seasons younger than Lavon himself. If he was old, it was only in knowledge.

'Lavon, I'm going to have to be honest with you,' Shar said at last, still looking out of the tall, irregular window. 'You've come to me for the secrets on the metal plates, just as your predecessors did to me. I can give some of them to you – but for the most part, I don't know what they mean.'

'After so many generations?' Lavon asked, surprised. 'Wasn't it Shar III who first found out how to read them? That was a long time ago.'

The young man turned and looked at Lavon with eyes made dark and wide by the depths into which they had been staring. 'I can read what's on the plates, but most of it seems to make no sense. Worst of all, the plates are incomplete. You didn't know that? They are. One of them was lost in a battle during the final war with the Eaters, while these castles were still in their hands.'

'What am I here for, then?' Lavon said. 'Isn't there anything of value on the remaining plates? Do they really contain "the wisdom of the Creators" or is that another myth?'

'No. No, that's true,' Shar said slowly, 'as far as it goes.'

He paused, and both men turned and gazed at the ghostly creature which had appeared suddenly outside the window. Then Shar said gravely, 'Come in, Para.'

The slipper-shaped organism, nearly transparent except for the thousands of black-and-silver granules and frothy bubbles which packed its interior, glided into the chamber and hovered, with a muted whirring of cilia. For a moment it remained silent, probably speaking telepathically to the Noc floating in the vault, after the ceremonious fashion of all the protos. No human had ever intercepted one of these colloquies, but there was no doubt about their reality: humans had used them for long-range communication for generations.

Then the Para's cilia buzzed once more. Each separate hair-like process vibrated at an independent, changing rate; the resulting sound waves spread through the water, intermodulating, reinforcing or canceling each other. The aggregate wavefront, by the time it reached human ears, was recognizable human speech.

'We are arrived, Shar and Lavon, according to the custom.'

'And welcome,' said Shar. 'Lavon, let's leave this matter of the plates for a while, until you hear what Para has to say; that's a part of the knowledge Lavons must have as they come of age, and it comes before the plates. I can give you some hints of what we are. First Para has to tell you something about what we aren't.'

Lavon nodded, willingly enough, and watched the proto as it settled gently to the surface of the hewn table at which Shar had been sitting. There was in the entity such a perfection and economy of organization, such a grace and surety of movement, that he could hardly believe in his own new-won maturity. Para, like all the protos, made him feel not, perhaps, poorly thought-out, but at least unfinished.

'We know that in this universe there is logically no place for man,' the gleaming, now immobile cylinder upon the table droned abruptly. 'Our memory is the common property to all our races. It reaches back to a time when there were no such creatures as men here. It remembers also that once upon a day there were men here, suddenly, and in some numbers. Their spores littered the bottom; we found the spores only a short time after our season's Awakening, and in them we saw the forms of men slumbering.

'Then men shattered their spores and emerged. They were intelligent, active. And they were gifted with a trait, a character, possessed by no other creature in this world. Not even the savage Eaters had it. Men organized us to exterminate the Eaters and therein lay the difference. Men had initiative. We have the word now, which you gave us, and we apply it, but we still do not know what the thing is that it labels.'

'You fought beside us,' Lavon said.

'Gladly. We'd never have thought of that war by ourselves,

but it was good and brought good. Yet we wondered. We saw that men were poor swimmers, poor walkers, poor crawlers, poor climbers. We saw that men were formed to make and use tools, a concept we still do not understand, for so wonderful a gift is largely wasted in this universe, and there is no other. What good are too-useful members such as the hands of men? We do not know. It seems plain that so radical a thing should lead to a much greater rulership over worlds than has, in fact, proven to be possible for men.'

Lavon's head was spinning. 'Para, I had no notion that you people were philosophers.'

'The protos are old,' Shar said. He had again turned to look out the window, his hands locked behind his back. 'They aren't philosophers, Lavon, but they are remorseless logicians. Listen to Para.'

'To this reasoning there could be not one outcome,' the Para said. 'Our strange ally, Man, was like nothing else in this universe. He was and is ill-fitted for it. He does not belong here; he has been – adopted. This drives us to think that there are other universes besides this one, but where these universes might lie, and what their properties might be, it is impossible to imagine. We have no imagination, as men know.'

Was the creature being ironic? Lavon could not tell. He said slowly: 'Other universes? How could that be true?'

'We do not know,' the Para's uninflected voice hummed. Lavon waited, but obviously the proto had nothing more to say.

Shar had resumed sitting on the window sill, clasping his knees, watching the come and go of dim shapes in the lighted gulf. 'It is quite true,' he said. 'What is written on the remaining plates makes it plain. Let me tell you now what they say.

'*We were made*, Lavon. We were made by men who are not as we are, but men who were our ancestors all the same. They were caught in some disaster, and they made us, and put us here in our universe – so that, even though they had to die, the race of men would live.'

Lavon surged up from the woven spyrogyra mat upon which he had been sitting. 'You must think I'm a fool!' he said sharply.

'No. You're our Lavon; you have a right to know the facts. Make what you like of them.' Shar swung his webbed toes back into the chamber. 'What I've told you may be hard to believe, but it seems to be so; what Para says backs it up. Our unfitness to live here is selfevident. I'll give you some examples:

'The past four Shars discovered that we won't get any further in our studies until we learn how to control heat. We've produced enough heat chemically to show that even the water around us changes when the temperature gets high enough. But there we're stopped.'

'Why?'

'Because heat produced in open water is carried off as rapidly as it's produced. Once we tried to enclose that heat, and we blew up a whole tube of the castle and killed everything in range; the shock was terrible. We measured the pressures that were involved in that explosion, and we discovered that no substance we know could have resisted them. Theory suggest some stronger substances – *but we need heat to form them!*

'Take our chemistry. We live in water. Everything seems to dissolve in water, to some extent. How do we confine a chemical test to the crucible we put it in? How do we maintain a solution at one dilution? I don't know. Every avenue leads me to the same stone door. We're thinking creatures, Lavon, but there's something drastically wrong in the way we think about this universe we live in. It just doesn't seem to lead to results.'

Lavon pushed back his floating hair futilely. 'Maybe you're thinking about the wrong results. We've had no trouble with warfare, or crops, or practical things like that. If we can't create much heat, well, most of us won't miss it; we don't need any. What's the other universe supposed to be like, the one our ancestors lived in? Is it better than this one?'

'I don't know,' Shar admitted. 'It was so different that it's hard to compare the two. The metal plates tell a story about men who were traveling from one place to another in a container that moved by itself. The only analogy I can think of is the shallops of diatom shells that our youngsters use to sled along the thermocline; but evidently what's meant is something much bigger.

'I picture a huge shallop, closed on all sides, big enough to hold many people – maybe twenty or thirty. It had to travel for generations through some kind of space where there wasn't any water to breathe, so that the people had to carry their own water and renew it constantly. There were no seasons; no yearly turnover; no ice forming on the sky, because there wasn't any sky in a closed shallop; no spore formation.

'Then the shallop was wrecked somehow. The people in it knew they were going to die. They made us, and put us here, as if we were their children. Because they had to die, they wrote their story on the plates, to tell us what had happened. I suppose we'd understand it better if we had the plate Shar III lost during the war, but we don't.'

'The whole thing sounds like a parable,' Lavon said, shrugging. 'Or a song. I can see why you don't understand it. What I can't see is why you bother to try.'

'Because of the plates,' Shar said. 'You've handled them yourself, so you know that we've nothing like them. We have crude, impure metals we've hammered out, metals that last for a while and then decay. But the plates shine on and on.

'They don't change; our hammers and graving tools break against them; the little heat we can generate leaves them unharmed. Those plates weren't formed in our universe – and that one fact makes every word on them important to me. Someone went to a great deal of trouble to make those plates indestructible to give them to us. Someone to whom the word "stars" was important enough to be worth fourteen repetitions, despite the fact that the word doesn't seem to mean anything. I'm ready to think that if our makers repeated the word even twice on a record that seems likely to last forever, it's important for us to know what it means.'

'All these extra universes and huge shallops and meaningless words – I can't say that they don't exist, but I don't see what difference it makes. The Shars of a few generations ago spent their whole lives breeding better algae crops for us, and showing us how to cultivate them instead of living haphazardly off bacteria. That was well worth doing. The Lavons of those days evidently got along without the metal plates, and saw to it that the Shars did, too: Well, as far as I'm concerned, you're welcome to the plates, if you like them better than crop improvement – but I think they ought to be thrown away.'

'All right,' Shar said, shrugging. 'If you don't want them, that ends the traditional interview. We'll go our . . .'

There was a rising drone from the table-top. The Para was lifting itself, waves of motion passing over its cilia, like the waves which went across the fruiting stalks of the fields of delicate fungi with which the bottom was planted. It had been so silent that Lavon had forgotten it; he could tell from Shar's startlement that Shar had, too.

'This is a great decision,' the waves of sound washing from the creature throbbed. 'Every proto has heard it and agrees with it. We have been afraid of these metal plates for a long time, afraid that men would learn to understand them and to follow what they say to some secret place, leaving the protos behind. Now we are not afraid.'

'There wasn't anything to be afraid of,' Lavon said indulgently.

'No, Lavon, before you had said so,' Para said. 'We are glad. We will throw the plates away.'

With that, the shining creature swooped toward the embrasure. With it, it bore away the remaining plates, which had been resting under it on the table-top, suspended delicately in the curved tips of its supple cilia. With a cry, Shar plunged through the water toward the opening.

'Stop, Para!'

But Para was already gone, so swiftly that he had not even heard the call. Shar twisted his body and brought up on one shoulder against the tower hall. He said nothing. His face was enough. Lavon could not look at it for more than an instant.

The shadows of the two men moved slowly along the uneven cobbled floor. The Noc descended toward them from the vault, its single thick tentacle stirring the water, its internal light flaring and fading irregularly. It, too, drifted through the window after its cousin, and sank slowly away toward the bottom. Gently its living glow dimmed, flickered, winked out.

II

For many days, Lavon was able to avoid thinking much about the loss. There was always a great deal of work to be done. Maintenance of the castles, which had been built by the now-extinct Eaters rather than by human hands, was a never-ending task. The thousand dichotomously branching wings tended to crumble, especially at their bases where they spouted from each other, and no Shar had yet come forward with a mortar as good as the rotifer-spittle which had once held them together. In addition, the breaking through of windows and the construction of chambers in the early days had been haphazard and often unsound. The instinctive architecture of the rotifers, after all, had not been meant to meet the needs of human occupants.

And then there were the crops. Men no longer fed precariously upon passing bacteria; now there were the drifting mats of specific water-fungi, rich and nourishing, which had been bred by five generations of Shars. These had to be tended constantly to keep the strains pure, and to keep the older and less intelligent species of the protos from grazing on them. In this latter task, to be sure, the more intricate and far-seeing proto types cooperated, but men were needed to supervise.

There had been a time, after that of the Eaters, when it had been customary to prey upon the slow-moving and stupid diatoms, whose exquisite and fragile glass shells were so easily burst, and who were unable to learn that a friendly voice did not necessarily mean a friend. There were still people who would crack open a diatom when no one else was looking, but they were regarded as barbarians, to the puzzlement of the protos. The blurred and simple-minded speech of the gorgeously engraved plants had brought them into the category of pets – a concept which the protos were utterly unable to grasp, especially since men admitted that diatoms on the half-frustrule were delicious.

Lavon had had to agree, very early, that the distinction was tiny. After all, humans did eat the desmids, which differed from the diatoms only on three particulars: their shells were flexible, they could not move, and they did not speak. Yet to Lavon, as to most men, there did seem to be some kind of distinction, whether the protos could see it or not, and that was that. Under the circumstances he felt that it was a part of his duty, as a leader of men, to protect the diatoms from the occasional poachers who browsed upon them, in defiance of custom, in the high levels of the sunlit sky.

Yet Lavon found it impossible to keep himself busy enough to forget that moment when the last clues to Man's origin and destination had been seized and borne away into dim space.

It might be possible to ask Para for the return of the plates, explain that a mistake had been made. The protos were creatures of implacable logic, but they respected Man, were used to illogic in Man, and might reverse their decision if pressed —

We are sorry. The plates were carried over the bar and released in the gulf. We will have the bottom there searched, but ...

With sick feeling he could not repress, Lavon knew that when the protos decided something was worthless, they did not hide it in some chamber like old women. They threw it away – efficiently.

Yet despite the tormenting of his conscience, Lavon was convinced that the plates were well lost. What had they ever done for man, except to provide Shars with useless things to think about in the late seasons of their lives? What the Shars themselves had done to benefit Man, here, in the water, in the world, in the universe, had been done by direct experimentation. No bit of useful knowledge ever had come from the plates. There had never been anything in the plates but things left unthought. The protos were right.

Lavon shifted his position on the plant frond, where he had been sitting in order to overlook the harvesting of an experimental crop of blue-green, oil-rich algae drifting in a clotted mass close to the top of the sky, and scratched his back gently against the coarse bole. The protos were seldom wrong, after all. Their lack of creativity, their inability to think an original thought, was a gift as well as a limitation. It allowed them to see and feel things at all times as they were – not as they hoped they might be, for they had no ability to hope, either.

'La-von! Laa-vah-on!'

The long halloo came floating up from the sleepy depths. Propping one hand against the top of the frond, Lavon bent and looked down. One of the harvesters was looking up at him, holding loosely the adze with which he had been splitting free the glutinous tetrads of the algae.

'Up here. What's the matter?'

'We have the ripened quadrant cut free. Shall we tow it away?'

'Tow it away,' Lavon said, with a lazy gesture. He leaned back again. At the same instant, a brilliant reddish glory burst into being above him and cast itself down toward the depths like mesh after mesh of the finest-drawn gold. The great light which lived above the sky during the day, brightening or dimming according to some pattern no Shar ever had fathomed, was blooming again.

Few men, caught in the warm glow of that light, could resist looking up at it – especially when the top of the sky itself wrinkled and smiled just a moment's climb or swim away. Yet, as always, Lavon's bemused upward look gave him back nothing but his own distorted, bobbling reflection, and a reflection of the plant on which he rested.

Here was the upper limit, the third of the three surfaces of the universe.

The first surface was the bottom, where the water ended.

The second surface was the thermocline, the invisible division between the colder waters of the bottom and the warm, light waters of the sky. During the height of the warm weather, the thermocline was so definite a division as to make for good sledding and for chilly passage. A real interface formed between the cold, denser bottom waters and the warm reaches and maintained itself almost for the whole of the warm season.

The third surface was the sky. One could no more pass through that surface than one could penetrate the bottom, nor was there any better reason to try. There universe ended. The light which played over it daily, waxing and waning as it chose, seemed to be one of its properties.

Toward the end of the season, the water gradually grew colder and more difficult to breathe, while at the same time the light became duller and stayed for shorter periods between darknesses. Slow currents started to move. The high waters turned chill and began to fall. The bottom mud stirred and smoked away, carrying with it the spores of the fields of fungi. The thermocline tossed, became choppy, and melted away. The sky began to fog with particles of soft silt carried up from the bottom, the walls, the corners of the universe. Before very long, the whole world was cold, inhospitable, flocculent with yellowing, dying creatures.

Then the protos encysted; the bacteria, even most of the plants and, not long afterward, men, too, curled up in their oil-filled amber shells. The world died until the first tentative current of warm water broke the winter silence.

'La-von!'

Just after the long call, a shining bubble rose past Lavon. He reached out and poked it, but it bounded away from his sharp thumb. The gas-bubbles which rose from the bottom in late summer were almost invulnerable – and when some especially hard blow or edge did penetrate them, they broke into smaller bubbles which nothing could touch, and fled toward the sky, leaving behind a remarkably bad smell.

Gas. There was no water inside a bubble. A man who got inside a bubble, would have nothing to breathe.

But, of course, it was impossible to penetrate a bubble. The surface tension was too strong. As strong as Shar's metal plates. As strong as the top of the sky.

As strong as the top of the sky. And above that – once the bubble was broken – a world of gas instead of water? Were all worlds bubbles of water drifting in gas?

If it were so, travel between them would be out of the question, since it would be impossible to pierce the sky to begin with. Nor did the infant cosmology include any provisions for bottoms for the worlds.

And yet some of the local creatures did burrow *into* the bottom, quite deeply, seeking something in those depths which was beyond the reach of Man. Even the surface of the ooze, in high summer, crawled with tiny creatures for which mud was a natural medium. Man, too, passed freely between the two countries of water which were divided by the thermocline, though many of the creatures with which he lived could not pass that line at all, once it had established itself.

And if the new universe of which Shar had spoken existed at all, it had to exist beyond the sky, where the light was. Why could not the sky be passed, after all? The fact that bubbles could be broken showed that the surface skin that formed between water and gas wasn't completely invulnerable. Had it ever been tried?

Lavon did not suppose that one man could butt his way through the top of the sky, any more than he could burrow into the bottom, but there might be ways around the difficulty. Here at his back, for instance, was a plant which gave every appearance of continuing beyond the sky: its uppermost fronds broke off and were bent back only by a trick of reflection.

It had always been assumed that the plants died where they touched the sky. For the most part, they did, for frequently the dead extension could be seen, leached and yellow, the boxes of its component cells empty, floating imbedded in the perfect mirror. But some were simply chopped off, like the one which sheltered him now. Perhaps that was only an illusion, and instead it soared indefinitely into some other place – some place where men might once have been born, and might still live . . .

The plates were gone. There was only one other way to find out.

Determinedly, Lavon began to climb toward the wavering mirror of the sky. His thorn-thumbed feet trampled obliviously upon the clustered sheaves of fragile stippled diatoms. The tulip-heads of Vortae, placid and murmurous cousins of Para, retracted startledly out of his way upon coiling stalks, to make silly gossip behind him.

Lavon did not hear them. He continued to climb doggedly toward the light, his fingers and toes gripping the plant-bole.

'Lavon! Where are you going? Lavon!'

He leaned out and looked down. The man with the adze, a doll-like figure, was beckoning to him from a patch of blue-green retreating over a violet abyss. Dizzily he looked away, clinging to the bole; he had never been so high before. Then he began to climb again.

After a while, he touched the sky with one hand. He stopped to breathe. Curious bacteria gathered about the base of his thumb where blood from a small cut was fogging away, scattered at his gesture, and wriggled mindlessly back toward the dull red lure.

He waited until he no longer felt winded, and resumed climbing. The sky pressed down against the top of his head, against the back of his neck, against his shoulders. It seemed to give slightly, with a tough, frictionless elasticity. The water here was intensely bright, and quite colorless. He climbed another step, driving his shoulders against that enormous weight.

It was fruitless. He might as well have tried to penetrate a cliff.

Again he had to rest. While he panted, he made a curious discovery. All around the bole of the water plant, the steel surface of the sky curved upward, making a kind of sheath. He found that he could insert his hand into it – there was almost enough space to admit his head as well. Clinging closely to the bole, he looked up into the inside of the sheath, probing with his injured hand. The glare was blinding.

There was a kind of soundless explosion. His whole wrist was suddenly encircled in an intense, impersonal grip, as if it were being cut in two. In blind astonishment, he lunged upward.

The ring of pain traveled smoothly down his upflung arm as

he rose, was suddenly around his shoulders and chest. Another lunge and his knees were being squeezed in the circular vine. Another —

Something was horribly wrong. He clung to the bole and tried to gasp, but there was – nothing to breathe.

The water came streaming out of his body, from his mouth, his nostrils, the spiracles in his sides, spurting in tangible jets. An intense and fiery itching crawled over the entire surface of his body. At each spasm, long knives ran into him, and from a great distance he heard more water being expelled from his book-lungs in an obscene, frothy sputtering.

Lavon was drowning.

With a final convulsion, he kicked himself away from the splintery bole, and fell. A hard impact shook him; and then the water, which had clung to him so tightly when he had first attempted to leave it, took him back with cold violence.

Sprawling and tumbling grotesquely, he drifted, down and down and down, toward the bottom.

III

For many days, Lavon lay curled insensibly in his spore, as if in the winter sleep. The shock of cold which he had felt on re-entering his native universe had been taken by his body as a sign of coming winter, as it had taken the oxygen-starvation of his brief sojourn above the sky. The spore-forming glands had at once begun to function.

Had it not been for this, Lavon would surely have died. The danger of drowning disappeared even as he fell, as the air bubbled out of his lungs and readmitted the life-giving water. But for acute desiccation and third degree sunburn, the sunken universe knew no remedy. The healing amnionic fluid generated by the spore-forming glands, after the transparent amber sphere had enclosed him, offered Lavon his only chance.

The brown sphere was spotted after some days by a prowling amoeba, quiescent in the eternal winter of the bottom. Down there the temperature was always an even 4°, no matter what the season, but it was unheard of that a spore should be found there while the high epilimnion was still warm and rich in oxygen.

Within an hour, the spore was surrounded by scores of astonished protos, jostling each other to bump their blunt eyeless prows against the shell. Another hour later, a squad of worried men came plunging from the castles far above to press their own noses against the transparent wall. Then swift orders were given.

Four Para grouped themselves about the amber sphere, and there was a subdued explosion as the trichocysts which lay embedded at the bases of their cilia, just under the pellicle, burst and cast fine lines of a quickly solidifying liquid into the water. The four Paras thrummed and lifted, tugging.

Lavon's spore swayed gently in the mud and then rose slowly, entangled in the web. Nearby, a Noc cast a cold pulsating glow over the operation – not for the Paras, who did not need the light, but for the baffled knot of men. The sleeping figure of Lavon, head bowed, knees drawn up to its chest, revolved with an absurd solemnity inside the shell as it was moved.

'Take him to Shar, Para.'

The young Shar justified, by minding his own business, the traditional wisdom with which his hereditary office had invested him. He observed at once that there was nothing he could do for the encysted Lavon which would not be classifiable as simple meddling.

He had the sphere deposited in a high tower room of his castle, where there was plenty of light and the water was warm, which should suggest to the hibernating form that spring was again on the way. Beyond that, he simply sat and watched, and kept his speculations to himself.

Inside the spore, Lavon's body seemed rapidly to be shedding its skin, in long strips and patches. Gradually, his curious shrunkenness disappeared. His withered arms and legs and sunken abdomen filled out again.

The days went by while Shar watched. Finally he could discern no more changes, and, on a hunch, had the spore taken up to the topmost battlements of the tower, into the direct daylight.

An hour later, Lavon moved in his amber prison.

He uncurled and stretched, turned blank eyes up toward the light. His expression was that of a man who had not yet awakened from a ferocious nightmare. His whole body shone with a strange pink newness.

Shar knocked gently on the wall of the spore. Lavon turned

his blind face toward the sound, life coming into his eyes. He smiled tentatively and braced his hands and feet against the inner wall of the shell.

The whole sphere fell abruptly to pieces with a sharp crackling. The amnionic fluid dissipated around him and Shar, carrying away with it the suggestive odor of a bitter struggle against death.

Lavon stood among the bits of shell looked at Shar silently. At last he said:

'Shar — I've been beyond the sky.'

'I know,' Shar said gently.

Again Lavon was silent. Shar said, 'Don't be humble, Lavon. You've done an epoch-making thing. It nearly cost you your life. You must tell me the rest — all of it.'

'The rest?'

'You taught me a lot while you slept. Or are you still opposed to useless knowledge?'

Lavon could say nothing. He no longer could tell what he knew from what he wanted to know. He had only one question left, but he could not utter it. He could only look dumbly into Shar's delicate face.

'You have answered me,' Shar said, even more gently. 'Come, my friend; join me at my table. We will plan our journey to the stars.'

It was two winter sleeps after Lavon's disastrous climb beyond the sky that all work on the spaceship stopped. By then, Lavon knew that he had hardened and weathered into that temporarily ageless state a man enters after he has just reached his prime; and he knew also that there were wrinkles engraved upon his brow, to stay and to deepen.

'Old' Shar, too had changed, his features losing some of their delicacy as he came into his maturity. Though the wedge-shaped bony structure of his face would give him a withdrawn and poetic look for as long as he lived, participation in the plan had given his expression a kind of executive overlay, which at best gave it a masklike rigidity, and at worst coarsened it somehow.

Yet despite the bleeding away of the years, the spaceship was still only a hulk. It lay upon a platform built above the tumbled boulders of the sandbar which stretched out from one wall of the world. It was an immense hull of pegged wood, broken by regularly spaced gaps through which the raw beams of the skeleton could be seen.

Work upon it had progressed fairly rapidly at first, for it was not hard to visualize what kind of vehicle would be needed to crawl through empty space without losing its water. It had been recognized that the sheer size of the machine would enforce a long period of construction, perhaps two full seasons; but neither Shar nor Lavon had anticipated any serious snag.

For that matter, part of the vehicle's apparent incompleteness was an illusion. About a third of its fittings were to consist of living creatures, which could not be expected to install themselves in the vessel much before the actual takeoff.

Yet time and time again, work on the ship had had to be halted for long periods. Several times whole sections needed to be ripped out, as it became more and more evident that hardly a single normal, understandable concept could be applied to the problem of space travel.

The lack of the history plates, which the Para steadfastly refused to deliver up, was a double handicap. Immediately upon their loss, Shar had set himself to reproduce them from memory; but unlike the more religious of his people, he had never regarded them as holy writ, and hence had never set himself to memorizing them word by word. Even before the theft, he had accumulated a set of variant translations of passages presenting specific experimental problems, which were stored in his library, carved in wood. But most of these translations tended to contradict each other, and none of them related to spaceship construction, upon which the original had been vague in any case.

No duplicates of the cryptic characters of the original had ever been made, for the simple reason that there was nothing in the sunken universe capable of destroying the originals, nor of duplicating their apparently changeless permanence. Shar remarked too late that through simple caution they should have made a number of verbatim temporary records – but after generations of green-gold peace, simple caution no longer covers preparations against catastrophe. (Nor, for that matter, did a culture which had to dig each letter of its simple alphabet into pulpy waterlogged wood with a flake of stonewort, encourage the keeping of records in triplicate.)

As a result, Shar's imperfect memory of the contents of the history plates, plus the constant and millennial doubt as to the accuracy of the various translations proved finally to be the worst obstacle to progress on the spaceship itself.

'Men must paddle before they can swim,' Lavon observed belatedly, and Shar was forced to agree with him.

Obviously, whatever the ancients had known about spaceship construction, very little of that knowledge was usable to a people still trying to build its first spaceship from scratch. In retrospect, it was not surprising that the great hulk still rested incomplete upon its platform above the sand boulders, exuding a musty odor of wood steadily losing its strength, two generations after its flat bottom had been laid down.

The fat-faced young man who headed the strike delegation was Phil XX, a man two generations younger than Lavon, four younger than Shar. There were crow's-feet at the corners of his eyes, which made him look both like a querulous old man and like an infant spoiled in the spore.

'We're calling a halt to this crazy project,' he said bluntly. 'We've slaved our youth away on it, but now that we're our own masters, it's over, that's all. Over.'

'Nobody's compelled you,' Lavon said angrily.

'Society does; our parents do,' a gaunt member of the delegation said. 'But now we're going to start living in the real world. Everybody these days knows that there's no other world but this one. You oldsters can hang on to your superstitions if you like. We don't intend to.'

Baffled, Lavon looked over at Shar. The scientist smiled and said, 'Let them go, Lavon. We have no use for the faint-hearted.'

The fat-faced young man flushed. 'You can't insult us into going back to work. We're through. Build your own ship to no place!'

'All right,' Lavon said evenly. 'Go on, beat it. Don't stand around here orating about it. You've made your decision and we're not interested in your self-justifications. Good-bye.'

The fat-faced young man evidently still had quite a bit of heroism to dramatize which Lavon's dismissal had short-circuited. An examination of Lavon's stony face, however, convinced him that he had to take his victory as he found it. He and the delegation trailed ingloriously out the archway.

'Now what?' Lavon asked when they had gone. 'I must admit, Shar, that I would have tried to persuade them. We do need the workers, after all.'

'Not as much as they need us,' Shar said tranquilly. 'How many volunteers have you got for the crew of the ship?'

'Hundreds. Every young man of the generation after Phil's wants to go along. Phil's wrong about that segment of the population, at least. The project catches the imagination of the very young.'

'Did you give them any encouragement?'

'Sure,' Lavon said. 'I told them we'd call on them if they were chosen. But you can't take that seriously! We'd do badly to displace our picked group of specialists with youths who have enthusiasm and nothing else.'

'That's not what I had in mind, Lavon. Didn't I see a Noc in your chambers somewhere? Oh, there he is, asleep in the dome. Noc!'

The creature stirred its tentacles lazily.

'Noc, I've a message,' Shar called. 'The protos are to tell all men that those who wish to go to the next world with the spaceship must come to the staging area right away. Say that we can't promise to take everyone, but that only those who help us build the ship will be considered at all.'

The Noc curled its tentacles again and appeared to go back to sleep. Actually, of course, it was sending its message through the water in all directions.

IV

Lavon turned from the arrangement of speaking-tube megaphones which was his control board and looked at the Para. 'One last try,' he said. 'Will you give us back the plates?'

'No, Lavon. We have never denied you anything before, but this we must.'

'You're going with us though, Para. Unless you give us the knowledge we need, you'll lose your life if we lose ours.'

'What is one Para?' the creature said. 'We are all alike. This cell will die; but the protos need to know how you fare on this journey. We believe you should make it without the plates.'

'Why?'

The proto was silent. Lavon stared at it a moment, then turned deliberately back to the speaking tubes. 'Everyone hang on,' he said. He felt shaky. 'We're about to start. Tol, is the ship sealed?'

'As far as I can tell, Lavon.'

Lavon shifted to another megaphone. He took a deep breath. Already the water seemed stifling, though the ship hadn't moved.

'Ready with one-quarter power. One, two, three, go.'

The whole ship jerked and settled back into place again. The raphe diatoms along the under hull settled into their niches, their jelly treads turning against broad endless belts of crude leather. Wooden gears creaked, stepping up the slow power of the creatures, transmitting it to the sixteen axles of the ship's wheels.

The ship rocked and began to roll slowly along the sandbar. Lavon looked tensely through the mica port. The world flowed painfully past him. The ship canted and began to climb the slope. Behind him, he could feel the electric silence of Shar, Para, the two alternate pilots, as if their gaze were stabbing directly through his body and on out the port. The world looked different, now that he was leaving it. How had he missed all this beauty before?

The slapping of the endless belts and the squeaking and groaning of the gears and axles grew louder as the slope steepened. The ship continued to climb, lurching. Around it, squadrons of men and protos dipped and wheeled, escorting it toward the sky.

Gradually the sky lowered and pressed down toward the top of the ship.

'A little more work from your diatoms, Tanol,' Lavon said. 'Boulder ahead.' The ship swung ponderously. 'All right, slow them up again. Give us a shove from your side, Than – no, that's too much – there, that's it. Back to normal; you're still turning us! Tanol, give us one burst to line us up again. Good. Allright, steady drive on all sides. Won't be long now.'

'How can you think in webs like that?' the Para wondered behind him.

'I just do, that's all. It's the way men think. Overseers, a little more thrust now; the grade's getting steeper.'

The gears groaned. The ship nosed up. The sky brightened in Lavon's face. Despite himself, he began to be frightened. His lungs seemed to burn, and in his mind he felt his long fall through nothingness toward the chill slap of water as if he were experiencing it for the first time. His skin itched and burned. Could he go up *there* again? Up there into the burning void, the great grasping agony where no life should go?

The sandbar began to level out and the going became a little easier. Up here, the sky was so close that the lumbering motion of the huge ship disturbed it. Shadows of wavelets ran across the sand. Silently, the thick-barreled bands of blue-green algae drank in the light and converted it to oxygen, writhing in their slow mindless dance just under the long mica skylight which ran along the spine of the ship. In the hold, beneath the latticed corridor and cabin floors, whirring Vortae kept the ship's water in motion, fuelling themselves upon drifting organic particles.

One by one, the figures wheeling about the ship outside waved arms or cilia and fell back, coasting down the slope of the sandbar toward the familiar world, dwindling and disappearing. There was at last only one single Euglena, half-plant cousin of the protos, forging along beside the spaceship into the marches of the shallows. It loved the light, but finally it, too, was driven away into cooler, deeper waters, its single whiplike tentacle undulating placidly as it went. It was not very bright, but Lavon felt deserted when it left.

Where they were going, though, none could follow.

Now the sky was nothing but a thin, resistant skin of water coating the top of the ship. The vessel slowed, and when Lavon called for more power, it began to dig itself in among the sandgrains.

'That's not going to work' Shar said tensely. 'I think we'd better step down the gear ratio, Lavon, so you can apply stress more slowly.'

'All right,' Lavon agreed. 'Full stop, everybody. Shar, will you supervise gear-changing, please?'

Insane brilliance of empty space looked Lavon full in the face just beyond his big mica bull's eye. It was maddening to be forced to stop here upon the threshold of infinity; and it was dangerous, too. Lavon could feel building in him the old fear of the outside. A few moments more of inaction, he knew with a gathering coldness at the pit of his stomach, and he would be unable to go through with it.

Surely, he thought, there must be a better way to change gear-ratios than the traditional one, which involved dismantling almost the entire gear-box. Why couldn't a number of gears of different sizes be carried on the same shaft, not necessarily all in action all at once, but awaiting use simply by shoving the axle back and forth longitudinally in its sockets? It would still be clumsy, but it could be worked on orders from the bridge and would not involve shutting down the entire machine – and throwing the new pilot into a blue-green funk.

Shar came lunging up through the trap and swam himself to a stop.

'All set,' he said. 'The big reduction gears aren't taking the strain too well, though.'

'Splintering?'

'Yes. I'd go it slow at first.'

Lavon nodded mutely. Without allowing himself to stop, even for a moment, to consider the consequences of his words, he called: 'Half power.'

The ship hunched itself down again and began to move, very slowly indeed, but more smoothly than before. Overhead, the sky thinned to complete transparency. The great light came blasting in. Behind Lavon there was an uneasy stir. The whiteness grew at the front ports.

Again the ship slowed, straining against the blinding barrier. Lavon swallowed and called for more power. The ship groaned like something about to die. It was now almost at a standstill.

'More power,' Lavon ground out.

Once more, with infinite slowness, the ship began to move. Gently, it tilted upward.

Then it lunged forward and every board and beam in it began to squall.

'Lavon! Lavon!'

Lavon started sharply at the shout. The voice was coming at him from one of the megaphones, the one marked for the port at the rear of the ship.

'Lavon!'

'What is it? Stop your damn yelling.'

'I can see the top of the sky! From the *other* side, from the top side! It's like a big flat sheet of metal. We're going away from it. We're above the sky, Lavon, we're above the sky!'

Another violent start swung Lavon around toward the forward port. On the outside of the mica, the water was evaporating with shocking swiftness, taking with it strange distortions and patterns made of rainbows.

Lavon saw Space.

It was at first like a deserted and cruelly dry version of the bottom. There were enormous boulders, great cliffs, tumbled, split, riven, jagged rocks going up and away in all directions.

But it had a sky of its own – a deep dome so far away that he could not believe in, let alone compute, what its distance might be. And in this dome was a ball of white fire that seared his eyeballs.

The wilderness of rock was still a long way away from the ship, which now seemed to be resting upon a level, glistening plain. Beneath the surface-shine, the plain seemed to be made of sand, nothing but familiar sand, the same substance which had heaped up to form a bar in Lavon's own universe, the bar along which the ship had climbed. But the glassy, colorful skin over it —

Suddenly Lavone became conscious of another shout from the megaphone banks. He shook his head savagely and asked, 'What is it now?'

'Lavon, this is Than. What have you gotten us into? The belts are locked. The diatoms can't move them. They aren't faking, either; we've rapped them hard enough to make them think we were trying to break their shells, but they still can't give us more power.'

'Leave them alone,' Lavon snapped. 'They can't fake; they haven't enough intelligence. If they say they can't give you more power, they can't.'

'Well, then, you get us out of it,' Than's voice said frightenedly.

Shar came forward to Lavon's elbow. 'We're on a space-water interface, where the surface tension is very high,' he said softly. 'This is why I insisted on our building the ship so that we could lift the wheels off the ground whenever necessary. For a long while I couldn't understand the reference of the history plates to "retractable landing gear," but it finally occurred to me that the tension along a space-water interface – or, to be more exact, a space-mud interface – would hold any large object tightly. If you order the wheels pulled up now, I think we'll make better progress for a while on the bellytreads.'

'Good enough,' Lavon said. 'Hello below – up landing gear. Evidently the ancients knew their business after all, Shar.'

Quite a few minutes later, for shifting power to the belly-treads involved another setting of the gear box, the ship was crawling along the shore toward the tumbled rock. Anxiously,

Lavon scanned the jagged, threatening wall for a break. There was a sort of rivulet off toward the left which might offer a route, though a dubious one, to the next world. After some thought, Lavon ordered his ship turned toward it.

'Do you suppose that thing in the sky is a "star"?' he asked, 'But there were supposed to be lots of them. Only one is up there – and one's plenty for *my* taste.'

'I don't know,' Shar admitted. 'But I'm beginning to get a picture of the way the universe is made, I think. Evidently our world is a sort of cup in the bottom of this huge one. This one has a sky of its own; perhaps it, too, is only a cup in the bottom of a still huger world, and so on and on without end. It's a hard concept to grasp, I'll admit. Maybe it would be more sensible to assume that all the worlds are cups in this one common surface, and that the great light shines on them all impartially.'

'Then what makes it seem to go out every night, and dim even in the day during winter?' Lavon demanded.

'Perhaps it travels in circles, over first one world, then another. How could I know yet?'

'Well, if you're right, it means that all we have to do is crawl along here for a while, until we hit the top of the sky of another world,' Lavon said. 'Then we dive in. Somehow it seems too simple, after all our preparations.'

Shar chuckled, but the sound did not suggest that he had discovered anything funny. 'Simple? Have you noticed the temperature yet?'

Lavon had noticed it, just beneath the surface of awareness, but at Shar's remark he realized that he was gradually being stifled. The oxygen content of the water, luckily, had not dropped, but the temperature suggested the shallows in the last and worst part of the autumn. It was like trying to breathe soup.

'Than, give us more action from the Vortae,' Lavon called. 'This is going to be unbearable unless we get more circulation.'

It was all he could do now to keep his attention on the business of steering the ship.

The cut or defile in the scattered razor-edged rocks was a little closer, but there still seemed to be many miles of rough desert to cross. After a while, the ship settled into a steady, painfully slow crawling, with less pitching and jerking than before, but also with less progress. Under it, there was now a sliding, grinding sound, rasping against the hull of the ship itself, as if it were treadmilling over some coarse lubricant whose particles were each as big as a man's head.

Finally Shar said, 'Lavon, we'll have to stop again. The sand this far up is dry, and we're wasting energy using the treads.'

'Are you sure we can take it?' Lavon asked, gasping for breath. 'At least we are moving. If we stop to lower the wheels and change gears again, we'll boil.'

'We'll boil if we don't,' Shar said calmly. 'Some of our algae are already dead and the rest are withering. That's a pretty good sign that we can't take much more. I don't think we'll make it into the shadows, unless we do change over and put on some speed.'

There was a gulping sound from one of the mechanics. 'We ought to turn back,' he said raggedly. 'We were never meant to be out here in the first place. We were made for the water, not this hell.'

'We'll stop,' Lavon said, 'but we're not turning back. That's final.'

The words made a brave sound, but the man had upset Lavon more than he dared to admit, even to himself. 'Shar,' he said, 'make it fast, will you?'

The scientist nodded and dived below.

The minutes stretched out. The great white globe in the sky blazed and blazed. It had moved down the sky, far down, so that the light was pouring in to the ship directly in Lavon's face, illuminating every floating particle, its rays like long milky streamers. The currents of water passing Lavon's cheek were almost hot.

How could they dare go directly forward into that inferno? The land directly under the 'star' must be even hotter than it was here!

'Lavon! Look at Para!'

Lavon forced himself to turn and look at his proto ally. The great slipper had settled to the deck, where it was lying with only a feeble pulsation of its cilia. Inside, its vacuoles were beginning to swell, to become bloated, pear-shaped bubbles, crowding the granulated protoplasm, pressing upon the dark nuclei.

'This cell is dying,' Para said, as coldly as always. 'But go on – go on. There is much to learn, and you may live, even though we do not. Go on.'

'You're ... for us now?' Lavon whispered.

'We have always been for you. Push your folly to its uttermost. We will benefit in the end, and so will Man.'

The whisper died away. Lavon called the creature again, but it did not respond.

There was a wooden clashing from below, and then Shar's voice came tinnily from one of the megaphones. 'Lavon, go ahead! The diatoms are dying, too, and then we'll be without power. Make it as quickly and directly as you can.'

Grimly, Lavon leaned forward. 'The "star" is directly over the land we're approaching.'

'It is? It may go lower still and the shadows will get longer. That's our only hope.'

Lavon had not thought of that. He rasped into the banked megaphones. Once more, the ship began to move. It got hotter.

Steadily, with a perceptible motion, the 'star' sank in Lavon's face. Suddenly a new terror struck him. Suppose it should continue to go down until it was gone entirely? Blasting though it was now, it was the only source of heat. Would not space become bitter cold on the instant – and the ship an expanding, bursting block of ice?

The shadows lengthened menacingly, stretched across the desert toward the forward-rolling vessel. There was no talking in the cabin, just the sound of ragged breathing and the creaking of the machinery.

Then the jagged horizon seemed to rush upon them. Stony teeth cut into the lower rim of the ball of fire, devoured it swiftly. It was gone.

They were in the lee of the cliffs. Lavon ordered the ship turned to parallel the rock-line; it responded heavily, sluggishly. Far above, the sky deepened steadily from blue to indigo.

Shar came silently up through the trap and stood beside Lavon, studying that deepening color and the lengthening of the shadows down the beach toward their world. He said nothing, but Lavon knew that the same chilling thought was in his mind.

'Lavon.'

Lavon jumped. Shar's voice had iron in it. 'Yes?'

'We'll have to keep moving. We must make the next world,

wherever it is, very shortly.'

'How can we dare move when we can't see where we're going? Why not sleep it over – if the cold will let us?'

'It will let us.' Shar said. 'It can't get dangerously cold up here. If it did, the sky – or what we used to think of as the sky – would have frozen over every night, even in summer. But what I'm thinking about is the water. The plants will go to sleep now. In our world that wouldn't matter; the supply of oxygen is enough to last through the night. But in this confined space, with so many creatures in it and no source of fresh water, we will probably smother.'

Shar seemed hardly to be involved at, all but spoke rather with the voice of implacable physical laws.

'Furthermore,' he said, staring unseeingly out at the raw landscape, 'the diatoms are plants, too. In other words, we must stay on the move for as long as we have oxygen and power – and pray that we make it.'

'Shar, we had quite a few protos on board this ship once. And Para there isn't quite dead yet. If he were, the cabin would be intolerable. The ship is nearly sterile of bacteria, because all the protos have been eating them as a matter of course and there's no outside supply of them, any more than there is for oxygen. But still and all there would have been some decay.'

Shar bent and tested the pellicle of the motionless Para with a probing finger. 'You're right, he's still alive. What does that prove?'

'The Vortae are also alive; I can feel the water circulating. Which proves it wasn't the heat that hurt Para. *It was the light.* Remember how badly my skin was affected after I climbed beyond the sky? Undiluted starlight is deadly. We should add that to the information on the plates.'

'I still don't see the point.'

'It's this. We've got three or four Noc down below. They were shielded from the light, and so must be alive. If we concentrate them in the diatom galleys, the dumb diatoms will think it's still daylight and will go on working. Or we can concentrate them up along the spine of the ship, and keep the algae putting out oxygen. So the question is: which do we need more, oxygen or power? Or can we split the difference?'

Shar actually grinned. 'A brilliant piece of thinking. We'll make a Shar of you yet, Lavon. No, I'd say that we can't split the difference. There's something about daylight, some quality, that the light Noc emits doesn't have. You and I can't detect it, but the green plants can, and without it they don't make oxygen. So we'll have to settle for the diatoms – for power.'

Lavon brought the vessel away from the rocky lee of the cliff, out onto the smoother sand. All trace of direct light was gone now, although there was still a soft, general glow on the sky.

'Now, then,' Shar said thoughtfully, 'I would guess that there's water over there in the canyon, if we can reach it. I'll go below and arrange —'

Lavon gasped, 'What's the matter?'

Silently, Lavon pointed, his heart pounding.

The entire dome of indigo above them was spangled with tiny, incredibly brilliant lights. There were hundreds of them, and more and more were becoming visible as the darkness deepened. And far away, over the ultimate edge of the rocks, was a dim red globe, crescented with ghostly silver. Near the zenith was another such body, much smaller, and silvered all over . . .

Under the two moons of Hydrot, and under the eternal stars, the two inch wooden spaceship and its microscopic cargo toiled down the slope toward the drying little rivulet.

V

The ship rested on the bottom of the canyon for the rest of the night. The great square doors were thrown open to admit the raw, irradiated, life-giving water from outside – and the wriggling bacteria which were fresh food.

No other creatures approached them, either with curiosity or with predatory intent, while they slept, though Lavon had posted guards at the doors. Evidently, even up here on the very floor of space, highly organized creatures were quiescent at night.

But when the first flush of light filtered through the water, trouble threatened.

First of all, there was the bug-eyed monster. The thing was green and had two snapping claws, either one of which could have broken the ship in two like a spyrogyra straw. Its eyes were black and globular, on the ends of short columns, and its long feelers were as thick as a plantbole. It passed in a kicking fury of motion, however, never noticing the ship at all.

'Is that – a sample of the kind of life we can expect in the next world?' Lavon whispered. Nobody answered, for the very good reason that nobody knew.

After a while, Lavon risked moving the ship forward against the current, which was slow but heavy. Enormous writhing worms whipped past them. One struck the hull a heavy blow, then thrashed on obliviously.

'They don't notice us,' Shar said. 'We're too small. Lavon, the ancients warned us of the immensity of space, but even when you see it, it's impossible to grasp. And all those stars – can they mean what I think they mean? It's beyond thought, beyond belief!'

'The bottom's sloping,' Lavon said, looking ahead intently. 'The walls of the canyon are retreating, and the water's becoming rather silty. Let the stars wait, Shar; we're coming toward the entrance of our new world.'

Shar subsided moodily. His vision of space had disturbed him, perhaps seriously. He took little notice of the great thing that was happening, but instead huddled worriedly over his own expanding speculations. Lavon felt the old gap between their two minds widening once more.

Now the bottom was tilting upward again. Lavon had no experience with delta-formation, for no rivulets left his own world, and the phenomenon worried him. But his worries were swept away in wonder as the ship topped the rise and nosed over.

Ahead, the bottom sloped away again, indefinitely, into glimmering depths. A proper sky was over them once more, and Lavon could see small rafts of plankton floating placidly beneath it. Almost at once, too, he saw several of the smaller kinds of protos, a few of which were already approaching the ship —

Then the girl came darting out of the depths, her features distorted with terror. At first she did not see the ship at all. She came twisting and turning lithely through the water, obviously hoping only to throw herself over the ridge of the delta and into the savage streamlet beyond.

Lavon was stunned. Not that there were men here – he had hoped for that – but at the girl's single-minded flight toward suicide.

'What —'

Then a dim buzzing began to grow in his ears, and he understood.

'Shar! Than! Tanol!' he bawled. 'Break out crossbows and spears! Knock out all the windows!' He lifted a foot and kicked through the big port in front of him. Someone thrust a crossbow into his hand.

'Eh? What's happening?' Shar blurted.

'*Rotifers!*'

The cry went through the ship like a galvanic shock. The rotifers back in Lavon's own world were vitually extinct, but everyone knew thoroughly the grim history of the long battle man and proto had waged against them.

The girl spotted the ship suddenly and paused, stricken by despair at the sight of the new monster. She drifted with her own momentum, her eyes alternately fixed hypnotically upon the ship and glancing back over her shoulder, toward where the buzzing snarled louder and louder in the dimness.

'Don't stop!' Lavon shouted. 'This way, this way! We're friends! We'll help!'

Three great semi-transparent trumpets of smooth flesh bored over the rise, the many thick cilia of their coronas whirring greedily. Dicrans – the most predacious of the entire tribe of Eaters. They were quarreling thickly among themselves as they moved, with the few blurred, presymbolic noises which made up their 'language.'

Carefully, Lavon wound the crossbow, brought it to his shoulder, and fired. The bolt sang away through the water. It lost momentum rapidly, and was caught by a stray current which brought it closer to the girl than to the Eater at which Lavon had aimed.

He bit his lip, lowered the weapon, wound it up again. It did not pay to underestimate the range; he would have to wait until he could fire with effect. Another bolt, cutting through the water from a side port, made him issue orders to cease firing.

The sudden irruption of the rotifers decided the girl. The motionless wooden monster was strange to her and had not yet menaced her – but she must have known what it would be like to have three Dicrans over her, each trying to grab away from the other the biggest share. She threw herself toward the big

115

port. The Eaters screamed with fury and greed and bored after her.

She probably would not have made it, had not the dull vision of the lead Dicran made out the wooden shape of the ship at the last instant. It backed off, buzzing, and the other two sheered away to avoid colliding with it. After that they had another argument, though they could hardly have formulated what it was that they were fighting about. They were incapable of saying anything much more complicated than the equivalent of 'Yaah,' 'Drop dead,' and 'You're another.'

While they were still snarling at each other, Lavon pierced the nearest one all the way through with an arablast bolt. It disintegrated promptly – rotifers are delicately organized creatures despite their ferocity – and the remaining two were at once involved in a lethal battle over the remains.

'Than, take a party out and spear me those two Eaters while they're still fighting,' Lavon ordered. 'Don't forget to destroy their eggs, too. I can see that this world needs a little taming.'

The girl shot through the port and brought up against the far wall of the cabin, flailing in terror. Lavon tried to approach her, but from somewhere she produced a flake of stonewort chipped to a nasty point. He sat down on the stool before his control board and waited while she took in the cabin, Lavon, Shar, the pilot, the senescent Para.

At last she said: 'Are – you – the gods from beyond the sky?'

'We're from beyond the sky, all right,' Lavon said. 'But we're not gods. We're human beings, like yourself. Are there many humans here?'

The girl seemed to assess the situation very rapidly, savage though she was. Lavon had the odd and impossible impression that he should recognize her. She tucked the knife back into her matted hair – ah, Lavon thought, that's a trick I may need to remember – and shook her head.

'We are few. The Eaters are everywhere. Soon they will have the last of us.'

Her fatalism was so complete that she actually did not seem to care.

'And you've never cooperated against them? Or asked the protos to help?'

'The protos?' She shrugged. 'They are as helpless as we are against the Eaters. We have no weapons which kill at a dis-

116

tance, like yours. And it is too late now for such weapons to do any good. We are too few, the Eaters too many.'

Lavon shook his head emphatically. 'You've had one weapon that counts, all along. Against it, numbers mean nothing. We'll show you how we've used it. You may be able to use it even better than we did, once you've given it a try.'

The girl shrugged again. 'We have dreamed of such a weapon now and then, but never found it. I do not think that what you say is true. What is this weapon?'

'Brains,' Lavon said. 'Not just one brain, but brains. Working together. Cooperation.'

'Lavon speaks the truth,' a weak voice said from the deep. The Para stirred feebly. The girl watched it with wide eyes. The sound of the Para using human speech seemed to impress her more than the ship or anything else it contained.

'The Eaters can be conquered,' the thin, buzzing voice said. 'The protos will help, as they helped in the world from which we came. They fought this flight through space, and deprived Man of his records; but Man made the trip without the records. The protos will never oppose men again. I have already spoken to the protos of this world and have told them what Man can dream, Man can do, whether the protos wish it or not.

'Shar, your metal records are with you. They were hidden in the ship. My brothers will lead you to them.

'This organism dies now. It dies in confidence of knowledge, as an intelligent creature dies. Man has taught us this. There is nothing that knowledge ... cannot do. With it, men ... have crossed ... have crossed space ...'

The voice whispered away. The shining slipper did not change, but something about it was gone. Lavon looked at the girl; their eyes met.

'We have crossed space,' Lavon repeated softly.

Shar's voice came to him across a great distance. The young-old man was whispering: 'But *have* we?'

'As far as I'm concerned, yes,' said Lavon.

The Deserter
by William Tenn

'*November 10, 2039 —*

'*Terran Supreme Command communiqué No. 18–673 for the twenty-four hours ending 0900 Monday, Terran capital time:*

... whereupon sector HQ on Fortress Satellite Five ordered a strategic withdrawal of all interceptor units. The withdrawal was accomplished without difficulty and with minimal loss.

'The only other incident of interest in this period was the surrender of an enemy soldier of undetermined rank, the first of these creatures from Jupiter to be taken alive by our forces. The capture was made in the course of defending Cochabamba, Bolivia, from an enemy commando raid. Four Jovians were killed in this unsuccessful assault upon a vital tin-supplying area after which the fifth laid down his arms and begged that his life be spared. Upon capture by our forces, the Jovian claimed to be a deserter and requested a safe-conduct to ...'

Mardin had been briefed on what to expect by the MP officer who'd escorted him into the cave. Inevitably, though, his first view of the tank in which the alien floated brought out a long, whimpering grunt of disbelief and remembered fear. It was at least sixty feet long by forty wide, and it reared off the rocky floor to twice the height of a man. Whatever incredible material its sides had been composed of had hours ago been covered by thick white layers of ice.

Cold air currents bouncing the foul, damp smell of methane back from the tank tweaked his nose and pricked at his ears. *Well, after all,* Mardin thought, *those things have a body temperature somewhere in the neighborhood of minus 200° Fahrenheit!*

And he had felt this cold once before ...

He shivered violently in response to the memory and zipped shut the fur-lined coveralls he'd been issued at the entrance. 'Must have been quite a job getting that thing in here.' The casualness of his voice surprised him and made him feel better.

'Oh, a special engineer task force did it in – let me see, now —' The MP lieutenant, a Chinese girl in her late teens, pursed soft, coral lips at his graying hair. 'Less than five hours, figuring from the moment they arrived. The biggest problem was finding a cell in the neighborhood that was big enough to hold the prisoner. This cave was perfect.'

Mardin looked up at the ledge above their heads. Every ten feet, a squad of three men, highly polished weapons ready for instant action. Atomic cannon squads alternating with men bent down under the weight of dem-dem grenades. Grim-faced young subalterns, very conscious of the bigness of the brass that occupied the platform at the far end of the cave, stamped back and forth along the ledge from squad to squad, deadly little Royster pistolettos tinkling and naked in their sweating hands. *Those kids*, he thought angrily, *so well adjusted to it all!*

The ledge ran along three sides of the cave; on the fourth, the low entrance from which Mardin had just come, he had seen five steel Caesars implanted, long, pointed snouts throbbingly eager to throw tremendous gusts of nuclear energy at the Jovian's rear. And amid the immense rock folds of the roof, a labyrinth of slender, pencil-like bombs had been laid, held in place by clamps that would all open simultaneously the moment a certain colonel's finger pressed a certain green button ...

'If our friend in the tank makes one wrong move,' Mardin muttered, 'half of South America goes down the drain.'

The girl started to chuckle, then changed her mind and frowned. 'I'm sorry, Major Mardin, but I don't like that. I don't like hearing them referred to as "friends." Even in a joke. Over a million and a half people – three hundred thousand of them Chinese – have been wiped out by those – those ammoniated flatworms!'

'And the first fifty of which,' he reminded her irritably, 'were my relatives and neighbors. If you're old enough to remember Mars and the Three Watertanks Massacre, young lady.'

She swallowed and looked stricken. An apology seemed to be in the process of composition, but Mardin moved past her in a long, disgusted stride and headed rapidly for the distant platform. He had a fierce dislike, he had discovered long ago, for people who were unable to hate wholesomely and intelligently, who had to jog their animus with special symbols and idiotic negations. Americans, during the War of 1914–18, changing sauerkraut into liberty cabbage; mobs of Turks, in the Gibraltar

120

Flare-up of 1985, lynching anyone in Ankara caught eating oranges. How many times had he seen aged men in the uniform of the oldster's service, the Infirm Civilian Corps, make the socially accepted gesture of grinding out a worm with their heels whenever they referred to the enemy from Jupiter!

He grimaced at the enormous expanse of ice-covered tank in which a blanket of living matter large enough to cover a city block pursued its alien processes. 'Let me see you lift your foot and step on *that*!' he told the astonished girl behind him. *Damn all simplicity-hounds, anyway,* he thought. *A week on the receiving end of a Jovian question-machine is exactly what they need. Make them nice and thoughtful and give them some inkling of how crazily complex this universe can be!*

That reminded him of his purpose in this place. He became thoughtful himself and – while the circular scar on his forehead wrinkled – very gravely reminiscent of how crazily complex the universe actually was . . .

So thoughtful, in fact, that he had to take a long, relaxing breath and wipe his hands on his coveralls before climbing the stairs that led up to the hastily constructed platform.

Colonel Liu, Mardin's immediate superior, broke away from the knot of men at the other end and came up to him with arms spread wide. 'Good to see you, Mardin,' he said rapidly. 'Now listen to me. Old Rockethead himself is here – you know how *he* is. So put a little snap into your salute and kind of pull back on those shoulders when you're talking to him. Know what I mean? Try to show him that when it comes to military bearing, we in Intelligence don't take a – Mardin, are you listening to me? This is *very* important.'

With difficulty, Mardin took his eyes away from the transparent un-iced top of the tank. 'Sorry, sir,' he mumbled. 'I'll – I'll try to remember.'

'This the interpreter, Colonel Liu? Major Mardin, eh?' the very tall, stiffly erect man in the jeweled uniform of a Marshal of Space yelled from the railing. 'Bring him over. On the double, sir!'

Colonel Liu grabbed Mardin's left arm and pulled him rapidly across the platform. Rockethead Billingsley cut the colonel's breathless introduction short. 'Major *Igor* Mardin, is it? Sounds Russian. You wouldn't be Russian now, would you? I hate Russians.'

Mardin noticed a broad-shouldered vice-marshal standing in

Billingsley's rear stiffen angrily. 'No, sir,' he replied. 'Mardin is a Croat name. My family is French and Yugoslav with possibly a bit of Arab.'

The Marshal of Space inclined his fur-covered head. 'Good! Couldn't stand you if you were Russian. Hate Russians, hate Chinese, hate Portuguese. Though the Chinese are worst of all, I'd say. Ready to start working on this devil from Jupiter? Come over here, then. And move, man, move!' As he swung around, the dozen or so sapphire-studded Royster pistolettos that swung picturesquely from his shoulder straps clinked and clanked madly, making him seem like a gigantic cat that the mice had belled again and again.

Hurrying after him, Mardin noticed with amusement that the stiff, angry backs were everywhere now. Colonel Liu's mouth was screwed up into a dark pucker in his face; at the far end of the platform, the young lieutenant who'd escorted him from the jet base was punching a tiny fist into an open palm. Marshal of Space Rudolfo Billingsley enjoyed a rank high enough to make tact a function of the moment's whim – and it was obvious that he rarely indulged such moments. 'Head thick as a rocket wall and a mouth as filthy as a burned-out exhaust, but he can figure out, down to the smallest wound on the greenest corporal, exactly how much blood any attack is going to cost.' That was what the line officers said of him.

And that, after all, Mardin reflected, was just the kind of man needed in the kind of world Earth had become in eighteen years of Jovian siege. He, himself, owed this man a very special debt. . . .

'You probably don't remember me, sir,' he began hesitantly as they paused beside a metal armchair that was suspended from an overhead wire. 'But we met once before, about sixteen years ago. It was aboard your spaceship, the *Euphrates*, that I —'

'The *Euphrates* wasn't a spaceship. It was an interceptor, third class. Learn your damned terminology if you're going to dishonor a major's uniform, mister! And pull that zipper up tight. Of course, you were one of that mob of mewling civilians I pulled out of Three Watertanks right under the Jovians' noses. Let's see: that young archaeologist fellow. Didn't know then that we were going to get a real, first-class, bang-up, slaughter-em-dead war out of that incident, did we? Hah! You thought you had an easy life ahead of you, eh? Didn't suspect you'd be spending the rest of it in uniform, standing up straight and jumping when you got an order! This war's made men out of a lot of wet jellyfish like you, mister, and you can be grateful for the privilege.'

Mardin nodded with difficulty, sardonically conscious of the abrupt stiffness of his own back, of the tightly clenched fingers scraping his palm. He wondered about the incidence of court-martial, for striking a superior officer, in Billingsley's personal staff.

'All right, hop into it. Hop *in*, man!' Mardin realized the significance of the cupped hands being extended to him. A Marshal of Space was offering him a boost! Billingsley believed nobody could do *anything* better than Billingsley. Very gingerly, he stepped into it, was lifted up so that he could squirm into the chair. Automatically, he fastened the safety belt across his middle, strapped the headset in place.

Below him, Old Rockethead pulled the clamps tight around his ankles and called up: 'You've been briefed? Arkhnatta contacted you?'

'Yes. I mean yes, *sir*. Professor Arkhnatta traveled with me all the way from Melbourne Base. He managed to cover everything, but of course it wasn't the detail he'd have liked.'

'Hell with the detail. Listen to me, Major Mardin. Right there in front of you is the only Jovian flatworm we've managed to take alive. I don't know how much longer we can *keep* him alive – engineers are building a methane plant in another part of the cave so he'll have some stink to breathe when his own supply runs out, and the chemistry johnnies are refrigerating ammonia for him to drink – but I intend to rip every bit of useful military information out of his hide before he caves in. And your mind is the only chisel I've got. Hope I don't break the chisel, but the way I figure it you're not worth as much as a secondary space fleet. And I sacrificed one of those day before yesterday – complement of two thousand men – just to find out what the enemy was up to. So, mister, you pay attention to me and keep asking him questions. And shout your replies, good and loud for the recording machines. Swing him out, Colonel! Didn't you *hear* me? How the hell long does it take to swing him out?'

As the cable pulled the chair away from the platform and over the immense expanse of monster, Mardin felt something in his belly go far away and something in his brain try to hide.

In a few moments – at the thought of what he'd be doing in a minute or two he shut his eyes tightly as he had in childhood, trying to wish the bad thing away.

He should have done what all his instincts urged way back in Melbourne Base when he'd gotten the orders and realized what they meant. He should have deserted. Only trouble, where do you desert in a world under arms, on a planet where every child has its own military responsibilities? But he should have done something. *Something*. No man should have to go through this twice in one lifetime.

Simple enough for Old Rockethead. This was *his* life, negative as its goals were; moments like these of incipient destruction were the fulfillment for which he'd trained and worked and studied. He remembered something else now about Marshal of Space Billingsley. The beautiful little winged creatures of Venus – *Griggoddon*, they'd been called – who'd learned human languages and begun pestering the early colonists of that planet with hundreds of questions. Toleration of their high-pitched, ear-splitting voices had turned into annoyance and they'd been locked out of the settlements, whereupon they'd made the nights hideous with their curiosity. Since they'd refused to leave, and since the hard-working colonists found themselves losing more and more sleep, the problem had been turned over to the resident military power on Venus. Mardin recalled the uproar even on Mars when a laconic order of the day – 'Venus has been rendered permanently calm: Commodore R. Billingsley.' – announced that the first intelligent extra-terrestrial life to be discovered had been destroyed down to the last crawling segmented infant by means of a new insecticide spray.

Barely six months later the attack on sparsely settled Mars had underlined with human corpses the existence of another intelligent race in the solar system – and a much more powerful one. Who remembered the insignificant *Griggoddon* when Commodore Rudolfo Billingsley slashed back into the enemy-occupied capital of Southern Mars and evacuated the few survivors of Jupiter's initial assault? Then the Hero of Three Watertanks had even gone back and rescued one of the men captured alive by the Jovian monsters – a certain Igor Mardin, proud possessor of the first, and, as it eventually turned out, also the only Ph.D. in Martian archaeology.

No, for Old Rockethead this horrendous planet-smashing

was more than fulfillment, much more than a wonderful opportunity to practice various aspects of his trade: it represented reprieve. If mankind had not blundered into and alerted the outposts of Jovian empire in the asteroid belt, Billinglsey would have worked out a miserable career as a police officer in various patrol posts, chained for the balance of his professional life to a commodore's rank by the *Griggoddon* blunder. Whenever he appeared at a party some fat woman would explain to her escort in a whisper full of highly audible sibilants that this was the famous Beast of Venus – and every uniformed man in the place would look uncomfortable. The Beast of Venus it would have been instead of the Hero of Three Watertanks, Defender of Luna, the Father of the Fortress Satellite System.

As for himself – well, Dr. Mardin would have plodded out the long years tranquilly and usefully, a scholar among scholars, not the brightest and best, possibly – here, a stimulating and rather cleverly documented paper, there a startling minor discovery of interest only to specialists – but a man respected by his colleagues, doing work he was fitted for and liked, earning a secure place for himself in the textbooks of another age as a secondary footnote or additional line in a bibliography. But instead the Popa Site Diggings were disintegrated rubble near the ruins of what had once been the human capital of Southern Mars and Major Igor Marden's civilian skills had less relevance and value than those of a dodo breeder or a veterinarian to mammoths and mastodons. He was now a mildly incompetent field grade officer in an unimportant section of Intelligence whose attempts at military bearing and deportment amused his subordinates and caused his superiors a good deal of pain. He didn't like the tasks he was assigned; frequently he didn't even understand them. His value lay only in the two years of psychological hell he'd endured as a prisoner of the Jovians and even that could be realized only in peculiarly fortuitous circumstances such as those of the moment. He could never be anything but an object of pathos to the snappy, single-minded generation grown up in a milieu of no-quarter interplanetary war: and should the war end tomorrow with humanity, by some unimaginable miracle, victorious, he would have picked up nothing in the eighteen years of conflict but uncertainty about himself and a few doubtful moments for some drab little memoirs.

He found that, his fears forgotten, he had been glaring down at the enormous hulk of the Jovian rippling gently under the transparent tank-surface. This quiet-appearing sea of turgid scarlet soup in which an occasional bluish-white dumpling bobbed to the surface only to dwindle in size and disappear – this was one of the creatures that had robbed him of the life he should have had and had hurled him into a by-the-numbers purgatory. And why? So that their own peculiar concepts of mastery might be maintained, so that another species might not arise to challenge their dominion of the outer planets. No attempt at arbitration, at treaty-making, at any kind of discussion – instead an overwhelming and relatively sudden onslaught, as methodical and irresistible as the attack of an anteater on an anthill.

A slender silvery tendril rose from the top of the tank to meet him and the chair came to an abrupt halt in its swaying journey across the roof of the gigantic cave. Mardin's shoulders shot up against his neck convulsively, he found himself trying to pull his head down into his chest – just as he had scores of times in the prison cell that had once been the Three Watertanks Public Library.

At the sight of the familiar questing tendril, a panic eighteen years old engulfed and nauseated him.

It's going to hurt inside, his mind wept, twisting and turning and dodging in his brain. *The thoughts are going to be rubbed against each other so that the skin comes off them and they hurt and hurt and hurt....*

The tendril came to a stop before his face and the tip curved interrogatively. Mardin squirmed back against the metal chair back.

I won't! This time I don't have to! You can't make me – this time you're our prisoner – you can't make me – you can't make me —

'Mardin!' Billingsley's voice bellowed in his headphones. 'Put the damn thing on and let's get going! Move, man, *move!*'

And almost before he knew he had done it, as automatically as he had learned to go rigid at the sound of *atten-shun!* Mardin's had reached out for the tendril and placed the tip of it against the old scar on his forehead.

There was that anciently familiar sensation of inmost rapport, of new-found completeness, of belonging to a higher order of being. There were the strange double memories: a river of green fire arching off a jet-black trembling cliff hundreds of miles high, somehow blending in with the feel of delighted shock as Dave Weiner's baseball hit the catcher's mitt you'd gotten two hours ago for a birthday present; a picture of a very lovely and very intent young female physicist explaining to you just how somebody named Albert Fermi Vannevar derived $E = MC^2$, getting all confused with the time to begin the many-scented dance to the surface because of the myriad of wonderful soft spots you could feel calling to each other on your back.

But, Mardin realized with amazement in some recess of autonomy still left in his mind, this time there was a difference. This time there was no feeling of terror as of thorough personal violation, there was no incredibly ugly sensation of tentacles armed with multitudes of tiny suckers speeding through his nervous system and feeding, feeding, greedily feeding. ... This time none of his thoughts were dissected, kicking and screaming, in the operating theater of his own skull while his ego shuddered fearfully at the bloody spectacle from a distant psychic cranny.

This time he was *with* – not *of*.

Of course, a lot of work undoubtedly had been done on the Jovian question-machine in the past decade. The single tendril that contained all of the intricate mechanism for telepathic communication between two races had probably been refined far past the coarse and blundering gadget that had gouged at his mind eighteen years ago.

And, of course, this time *he* was the interrogator. This time it was a Jovian that lay helpless before the probe, the weapons, the merciless detachment of an alien culture. This time it was a Jovian, not Igor Mardin, who had to find the right answers to the insistent questions – and the right symbols with which to articulate those answers.

All that made a tremendous difference. Mardin relaxed and was amused by the feeling of power that roared through him.

Still – there was something else. This time he was dealing with a totally different personality.

There was a pleasant, undefinable quality to this individual from a world whose gravity could smear Mardin across the landscape in a fine liquid film. A character trait like – no, not simple tact – certainly not timidity – and you couldn't just call it gentleness and warmth —

Mardin gave up. Certainly, he decided, the difference between this Jovian and his jailer on Mars was like the difference between two entirely different breeds. Why, it was a pleasure to share part of his mental processes temporarily with this kind of person! As from a distance, he heard the Jovian reply that the pleasure was mutual. He felt instinctively they had much in common.

And they'd have to – if Billingsley were to get the information he wanted. Superficially, it might seem that a mechanism for sharing thoughts was the ideal answer to communication between races as dissimilar as the Jovian and Terrestrial. In practice, Mardin knew from long months of squeezing his imagination under orders in Three Watertanks, a telepathy machine merely gave you a communication potential. An individual thinks in pictures and symbols based on his life experiences – if two individuals have no life experiences in common, all they can share is confusion. It had taken extended periods of desperate effort before Mardin and his Jovian captor had established that what passed for the digestive process among humans was a combination of breathing and strenuous physical exercise to a creature born on Jupiter, that the concept of taking a bath could be equated with a Jovian activity so shameful and so overlaid with pain that Mardin's questioner had been unable to visit him for five weeks after the subject came up and thenceforth treated him with the reserve one might maintain toward an intelligent blob of fecal matter.

But mutually accepted symbols eventually had been established – just before Mardin's rescue. And ever since then, he'd been kept on ice in Intelligence, for a moment like this. . . .

'Mardin!' Old Rockethead's voice ripped out of his earphones. 'Made contact yet?'

'Yes. I think I have, sir.'

'Good! Feels like a reunion of the goddam old regiment, eh? All set to ask questions? The slug's cooperating? Answer me, Mardin! Don't sit there gaping at him!'

'Yes, sir,' Mardin said hurriedly. 'Everything's all set.'

'Good! Let's see now. First off, ask him his name, rank and serial number.'

Mardin shook his head. The terrifying, straight-faced orderliness of the military mind! The protocol was unalterable: you asked a Japanese prisoner-of-war for his name, rank and serial number; obviously, you did the same when the prisoner was a Jovian! The fact that there was no interplanetary Red Cross to notify his family that food packages might now be sent...

He addressed himself to the immense blanket of quiescent living matter below him, phrasing the question in as broad a set of symbols as he could contrive. Where would the answer be worked out, he wondered? On the basis of their examination of dead Jovians, some scientists maintained that the creatures were really vertebrates, except that they had nine separate brains and spinal columns; other biologists insisted that the 'brains' were merely the kind of ganglia to be found in various kinds of invertebrates and that thinking took place on the delicately convoluted surface of their bodies. And no one had ever found anything vaguely resembling a mouth or eyes, not to mention appendages that could be used in locomotion.

Abruptly, he found himself on the bottom of a noisy sea of liquid ammonia, clustered with dozens of other newborn around the neuter 'mother.' Someone flaked off the cluster and darted away; he followed. The two of them met in the appointed place of crystallization and joined into one individual. The pride he felt in the increase of self was worth every bit of effort.

Then he was humping along a painful surface. He was much larger now – and increased in self many times over. The Council of Unborn asked him for his choice. He chose to become a male. He was directed to a new fraternity.

Later, there was a mating with tiny silent females and enormous, highly active neuters. He was given many presents. Much later, there was a songfest in a dripping cavern that was interrupted by a battle scene with rebellious slaves on one of Saturn's moons. With a great regret he seemed to go into suspended animation for a number of years. *Wounded?* Mardin wondered. *Hospitalized?*

In conclusion, there was a guided tour of an undersea hatchery which terminated in a colorful earthquake.

Mardin slowly assimilated the information in terms of human symbology.

'Here it is, sir,' he said at last hesitantly into the mouthpiece. 'They don't have any actual equivalents in this area, but you might call him Ho-Par XV, originally of the Titan garrison and sometime adjutant to the commanders of Ganymede.' Mardin paused a moment before going on. 'He'd like it on the record that he's been invited to reproduce five times – and twice in public.'

Billingsley grunted. 'Nonsense! Find out why he didn't fight to the death like the other four raiders. If he still claims to be a deserter, find out why. Personally, I think these Jovians are too damn fine soldiers for that sort of thing. They may be worms, but I can't see one of them going over to the enemy.'

Mardin put the question to the prisoner. . . .

Once more he wandered on worlds where he could not have lived for a moment. He superintended a work detail of strange dustmotes, long ago conquered and placed under Jovian hegemony. He found himself feeling about them the way he had felt about the *Griggoddon* eighteen years ago: they were too wonderful to be doomed, he protested. Then he realized that the protest was not his, but that of the sorrowing entity who had lived these experiences. And they went on to other garrisons, other duties.

The reply he got this time made Mardin gasp. 'He says all five of the Jovians were deserting! They had planned it for years, all of them being both fraternity-brothers and brood-brothers. He says that they – well, you might say *parachuted* down together – and not one of them had a weapon. They each tried in different ways, as they had planned beforehand, to make their surrender known. Ho-Par XV was the only successful one. He brings greetings from clusters as yet unsynthesized.'

'Stick to the facts, Mardin. No romancing. Why did they desert?'

'I am sticking to the facts, sir: I'm just trying to give you the flavor as well as the substance. According to Ho-Par XV, they deserted because they were all violently opposed to militarism.'

'*Wha-at?*'

'That, as near as I can render it, is exactly what he says. He says that militarism is ruining their race. It has resulted in all kinds of incorrect choices on the part of the young as to which sex they will assume in the adult state (I don't understand that part at all myself, sir) – it has thrown confusion into an art somewhere between cartography and horticulture that Ho-Par thinks is very important to the future of Jupiter – and it has weighed every Jovian down with an immense burden of guilt because of what their armies and military administration have done to alien life-forms on Ganymede, Titan, and Europa, not to mention the half-sentient bubbles of the Saturnian core.'

'To hell with the latrine-blasted half-sentient bubbles of the Saturnian core!' Billingsley bellowed.

'Ho-Par XV feels,' the man in the suspended metal armchair went on relentlessly, staring down with delight at the flat stretch of red liquid whose beautifully sane, delicately balanced mind he was paraphrasing, 'that his race needs to be stopped for its own sake as well as that of the other forms of life in the Solar System. Creatures trained in warfare are what he calls "philosophically anti-life." The young Jovians had just about given up hope that Jupiter *could* be stopped, when humanity came busting through the asteroids. Only trouble is that while we do think and move about three times as fast as they do, the Jovian females – who are the closest thing they have to theoretical scientists – know a lot more than we, dig into a concept more deeply than we can imagine and generally can be expected to keep licking us as they have been, until we are either extinct or enslaved. Ho-Par XV and his brood-brothers decided after the annual smelling session in the Jovian fleet this year to try to change all this. They felt that with our speedier metabolism, we might be able to take a new weapon, which the Jovians have barely got into production, and turn it out fast enough to make a slight —'

At this point there was a certain amount of noise in the headphones. After a while, Old Rockethead's voice, suavity gone, came through more or less distinctly: '– and if you don't start detailing that weapon immediately, you mangy son of a flea-bitten cur, I will have you broken twelve grades below Ordinary Spaceman and strip the skin off your pimply backside with my own boot the moment I get you back on this platform. I'll personally see to it that you spend all of your leaves cleaning the filthiest latrines the space fleet can find! Now jump to it!'

Major Mardin wiped the line of sweat off his upper lip and began detailing the weapon. *Who does he think he's talking to?* his mind asked bitterly. *I'm no kid, no applecheeked youngster, to be snapped at and dressed down with that line of frowsy, ugly, barracks-corporal humor! I got a standing ovation from the All-Earth Archaeological Society once, and Dr. Emmanuel Hozzne himself congratulated me on my report.*

But his mouth began detailing the weapon, his mouth went

on articulating the difficult ideas which Ho-Par XV and his fellow deserters had painfully translated into faintly recognizable human terms, his mouth dutifully continued to explicate mathematical and physical concepts into the black speaking cone near his chin.

His mouth went about its business and carried out its orders – but his mind lay agonized at the insult. And then, in a corner of his mind where tenancy was joint, so to speak, a puzzled, warm, highly sensitive and extremely intelligent personality asked a puzzled, tentative question.

Mardin stopped in mid-sentence, overcome with horror at what he'd almost given away to the alien. He tried to cover up, to fill his mind with memories of contentment, to create *non-sequiturs* as psychological camouflage. What an idiot to forget that he wasn't alone in his mind!

And the question was asked again. *Are you not the representative of your people? Are – are there others ... unlike you?*

Of course not! Mardin told him desperately. *Your confusion is due entirely to the fundamental differences between Jovian and Terrestrial thinking —*

'Mardin! Will you stop drooling out of those nearsighted eyes and come the hell to attention? Keep talking, chowderhead, we want the rest of that flatworm's brain picked!'

What fundamental differences? Mardin asked himself suddenly, his skull a white-hot furnace of rage. There were more fundamental differences between someone like Billingsley and himself, than between himself and this poetic creature who had risked death and become a traitor to his own race – to preserve the dignity of the life-force. What did he have in common with that Cain come to judgment, this bemedaled swaggering boor who rejoiced in having reduced all the subtleties of conscious thought to rigidly simple, unavoidable alternatives: kill or be killed! damn or be damned! be powerful or be overpowered! The monster who had tortured his mind endlessly, dispassionately, in the prison on Mars would have found Old Rockethead much more of a friend than Ho-Par XV.

That is true, that is so! The Jovian's thought came down emphatically on his mind. *And now, friend, blood-brother, whatever you may choose to call yourself, please let me know what kind of creature I have given this weapon to. Let me know what he has done in the past with power, what he may*

132

be expected to do in hatching cycles yet to come. Let me know through your mind and your memories and your feelings – for you and I understand each other.

Mardin let him know.

'... to the nearest legal representative of the entire human race. As the result of preliminary interrogation by the military authorities a good deal was learned about the life and habits of the enemy. Unfortunately, in the course of further questioning, the Jovian evidently came to regret being taken alive and opened the valves of the gigantic tank which was his space suit, thus committing suicide instantly and incidentally smothering his human interpreter in a dense cloud of methane gas. Major Igor Mardin, the interpreter, has been posthumously awarded the Silver Lunar Circlet with doubled jets. The Jovian's suicide is now being studied by space fleet psychologists to determine whether this may not indicate an unstable mental pattern which will be useful to our deepspace armed forces in the future. ...'

Mother
by Philip José Farmer

I

'Look, mother. The clock is running backwards.'

Eddie Fetts pointed to the hands on the pilot room dial.

Dr. Paula Fetts said, 'The crash must have reversed it.'

'How could it do that?'

'I can't tell you. I don't know everything, son.'

'Oh!'

'Well, don't look at me so disappointedly. I'm a pathologist, not an electronician.'

'Don't be so cross, mother. I can't stand it. Not now.'

He walked out of the pilot room. Anxiously, she followed him. The burial of the crew and her fellow scientists had been very trying for him. Spilled blood had always made him dizzy and sick; he could scarcely control his hands enough to help her sack the scattered bones and entrails.

He had wanted to put the corpses in the nuclear furnace, but she had forbidden that. The Geigers amidships were ticking loudly, warning that there was invisible death in the stern.

The meteor that struck the moment the ship come out of Translation into normal space had probably wrecked the engineroom. So she had understood from the incoherent high-pitched phrases of a colleague before he fled to the pilotroom. She had hurried to find Eddie. She feared his cabin door would still be locked, as he had been making a tape of the aria 'Heavy Hangs the Albatross' from Gianelli's *Ancient Mariner*.

Fortunately, the emergency system had automatically thrown out the locking circuits. Entering, she had called out his name in fear he'd been hurt. He was lying half-unconscious on the floor, but it was not the accident that had thrown him there. The reason lay in the corner, released from his lax hand; a quart freefall thermos, rubber-nippled. From Eddie's open mouth charged a breath of rye that not even Nodor pills had been able to conceal.

Sharply she had commanded him to get up and on to the bed. Her voice, the first he had ever heard, pierced through the phalanx of Old Red Star. He struggled up, and she though

135

smaller, had thrown every ounce of her weight into getting him up and on to the bed.

There she had lain down with him and strapped them both in. She understood that the lifeboat had been wrecked also, and that it was up to the captain to bring the yacht down safely to the surface of this charted but unexplored planet, Baudelaire. Everybody else had gone to sit behind the captain, strapped in crashchairs, unable to help except with their silent backing.

Moral support had not been enough. The ship had come in on a shallow slant. Too fast. The wounded motors had not been able to hold her up. The prow had taken the brunt of the punishment. So had those seated in the nose.

Dr. Fetts had held her son's head on her bosom and prayed out loud to her God. Eddie had snored and muttered. Then there was a sound like the clashing of the gates of doom – a tremendous bong as if the ship were a clapper in a gargantuan bell tolling the most frightening message human ears may hear – a blinding blast of light – and darkness and silence.

A few moments later Eddie began crying out in a childish voice. 'Don't leave me to die, mother! Come back! Come back!'

Mother was unconscious by his side, but he did not know that. He wept for a while, then he lapsed back into his rye-fogged stupor – if he had ever been out of it – and slept. Again, darkness and silence.

It was the second day since the crash, if 'day' could describe that twilight state on Baudelaire. Dr. Fetts followed her son wherever he went. She knew he was very sensitive and easily upset. All his life she had known it and had tried to get between him and anything that would cause trouble. She had succeeded, she thought, fairly well until three months ago when Eddie had eloped.

The girl was Polina Fameux, the ash-blonde long-legged actress whose tridi image, taped, had been shipped to frontier stars where a small acting talent meant little and a large and shapely bosom much. Since Eddie was a well-known Metro tenor, the marriage made a big splash whose ripples ran around the civilized Galaxy.

Dr. Fetts had felt very bad about the elopement, but she had, she hoped, hidden her grief very well beneath a smiling mask. She didn't regret having to give him up; after all, he was a full-grown man, no longer her little boy. But, really, aside from the seasons at the Met and his tours, he had not been parted from her since he was eight.

That was when she went on a honeymoon with her second husband. And then she and Eddie had not been separated long, for Eddie had got very sick, and she'd had to hurry back and take care of him, as he had insisted she was the only one who could make him well.

Moreover, you couldn't count his days at the opera as a total loss, for he vised her every noon and they had a long talk – no matter how high the vise bills ran.

The ripples caused by her son's marriage were scarcely a week old before they were followed by even bigger ones. They bore the news of the separation of Eddie and his wife. A fortnight later, Polina applied for divorce on grounds of incompatibility. Eddie was handed the papers in his mother's apartment. He had come back to her the day he and Polina had agreed they 'couldn't make a go of it,' or, as he phrased it to his mother, 'couldn't get together.'

Dr. Fetts was, of course, very curious about the reason for their parting, but, as she explained to her friends, she 'respected' his silence. What she didn't say was that she had told herself the time would come when he would tell her all.

Eddie's 'nervous breakdown' started shortly afterwards. He had been very irritable, moody, and depressed, but he got worse the day a so-called friend told Eddie that whenever Polina heard his name mentioned, she laughed loud and long. The friend added that Polina had promised to tell someday the true story of their brief merger.

That night his mother had to call in a doctor.

In the days that followed, she thought of giving up her position as research pathologist at De Kruif and taking all her time to help him 'get back on his feet.' It was a sign of the struggle going on in her mind that she had not been able to decide within a week's time. Ordinarily given to swift consideration and resolution of a problem, she could not agree to surrender her beloved quest into tissue-regeneration.

Just as she was on the verge of doing what was for her the incredible and the shameful, tossing a coin, she had been vised by her superior. He told her she had been chosen to go with a group of biologists on a research cruise to ten preselected planetary systems.

Joyfully, she had thrown away the papers that would turn Eddie over to a sanatorium. And, since he was quite famous, she had used her influence to get government to allow him to go along. Ostensibly, he was to make a survey of the development of opera on planets colonized by Terrans. That the yacht was not visiting any colonized globes seemed to have been missed by the bureaus concerned. But it was not the first time in the history of a government that its left hand knew not what its right was doing.

Actually, he was to be 'rebuilt' by his mother, who thought herself better than S, K, or H therapies. True, some of her friends reported amazing results with some of the symbol-chasing techniques. On the other hand, two of her close companions had tried them all and had got no benefits from any of them. She was his mother; she could do more for him than any of those 'alphabatties'; he was flesh of her flesh, blood of her blood. Besides, he wasn't so sick. He just got awfully blue sometimes and made theatrical but insincere threats of suicide or else just sat and stared into space. But she could handle him.

II

So now it was that she followed him from the backward-running clock to his room. And saw him step inside, look for a second, and then turn to her with a twisted face.

'Neddies is ruined, mother. Absolutely ruined.'

She glanced at the piano. It had torn loose from the wall-racks at the moment of impact and smashed itself against the opposite wall. To Eddie it wasn't just a piano; it was Neddie. He had a pet name for everything he contacted for more than a brief time. It was as if he hopped from one appellation to the next, like an ancient sailor who felt lost unless he was close to the familiar and designated points of the shoreline. Otherwise, Eddie seemed to be drifting helplessly in a chaotic ocean, one that was anonymous and amorphous.

Or, analogy more typical of him, he was like the night-clubber who feels submerged, drowning, unless he hops from table to table, going from one well-known group of faces to the next, avoiding the featureless and unnamed dummies at the strangers' tables.

He did not cry over Neddie. She wished he would. He had

been so apathetic during the voyage. Nothing, not even the unparalleled splendour of the naked stars nor the inexpressible alienness of strange planets had seemed to lift him very long. If he would only weep or laugh loudly or display some sign that he was reacting violently to what was happening. She would even have welcomed his striking her in anger or calling her 'bad' names.

But no, not even during the gathering of the mangled corpses, when he looked for a while as if he were going to vomit, would he give way to his body's demand for expression. She understood that if he were to throw up, he would be much better for it, would have got rid of much of the psychic disturbance along with the physical.

He would not. He had kept on raking flesh and bones into the large plastic bags and kept a fixed look of resentment and sullenness.

She hoped now that the loss of his piano would bring tears and shaking shoulders. Then she could take him in her arms and give him sympathy. He would be her little boy again, afraid of the dark, afraid of the dog killed by a car, seeking her arms for the sure safety, the sure love.

'Never mind, baby,' she said. 'When we're rescued, we'll get you a new one.'

'When —!'

He lifted his eyebrows and sat down on the bed's edge. 'What do we do now?'

She became very brisk and efficient.

'The ultrad automatically started working the moment the meteor struck. If it's survived the crash, it's still sending SOS's. If not, then there's nothing we can do about it. Neither of us knows how to repair it.

'However, it's possible that in the last five years since this planet was located, other expeditions may have landed here. Not from Earth but from some of the colonies. Or from non-human globes. Who knows? It's worth taking a chance. Let's see.'

A single glance was enough to wreck their hopes. The ultrad had been twisted and broken until it was no longer recognizable as the machine that sent swifter-than-light waves through the no-ether.

Dr. Fetts said with false cheeriness. 'Well, that's that! So what? It makes things too easy. Let's go into the storeroom and see what we can see.'

Eddie shrugged and followed her. There she insisted that each take a panrad. If they had to separate for any reason, they could always communicate and also using the DF's – the built-in direction finders – locate each other. Having used them before, they knew the instruments' capabilities and how essential they were on scouting or camping trips.

The panrads were lightweight cylinders about two feet high and eight inches in diameter. Crampacked, they held the mechanisms of two dozen different utilities. Their batteries lasted a year without recharging, they were practically indestructible and worked under almost any conditions.

Keeping away from the inside of the ship that had the huge hole in it, they took the panrads outside. The long wave bands were searched by Eddie while his mother moved the dial that ranged up and down the shortwaves. Neither really expected to hear anything, but to search was better than doing nothing.

Finding the modulated wave-frequencies empty of any significant noise, he switched to the continuous waves. He was startled by a dot-dashing.

'Hey, mom! Something in the 1000 kilocycles! Unmodulated!'

'Naturally, son,' she said with some exasperation in the midst of her elation. 'What would you expect from a radio-telegraphic signal?'

She found the band on her own cylinder. He looked blankly at her. 'I know nothing about radio, but that's not Morse.'

'What? You must be mistaken!'

'I – I don't think so.'

'Is it or isn't it? Good God, son, can't you be certain of *anything*!'

She turned the amplifier up. As both of them had learned Galacto-Morse through sleeplearn techniques, she checked him at once.

'You're right. What do you make of it?'

His quick ear sorted out the pulses.

'No simple dot and dash. Four different time-lengths.'

He listened some more.

'They've got a certain rhythm, all right. I can make out definite groupings. Ah! That's the sixth time I've caught that particular one. And there's another. And another.'

Dr. Fetts shook her ash-blonde head. She could make out nothing but a series of zzt-zzt-zzt's.

Eddie glanced at the DF needle.

'Coming from NE by E. Should we try to locate?'

'Naturally,' she replied. 'But we'd better eat first. We don't know how far away it is, or what we'll find there. While I fix a hot meal, you get our field trip stuff ready.'

'O.K.,' he said with more enthusiasm than he had shown for a long time.

When he came back he ate everything in the large dish his mother had prepared on the unwrecked galley stove.

'You alway did make the best stew,' he said.

'Thank you. I'm glad you're eating again, son. I am surprised. I thought you'd be sick about all this.'

He waved vaguely but energetically.

'The challenge of the unknown. I have a sort of feeling this is going to turn out much better than we thought. Much better.'

She came close and sniffed his breath. It was clean, innocent even of stew. That meant he'd taken Nodor, which probably meant he'd been sampling some hidden rye. Otherwise, how explain his reckless disregard of the possible dangers? It wasn't like him.

She said nothing, for she knew that if he tried to hide a bottle in his clothes or field sack while they were tracking down the radio signals, she would soon find it. And take it away. He wouldn't even protest, merely let her lift it from his limp hand while his lips swelled with resentment.

III

They set out. Both wore knapsacks and carried the panrads. He carried a gun over his shoulder, and she had snapped onto her sack her small black bag of medical and lab supplies.

High noon of late autumn was topped by a weak red sun that barely managed to make itself seen through the eternal double layer of clouds. Its companion, an even smaller blob of lilac, was setting on the northwestern horizon. They walked in a sort of bright twilight, the best that Baudelaire ever achieved. Yet, despite the lack of light, the air was warm. It was a phenomenon common to certain planets behind the Horsehead Nebula, one being investigated but as yet unexplained.

The country was hilly, with many deep ravines. Here and there were prominences high enough and steep-sided enough to be called embryo mountains. Considering the roughness of the land, however, there was a surprising amount of vegetation. Pale green, red and yellow bushes, vines, and little trees clung to every bit of ground, horizontal or vertical. All had comparatively broad leaves that turned with the sun to catch the light.

From time to time, as the two Terrans strode noisily through the forest, small multicoloured insect-like and mammal-like creatures scuttled from hiding place to hiding place. Eddie decided to carry his gun in the crook of his arm. Then, after they were forced to scramble up and down ravines and hills and fight their way through thickets that became unexpectedly tangled, he put it back over his shoulder, where it hung from a strap.

Despite their exertions, they did not tire quickly. They weighed about twenty pounds less than they would have on Earth and, though the air was thinner, it was richer in oxygen.

Dr. Fetts kept up with Eddie. Thirty years the senior of the twenty-three-year-old, she passed even at close inspection for his older sister. Longevity pills took care of that. However, he treated her with all the courtesy and chivalry that one gave one's mother and helped her up the steep inclines, even though the climbs did not appreciably cause her deep chest to demand more air.

They paused once by a creek bank to get their bearings.

'The signals have stopped,' he said.

'Obviously,' she replied.

At that moment the radar-detector built into the panrad began to ping. Both of them automatically looked upwards.

'There's no ship in the air.'

'It can't be coming from either of those hills,' she pointed out. 'There's nothing but a boulder on top of each one. Tremendous rocks.'

'Nevertheless, it's coming from there, I think. Oh! Oh! Did you see what I saw? Looked like a tall stalk of some kind being pulled down behind that big rock.'

She peered through the dim light. 'I think you were imagining things, son. I saw nothing.'

Then, even as the pinging kept up, the zzting started again.

But after a burst of noise, both stopped.

'Let's go up and see what we shall see,' she said.

'Something screwy,' he commented. She did not answer.

They forded the creek and began the ascent. Half-way up, they stopped to sniff in puzzlement at a gust of some heavy odour coming downwind.

'Smells like a cageful of monkeys,' he said.

'In heat,' she added. If his was the keener ear, hers was the sharper nose.

They went on up. The RD began sounding its tiny hysterical gonging. Nonplussed, Eddie stopped. The DF indicated the radar pulses were not coming from the top of the hill they were climbing, as formerly, but from the other hill across the valley. Abruptly, the panrad fell silent.

'What do we do now?'

'Finish what we started. This hill. Then we go to the other one.'

He shrugged and then hastened after her tall slim body in its long-legged coveralls. She was hot on the scent, literally, and nothing could stop her. Just before she reached the bungalow-sized boulder topping the hill, he caught up with her. She had stopped to gaze intently at the DF needle, which swung wildly before it stopped at neutral. The monkey-cage odour was very strong.

'Do you suppose it could be some sort of radio-generating mineral?' she asked, disappointedly.

'No. Those groupings were semantic. And that smell. . . .'

'Then what —'

He didn't know whether to feel pleased or not that she had so obviously and suddenly thrust the burden of responsibility and action on him. Both pride and a curious shrinking affected him. But he did feel exhilarated. Almost, he thought, he felt as if were he on the verge of discovering what he had been looking for for a long time. What the object of his search had been, he could not say. But he was excited and not very much afraid.

He unslung his weapon, a two-barrelled combination shotgun and rifle. The panrad was still quiet.

'Maybe the boulder is camouflage for a spy outfit,' he said. He sounded silly, even to himself.

Behind him, his mother gasped and screamed. He whirled and raised his gun, but there was nothing to shoot. She was pointing at the hilltop across the valley, shaking, and saying something incoherent.

He could make out a long slim antenna seemingly projecting from a monstrous boulder crouched there. At the same time two thoughts struggled for first place in his mind: one, that it was more than a coincidence that both hills had almost identical stone structures on their brows, and, two, that the antenna must have been recently struck out, for he was sure he had not seen it the last time he looked.

He never got to tell her his conclusions, for something thin and flexible and irresistible seized him from behind. Lifted into the air, he was borne backwards. He dropped the gun and tried to grab the bands or tentacles around him and tear them off with his bare hands. No use.

He caught one last glimpse of his mother running off down the hillside. Then a curtain snapped down, and he was in total darkness.

IV

Eddie sensed himself, still suspended, twirled around. He could not know for sure, of course, but he thought he was facing in exactly the opposite direction. Simultaneously the tentacles binding his legs and arms were released. Only his waist was still gripped. It was pressed so tightly that he cried out in pain.

Then, boot-toes bumping on some resilient substance, he was carried forward. Halted, facing he knew not what horrible monster, he was suddenly assailed – not by a sharp beak or tooth or knife or some other cutting or mangling instrument – but by a dense cloud of that same monkey perfume.

In other circumstances, he might have vomited. Now his stomach was not given the time to consider whether it should clean house or not. The tentacle lifted him higher and thrust him against something soft and yielding – something fleshlike and womanly – almost breastlike in texture and smoothness and warmth and in its hint of gentle curving.

He put his hands and feet out to brace himself, for he thought for a moment he was going to sink in and be covered up – enfolded – ingested. The idea of a gargantuan amoeba-thing hiding within a hollow rock – or a rocklike shell – made him writhe and yell and shove at the protoplasmic substance.

But nothing of the kind happened. He was not plunged into

144

a smothering and slimy jelly that would strip him of his skin and then his flesh and then dissolve his bones. He was merely shoved repeatedly against the soft swelling. Each time, he pushed or kicked or struck at it. After a dozen of these seemingly purposeless acts, he was held away, as if whatever was doing it was puzzled by his behaviour.

He had quit screaming. The only sounds were his harsh breathing and the zzzts and pings from the panrad. Even as he became aware of them, the zzzts changed tempo and settled into a recognizable pattern of bursts – three units that crackled out again and again.

'Who are you? Who are you?'

Of course, it could just as easily have been, 'What are you?' or 'What the hell!' or 'Nor smoz ka pop?'

Or nothing – semantically speaking.

But he didn't think the latter. And when he was gently lowered to the floor, and the tentacle went off to only-God-knew-where in the dark, he was sure that the creature was communicating – or trying to – with him.

It was this thought that kept him from screaming and running around in the lightless and fetid chamber, brainlessly seeking an outlet. He mastered his panic and snapped open a little shutter in the panrad's side and thrust in his right-hand index finger. There he poised it above the key and in a moment, when the thing paused in transmitting, he sent back, as best he could, the pulses he had received. It was not necessary for him to turn on the light and spin the dial that would put him on the 1000 kc. band. The instrument would automatically key that frequency in with the one he had just received.

The oddest part of the whole procedure was that his whole body was trembling almost uncontrollably – one part excepted. That was his index finger, his one unit that seemed to him to have a definite function in this otherwise meaningless situation. It was the section of him that was helping him to survive – the only part that knew how – at that moment. Even his brain seemed to have no connexion with his finger. That digit was himself, and the rest just happened to be linked to it.

When he paused, the transmitter began again. This time the units were unrecognizable. There was a certain rhythm to them, but he could not know what they meant. Meanwhile, the RD was pinging. Something somewhere in the dark hole had a beam held tightly on him.

He pressed a button on the panrad's top, and the built-in flash-light illuminated the area just in front of him. He saw a wall of reddish-grey rubbery substance. On the wall was a roughly circular, light grey swelling about four feet in diameter. Around it, giving it a Medusa apperance, were coiled twelve very long, very thin tentacles.

Though he was afraid that if he turned his back to them the tentacles would seize him once more, his curiosity forced him to wheel about and examine his surroundings with the bright beam. He was in an egg-shaped chamber about thirty feet long, twelve wide, and eight to ten high in the middle. It was formed of a reddish-grey material, smooth except for irregular intervals of blue or red pipes. Veins and arteries?

A door-sized portion of the wall had a vertical slit running down it. Tentacles fringed it. He guessed it was a sort of iris and that it had opened to drag him inside. Starfish-shaped groupings of tentacles were scattered on the walls or hung from the ceiling. On the wall opposite the iris was a long and flexible stalk with a cartilaginous ruff around its free end. When Eddie moved, it moved, its blind point following him as a radar antenna tracks the thing it is locating. That was what it was. And unless he was wrong, the stalk was also a C.W. transmitter-receiver.

He shot the light around. When it reached the end farthest from him, he gasped. Ten creatures were huddled together facing him! About the size of half-grown pigs, they looked like nothing so much as unshelled snails; they were eyeless, and the stalk growing from the forehead of each was a tiny duplicate of that on the wall. They didn't look dangerous. Their open mouths were little and toothless, and their rate of locomotion must be slow, for they moved like snails, on a large pedestal of flesh – a foot-muscle.

Nevertheless, if he were to fall asleep they could overcome him by force of numbers, and those mouths might drip an acid to digest him, or they might carry a concealed poisonous sting.

His speculations were interrupted violently. He was seized, lifted, and passed on to another group of tentacles. He was carried beyond the antenna-stalk and towards the snail-beings. Just before he reached them, he was halted, facing the wall. An iris, hitherto invisible, opened. His light shone into it, but he could see nothing but convolutions of flesh.

The panrad gave off a new pattern of dit-dot-deet-dats. The iris widened until it was large enough to admit his body, if he were shoved in head first. Or feet first. It didn't matter. The convolutions straightened out and became a tunnel. Or a throat. From thousands of little pits emerged thousands of tiny, razor-sharp teeth. They flashed out and sank back in, and before they had disappeared thousands of other wicked little spears darted out and past the receding fangs.

Meat-grinder.

Beyond the murderous array, at the end of the throat, was a huge pouch of water. Steam came from it, and with it an odour like that of his mother's stew. Dark bits, presumably meat, and pieces of vegetables floated on the seething surface.

Then the iris closed, and he was turned around to face the slugs. Gently, but unmistakably, a tentacle spanked his buttocks. And the panrad zzzted a warning.

Eddie was not stupid. He knew now that the creatures were not dangerous unless he molested them. In which case he had just seen where he would go if he did not behave.

Again he was lifted and carried along the wall until he was shoved against the light grey spot. The monkey-cage odour, which had died out, became strong again. Eddie identified its source with a very small hole which appeared in the wall.

When he did not respond – he had no idea yet how he was supposed to act – the tentacles dropped him so unexpectedly that he fell on his back. Unhurt by the yielding flesh, he rose.

What was the next step? Exploration of his resources. Itemization: The panrad. A sleeping-bag, which he wouldn't need as long as the present too-warm temperature kept up. A bottle of Old Red Star capsules. A free-fall thermos with attached nipple. A box of A-2-Z rations. A Foldstove. Cartridges for his double-barrel, now lying outside the creature's boulder-ish shell. A roll of toilet paper. Toothbrush. Paste. Soap. Towel. Pills: Nodor, hormone, vitamin, longevity, reflex, and sleeping. And a thread-thin wire, a hundred feet long when uncoiled that held prisoner in its molecular structure a hundred symphonies, eighty operas, a thousand different types of musical pieces, and two thousand great books ranging from Sophocles and Dostoyevsky to the latest bestseller. It could be played inside the panrad.

He inserted it, pushed a button, and spoke. 'Eddie Fetts's recording of Puccini's *Che gelida manina*, please.'

And while he listened approvingly to his own magnificent voice, he zipped open a can he had found in the bottom of the sack. His mother had put into it the stew left over from their last meal in the ship.

Not knowing what was happening, yet for some reason sure he was for the present safe, he munched meat and vegetables with a contented jaw. Transition from abhorrence to appetite sometimes came easily for Eddie.

He cleaned out the can and finished with some crackers and a chocolate bar. Rationing was out. As long as the food lasted, he would eat well. Then, if nothing turned up, he would ... But then, he reassured himself as he licked his fingers, his mother, who was free, would find some way to get him out of his trouble.

She always had.

V

The panrad, silent for a while, began signalling. Eddie spotlighted the antenna and saw it was pointing at the snailbeings, which he had, in accordance with his custom, dubbed familiarly. Sluggos he called them.

The Sluggos crept towards the wall and stopped close to it. Their mouths, placed on the tops of their heads gaped like so many hungry young birds. The iris opened, and two lips formed into a spout. Out of it streamed steaming-hot water and chunks of meat and vegetables. Stew! Stew that fell exactly into each waiting mouth.

That was how Eddie learned the second phrase of Mother Polyphema's language. The first message had been. 'What are you?' This was, 'Come and get it!'

He experimented. He tapped out a repetition of what he'd last heard. As one, the Sluggos – except the one then being fed – turned to him and crept a few feet before halting, puzzled.

Inasmuch as Eddie was broadcasting, the Sluggos must have had some sort of built-in DF. Otherwise they wouldn't have been able to distinguish between his pulses and their Mother's.

Immediately after, a tentacle smote Eddie across the shoulders and knocked him down. The panrad zzzted its third intelligible message: 'Don't ever do that!'

And then a fourth, to which the ten young obeyed by wheeling and resuming their former positions.

'This way, children.'

Yes, they were the offspring, living, eating, sleeping, playing, and learning to communicate in the womb of their mother – the Mother. They were the mobile brood of this vast immobile entity that had scooped up Eddie as a frog scoops up a fly. This Mother. She who had once been just such a Sluggo until she had grown hog-size and had been pushed out of her Mother's womb. And who, rolled into a tight ball, had freewheeled down her natal hill, straightened out at the bottom, inched her way up the next hill, rolled down, and so on. Until she found the empty shell of an adult who had died. Or, if she wanted to be a first class citizen in her society and not a prestigeless *occupée*, she found the bare top of a tall hill – any eminence that commanded a big sweep of territory – and there squatted.

And there she put out many thread-thin tendrils into the soil and into the cracks in the rocks, tendrils that drew sustenance from the fat of her body and grew and extended downwards and ramified into other tendrils. Deep underground the rootlets worked their instinctive chemistry; searched for and found the water, the calcium, the iron, the copper, the nitrogen, the carbons, fondled earthworms and grubs and larvae, teasing them for the secrets of their fats and proteins; broke down the wanted substance into shadowy colloidal particles; sucked them up the thready pipes of the tendrils and back to the pale and slimming body crouching on a flat space atop a ridge, a hill, a peak.

There, using the blueprints stored in the molecules of the cerebellum, her body took the building blocks of elements and fashioned them into a very thin shell of the most available material, a shield large enough so she could expand to fit it while her natural enemies – the keen and hungry predators that prowled twilighted Baudelaire – nosed and clawed it in vain.

Then, her evergrowing bulk cramped, she would resorb the hard covering. And if no sharp tooth found her during that process of a few days, she would cast another and a larger. And so on through a dozen or more.

Until she had become the monstrous and much reformed body of an adult and virgin female. Outside would be the stuff that so much resembled a boulder, that was, actually, rock: either granite, diorite, marble, basalt, or maybe just plain limestone. Or sometimes iron, glass, or cellulose.

Within was the centrally located brain, probably as large as a man's. Surrounding it, the tons of organs: the nervous system, the mighty heart, or hearts, the four stomachs, the microwave and longwave generators, the kidneys, bowels, tracheae, scent and taste organs, the perfume factory which made odours to attract animals and birds close enough to be seized, and the huge womb. And the antennae – the small one inside for teaching and scanning the young, and a long and powerful stalk on the outside, projecting from the shelltop, retractable if danger came.

The next step was from virgin to Mother, lower case to uppercase as designated in her pulse-language by a longer pause before a word. Not until she was deflowered could she take a high place in her society. Immodest, unblushing, she herself made the advances, the proposals, and the surrender.

After which, she ate her mate.

The clock in the panrad told Eddie he was in his thirtieth day of imprisonment when he found out that little bit of information. He was shocked, not because it offended his ethics, but because he himself had been intended to be the mate. And the dinner.

His finger tapped, 'Tell me, Mother, what you mean.'

He had not wondered before how a species that lacked males could reproduce. Now he found that, to the Mothers, all Creatures except themselves were male. Mothers were immobile and female. Mobiles were male. Eddie had been mobile. He was, therefore, a male.

He had approached this particular Mother during the mating season, that is, midway through raising a litter of young. She had scanned him as he came along the creekbanks at the valley bottom. When he was at the foot of the hill, she had detected his odour. It was new to her. The closest she could come to it in her memorybanks was that of a beast similar to him. From her description, he guessed it to be an ape. So she had released from her repertoire its rut stench. When he seemingly fell into the trap, she had caught him.

He was supposed to attack the conception-spot, that light grey swelling on the wall. After he had ripped and torn it enough to begin the mysterious working of pregnancy, he would have been popped into her stomach-iris.

Fortunately, he had lacked the sharp beak, the fang, the

claw. And she had received her own signals back from the panrad.

Eddie did not understand why it was necessary to use a mobile for mating. A Mother was intelligent enough to pick up a sharp stone and mangle the spot herself.

He was given to understand that conception would not start unless it was accompanied by a certain titillation of the nerves – a frenzy and its satisfaction. Why this emotional state was needed, Mother did not know.

Eddie tried to explain about such things as genes and chromosomes and why they had to be present in highly-developed species.

Mother did not understand.

Eddie wondered if the number of slashes and rips in the spot corresponded to the number of young. Or if there were a large number of potentialities in the heredity-ribbons spread out under the conception-skin. And if the haphazard irritation and consequent stimulation of the genes paralleled the chance combining of genes in human male-female mating. Thus resulting in offspring with traits that were combinations of their parents.

Or did the inevitable devouring of the mobile after the act indicate more than an emotional and nutritional reflex? Did it hint that the mobile caught up scattered gene-nodes, like hard seeds, along with the torn skin, in its claws and tusks, that these genes survived the boiling in the stew-stomach, and were later passed out in the faeces? Where animals and birds picked them up in beak, tooth, or foot, and then, seized by other Mothers in this oblique rape, transmitted the heredity-carrying agents to the conception-spots while attacking them, the nodules being scraped off and implanted in the skin and blood of the swelling even as others were harvested? Later, the mobiles were eaten, digested, and ejected in the obscure but ingenious and never-ending cycle? Thus ensuring the continual, if haphazard, recombining of genes, chances for variations in offspring, opportunities for mutations, and so on?

Mother pulsed that she was nonplussed.

Eddie gave up. He'd never know. After all, did it matter?

He decided not, and rose from his prone position to request water. She pursed up her iris and spouted a tepid quartful into his thermos. He dropped in a pill, swished it around till it dissolved, and drank a reasonable fascimile of Old Red Star.

He preferred the harsh and powerful rye, though he could have afforded the smoothest. Quick results were what he wanted. Taste didn't matter, as he disliked all liquor tastes. Thus he drank what the Skid Row bums drank and shuddered even as they did, renaming it Old Rotten Tar and cursing the fate that had brought them so low they had to gag such stuff down.

The rye glowed in his belly and spread quickly through his limbs and up to his head, chilled only by increasing scarcity of the capsules. When he ran out – then what? It was at times like this that he most missed his mother.

Thinking about her brought a few large tears. He snuffled and drank some more and when the biggest of the Sluggos nudged him for a back-scratching, he gave it instead a shot of Old Red Star. A slug for Sluggo. Idly, he wondered what effect a taste for rye would have on the future of the race when these virgins became Mothers.

At that moment he was shaken by what seemed a life-saving idea. These creatures could suck up the required elements from the earth and with them duplicate quite complex molecular structures. Provided, of course, they had a sample of the desired substance to brood over in some cryptic organ.

Well, what easier to do than give her one of the cherished capsules? One could become any number. Those, plus the abundance of water pumped up through hollow underground tendrils from the nearby creek, would give enough to make a master-distiller green!

He smacked his lips and was about to key her his request when what she was transmitting penetrated his mind.

Rather cattily, she remarked that her neighbour across the valley was putting on airs because she, too, held prisoner a communicating mobile.

VI

The Mothers had a society as hierarchical as table-protocol in Washington or peck-order in a barnyard. Prestige was what counted, and prestige was determined by the broadcasting power, the height of the eminence on which the Mother sat, which governed the extent of her radar-territory, and the abundance and novelty and wittiness of her gossip. The creature that had snapped Eddie up was a queen. She had precedence over thirty-odd of her kind; they all had to let her broadcast first, and none dared start pulsing until she quit. Then, the next in order began, and so on down the line. Any of them could be interrupted at any time by Number One, and if any of the lower echelon had something interesting to transmit, she could break in on the one then speaking and get permission from the queen to tell her tale.

Eddie knew this, but he could not listen in directly to the hilltop-gabble. The thick pseudo-granite shell barred him from that and made him dependent upon her womb-stalk for relayed information.

Now and then Mother opened the door and allowed her young to crawl out. There they practised beaming and broadcasting at the Sluggos of the Mother across the valley. Occasionally that Mother deigned herself to pulse the young, and Eddie's keeper reciprocated to her offspring.

Turnabout.

The first time the children had inched through the exit-iris, Eddie had tried, Ulysses-like, to pass himself off as one of them and crawl out in the midst of the flock. Eyeless, but no Polyphemus, Mother had picked him out with her tentacles and hauled him back in.

It was following that incident that he had named her Polyphema.

He knew she had increased her own already powerful prestige tremendously by possession of that unique thing – a transmitting mobile. So much had her importance grown that the Mothers on the fringes of her area passed on the news to others. Before he had learned her language, the entire continent was hooked-up. Polyphema had become a veritable gossip columnist; tens of thousands of hillcrouchers listened in eagerly to her accounts of her dealings with the walking paradox: a semantic male.

That had been fine. Then, very recently, the Mother across the valley had captured a similar creature. And in one bound she had become Number Two in the area and would, at the slightest weakness on Polyphema's part, wrest the top position away.

Eddie became wildly excited at the news. He had often day-dreamed about his mother and wondered what she was doing. Curiously enough, he ended many of his fantasies with lip-mutterings, reproaching her almost audibly for having left him and for making no try to rescue him. When he became aware of his attitude, he was ashamed. Nevertheless, the sense of desertion coloured his thoughts.

Now that he knew she was alive and had been caught, probably while trying to get him out, he rose from the lethargy that had lately been making him doze the clock around. He asked Polyphema if she would open the entrance so he could talk directly with the other captive. She said yes. Eager to listen in on a conversation between two mobiles, she was very cooperative. There would be a mountain of gossip in what they would have to say. The only thing that dented her joy was that the other Mother would also have access.

Then, remembering she was still Number One and would broadcast the details first, she trembled so with pride and ecstasy that Eddie felt the floor shaking.

Iris open, he walked through it and looked across the valley. The hillsides were still green, red, and yellow, as the plants on Baudelaire did not lose their leaves during winter. But a few white patches showed that winter had begun. Eddie shivered from the bite of cold air on his naked skin. Long ago he had taken off his clothes. The womb-warmth had made garments too uncomfortable; moreover, Eddie, being human, had had to get rid of waste products. And Polyphema, being a Mother, had had periodically to flush out the dirt with warm water from one of her stomachs. Every time the tracheae-vents exploded streams that swept the undesirable elements out through her door-iris, Eddie had become soaked. When he abandoned dress, his clothes had gone floating out. Only by sitting on his pack did he keep it from a like fate.

Afterwards, he and the Sluggos had been dried off by warm air pumped through the same vents and originating from the mighty battery of lungs. Eddie was comfortable enough – he'd always liked showers – but the loss of his garments had been one more thing that kept him from escaping. He would soon freeze to death outside unless he found the yacht quickly. And he wasn't sure he remembered the path back.

So now, when he stepped outside, he retreated a pace or two and let the warm air from Polyphema flow like a cloak from his shoulders.

Then he peered across the half-mile that separated him from his mother, but he could not see her. The twilight state and the dark of the unlit interior of her captor hid her.

He tapped in Morse, 'Switch to the talkie, same frequency.' Paula Fetts did so. She began asking him frantically if he were all right.

He replied he was fine.

'Have you missed me terribly, son?'

'Oh, very much.'

Even as he said this he wondered vaguely why his voice sounded so hollow. Despair at never again being able to see her, probably.

'I've almost gone crazy, Eddie. When you were caught I ran away as fast as I could. I had no idea what horrible monster it was that was attacking us. And then, half-way down the hill, I fell and broke my leg. . . .'

'Oh, no mother!'

'Yes. But I managed to crawl back to the ship. And there, after I'd set it myself, I gave myself B.K. shots. Only, my system didn't react like it's supposed to. There are people that way, you know, and the healing took twice as long.

'But when I was able to walk, I got a gun and a box of dynamite. I was going to blow up what I thought was a kind of rockfortress, an outpost for some kind of extee. I'd no idea of the true nature of these beasts. First, though, I decided to reconnoitre. I was going to spy on the boulder from across the valley. But I was trapped by this thing.

'Listen, son. Before I'm cut off, let me tell you not to give up hope. I'll be out of here before long and over to rescue you.'

'How?'

'If you remember, my lab kit holds a number of carcinogens for field work. Well, you know that sometimes a Mother's conception-spot when it is torn up during mating, instead of begetting young, goes into cancer – the opposite of pregnancy. I've injected a carcinogen into the spot and a beautiful carcinoma has developed. She'll be dead in a few days.'

'Mom! You'll be buried in that rotting mass!'

'No. This creature has told me that when one of her species dies, a reflex opens the labia. That's to permit their young – if any – to escape. Listen, I'll —'

A tentacle coiled about him and pulled him back through the iris, which shut.

When he switched back to C.W., he heard, 'Why did you communicate? What were you doing? Tell me! Tell me!'

Eddie told her. There was a silence that could only be interpreted as astonishment. After Mother had recovered her wits, she said, 'From now on, you will talk to the other male through me.'

Obviously, she envied and hated his ability to change wavebands, and, perhaps had a struggle to accept the idea.

'Please,' he persisted, not knowing how dangerous were the waters he was wading in, 'please let me talk to my mother di —'

For the first time, he heard her stutter.

'Wha-wha-what? Your Mo-Mo-Mother?'

'Yes. Of course.'

The floor heaved violently beneath his feet. He cried out and braced himself to keep from falling and then flashed on the light. The walls were pulsating like shaken jelly, and the vascular columns had turned from red and blue to grey. The entrance-iris sagged open, like a lax mouth, and the air cooled. He could feel the drop in temperature in her flesh with the soles of his feet.

It was some time before he caught on.

Polyphema was in a state of shock.

What might have happened had she stayed in it, he never knew. She might have died and thus forced him out into the winter before his mother could escape. If so, and he couldn't find the ship, he would die. Huddled in the warmest corner of the egg-shaped chamber, Eddie contemplated that idea and shivered to a degree for which the outside air couldn't account.

VII

However, Polyphema had her own method of recovery. It consisted of spewing out the contents of her stew-stomach, which had doubtless become filled with the poisons draining out of her system from the blow. Her ejection of the stuff was the physical manifestation of the psychical catharsis. So furious was the flood that her foster son was almost swept out in the hot tide, but he, reacting instinctively, had coiled tentacles about him and the Sluggos. Then she followed the first upchucking by emptying her other three waterpouches, the second hot and the third luke-warm and the fourth, just filled, cold.

Eddie yelped as the icy water doused him.

Polyphema's irises closed again. The floor and walls gradually quit quaking; the temperature rose; and her veins and arteries regained their red and blue. She was well again. Or so she seemed.

But when, after waiting twenty-four hours he cautiously approached the subject, he found she not only would not talk about it, she refused to acknowledge the existence of the other mobile.

Eddie, giving up hope of conversation, thought for quite a while. The only conclusion he could come to, and he was sure he'd grasped enough of her psychology to make it valid, was that the concept of a mobile female was utterly unacceptable.

Her world was split into two: mobile and her kind, the immobile. Mobile meant food and mating. Mobile meant – male. The Mothers were – female.

How the mobiles reproduced had probably never entered the hillcrouchers' minds. Their science and philosophy were on the instinctive body-level. Whether they had some notion of spontaneous generation or amoeba-like fission being responsible for the continued population of mobiles, or they'd just taken for granted they 'growed', like Topsy, Eddie never found out. To them, they were female and the rest of the protoplasmic cosmos was male.

That was that. Any other idea was more than foul and obscene and blasphemous. It was – unthinkable.

Polyphema had received a deep trauma from his words. And though she seemed to have recovered, somewhere in those tons of unimaginably complicated flesh a bruise was buried. Like a hidden flower, dark purple, it bloomed, and the shadow it cast was one that cut off a certain memory, a certain tract, from the light of consciousness. That bruise-stained shadow covered that time and event which the Mother, for reasons unfathomable to the human being, found necessary to mark KEEP OFF.

Thus, though Eddie did not word it, he understood in the cells of his body, he felt and knew, as if his bones were prophesying and his brain did not hear, what came to pass.

Sixty-six hours later by the panrad clock, Polyphema's entrance-lips opened. Her tentacles darted out. They came back in, carrying his helpless and struggling mother.

Eddie, roused out of a doze, horrified, paralysed, saw her toss her lab kit at him and heard an inarticulate cry from her. And saw her plunged, headforemost, into the stomach-iris.

Polyphema had taken the one sure way of burying the evidence.

Eddie lay face down, nose mashed against the warm and faintly throbbing flesh of the floor. Now and then his hands clutched spasmodically as if he were reaching for something that someone kept putting just within his reach and then moving away.

How long he was there he didn't know, for he never again looked at the clock.

Finally, in the darkness, he sat up and giggled insanely, 'Mother always did make good stew.'

That set him off. He leaned back on his hands and threw his head back and howled like a wolf under a full moon.

Polyphema, of course, was dead-deaf, but she could radar his posture, and her keen nostrils deduced from his body-scent that he was in terrible fear and anguish.

A tentacle glided out and gently enfolded him.

'What is the matter?' zzted the panrad.

He stuck his finger in the keyhole.

'I have lost my mother!'

'?'

'She's gone away, and she'll never come back.'

'I don't understand. *Here I am.*'

Eddie quit weeping and cocked his head as if he were listening to some inner voice. He snuffled a few times and wiped away the tears, slowly disengaged the tentacle, patted it, walked over to his pack in a corner, and took out the bottle of Old Red Star capsules. One he popped into the thermos; the other he gave to her with the request she duplicate it, if possible. Then he stretched out on his side, propped on one elbow like a Roman in his sensualities, sucked the rye through the nipple, and listened to a medley of Beethoven, Moussorgsky, Verdi, Strauss, Porter, Feinstein, and Waxworth.

So the time – if there were such a thing there – flowed around Eddie. When he was tired of music or plays or books, he listened in on the area hookup. Hungry, he rose and walked – or often just crawled – to the stew-iris. Cans of rations lay in his pack; he had planned to eat those until he was sure that – what was it he was forbidden to eat? Poison? Something had been devoured by Polyphema and the Sluggos. But sometime during the music-rye orgy, he had forgotten. He now ate quite hungrily and with thought for nothing but the satisfaction of his wants.

Sometimes the door-iris opened, and Billy Greengrocer hopped in. Billy looked like a cross between a cricket and a kangaroo. He was the size of a collie, and he bore in a marsupialian pouch vegetables and fruit and nuts. These he extracted with shiny green, chitinous claws and gave to Mother in return for meals of stew. Happy symbiote, he chirruped merrily while his many-faceted eyes, revolving independently of each other, looked one at the Sluggos and the other at Eddie.

Eddie, on impulse, abandoned the 100 kc. band and roved the frequencies until he found that both Polyphema and Billy were emitting a 108 wave. That, apparently, was their natural signal.

When Billy had his groceries to deliver, he broadcast. Polyphema, in turn, when she needed them, sent back to him. There was nothing intelligent on Billy's part; it was just his instinct to transmit. And the Mother was, aside from the 'semantic' frequency, limited to that one band. But it worked out fine.

VIII

Everything was fine. What more could a man want? Free food, unlimited liquor, soft bed, air-conditioning, showerbaths, music, intellectual works (on the tape), interesting conversation (much of it was about him), privacy, and security.

If he had not already named her, he would have called her Mother Gratis.

Nor were creature comforts all. She had given him the answers to all his questions, all. . . .

Except one.

That was never expressed vocally by him. Indeed, he would have been incapable of doing so. He was probably unaware that he had such a question.

But Polyphema voiced it one day when she asked him to do her a favour.

Eddie reacted as if outraged.

'One does not —! One does not —! '

He choked, and then he thought, how ridiculous! She is not —

And looked puzzled, and said, 'But she is.'

He rose and opened the lab kit. While he was looking for a scalpel, he came across the carcinogens. He threw them through the half-opened labia far out and down the hillside.

Then he turned and, scalpel in hand, leaped at the light grey swelling on the wall. And stopped, staring at it, while the instrument fell from his hand. And picked it up and stabbed feebly and did not even scratch the skin. And again let it drop.

'What is it? What is it?' crackled the panrad hanging from his wrist.

Suddenly, a heavy cloud of human odour – mansweat – was puffed in his face from a nearby vent.

'? ? ? ?'

And he stood, bent in a half-crouch, seemingly paralysed. Until tentacles seized him in fury and dragged him toward the stomach-iris, yawning man-sized.

Eddie screamed and writhed and plunged his finger in the panrad and tapped, 'All right! All right!'

And once back before the spot, he lunged with a sudden and wild joy, he lashed savagely; he yelled. 'Take that! And that, P . . .' and the rest was lost in a mindless shout.

He did not stop cutting, and he might have gone on and on until he had quite excised the spot had not Polyphema interferred by dragging him toward her stomach-iris again. For ten seconds he hung there, helpless and sobbing with a mixture of fear and glory.

Polyphema's reflexes had almost overcome her brain. Fortunately, a cold spark of reason lit up a corner of the vast, dark, and hot chapel of frenzy.

The convolutions leading to the steaming, meat-laden pouch closed and the foldings of flesh rearranged themselves. Eddie was suddenly hosed with warm water from what he called the 'sanitation' stomach. The iris closed. He was put down. The scalpel was put back in the bag.

For a long time Mother seemed to be shaken by the thought of what she might have done to Eddie. She did not trust herself to transmit until her nerves were settled. When they were, she did not refer to his narrow escape. Nor did he.

He was happy. He felt as if a spring, tight-coiled against his bowels since he and his wife had parted, was now, for some reason, released. The dull vague pain of loss and discontent, the slight fever and cramp in his entrails, and the apathy that sometimes afflicted him, were gone. He felt fine.

Meanwhile, something akin to deep affection had been lighted, like a tiny candle under the draughty and overtowering roof of a cathedral. Mother's shell housed more than Eddie; it now curved over an emotion new to her kind. This was evident by the next event that filled him with terror.

For the wounds in the spot healed and the swelling increased into a large bag. Then the bag burst and ten mousesized Sluggos struck the floor. The impact had the same effect as a doctor spanking a newborn baby's bottom; he drew in their first breath with shock and pain; their uncontrolled and feeble pulses filled the ether with shapeless SOS's.

When Eddie was not talking with Polyphema or listening in or drinking or sleeping or eating or bathing or running off the tape, he played with the Sluggos. He was, in a sense, their father. Indeed, as they grew to hog-size, it was hard for their female parent to distinguish him from her young. As he seldom walked any more, and was often to be found on hands and knees in their midst, she could not scan him too well. Moreover, something in the heavywet air or in the diet had caused every hair on his body to drop off. He grew very fat. Generally speaking, he was one with the pale, soft, round, and bald offspring. A family likeness.

There was one difference. When the time came for the virgins to be expelled, Eddie crept to one end, whimpering, and stayed there until he was sure Mother was not going to thrust him out into the cold, hard, and hungry world.

That final crisis over, he came back to the centre of the floor. The panic in his breast had died out, but his nerves were still quivering. He filled his thermos and then listened for a while to his own tenor singing the 'Sea Things' aria from his favourite opera, Gianelli's *Ancient Mariner*. Suddenly, he burst out and accompanied himself, finding himself thrilled as never before by the concluding words.

> *And from my neck so free*
> *The Albatross fell off, and sank*
> *Like lead into the sea.*

Afterward, voice silent but heart singing, he switched off the wire and cut in on Polyphema's broadcast.

Mother was having trouble. She could not precisely describe to the continent-wide hook-up this new and almost inexpressible emotion she felt about the mobile. It was a concept her language was not prepared for. Nor was she helped any by the gallons of Old Red Star in her bloodstream.

Eddie sucked at the plastic nipple and nodded sympathetically and drowsily at her search for words. Presently, the thermos rolled out of his hand.

He slept on his side, curled in a ball, knees on his chest and arms crossed, neck bent forward. Like the pilot room chronometer whose hands reversed after the crash, the clock of his body was ticking backwards, ticking backwards...

In the darkness, in the moistness, safe and warm, well fed, much loved.

Stranger Station
by Damon Knight

The clang of metal echoed hollowly down through the Station's many vaulted corridors and rooms. Paul Wesson stood listening for a moment as the rolling echoes died away. The maintenance rocket was gone, heading back to Home; they had left him alone in Stranger Station.

Stranger Station! The name itself quickened his imagination. Wesson knew that both orbital stations had been named a century ago by the then-British administration of the satellite service; 'Home' because the larger, inner station handled the traffic of Earth and its colonies; 'Stranger' because the outer station was designed specifically for dealings with foreigners – beings from outside the solar system. But even that could not diminish the wonder of Stranger Station, whirling out here alone in the dark – waiting for its once-in-two-decades visitor...

One man, out of all Sol's billions, had the task and privilege of enduring the alien's presence when it came. The two races, according to Wesson's understanding of the subject, were so fundamentally different that it was painful for them to meet. Well, he had volunteered for the job, and he thought he could handle it – the rewards were big enough.

He had gone through all the tests, and against his own expectations he had been chosen. The maintenance crew had brought him up as dead weight, drugged in a survival hamper; they had kept him the same way while they did their work and then had brought him back to consciousness. Now they were gone. He was alone.

But not quite.

'Welcome to Stranger Station, Sergeant Wesson,' said a pleasant voice. 'This is your alpha network speaking. I'm here to protect and serve you in every way. If there's anything you want, just ask me.' It was a neutral voice, with a kind of professional friendliness in it, like that of a good schoolteacher or rec supervisor.

Wesson had been warned, but he was still shocked at the human quality of it. The alpha networks were the last word in robot brains – computers, safety devices, personal servants, libraries, all wrapped up in one, with something so close to 'personality' and 'free will' that experts were still arguing the question. They were rare and fantastically expensive; Wesson had never met one before.

'Thanks,' he said now, to the empty air. 'Uh – what do I call you, by the way. I can't keep saying, "Hey, alpha network." '

'One of your recent predecessors called me Aunt Nettie,' was the response.

Wesson grimaced. Apha network – Aunt Nettie. He hated puns; that wouldn't do. 'The aunt part is all right,' he said. 'Suppose I call you Aunt Jane. That was my mother's sister; you sound like her, a little bit.'

'I am honored,' said the invisible mechanism politely. 'Can I serve you any refreshments now? Sandwiches? A drink?'

'Not just yet,' said Wesson. 'I think I'll look the place over first.'

He turned away. That seemed to end the conversation as far as the network was concerned. A good thing; it was all right to have it for company, speaking when spoken to, but if it got talkative...

The human part of the Station was in four segments: bedroom, living room, dining room, bath. The living room was comfortably large and pleasantly furnished in greens and tans; the only mechanical note in it was the big instrument console in one corner. The other rooms, arranged in a ring around the living room, were tiny; just space enough for Wesson, a narrow encircling corridor, and the mechanisms that would serve him. The whole place was spotlessly clean, gleaming and efficient in spite of its twenty-year layoff.

This is the gravy part of the run, Wesson told himself. The month before the alien came – good food, no work, and an alpha network for conversation. 'Aunt Jane, I'll have a small steak now,' he said to the network. 'Medium rare, with hashed brown potatoes, onions, and mushrooms, and a glass of lager. Call me when it's ready.'

'Right,' said the voice pleasantly. Out in the dining room, the autochef began to hum and cluck self-importantly. Wesson wandered over and inspected the instrument console. Air locks were sealed and tight, said the dials; the air was cycling. The station was in orbit and rotating on its axis with a force at the perimeter, where Wesson was, of one g. The internal temperature of this part of the Station was an even 73°.

The other side of the board told a different story; all the dials were dark and dead. Sector Two, occupying a volume some eighty-eight thousand times as great as this one, was not yet functioning.

Wesson had a vivid mental image of the Station, from photographs and diagrams – a five-hundred-foot Duralumin sphere, onto which the shallow thirty-foot disk of the human section had been stuck apparently as an afterthought. The whole cavity of the sphere, very nearly – except for a honeycomb of supply and maintenance rooms and the all-important, recently enlarged vats – was one cramped chamber for the alien...

'Steak's ready!' said Aunt Jane.

The steak was good, bubbling crisp outside the way he liked it, tender and pink inside. 'Aunt Jane,' he said with his mouth full, 'this is pretty soft, isn't it?'

'The steak?' asked the voice, with a faintly anxious note.

Wesson grinned. 'Never mind,' he said. 'Listen, Aunt Jane, you've been through this routine – how many times? Were you installed with the Station, or what?'

'I was not installed with the Station,' said Aunt Jane primly. 'I have assisted at three contacts.'

'Um. Cigarette,' said Wesson, slapping his pockets. The autochef hummed for a moment, and popped a pack of G.I.'s out of a vent. Wesson lighted up. 'All right,' he said, 'you've been through this three times. There are a lot of things you can tell me, right?'

'Oh, yes, certainly. What would you like to know?'

Wesson smoked, leaning back reflectively, green eyes narrowed. 'First,' he said, 'read me the Pigeon report – you know, from the *Brief History*. I want to see if I remember it right.'

'Chapter Two,' said the voice promptly. 'First contact with a non-Solar intelligence was made by Commander Ralph C. Pigeon on July 1, 1987, during an emergency landing on Titan. The following is an excerpt from his official report:

' "While searching for a possible cause for our mental disturbance, we discovered what appeared to be a gigantic construction of metal on the far side of the ridge. Our distress grew stronger with the approach to this construction, which was polyhedral and approximately five times the length of the *Cologne*.

' "Some of those present expressed a wish to retire, but Lt.

Acuff and myself had a strong sense of being called or summoned in some indefinable way. Although our uneasiness was not lessened, we therefore agreed to go forward and keep radio contact with the rest of the party while they returned to the ship.

' "We gained access to the alien construction by way of a large, irregular opening.... The internal temperature was minus seventy-five degrees Fahrenheit; the atmosphere appeared to consist of methane and ammonia.... Inside the second chamber, an alien creature was waiting for us. We felt the distress, which I have tried to describe, to a much greater degree than before, and also the sense of summoning or pleading.... We observed that the creature was exuding a thick yellowish fluid from certain joints or pores in its surface. Though disgusted, I managed to collect a sample of this exudate, and it was later forwarded for analysis...."

'The second contact was made ten years later by Commodore Crawford's famous Titan Expedition—'

'No, that's enough,' said Wesson. 'I just wanted the Pigeon quote.' He smoked, brooding. 'It seems kind of chopped off. doesn't it! Have you got a longer version in your memory banks anywhere?'

There was a pause. 'No,' said Aunt Jane.

'There was more to it when I was a kid,' Wesson complained nervously. 'I read that book when I was twelve, and I remember a long description of the alien – that is, I remember its being there.' He swung around. 'Listen, Aunt Jane – you're a sort of universal watchdog, that right? You've got cameras and mikes all over the Station?'

'Yes,' said the network, sounding – was it Wesson's imagination? – faintly injured.

'Well, what about Sector Two? You must have cameras up there, too, isn't so?'

'Yes.'

'All right, then you can tell me. What do the aliens look like?'

There was a definite pause. 'I'm sorry, I can't tell you that,' said Aunt Jane.

'No,' said Wesson, 'I didn't think you could. You've got orders not to, I guess, for the same reason those history books have been cut since I was a kid. Now, what would the reason be? Have you got any idea, Aunt Jane?'

There was another pause. 'Yes,' the voice admitted.

'Well?'

'I'm sorry, I can't —'

'— tell you that.' Wesson repeated along with it. 'All right. At least we know where we stand.'

'Yes, Sergeant. Would you like some dessert?'

'No dessert. One other thing. *What happens to Station watchmen, like me, after their tour of duty?*'

'They are upgraded to Class Seven, students with unlimited leisure, and receive outright gifts of seven thousand stellors, plus free Class One housing....'

'Yeah, I know all that,' said Wesson, licking his dry lips. 'But here's what I'm asking you. The one you know — what kind of shape were they in when they left here?'

'The usual human shape,' said the voice brightly. 'Why do you ask, Sergeant?'

Wesson made a discontented gesture. 'Something I remember from a bull session at the Academy. I can't get it out of my head; I know it had something to do with the Station. Just a part of a sentence: "... blind as a bat and white bristles all over ..." Now, would that be a description of the alien — or the watchman when they came to take him away?'

Aunt Jane went into one of her heavy pauses. 'All right, I'll save you the trouble,' said Wesson. 'You're sorry, you can't tell me that.'

'I *am* sorry,' said the robot sincerely.

As the slow days passed into weeks, Wesson grew aware of the Station almost as a living thing. He could feel its resilient metal ribs enclosing him, lightly bearing his weight with its own as it swung. He could feel the waiting emptiness 'up there,' and he sensed the alert electronic network that spread around him everywhere, watching and probing, trying to anticipate his needs.

Aunt Jane was a model companion. She had a record library of thousands of hours of music; she had films to show him, and microprinted books that he could read on the scanner in the living room; or if he preferred, she would read to him. She controlled the Station's three telescopes, and on request would give him a view of Earth or the Moon or Home....

But there was no news. Aunt Jane would obligingly turn on the radio receiver if he asked her, but nothing except static came out. That was the thing that weighed most heavily on

167

Wesson, as time passed – the knowledge that radio silence was being imposed on all ships in transit, on the orbital stations, and on the planet-to-space transmitters. It was an enormous, almost a crippling handicap. Some information could be transmitted over relatively short distances by photophone, but ordinarily the whole complex traffic of the space lanes depended on radio.

But this coming alien contact was so delicate a thing that even a radio voice, out here where the Earth was only a tiny disk twice the size of the Moon, might upset it. It was so precarious a thing, Wesson thought, that only one man could be allowed in the Station while the alien was there, and to give that man the company that would keep him sane, they had to install an alpha network. . . .

'Aunt Jane?'

The voice answered promptly, 'Yes, Paul.'

'This distress that the books talk about – you wouldn't know what it is, would you?'

'No, Paul.'

'Because robot brains don't feel it, right?'

'Right, Paul.'

'So tell me this – why do they need a man here at all? Why can't they get along with just you?'

A pause. 'I don't know, Paul.' The voice sounded faintly wistful. Were those gradations of tone really in it, Wesson wondered, or was his imagination supplying them?

He got up from the living room couch and paced restlessly back and forth. 'Let's have a look at Earth,' he said. Obediently, the viewing screen on the console glowed into life: there was the blue Earth, swimming deep below him, in its first quarter, jewel bright. 'Switch it off,' Wesson said.

'A little music?' suggested the voice, and immediately began to play something soothing, full of woodwinds.

'No,' said Wesson. The music stopped.

Wesson's hands were trembling; he had a caged and frustrated feeling.

The fitted suit was in its locker beside the air lock. Wesson had been topside in it once or twice; there was nothing to see up there, just darkness and cold. But he had to get out of this squirrel cage. He took the suit down and began to get into it.

'Paul,' said Aunt Jane anxiously, 'are you feeling nervous?'

'Yes,' he snarled.

'Then don't go into Sector Two,' said Aunt Jane.

'Don't tell me what to do, you hunk of tin!' said Wesson with sudden anger. He zipped up the front of his suit with a vicious motion.

Aunt Jane was silent.

Seething, Wesson finished his check-off and opened the lock door.

The air lock, an upright tube barely large enough for one man, was the only passage between Sector One and Sector Two. It was also the only exit from Sector One; to get here in the first place, Wesson had had to enter the big lock at the 'south' pole of the sphere, and travel all the way down inside, by drop hole and catwalk. He had been drugged unconscious at the time, of course. When the time came, he would go out the same way; neither the maintenance rocket nor the tanker had any space, or time, to spare.

At the 'north' pole, opposite, there was a third air lock, this one so huge it could easily have held an interplanet freighter. But that was nobody's business – no human being's.

In the beam of Wesson's helmet lamp, the enormous central cavity of the Station was an inky gulf that sent back only remote mocking glimmers of light. The near walls sparkled with hoarfrost. Sector Two was not yet pressurized; there was only a diffuse vapor that had leaked through the airseal and had long since frozen into the powdery deposit that lined the walls. The metal rang cold under his shod feet; the vast emptiness of the chamber was the more depressing because it was airless, unwarmed and unlit. *Alone*, said his footsteps; *alone* . . .

He was thirty yards up the catwalk when his anxiety suddenly grew stronger. Wesson stopped in spite of himself and turned clumsily, putting his back to the wall. The support of the solid wall was not enough. The catwalk seemed threatening to tilt underfoot, dropping him into the lightless gulf.

Wesson recognized this drained feeling, this metallic taste at the back of his tongue. It was fear.

The thought ticked through his head: *They want me to be afraid*. But why? Why now? Of What?

Equally suddenly, he knew. The nameless pressure tightened, like a great fist closing, and Wesson had the appalling sense of something so huge that it had no limits at all, descend-

169

ing, with a terrible endless swift slowness. . . .

It was time.

His first month was up.

The alien was coming.

As Wesson turned, gasping, the whole huge structure of the Station around him seemed to dwindle to the size of an ordinary room – and Wesson with it, so that he seemed to himself like a tiny insect, frantically scuttling down the walls toward safety.

Behind him as he ran, the Station *boomed*.

In the silent rooms, all the lights were burning dimly. Wesson lay still, looking at the ceiling. Up there his imagination formed a shifting, changing image of the alien – huge, shadowy, formlessly menacing.

Sweat had gathered in globules on his brow. He stared, unable to look away.

'That was why you didn't want me to go topside, huh, Aunt Jane?' he said hoarsely.

'Yes. The nervousness is the first sign. But you gave me a direct order, Paul.'

'I know it,' he said vaguely, still staring fixedly at the ceiling. 'A funny thing . . . Aunt Jane?'

'Yes, Paul?'

'You won't tell me what it looks like, right?'

'No, Paul.'

'I don't want to know. Lord, I don't *want* to know. . . . Funny thing. Aunt Jane, part of me is just pure funk – I'm so scared I'm nothing but a jelly.'

'I know,' said the voice gently.

'– And part is real cool and calm, as if it didn't matter. Crazy, the things you think about. You know?'

'What things, Paul?'

He tried to laugh. 'I'm remembering a kid's party I went to twenty, twenty-five years ago. I was – let's see – I was nine. I remember, because that was the same year my father died.

'We were living in Dallas then, in a rented mobile house, and there was a family in the next tract with a bunch of redheaded kids. They were always throwing parties; nobody liked them much, but everybody always went.'

'Tell me about the party, Paul.'

He shifted on the couch. 'This one – this one was a Halloween party. I remember the girls had on black and orange dresses, and the boys mostly wore spirit costumes. I was about the youngest kid there, and I felt kind of out of place. Then all of a sudden one of the redheads jumps up in a skull mask, hollering, "C'mon, everybody get ready for hide-and-seek." And he grabs *me*, and says, "*You* be it," and before I can even move, he shoves me into a dark closet. And I hear that door lock behind me.'

He moistened his lips. 'And then – you know, in the darkness – I feel something hit my *face*. You know, cold and clammy, like – I don't know – something dead. . . .

'I just hunched up on the floor of that closet, waiting for that thing to touch me again. You know? That thing, cold and kind of gritty, hanging up there. You know what it was? A cloth glove, full of ice and bran cereal. A joke. Boy, that was one joke I never forgot. . . . Aunt Jane?'

'Yes, Paul.'

'Hey, I'll bet you alpha networks made great psychs, huh? I could lie here and tell you anything, because you're just a machine – right?'

'Right, Paul,' said the network sorrowfully.

'Aunt Jane, Aunt Jane . . . It's no use kidding myself along. I can *feel* that thing up there, just a couple of yards away.'

'I know you can, Paul.'

'I can't stand it, Aunt Jane.'

'You can if you think you can, Paul.'

He writhed on the couch. 'It's – it's dirty, it's clammy. My God, is it going to be like that for *five* months? I can't, it'll kill me, Aunt Jane.'

There was another thunderous boom, echoing down through the structural members of the Station. 'What's that?' Wesson gasped. 'The other ship – casting off?'

'Yes. Now he's alone, just as you are.'

'Not like me. He can't be feeling what I'm feeling. Aunt Jane, you don't know. . . .'

Up there, separated from him only by a few yards of metal, the alien's enormous, monstrous body hung. It was that poised weight, as real as if he could touch it, that weighed down his chest.

Wesson had been a space dweller for most of his adult life and knew even in his bones that, if an orbital station ever collapsed, the 'under' part would not be crushed but would be hurled away by its own angular momentum. This was not the oppressiveness of planetside buildings, where the looming mass above you seemed always threatening to fall. This was something else, completely distinct, and impossible to argue away.

It was the scent of danger, hanging unseen up there in the dark, waiting, cold, and heavy. It was the recurrent nightmare of Wesson's childhood – the bloated unreal shape, no-color, no-size, that kept on hideously falling toward his face.... It was the dead puppy he had pulled out of the creek, that summer in Dakota – wet fur, limp head, cold, cold, *cold*....

With an effort, Wesson rolled over on the couch and lifted himself to one elbow. The pressure was an insistent chill weight on his skull; the room seemed to dip and swing around him in slow, dizzy circles.

Wesson felt his jaw muscles contorting with the strain as he knelt, then stood erect. His back and legs tightened; his mouth hung painfully open. He took one step, then another, timing them to hit the floor as it came upright.

The right side of the console, the one that had been dark, was lighted. Pressure in Sector Two, according to the indicator, was about one and a third atmospheres. The air-lock indicator showed a slightly higher pressure of oxygen and argon; that was to keep any of the alien atmosphere from contaminating Sector One, but it also meant that the lock would no longer open from either side. Wesson found that irrationally comforting.

'Lemme see Earth,' he gasped.

The screen lighted up as he stared into it. 'It's a long way down,' he said. A long, long way down to the bottom of that well.... He had spent ten featureless years as a servo tech in Home Station. Before that, he'd wanted to be a pilot, but had washed out the first year – couldn't take the math. But he had never once thought of going back to Earth.

Now, suddenly, after all these years, that tiny blue disk seemed infinitely desirable.

'Aunt Jane, Aunt Jane, it's beautiful,' he mumbled.

Down there, he knew, it was spring; and in certain places, where the edge of darkness retreated, it was morning – a watery blue morning like the sea light caught in an agate, a morning with smoke and mist in it, a morning of stillness and promise. Down there, lost years and miles away, some tiny dot of a woman was opening her microscopic door to listen to an atom's song. Lost, lost, and packed away in cotton wool, like a specimen slide – one spring morning on Earth.

Black miles above, so far that sixty Earths could have been piled one on another to make a pole for his perch, Wesson swung in his endless circle within a circle. Yet, vast as the gulf beneath him was, all this – Earth, Moon, orbital stations, ships; yes, the Sun and all the rest of his planets, too – was the merest sniff of space, to be pinched up between thumb and finger.

Beyond – there was the true gulf. In that deep night, galaxies lay sprawled aglitter, piercing a distance that could only be named in a meaningless number, a cry of dismay: O ... O ... O ...

Crawling and fighting, blasting with energies too big for them, men had come as far as Jupiter. But if a man had been tall enough to lie with his boots toasting in the Sun and his head freezing at Pluto, still he would have been too small for that overwhelming emptiness. Here, not at Pluto, was the outermost limit of man's empire; here the Outside funneled down to meet it, like the pinched waist of an hourglass; here, and only here, the two worlds came near enough to touch. Ours – and Theirs.

Down at the bottom of the board, now, the golden dials were faintly alight, the needles trembling ever so little on their pins.

Deep in the vats, the vats, the golden liquid was trickling down: *'Though disgusted, I took a sample of the exudate, and it was forwarded for analysis. . . .'*

Space-cold fluid, trickling down the bitter walls of the tubes, forming little pools in the cups of darkness; goldenly agleam there, half alive. The golden elixir. One drop of the concentrate would arrest aging for twenty years – keep your arteries soft, tonus good, eyes clear, hair pigmented, brain alert.

That was what the tests of Pigeon's sample had showed. That was the reason for the whole crazy history of the 'alien trading post' – first a hut on Titan, then later, when people understood more about the problem, Stranger Station.

Once every twenty years, an alien would come down out of Somewhere, and sit in the tiny cage we had made for him, and make us rich beyond our dreams – rich with life – and still we did not know why.

Above him, Wesson imagined he could see that sensed body awallow in the glacial blackness, its bulk passively turning with the Station's spin, bleeding a chill gold into the lips of the tubes

173

– drip ... drop ...

Wesson held his head. The pressure inside made it hard to think; it felt as if his skull were about to fly apart. 'Aunt Jane,' he said.

'Yes, Paul.' The kindly, comforting voice, like a nurse. The nurse who stands beside your cot while you have painful, necessary things done to you. Efficient, trained friendliness.

'Aunt Jane,' said Wesson, 'do you know why they keep coming back?'

'No,' said the voice precisely. 'It is a mystery.'

Wesson nodded. 'I had,' he said, 'an interview with Gower before I left Home. You know Gower? Chief of the Outerworld Bureau. Came up especially to see me.'

'Yes?' said Aunt Jane encouragingly.

'Said to me, "Wesson, you got to find out. Find out if we can count on them to keep up the supply. You know? There's fifty million more of us," he says, "than when you were born. We need more of the stuff, and we got to know if we can count on it. Because," he says, "you know what would happen if it stopped?" Do you know. Aunt Jane?'

'It would be,' said the voice, 'a catastrophe.'

'That's right,' Wesson said respectfully. 'It would. Like, he says to me, "What if the people in the Nefud area were cut off from the Jordan Valley Authority? Why, there'd be millions dying of thirst in a week.

' "Or what if the freighters stopped coming to Moon Base? Why," he says, "there'd be thousands starving and smothering to death."

'He says, "Where the water is, where you can get food and air, people are going to settle and get married, you know? And have kids."

'He says, "If the so-called longevity serum stopped coming. . . ." Says, "Every twentieth adult in the Sol family is due for his shot this year." Says, "Of those, almost twenty percent are one hundred fifteen or older." Says, "The deaths in that groups in the first year would be at least three times what the actuarial tables call for." ' Wesson raised a strained face. 'I'm thirty-four, you know?' he said. 'That Gower, he made me feel like a baby.'

Aunt Jane made a sympathetic noise.

'Drip, drip,' said Wesson hysterically. The needles of the tall golden indicators were infinitesimally higher. 'Every twenty years we need more of the stuff, so somebody like me has to come out and take it for five lousy months. And one of *them* has to come out and sit there, and *drip. Why*, Aunt Jane? What for? Why should it matter to them whether we live a long time or not? Why do they keep on coming back? What do they take *away* from here?'

But to these questions, Aunt Jane had no reply.

All day and every day, the lights burned cold and steady in the circular gray corridor around the rim of Sector One. The hard gray flooring had been deeply scuffed in that circular path before Wesson ever walked there – the corridor existed for that only, like a treadmill in a squirrel cage. It said 'Walk,' and Wesson walked. A man would go crazy if he sat still, with that squirming, indescribable pressure on his head; and so Wesson paced off the miles, all day and every day, until he dropped like a dead man in the bed at night.

He talked, too, sometimes to himself, sometimes to the listening alpha network; sometimes it was difficult to tell which. 'Moss on a rock,' he muttered, pacing. 'Told him, wouldn't give twenty mills, for any shell. . . . Little pebbles down there, all colors.' He shuffled on in silence for a while. Abruptly: 'I don't see *why* they couldn't have given me a cat.'

Aunt Jane said nothing. After a moment Wesson went on, 'Nearly everybody at Home has a cat, for God's sake, or a goldfish or something. You're all right, Aunt Jane, but I can't *see* you. My God, I mean if they couldn't send a man a woman for company – what I mean, my God, I never liked *cats*.' He swung around the doorway into the bedroom, and absentmindedly slammed his fist into the bloody place on the wall.

'But a cat would have been *something*,' he said.

Aunt Jane was still silent.

'Don't pretend your feelings are hurt. I know you, you're only a machine,' said Wesson. 'Listen, Aunt Jane, I remember a cereal package one time that had a horse and a cowboy on the side. There wasn't much room, so about all you saw was their faces. It used to strike me funny how much they looked alike. Two ears on the top with hair in the middle. Two eyes. Nose. Mouth with teeth in it. I was thinking, we're kind of distant cousins, aren't we, us and the horses. But compared to that thing up there – we're *brothers*. You know?'

'Yes,' said Aunt Jane quietly.

'So I keep asking myself, why couldn't they have sent a horse or a cat *instead* of a man? But I guess the answer is because only a man could take what I'm taking. God, only a man. Right?'

'Right,' said Aunt Jane with deep sorrow.

Wesson stopped at the bedroom doorway again and shuddered, holding onto the frame. 'Aunt Jane,' he said in a low, clear voice, 'you take pictures of *him* up there, don't you?'

'Yes, Paul.'

'And you take pictures of me. And then what happens? After it's all over, who looks at the pictures?'

'I don't know,' said Aunt Jane humbly.

'You don't know. But whoever looks at 'em, it doesn't do any good. Right? We got to find out why, why, why.... And we never do find out, do we?'

'No,' said Aunt Jane.

'But don't they figure that if the man who's going through it could see him, he might be able to tell something? That other people couldn't? Doesn't that make sense?'

'That's out of my hands, Paul.'

He sniggered. 'That's funny. Oh, that's funny.' He chortled in his throat, reeling around the circuit.

'Yes, that's funny,' said Aunt Jane.

'Aunt Jane, tell me what happens to the watchmen.'

'I can't tell you that, Paul.'

He lurched into the living room, sat down before the console, beat on its smooth, cold metal with his fists. 'What are you, some kind of monster? Isn't there any blood in your veins, or oil or *anything*?'

'Please, Paul —'

'Don't you see, all I want to know, can they talk? Can they tell anything after their tour is over?'

'No, Paul.'

He stood upright, clutching the console for balance. 'They can't? No, I figured. And you know why?'

'No.'

'Up there,' said Wesson obscurely. 'Moss on the rock.'

'Paul, what?'

'We get changed,' said Wesson, stumbling out of the room again. 'We get changed. Like a piece of iron next to a magnet. Can't help it. You – nonmagnetic, I guess. Goes right through you, huh. Aunt Jane? You don't get changed. You stay here, wait for the next one.'

'Yes,' said Aunt Jane.

'You know,' said Wesson, pacing. 'I can tell how he's lying up there. Head *that* way, tail the other. Am I right?'

'Yes,' said Aunt Jane.

Wesson stopped. 'Yes,' he said intently. 'So you *can* tell me what you see up there, can't you, Aunt Jane?'

'No. Yes. It isn't allowed.'

'Listen, Aunt Jane, *we'll die* unless we can find out what makes those aliens tick! Remember that.' Wesson leaned against the corridor wall, gazing up. 'He's turning now – around this way. Right?'

'Yes.'

'Well, what else is he doing? Come on, Aunt Jane, tell me!'

A pause. 'He is twitching his —'

'What?'

'I don't know the words.'

'My God, my God,' said Wesson, clutching his head, 'of course there aren't any words.' He ran into the living room, clutched the console, and stared at the blank screen. He pounded the metal with his fist. 'You've got to show me, Aunt Jane, come on and show me – show me!'

'It isn't allowed,' Aunt Jane protested.

'You've got to do it just the same, or we'll *die*, Aunt Jane – millions of us, billions, and it'll be your fault, get it? *Your fault*, Aunt Jane!'

'*Please,*' said the voice. There was a pause. The screen flickered to life, for an instant only. Wesson had a glimpse of something massive and dark, but half transparent, like a magnified insect – a tangle of nameless limbs, whiplike filaments, claws, wings. . . .

He clutched the edge of the console.

'Was that all right?' Aunt Jane asked.

'Of course! What do you think, it'll kill me to look at it? Put it back, Aunt Jane, put it back!'

Reluctantly, the screen lighted again. Wesson stared and went on staring. He mumbled something.

'What?' said Aunt Jane.

'*Life of my love, I loathe thee,*' said Wesson, staring. He roused himself after a moment and turned away. The image of the alien stayed with him as he went reeling into the corridor again; he was not surprised to find that it reminded him of all the loathsome, crawling, creeping things the Earth was full of. That explained why he was not supposed to see the alien, or even know what it looked like – because that fed his hate. And it was all right for him to be afraid of the alien, but he was not supposed to hate it. . . . Why not? Why not?

His fingers were shaking. He felt drained, steamed, dried up and withered. The one daily shower Aunt Jane allowed him was no longer enough. Twenty minutes after bathing the acid sweat dripped again from his armpits, the cold sweat was beaded on his forehead, the hot sweat was in his palms. Wesson felt as if there were a furnace inside him, out of control, all the dampers drawn. He knew that, under stress, something of the kind did happen to a man; the body's chemistry was altered – more adrenalin, more glycogen in the muscles, eyes brighter, digestion retarded. That was the trouble – he was burning himself up, unable to fight the thing that tormented him, not run from it.

After another circuit, Wesson's steps faltered. He hesitated, and went into the living room. He leaned over the console, staring. From the screen, the alien stared blindly up into space. Down in the dark side, the golden indicators had climbed: the vats were more than two thirds filled.

To *fight* or *run* . . .

Slowly Wesson sank down in front of the console. He sat hunched, head bent, hands squeezed tight between his knees, trying to hold onto the thought that had come to him.

If the alien felt a pain as great as Wesson's – or greater —

Stress might alter the alien's body chemistry, too.

Life of my love, I loathe thee.

Wesson pushed the irrelevant thought aside. He stared at the screen, trying to envisage the alien up there, wincing in pain and distress – sweating a golden sweat of horror. . . .

After a long time, he stood up and walked into the kitchen. He caught the table edge to keep his legs from carrying him on around the circuit. He sat down.

Humming fondly, the autochef slid out a try of small glasses – water, orange juice, milk. Wesson put the water glass to his stiff lips; the water was cool and hurt his throat. Then the juice, but he could drink only a little of it; then he sipped the milk. Aunt Jane hummed approvingly.

Dehydrated. How long had it been since he had eaten or

drunk? He looked at his hands. They were thin bundles of sticks, ropy-veined, with hard yellow claws. He could see the bones of his forearms under the skin, and his heart's beating stirred the cloth at his chest. The pale hairs on his arms and thighs – were they blond or white?

The blurred reflections in the metal trim of the dining room gave him no answers – only pale faceless smears of gray. Wesson felt light-headed and very weak, as if he had just ended a bout of fever. He fumbled over his ribs and shoulder bones. He was thin.

He sat in front of the autochef for a few minutes more, but no food came out. Evidently Aunt Jane did not think he was ready for it, and perhaps she was right. *Worse for them than for us*, he thought dizzily. *That's why the Station's so far out, why radio silence, and only one man aboard. They couldn't stand it at all, otherwise....* Suddenly he could think of nothing but sleep – the bottomless pit, layer after layer of smothering velvet, numbing and soft.... His leg muscles quivered and twitched when he tried to walk, but he managed to get to the bedroom and all on the mattress. The resilient block seemed to dissolve under him. His bones were melting.

He woke with a clear head, very weak, thinking cold and clear: *When two alien cultures meet, the stronger must transform the weaker with love or hate.* 'Wesson's Law,' he said aloud. He looked automatically for pencil and paper, but there was none, and he realized he would have to tell Aunt Jane, and let her remember it.

'I don't understand,' she said.

'Never mind, remember it anyway. You're good at that, aren't you?'

'Yes, Paul.'

'All right – I want some breakfast.'

He thought about Aunt Jane, so nearly human, sitting up here in her metal prison, leading one man after another through the torments of hell – nursemaid, protector, torturer. They must have known that something would have to give.... But, the alphas were comparatively new; nobody understood them very well. Perhaps they really thought that an absolute prohibition could never be broken.

... the stronger must transform the weaker....

I'm the stronger, he thought. *And that's the way it's going to be*. He stopped at the console, and the screen was blank. He said angrily, 'Aunt Jane!' And with a guilty start, the screen flickered into life.

Up there, the alien had rolled again in his pain. Now the great clustered eyes were staring directly into the camera; the coiled limbs threshed in pain; the eyes were staring, asking, pleading. . . .

'*No*,' said Wesson, feeling his own pain like an iron cap, and he slammed his hand down on the manual control. The screen went dark. He looked up, sweating, and saw the floral picture over the console.

The thick stems were like antennae, the leaves thoraxes, the buds like blind insect eyes. The whole picture moved slightly, endlessly, in a slow waiting rhythm.

Wesson clutched the hard metal of the console and stared at the picture, with sweat cold on his brow, until it turned into a calm, meaningless arrangement of lines again. Then he went into the dining room, shaking, and sat down.

After a moment he said, 'Aunt Jane, does it get worse?'

'No. From now on, it gets better.'

'How long?' he asked vaguely.

'One month.'

A month, getting 'better' – that was the way it had always been, with the watchman swamped and drowned, his personality submerged. Wesson thought about the men who had gone before him – Class Seven citizenship, with unlimited leisure, and Class One housing. Yes, sure – in a sanatorium.

His lips peeled back from his teeth, and his fists clenched hard. *Not me!* he thought.

He spread his hands on the cool metal to steady them. He said, 'How much longer do they usually stay able to talk?'

'You are already talking longer than any of them. . . .'

Then there was a blank. Wesson was vaguely aware, in snatches, of the corridor walls moving past and the console glimpsed and of a thunderous cloud of ideas that swirled around his head in a beating of wings. The aliens – what did they want? And what happened to the watchmen in Stranger Station?

The haze receded a little, and he was in the dining room again, staring vacantly at the table. Something was wrong.

He ate a few spoonfuls of the gruel the autochef served him, then pushed it away; the stuff tasted faintly unpleasant. The machine hummed anxiously and thrust a poached egg at him, but Wesson got up from the table.

The Station was all but silent. The resting rhythm of the household machines throbbed in the walls, unheard. The blue-lighted living room was spread out before him like an empty stage setting, and Wesson stared as if he had never seen it before.

He lurched to the console and stared down at the pictured alien on the screen – heavy, heavy, asprawl with pain in the darkness. The needles of the golden indicators were high, the enlarged vats almost full. *It's too much for him*, Wesson thought with grim satisfaction. The peace that followed the pain had not descended as it was supposed to; no, not this time!

He glanced up at the painting over the console – heavy crustacean limbs that swayed gracefully in the sea. . . .

He shook his head violently. *I won't let it; I won't give in!* He held the back of one hand close to his eyes. He saw the dozens of tiny cuneiform wrinkles stamped into the skin over the knuckles, the pale hairs sprouting, the pink shiny flesh of recent scars. *I'm human*, he thought. But when he let his hand fall onto the console, the bony fingers seemed to crouch like crustaceans' legs, ready to scuttle.

Sweating, Wesson stared into the screen. Pictured there, the alien met his eyes, and it was as if they spoke to each other, mind to mind, an instantaneous communication that needed no words. There was a piercing sweetness to it, a melting, dissolving luxury of change into something that would no longer have any pain. . . . A pull, a calling.

Wesson straightened up slowly, carefully, as if he held some fragile thing in his mind that must not be handled roughly, or it would distintegrate. He said hoarsely, 'Aunt Jane!'

She made some responsive noise.

He said, 'Aunt Jane, I've got the answer! The whole thing! Listen, now wait – listen!' He paused a moment to collect his thoughts. '*When two alien cultures meet, the stronger must transform the weaker with love or hate*. Remember? You said you didn't understand what that meant. I'll *tell* you what it means. When these – monsters – met Pigeon a hundred years ago on Titan, *they knew* we'd have to meet again. They're spreading out, colonizing, and so are we. We haven't got inter-stellar flight yet, but give us another hundred years, we'll *get* it.

We'll wind up out there, where they are. And they can't stop us. Because they're not killers. Aunt Jane, it isn't in them. They're *nicer* than us. See, they're like the missionaries, and we're the South Sea Islanders. *They* don't kill their enemies, oh, no – perish the thought!'

She was trying to say something, to interrupt him, but he rushed on. 'Listen! The longevity serum – that was a lucky accident. But they played it for all it's worth. Slick and smooth. They come and give us the stuff free – they don't ask for a thing in return. Why not? Listen.

'They come here, and the shock of that first contact makes them sweat out that golden gook we need. Then, the last month or so, the pain always eases off. Why? Because the two minds, the human and alien, they stop fighting each other. Something gives way, it goes soft, and there's a mixing together. And that's where you get the human casualties of this operation – the bleary men that come out of here not even able to talk human language anymore. Oh, I suppose they're happy – happier than I am! – because they've got something big and wonderful inside 'em. Something that you and I can't even understand. But if you took them and put them together again with the aliens who spent time here, *they could all live together – they're adapted.*

'That's what they're aiming for!' He struck the console with his fist. 'Not now – but a hundred, two hundred years from now! When we start expanding out to the stars – when we go a-conquering – we'll have already been conquered! Not by weapons, Aunt Jane, not by hate – by love! Yes, love! *Dirty, stinking,* low-down, sneaking love!'

Aunt Jane said something, a long sentence, in a high, anxious voice.

'What?' said Wesson irritably. He couldn't understand a word.

Aunt Jane was silent. 'What, what?' Wesson demanded, pounding the console. 'Have you got it through your tin head or not? *What?*'

Aunt Jane said something else, tonelessly. Once more, Wesson could not make out a single word.

He stood frozen. Warm tears started suddenly out of his eyes. 'Aunt Jane —' he said. He remembered, *You are already talking longer than any of them.* Too late? Too late? He tensed, then whirled and sprang to the closet where the paper

182

books were kept. He opened the first one his hand struck.

The black letters were alien squiggles on the page, little humped shapes, without meaning.

The tears were coming faster, he couldn't stop them – tears of weariness, tears of frustration, tears of hate. '*Aunt Jane!*' he roared.

But it was no good. The curtain of silence had come down over his head. He was one of the vanguard – the conquered men, the ones who would get along with their strange brothers, out among the alien stars.

The console was not working anymore; nothing worked when he wanted it. Wesson squatted in the shower stall, naked, with a soup bowl in his hands. Water droplets glistened on his hands and forearms; the pale short hairs were just springing up, drying.

The silvery skin of reflection in the bowl gave him back nothing but a silhouette, a shadow man's outline. He could not see his face.

He dropped the bowl and went across the living room, shuffling the pale drifts of paper underfoot. The black lines on the paper, when his eye happened to light on them, were worm shapes, crawling things, conveying nothing. He rolled slightly in his walk; his eyes were glazed. His head twitched, every now and then, sketching a useless motion to avoid pain.

Once the bureau chief, Gower, came to stand in his way. 'You fool,' he said, his face contorted in anger, 'you were supposed to go on to the end, like the rest. Now look what you've done!'

'I found out, didn't I?' Wesson mumbled, and as he brushed the man aside like a cobweb, the pain suddenly grew more intense. Wesson clasped his head in his hands with a grunt, and rocked to and fro a moment, uselessly, before he straightened and went on. The pain was coming in waves now, so tall that at their peak his vision dimmed out, violet then gray.

It couldn't go on much longer. Something had to burst.

He paused at the bloody place and slapped the metal with his palm, making the sound ring dully up into the frame of the Station: *rroom ... rroom ...*

Faintly an echo came back: *boo-oom ...*

Wesson kept going, smiling a faint and meaningless smile. He was only marking time now, waiting. Something was about to happen.

The kitchen doorway sprouted a sudden sill and tripped him. He fell heavily, sliding on the floor, and lay without moving beneath the slick gleam of the autochef.

The pressure was too great – the autochef's clucking was swallowed up in the ringing pressure, and the tall gray walls buckled slowly in. . . .

The Station lurched.

Wesson felt it through his chest, palms, knees, and elbows: the floor was plucked away for an instant and then swung back.

The pain in his skull relaxed its grip a little. Wesson tried to get to his feet.

There was an electric silence in the Station. On the second try, he got up and leaned his back against, a wall. *Cluck*, said the autochef suddenly, hysterically, and the vent popped open, but nothing came out.

He listened, straining to hear. What?

The Station bounced beneath him, making his feet jump like a puppet's; the wall slapped his back hard, shuddered, and was still; but far off through the metal cage came a long angry groan of metal, echoing, diminishing, dying. Then silence again.

The Station held its breath. All the myriad clickings and pulses in the walls were suspended; in the empty rooms the lights burned with a yellow glare, and the air hung stagnant and still. The console lights in the living room glowed like witch fires. Water in the dropped bowl, at the bottom of the shower stall, shone like quicksilver, waiting.

The third shock came. Wesson found himself on his hands and knees, the jolt still tingling in the bones of his body, staring at the floor. The sound that filled the room ebbed away slowly and ran down into the silences – a resonant metallic sound, shuddering away now along the girders and hull plates, rattling tinnily into bolts and fittings, diminishing, noiseless, gone. The silence pressed down again.

The floor leaped painfully under his body, one great resonant blow that shook him from head to foot.

A muted echo of that blow came a few seconds later, as if the shock had traveled across the Station and back.

The bed, Wesson thought, and scrambled on hands and knees through the doorway, along a floor curiously tilted, until he reached the rubbery block.

The room burst visibly upward around him, squeezing the block flat. It dropped back as violently, leaving Wesson bouncing helplessly on the mattress, his limbs flying. It came to rest, in a long reluctant groan of metal.

Wesson rolled up on one elbow, thinking incoherently, *Air, the air lock*. Another blow slammed him down into the mattress, pinched his lungs shut, while the room danced grotesquely over his head. Gasping for breath in the ringing silence, Wesson felt a slow icy chill rolling toward him across the room – and there was a pungent smell in the air. *Ammonia!* he thought, and the odorless, smothering methane with it.

His cell was breached. The burst membrane was fatal – the alien's atmosphere would kill him.

Wesson surged to his feet. The next shock caught him off balance, dashed him to the floor. He arose again, dazed and limping; he was still thinking confusedly, *The air lock – get out*.

When he was halfway to the door, all the ceiling lights went out at once. The darkness was like a blanket around his head. It was bitter cold now in the room, and the pungent smell was sharper. Coughing, Wesson hurried forward. The floor lurched under his feet.

Only the golden indicators burned now – full to the top, the deep vats brimming, golden-lipped, gravid, a month before the time. Wesson shuddered.

Water spurted in the bathroom, hissing steadily on the tiles, rattling in the plastic bowl at the bottom of the shower stall. The light winked on and off again. In the dining room, he heard the autochef clucking and sighing. The freezing wind blew harder; he was numb with cold to the hips. It seemed to Wesson abruptly that he was not at the top of the sky at all, but down, *down* at the bottom of the sea – trapped in this steel bubble, while the dark poured in.

The pain in his head was gone, as if it had never been there, and he understood what that meant: Up there, the great body was hanging like butcher's carrion in the darkness. Its death struggles were over, the damage done.

Wesson gathered a desperate breath, shouted, 'Help me! The alien's dead! He kicked the Station apart – the methane's coming in! Get help, do you hear me? *Do you hear me?*'

Silence. In the smothering blackness, he remembered: *She*

185

can't understand me anymore. Even if she's alive.

He turned, making an animal noise in his throat. He groped his way on around the room, past the second doorway. Behind the walls, something was dripping with a slow cold tinkle and splash, a forlorn night sound. Small, hard, floating things rapped against his legs. Then he touched a smooth curve of metal – the air lock.

Eagerly he pushed his feeble weight against the door. It didn't move. Cold air was rushing out around the door frame, a thin knife-cold stream, but the door itself was jammed tight.

The suit! He should have thought of that before. If he just had some pure air to breathe and a little warmth in his fingers . . . But the door of the suit locker would not move, either. The ceiling must have buckled.

And that was the end, he thought, bewildered. There were no more ways out. But there *had* to be. . . . He pounded on the door until his arms would not lift anymore; it did not move. Leaning against the chill metal, he saw a single light blink on overhead.

The room was a wild place of black shadows and swimming shapes – the book leaves, fluttering and darting in the air stream. Schools of them beat wildly at the walls, curling over, baffled, trying again; others were swooping around the outer corridor, around and around; he could see them whirling past the doorways, dreamlike, a white drift of silent paper in the darkness.

The acrid smell was harsher in his nostrils. Wesson choked, groping his way to the console again. He pounded it with his open hand, crying weakly – he wanted to see Earth.

But when the little square of brightness leaped up, it was the dead body of the alien that Wesson saw.

It hung motionless in the cavity of the Station, limbs dangling stiff and still, eyes dull. The last turn of the screw had been too much for it. But Wesson had survived. . . .

For a few minutes.

The dead alien face mocked him; a whisper of memory floated into his mind: *We might have been brothers.* . . . All at once Wesson passionately wanted to believe it – wanted to give in, turn back. That passed. Wearily he let himself sag into the bitter *now*, thinking with thin defiance, *It's done – hate wins. You'll have to stop this big giveaway – can't risk this happen-*

ing again. And we'll hate you for that – and when we get out to the stars —

The world was swimming numbly away out of reach. He felt the last fit of coughing take his body, as if it were happening to someone else besides him.

The last fluttering leaves of paper came to rest. There was a long silence in the drowned room.

Then:

'Paul,' said the voice of the mechanical woman brokenly; 'Paul,' it said again, with the hopelessness of lost, unknown, impossible love.

Greenslaves
by Frank Herbert

He looked pretty much like the bastard offspring of a Guarani Indio and some backwoods farmer's daughter, some *sertanista* who had tried to forget her enslavement to the *encomendero* system by 'eating the iron' – which is what they call lovemaking through the grill of a consel gate.

The type-look was almost perfect except when he forgot himself while passing through one of the deeper jungle glades.

His skin tended to shade down to green then, fading him into the background of leaves and vines, giving a strange disembodiment to the mud-gray shirt and ragged trousers, the inevitable frayed straw hat and rawhide sandals soled with pieces cut from worn tires.

Such lapses became less and less frequent the farther he got from the Parana headwaters, the *sertao* hinterland of Goyaz where men with his bang-cut black hair and glittering dark eyes were common.

By the time he reached *bandeirantes* country, he had achieved almost perfect control over the chameleon effect.

But now he was out of the jungle growth and into the brown dirt tracks that separated the parceled farms of the resettlement plan. In his own way, he knew he was approaching the *bandeirante* checkpoints. and with an almost human gesture, he fingered the *cedula de gracias al sacar*, the certificate of white blood, tucked safely beneath his shirt. Now and again, when humans were not near, he practised speaking aloud the name that had been chosen for him – 'Antonio Raposo Tavares.'

The sound was a bit stridulant, harsh on the edges, but he knew it would pass. It already had. Goyaz Indios were notorious for the strange inflection of their speech. The farm folk who had given him a roof and fed him the previous night had said as much.

When their questions had become pressing, he had squatted on the doorstep and played his flute, the *qena* of the Andes Indian that he carried in a leather purse hung from his shoulder. He had kept the sound to a conventional non-dangerous pitch. The gesture of the flute was a symbol of the region.

189

When a Guarani put flute to nose and began playing, that was a sign words were ended.

The farm folk had shrugged and retired.

Now, he could see red-brown rooftops ahead and the white crystal shimmering of a *bandeirante* tower with its aircars alighting and departing. The scene held an odd hive-look. He stopped, finding himself momentarily overcome by the touch of instincts that he knew he had to master or fail in the ordeal to come.

He united his mental identity then, thinking, *We are green-slaves subservient to the greater whole.* The thought lent him an air of servility that was like a shield against the stares of the humans trudging past all around him. His kind knew many mannerisms and had learned early that servility was a form of concealment.

Presently, he resumed his plodding course toward the town and the tower.

The dirt track gave way to a two-lane paved market road with its footpaths in the ditches on both sides. This, in turn, curved alongside a four-deck commercial transport highway where even the footpaths were paved. And now there were groundcars and aircars in greater number, and he noted that the flow of people on foot was increasing.

Thus far, he had attracted no dangerous attention. The occasional snickering side-glance from natives of the area could be safely ignored, he knew. Probing stares held peril, and he had detected none. The servility shielded him.

The sun was well along toward mid-morning and the day's heat was beginning to press down on the earth, raising a moist hothouse stink from the dirt beside the pathway, mingling the perspiration odors of humanity around him.

And they were around him now, close and pressing, moving slower and slower as they approached the checkpoint bottleneck. Presently, the forward motion stopped. Progress resolved itself into shuffle and stop, shuffle and stop.

This was the critical test now and there was no avoiding it. He waited with something like an Indian's stoic patience. His breathing had grown deeper to compensate for the heat, and he adjusted it to match that of the people around him, suffering the temperature rise for the sake of blending into his surroundings.

Andes Indians didn't breathe deeply here in the lowlands.

Shuffle and stop.

Shuffle and stop.

He could see the checkpoint now.

Fastidious bandeirantes in sealed white cloaks with plastic helmets, gloves and boots stood in a double row within a shaded brick corridor leading into the town. He could see sunlight hot on the street beyond the corridor and people hurrying away there after passing the gantlet.

The sight of that free area beyond the corridor sent an ache of longing through all the parts of him. The suppression warning flashed out instantly on the heels of that instinctive reaching emotion.

No distraction could be permitted now; he was into the hands of the first bandeirante, a hulking blond fellow with pink skin and blue eyes.

'Step along now! Lively now!' the fellow said.

A gloved hand propelled him toward two bandeirantes standing on the right side of the line.

'Give this one an extra treatment,' the blond giant called. 'He's from the upcountry by the look of him.'

The other two bandeirantes had him now, one jamming a breather mask over his face, the other fitting a plastic bag over him. A tube trailed from the bag out to machinery somewhere in the street beyond the corridor.

'Double shot!' one of the bandeirantes called.

Fuming blue gas puffed out the bag around him, and he took a sharp, gasping breath through the mask.

Agony!

The gas drove through every multiple linkage of his being with needles of pain.

We must not weaken, he thought.

But it was a deadly pain, killing. The linkages were beginning to weaken.

'Okay on this one,' the bag handler called.

The mask was pulled away. The bag was slipped off. Hands propelled him down the corridor toward the sunlight.

'Lively now! Don't hold up the line.'

The stink of the poison gas was all around him. It was a new one – a dissembler. They hadn't prepared him for this poison!

Now, he was into the sunlight and turning down a street lined with fruit stalls, merchants bartering with customers or standing fat and watchful behind their displays.

In his extremity, the fruit beckoned to him with the promise of life-saving sanctuary for a few parts of him, but the integrating totality fought off the lure. He shuffled as fast as he dared, dodging past the customers, through the knots of idlers.

'You like to buy some fresh oranges?'

An oily dark hand thrust two oranges toward his face.

'Fresh oranges from the green country. Never been a bug anywhere near these.'

He avoided the hand, although the odor of the oranges came near overpowering him.

Now, he was clear of the stalls, around a corner down a narrow side street. Another corner and he saw far away to his left, the lure of greenery in open country, the free area beyond the town.

He turned toward the green, increasing his speed, measuring out the time still available to him. There was still a chance. Poison clung to his clothing, but free air was filtering through the fabric and the thought of victory was like an antidote.

We can make it yet!

The green drew closer and closer – trees and ferns beside a river bank. He heard the running water. There was a bridge thronging with foot traffic from converging streets.

No help for it: he joined the throng, avoided contact as much as possible. The linkages of his legs and back were beginning to go, and he knew the wrong kind of blow could dislodge whole segments. He was over the bridge without disaster. A dirt track led off the path and down toward the river.

He turned toward it, stumbled against one of two men carrying a pig in a net slung between them. Part of the shell on his right upper leg gave way and he could feel it begin to slip down inside his pants.

The man he had hit took two backward steps, almost dropped the end of the burden.

'Careful!' the man shouted.

The man at the other end of the net said: 'Damn' drunks.'

The pig set up a squirming, squealing distraction.

In this moment, he slipped past them onto the dirt track leading down toward the river. He could see the water down there now, boiling with aeration from the barrier filters.

Behind him, one of the pig carriers said: 'I don't think he was drunk, Carlos. His skin felt dry and hot. Maybe he was sick.'

The track turned around an embankment of raw dirt dark brown with dampness and dipped toward a tunnel through ferns and bushes. The men with the pig could no longer see him, he knew, and he grabbed at his pants where the part of his leg was slipping, scurried into the green tunnel.

Now, he caught sight of his first mutated bee. It was dead, having entered the barrier vibration area here without any protection against that deadliness. The bee was one of the butterfly type with iridescent yellow and orange wings. It lay in the cup of a green leaf at the center of a shaft of sunlight.

He shuffled past, having recorded the bee's shape and color. They had considered the bees as a possible answer, but there were serious drawbacks to this course. A bee could not reason with humans, that was the key fact. And humans had to listen to reason soon, else all life would end.

There came the sound of someone hurrying down the path behind him, heavy footsteps thudding on the earth.

Pursuit? . . .

He was reduced to a slow shuffling now and soon it would be only crawling progress, he knew. Eyes searched the greenery around him for a place of concealment. A thin break in the fern wall on his left caught his attention. Tiny human footprints led into it – children. He forced his way through the ferns, found himself on a low narrow path along the embankment. Two toy aircars, red and blue, had been abandoned on the path. His staggering foot pressed them into the dirt.

The path led close to a wall of black dirt festooned with creepers, around a sharp turn and onto the lip of a shallow cave. More toys lay in the green gloom at the cave's mouth.

He knelt, crawled over the toys into the blessed dankness, lay there a moment, waiting.

The pounding footsteps hurried past a few feet below.

Voices reached up to him.

'He was headed toward the river. Think he was going to jump in?'

'Who knows? But I think me for sure he was sick.'

'Here; down this way. Somebody's been down this way.'

The voices grew indistinct, blended with the bubbling sound of the river.

The men were going on down the path. They had missed his hiding place. But why had they pursued him? He had not seriously injured the one by stumbling against him. Surely, they did not suspect.

Slowly, he steeled himself for what had to be done, brought his specialized parts into play and began burrowing into the earth at the end of the cave. Deeper and deeper he burrowed, thrusting the excess dirt behind and out to make it appear the cave had collapsed.

Ten meters in he went before stopping. His store of energy contained just enough reserve for the next stage. He turned on his back, scattering the dead parts of his legs and back, exposing the queen and her guard cluster to the dirt beneath his chitinous spine. Orifices opened at his thighs, exuded the cocoon foam, the soothing green cover that would harden into a protective shell.

This was victory; the essential parts had survived.

Time was the thing now – ten and one half days to gather new energy, go through the metamorphosis and disperse. Soon, there would be thousands of him – each with its carefully mimicked clothing and identification papers and appearance of humanity.

Identical – each of them.

There would be other checkpoints, but not as severe; other barriers, lesser ones.

This human copy had proved a good one. They had learned many things from study of their scattered captives and from the odd crew directed by the red-haired human female they'd trapped in the *sertao*. How strange she was: like a queen and not like a queen. It was so difficult to understand human creatures, even when you permitted them limited freedom ... almost impossible to reason with them. Their slavery to the planet would have to be proved dramatically, perhaps.

The queen stirred near the cool dirt. They had learned new things this time about escaping notice. All of the subsequent colony clusters would share that knowledge. One of them – at least – would get through to the city by the Amazon 'River Sea' where the death-for-all originated. One had to get through.

Senhor Gabriel Martinho, prefect of the Mato Grosso Barrier Compact, paced his study, muttering to himself as he passed the tall, narrow window that admitted the evening sunlight. Occasionally, he paused to glare down at his son, Joao, who sat on a tapir-leather sofa beneath one of the tall bookcases that lined the room.

194

The elder Martinho was a dark wisp of a man, limb thin, with gray hair and cavernous brown eyes above an eagle nose, slit mouth and boot-toe chin. He wore old style black clothing as befitted his position, his linen white against the black, and with golden cuffstuds glittering as he waved his arms.

'I am an object of ridicule!' he snarled.

Joao, a younger copy of the father, his hair still black and wavy, absorbed the statement in silence. He wore a bandeirante's white coverall suit sealed into plastic boots at the calf.

'An object of ridicule!' the elder Martinho repeated.

It began to grow dark in the room, the quick tropic darkness hurried by thunderheads piled along the horizon. The waning daylight carried a hazed blue cast. Heat lightning spattered the patch of sky visible through the tall window, sent dazzling electric radiance into the study. Drumming thunder followed. As though that were the signal, the house sensors turned on lights wherever there were humans. Yellow illumination filled the study.

The Prefect stopped in front of his son. 'Why does my own son, a bandeirante, a jefe of the Irmandades, spout these Carsonite stupidities?'

Joao looked at the floor between his boots. He felt both resentment and shame. To disturb his father this way, that was a hurtful thing, with the elder Martinho's delicate heart. But the old man was so blind!

'Those rabble farmers laughed at me,' the elder Martinho said. 'I told them we'd increase the green area by ten thousand hectares this month, and they laughed. "Your own son does not even believe this!" they said. And they told me some of the things you had been saying.'

'I am sorry I have caused you distress, father,' Joao said.

'The fact that I'm a bandeirante . . .' He shrugged. 'How else could I have learned the truth about this extermination program?'

His father quivered.

'Joao! Do you sit there and tell me you took a false oath when you formed your Irmandades band?'

'That's not the way it was, father.'

Joao pulled a sprayman's emblem from his breast pocket, fingered it. 'I believed it . . . then. We could shape mutated bees to fill every gap in the insect ecology. This I believed. Like the Chinese, I said: "Only the useful shall live!" But that was several years ago, father, and since then I have come to realize we don't have a complete understanding of what usefulness means.'

'It was a mistake to have you educated in North America,' his father said. 'That's where you absorbed this Carsonite heresy. It's all well and good for *them* to refuse to join the rest of the world in the Ecological Realignment; they do not have as many million mouths to feed. But my own son!'

Joao spoke defensively: 'Out in the red areas you see things, father. These things are difficult to explain. Plants look healthier out there and the fruit is...'

'A purely temporary thing,' his father said. 'We will shape bees to meet whatever need we find. The destroyers take food from our mouths. It is very simple. They must die and be replaced by creatures which serve a function useful to mankind.'

'The birds are dying, father,' Joao said.

'We are saving the birds! We have specimens of every kind in our sanctuaries. We will provide new foods for them to...'

'But what happens if our barriers are breached ... before we can replace the population of natural predators? What happens then?'

The elder Martinho shook a thin finger under his son's nose. 'This is nonsense! I will hear no more of it! Do you know what else those *mameluco* farmers said? They said they have seen bandeirantes reinfesting the green areas to prolong their jobs! That is what they said. This, too, is nonsense – but it is a natural consequence of defeatist talk just such as I have heard from you tonight. And every setback we suffer adds strength to such charges!'

'Setbacks, father?'

'I have said it: setbacks!'

Senhor Prefect Martinho turned, paced to his desk and back. Again, he stopped in front of his son, placed hands on hips. 'You refer to the Piratininga, of course?'

'You accuse me, father?'

'Your Irmandades were on that line.'

'Not so much as a flea got through us!'

'Yet, a week ago the Piratininga was green. Now, it is crawling. Crawling!'

'I cannot watch every bandeirante in the Mato Grosso,' Joao protested. 'If they...'

'The IEO gives us only six months to clean up,' the elder Martinho said. He raised his hands, palms up; his face was flushed. 'Six months! Then they throw an embargo around all Brazil – the way they have done with North America.' He lowered his hands. 'Can you imagine the pressures on me? Can you imagine the things I must listen to about the bandeirantes and especially about my own son?'

Joao scratched his chin with the sprayman's emblem. The reference to the International Ecological Organization made him think of Dr. Rhin Kelly, the IEO's lovely field director. His mind pictured her as he had last seen her in the A' Chigua nightclub at Bahia – red-haired, green-eyed ... so lovely and strange. But she had been missing almost six weeks now – somewhere in the *sertao*, and there were those who said she must be dead.

Joao looked at his father. If only the old man weren't so excitable. 'You excite yourself needlessly, father,' he said. 'The Piratininga was not a full barrier, just a ...'

'Excite myself!'

The Prefect's nostrils dilated; he bent toward his son. 'Already we have gone past two deadlines. We gained an extension when I announced you and the bandeirantes of Diogo Alvarez had cleared the Piratininga. How do I explain now that it is reinfested, that we have the work to do over?'

Joao returned the sprayman's emblem to his pocket. It was obvious he'd not be able to reason with his father this night. Frustration sent a nerve quivering along Joao's jaw. The old man had to be told, though; someone had to tell him. And someone of his father's stature had to get back to the Bureau, shake them up there and make *them* listen.

The Prefect returned to his desk, sat down. He picked up an antique crucifix, one that the great Aleihadinho had carved in ivory. He lifted it, obviously seeking to restore his serenity, but his eyes went on glaring. Slowly, he returned the crucifix to its position on the desk, keeping his attention on it.

'Joao,' he whispered.

It's his heart! Joao thought.

He leaped to his feet, rushed to his father's side. 'Father! What is it?'

The elder Martinho pointed, hand trembling.

Through the spiked crown of thorns, across the agonized ivory face, over the straining muscles of the Christ figure

197

crawled an insect. It was the color of the ivory, faintly reminiscent of a beetle in shape, but with a multi-clawed fringe along its wings and thorax, and with furry edging to its abnormally long antennae.

The elder Martinho reached for a roll of papers to smash the insect, but Joao put a hand restraining him. 'Wait. This is a new one. I've never seen anything like it. Give me a handlight. We must follow it, find where it nests.'

Senhor Prefect Martinho muttered under his breath, withdrew a small permalight from a drawer of the desk, handed the light to his son.

Joao peered at the insect, still not using the light. 'How strange it is,' he said. 'See how it exactly matches the tone of the ivory.'

The insect stopped, pointed its antennae toward the two men.

'Things have been seen,' Joao said. 'There are stories. Something like this was found near one of the barrier villages last month. It was inside the green area, on a path beside a river. Two farmers found it while searching for a sick man.' Joao looked at his father. 'They are very watchful of sickness in the newly green regions, you know. There have been epidemics ... and that is another thing.'

'There is no relationship,' his father snapped. 'Without insects to carry disease, we will have less illness.'

'Perhaps,' Joao said, and his tone said he did not believe it.

Joao returned his attention to the insect. 'I do not think our ecologists know all they say they do. And I mistrust our Chinese advisors. They speak in such flowery terms of the benefits from eliminating useless insects, but they will not let us go into their green areas and inspect. Excuses. Always excuses. I think they are having troubles they do not wish us to know.'

'That's foolishness,' the elder Martinho growled, but his tone said this was not a position he cared to defend. 'They are honorable men. Their way of life is closer to our socialism than it is to the decadent capitalism of North America. Your trouble is you see them too much through the eyes of those who educated you.'

'I'll wager this insect is one of the spontaneous mutations,' Joao said. 'It is almost as though they appeared according to some plan. Find me something in which I may capture this creature and take it to the laboratory.'

The elder Martinho remained standing by his chair. 'Where will you say it was found?'

'Right here,' Joao said.

'You will not hesitate to expose me to more ridicule?'

'But father . . .'

'Can't you hear what they will say? In his own home this insect is found. It is a strange new kind. Perhaps he breeds them there to reinfest the green.'

'Now *you* are talking nonsense, father. Mutations are common in a threatened species. And we cannot deny there is threat to insect species – the poisons, the barrier vibrations, the traps. Get me a container, father. I cannot leave this creature, or I'd get a container myself.'

'And you will tell where it was found?'

'I can do nothing else. We must cordon off this area, search it out. This could be . . . an accident . . .'

'Or a deliberate attempt to embarrass me.'

Joao took his attention from the insect, studied his father. *That* was a possibility, of course. The Carsonites had friends in many places . . . and some were fanatics who would stoop to any scheme. Still . . .

Decision came to Joao. He returned his attention to the motionless insect. His father had to be told, had to be reasoned with at any cost. Someone whose voice carried authority had to get down to the Capitol and make them listen.

'Our earliest poison killed off the weak and selected out those insects immune to this threat,' Joao said. 'Only the immune remained to breed. The poisons we use now . . . some of them do not leave such loopholes and the deadly vibrations at the barriers . . .' He shrugged. 'This is a form of beetle, father. I will show you a thing.'

Joao drew a long, thin whistle of shiny metal from his pocket. 'There was a time when this called countless beetles to their deaths. I had merely to tune it across their attraction spectrum.' He put the whistle to his lips, blew while turning the end of it.

No sound audible to human ears came from the instrument, but the beetle's antennae writhed.

Joao removed the whistle from his mouth.

The antennae stopped writhing.

'It stayed put, you see,' Joao said. 'And there are indications of malignant intelligence among them. The insects are far

199

from extinction, father ... and they are beginning to strike back.'

'Malignant intelligence, pah!'

'You must believe me father,' Joao said. 'No one else will listen. They laugh and say we are too long in the jungle. And where is our evidence? And they say such stories could be expected from ignorant farmers but not from bandeirantes. You must listen, father, and believe. It is why I was chosen to come here ... because you are my father and you might listen to your own son.'

'Believe what?' the elder Martinho demanded, and he was the Prefect now, standing erect, glaring coldly at his son.

'In the sertao of Goyaz last week,' Joao said, 'Antonil Lisboa's bandeirante lost three men who ...'

'Accidents.'

'They were killed with formic acid and oil of copahu.'

'They were careless with their poisons. Men grow careless when they ...'

'Father! The formic acid was a particularly strong type, but still recognizable as having been ... or being of a type manufactured by insects. And the men were drenched with it. While the oil of copahu ...'

'You imply that insects such as this ...' The Prefect pointed to the motionless creature on the crucifix. '... blind creatures such as this ...'

'They're not blind, father.'

'I did not mean literally blind, but without intelligence,' the elder Martinho said. 'You cannot be seriously implying that these creatures attacked humans and killed them.'

'We have yet to discover how the men were slain,' Joao said. 'We have only their bodies and the physical evidence at the scene. But there have been other deaths, father, and men missing and we grow more and more certain that ...'

He broke off as the beetle crawled off the crucifix onto the desk. Immediately, it darkened to brown, blending with the wood surface.

'Please, father. Get me a container.'

'I will get you a container only if you promise to use discretion in your story of where this creature was found,' the Prefect said.

'Father, I ...'

The beetle leaped off the desk far out into the middle of the room, scuttled to the wall, up the wall, into a crack beside a window.

Joao pressed the switch of the handlight, directed its beam into the hole which had swallowed the strange beetle.

'How long has this hole been here, father?'

'For years. It was a flaw in the masonry . . . an earth-quake, I believe.'

Joao turned, crossed to the door in three strides, went through an arched hallway, down a flight of stone steps, through another door and short hall, through a grillwork gate and into the exterior garden. He set the handlight to full intensity, washed its blue glare over the wall beneath the study window.

'Joao, what are you doing?'

'My job, father,' Joao said. He glanced back, saw that the elder Martinho had stopped just outside the gate.

Joao returned his attention to the exterior wall, washed the blue glare of light on the stones beneath the window. He crouched low, running the light along the ground, peering behind each clod, erasing all shadows.

His searching scrutiny passed over the raw earth, turned to the bushes, then the lawn.

Joao heard his father come up behind.

'Do you see it, son?'

'No, father.'

'You should have allowed me to crush it.'

From the outer garden that bordered the road and the stone fence, there came a piercing stridulation. It hung on the air in almost tangible waves, making Joao think of the hunting cry of jungle predators. A shiver moved up his spine. He turned toward the driveway where he had parked his airtruck, sent the blue glare of light stabbing there.

He broke off, staring at the lawn. 'What is that?'

The ground appeared to be in motion, reaching out toward them like the curling of a wave on a beach. Already, they were cut off from the house. The wave was still some ten paces away, but moving in rapidly.

Joao stood up, clutched his father's arm. He spoke quietly, hoping not to alarm the old man further. 'We must get to my truck, father. We must run across them.'

'Them?'

'Those are like the insect we saw inside, father – millions of them. Perhaps they are not beetles, after all. Perhaps they are like army ants. We must make it to the truck. I have equipment and supplies there. We will be safe inside. It is a bandeirante truck, father. You must run with me. I will help you.'

They began to run, Joao holding his father's arm, pointing the way with the light.

Let his heart be strong enough, Joao prayed.

They were into the creeping waves of insects then, but the creatures leaped aside, opening a pathway which closed behind the running men.

The white form of the airtruck loomed out of the shadows at the far curve of the driveway about fifteen meters ahead.

'Joao ... my heart,' the elder Martinho gasped.

'You can make it,' Joao panted. 'Faster!' He almost lifted his father from the ground for the last few paces.

They were at the wide rear door into the truck's lab compartment now. Joao yanked open the door, slapped the light switch, reached for a spray hood and poison gun. He stopped, stared into the yellow-lighted compartment.

Two men sat there – sertao Indians by the look of them, with bright glaring eyes and bang-cut black hair beneath straw hats. They looked to be identical twins – even to the mud-gray clothing and sandals, the leather shoulder bags. The beetle-like insects crawled around them, up the walls, over the instruments and vials.

'What the devil?' Joao blurted.

One of the pair held a qena flute. He gestured with it, spoke in a rasping, oddly inflected voice: 'Enter. You will not be harmed if you obey.'

Joao felt his father sag, caught the old man in his arms. How light he felt! Joao stepped up into the truck, carrying his father. The elder Martinho breathed in short, painful gasps. His face was a pale blue and sweat stood out on his forehead.

'Joao,' he whispered. 'Pain ... my chest.'

'Medicine, father,' Joao said. 'Where is your medicine?'

'House,' the old man said.

'It appears to be dying,' one of the Indians rasped.

Still holding his father in his arms, Joao, whirled toward the pair, blazed: 'I don't know who you are or why you loosed those bugs here, but my father's dying and needs help. Get out of my way!'

'Obey or both die,' said the Indian with the flute.

'He needs his medicine and a doctor,' Joao pleaded. He didn't like the way the Indian pointed that flute. The motion suggested the instrument was actually a weapon.

'What part has failed?' asked the other Indian. He stared curiously at Joao's father. The old man's breathing had become shallow and rapid.

'It's his heart,' Joao said. 'I know you farmers don't think he's acted fast enough for...'

'Not farmers,' said the one with the flute. 'Heart?'

'Pump,' said the other.

'Pump.' The Indian with the flute stood up from the bench at the front of the lab, gestured down. 'Put ... father here.'

The other one got off the bench, stood aside.

In spite of fear for his father, Joao was caught by the strange look of this pair, the fine, scale-like lines in their skin, the glittering brilliance of their eyes.

'Put father here,' repeated the one with the flute, pointing at the bench. 'Help can be...'

'Attained,' said the other one.

'Attained,' said the one with the flute.

Joao focused now on the masses of insects around the walls, the waiting quietude in their ranks. They *were* like the one in the study.

The old man's breathing was now very shallow, very rapid.

He's dying, Joao thought in desperation.

'Help can be attained,' repeated the one with the flute. 'If you obey, we will not harm.'

The Indian lifted his flute, pointed it at Joao like a weapon. 'Obey.'

There was no mistaking the gesture.

Slowly, Joao advanced, deposited his father gently on the bench.

The other Indian bent over the elder Martinho's head, raised an eyelid. There was a professional directness about the gesture. The Indian pushed gently on the dying man's diaphragm, removed the Prefect's belt, loosened his collar. A stubby brown finger was placed against the artery in the old man's neck.

'Very weak,' the Indian rasped.

Joao took another, closer look at this Indian, wondering at the sertao backwoodsman who behaved like a doctor.

'We've got to get him to a hospital,' Joao said. 'And his

medicine in . . .'

'Hospital,' the Indian agreed.

'Hospital?' asked the one with the flute.

A low, stridulant hissing came from the other Indian.

'Hospital,' said the one with the flute.

That stridulant hissing! Joao stared at the Indian beside the Prefect. The sound had been reminiscent of the weird call that had echoed across the lawn.

The one with the flute poked him, said: 'You will go into front and maneuver this . . .'

'Vehicle,' said the one beside Joao's father.

'Vehicle,' said the one with the flute.

'Hospital?' Joao pleaded.

'Hospital,' agreed the one with the flute.

Joao looked once more to his father. The other Indian already was strapping the elder Martinho to the bench in preparation for movement. How competent the man appeared in spite of his backwoods look.

'Obey,' said the one with the flute.

Joao opened the door into the front compartment, slipped through, feeling the other one follow. A few drops of rain spattered darkly against the curved windshield. Joao squeezed into the operator's seat, noted how the Indian crouched behind him, flute pointed and ready.

A dart gun of some kind, Joao guessed.

He punched the ignitor button on the dash, strapped himself in while waiting for the turbines to build up speed. The Indian still crouched behind him, vulnerable now if the airtruck were spun sharply. Joao flicked the communications switch on the lower left corner of the dash, looked into the tiny screen there giving him a view of the lab compartment. The rear doors were open. He closed them by hydraulic remote. His father was securely strapped to the bench now, Joao noted, but the other Indian was equally secured.

The turbines reached their whining peak. Joao switched on the lights, engaged the hydrostatic drive. The truck lifted six inches, angled upward as Joao increased pump displacement. He turned left onto the street, lifted another two meters to increase speed, headed toward the lights of a boulevard.

The Indian spoke beside his ear: 'You will turn toward the mountain over there.' A hand came forward, pointing to the right.

The Alejandro Clinic is there in the foothills, Joao thought.

He made the indicated turn down the cross street angling toward the boulevard.

Casually, he gave pump displacement another boost, lifted another meter and increased speed once more. In the same motion, he switched on the intercom to the rear compartment, tuned for the spare amplifier and pickup in the compartment beneath the bench where his father lay.

The pickup, capable of making a dropped pin sound like a cannon, gave forth only a distant hissing and rasping. Joao increased amplification. The instrument should have been transmitting the old man's heartbeats now, sending a noticeable drum-thump into the forward cabin.

There was nothing.

Tears blurred Joao's eyes, and he shook his head to clear them.

My father is dead, he thought. *Killed by these crazy backwoodsmen.*

He noted in the dash screen that the Indian back there had a hand under the elder Martinho's back. The Indian appeared to be massaging the dead man's back, and a rhythmic rasping matched the motion.

Anger filled Joao. He felt like diving the airtruck into an abutment, dying himself to kill these crazy men.

They were approaching the outskirts of the city, and ring-girders circled off to the left giving access to the boulevard. This was an area of small gardens and cottages protected by over-fly canopies.

Joao lifted the airtruck above the canopies, headed toward the boulevard.

To the clinic, yes, he thought. *But it is too late.*

In that instant, he realized there were no heartbeats at all coming from that rear compartment – only that slow, rhythmic grating, a faint susurration and a cicadalike hum up and down scale.

'To the mountains, there,' said the Indian behind him.

Again, the hand came forward to point off to the right.

Joao, with that hand close to his eyes and illuminated by the dash, saw the scale-like parts of a finger shift position slightly. In that shift, he recognized the scale shapes by their claw fringes.

The beetles!

The finger was composed of linked beetles working in unison!

Joao turned, stared into the *Indian's* eyes seeing now why they glistened so: they were composed of thousands of tiny facets.

'Hospital, there,' the creature beside him said, pointing.

Joao turned back to the controls, fighting to keep from losing composure. They were not Indians ... they weren't even human. They were insects – some kind of hive-cluster shaped and organized to mimic a man.

The implications of this discovery raced through his mind. How did they support their weight? How did they feed and breathe?

How did they speak?

Everything had to be subordinated to the urgency of getting this information and proof back to one of the big labs where the facts could be explored.

Even the death of his father could not be considered now. He had to capture one of these things, get out with it.

He reached overhead, flicked on the command transmitter, set its beacon for a homing call. *Let some of my Irmaos be awake and monitoring their sets*, he prayed.

'More to the right,' said the creature behind him.

Again, Joao corrected course.

The moon was high overhead now, illuminating a line of bandeirante towers off to the left. The first barrier.

They would be out of the green area soon and into the gray – then, beyond that, another barrier and the great red that stretched out in reaching fingers through the Goyaz and the Mato Grosso. Joao could see scattered lights of Resettlement Plan farms ahead, and darkness beyond.

The airtruck was going faster than he wanted, but Joao dared not slow it. They might become suspicious.

'You must go higher,' said the creature behind him.

Joao increased pump displacement, raised the nose. He leveled off at three hundred meters.

More bandeirante towers loomed ahead, spaced at closer intervals. Joao picked up the barrier signals on his meters, looked back at the *Indian*. The dissembler vibrations seemed not to affect the creature.

Joao looked out his side window and down. No one would challenge him, he knew. This was a bandeirante airtruck headed *into* the red zone ... and with its transmitter sending out a homing call. The men down there would assume he was a band leader headed out on a contract after a successful bid – and calling his men to him for the job ahead.

He could see the moon-silvered snake of the Sao Francisco winding off to his left, and the lesser water-ways like threads raveled out of the foothills.

I must find the nest – where we're headed, Joao thought. He wondered if he dared turn on his receiver – but if his men started reporting in ... No. That could make the creatures suspect; they might take violent counter-action.

My men will realize something is wrong when I don't answer, he thought. *They will follow.*

If any of them hear my call.

Hours droned past.

Nothing but moonlighted jungle sped beneath them now, and the moon was low on the horizon, near setting. This was the deep red region where broadcast poisons had been used at first with disastrous results. This was where the wild mutations had originated. It was here that Rhin Kelly had been reported missing.

This was the region being saved for the final assault, using a mobile barrier line when that line could be made short enough.

Joao armed the emergency charge that would separate the front and rear compartments of the truck when he fired it. The stub wings of the front compartment and its emergency rocket motors could get him back into bandeirante country.

With the *specimen* sitting behind him safely subdued, Joao hoped.

He looked up through the canopy, scanned the horizon as far as he could. Was that moonlight glistening on a truck far back to the right? He couldn't be sure.

'How much farther?' Joao asked.

'Ahead,' the creature rasped.

Now that he was alert for it, Joao heard the modulated stridulation beneath that voice.

'But how long?' Joao asked. 'My father ...'

'Hospital for ... the father ... ahead,' said the creature.

It would be dawn soon, Joao realized. He could see the first false line of light along the horizon behind. This night had passed so swiftly.

Then Joao wondered if these creatures had injected some

207

time-distorting drug into him without his knowing. He thought not. He was maintaining himself in the necessities of the moment. There was no time for fatigue or boredom when he had to record every landmark half-visible in the night, sense everything there was to sense about these creatures with him.

How did they coordinate all those separate parts?

Dawn came, revealing the plateau of the Mato Grosso. Joao looked out his windows. This region, he knew, stretched across five degrees of latitude and six degrees of longitude. Once, it has been a region of isolated *fazendas* farmed by independent blacks and by *sertanistos* chained to the *economendero* plantation system. It was hard-wood jungles, narrow rivers with banks overgrown by lush trees and ferns, savannahs and tangled life.

Even in this age it remained primitive, a fact blamed largely on insects and disease. It was one of the last strongholds of *teeming* insect life, if the International Ecological Organization's report could be believed.

Supplies for the bandeirantes making the assault on this insect stronghold would come by way of Sao Paulo, by air and by transport on the multi-decked highways, then on antique diesel trains to Itapira, on river runners to Bahus and by airtruck to Registo and Leopoldina on the Araguaya.

This area crawled with insects: wire worms in the roots of the savannahs, grubs digging in the moist black earth, hopping beetles, dart-like angita wasps, chalcis flies, chiggers, sphecidae, braconidae, fierce hornets, white termites, hemipteric crawlers, blood roaches, thrips, ants, lice, mosquitoes, mites, moths, exotic butterflies, mantidae – and countless unnatural mutations of them all.

This would be an expensive fight – unless it were stopped . . . because it already had been lost.

I mustn't think that way, Joao told himself. *Out of respect for my father*.

Maps of the IEO showed this region in varied intensities of red. Around the red ran a ring of gray with pink shading where one or two persistent forms of insect life resisted man's poisons, jelly flames, astringents, sonitoxics – the combination of flamant couroq and supersonics that drove insects from their hiding places into waiting death – and all the mechanical traps and lures in the bandeirante arsenal.

A grid map would be placed over this area and each thousand-acre square offered for bid to the independent bands to deinfest.

We bendeirantes are a kind of ultimate predator, Joao thought. *It's no wonder these creatures mimic us.*

But how good, really, was the mimicry? he asked himself. And how deadly to the predators?

'There,' said the creature behind him, and the multipart hand came forward to point toward a black scarp visible ahead in the gray light of morning.

Joao's foot kicked a trigger on the floor releasing a great cloud of orange dye-fog beneath the truck to mark the ground and forest for a mile around under this spot. As he kicked the trigger, Joao began counting down the five-second delay to the firing of the separation charge.

It came in a roaring blast that Joao knew would smear the creature behind him against the rear bulkhead. He sent the stub wings out, fed power to the rocket motors and backed hard around. He saw the detached rear compartment settling slowly earthward above the dye cloud, its fall cushioned as the pumps of the hydrostatic drive automatically compensated.

I will come back, father, Joao thought. *You will be buried among family and friends.*

He locked the controls, twisted in the seat to see what had happened to his captive.

A gasp escaped Joao's lips.

The rear bulkhead crawled with insects clustered around something white and pulsing. The mud-gray shirt and trousers were torn, but insects already were repairing it, spinning out fibers that meshed and sealed on contact. There was a yellow like extrusion near the pulsing white, and a dark brown skeleton with familiar articulation.

It looked like a human skeleton – but chitinous.

Before his eyes, the thing was reassembling itself, the long, furry antennae burrowing into the structure and interlocking.

The flute-weapon was not visible, and the thing's leather pouch had been thrown into the rear corner, but its eyes were in place in their brown sockets, staring at him. The mouth was reforming.

The yellow sac contracted, and a voice issued from the half-formed mouth.

'You must listen,' it rasped.

Joao gulped, whirled back to the controls, unlocked them

and sent the cab into a wild, spinning turn.

A high-pitched rattling buzz sounded behind him. The noise seemed to pick up every bone in his body and shake it. Something crawled on his neck. He slapped at it, felt it squash.

All Joao could think of was escape. He stared frantically out at the earth beneath, seeing a blotch of white in a savannah off to his right and, in the same instant, recognizing another airtruck banking beside him, the insignia of his own Irmandades band bright on its side.

The white blotch in the savannah was resolving itself into a cluster of tents with an IEO orange and green banner flying beside them.

Joao dove for the tents, praying the other airtruck would follow.

Something stung his cheek. They were in his hair – biting, stinging. He stabbed the braking rockets, aimed for open ground about fifty meters from the tent. Insects were all over the inside of the glass now, blocking his vision. Joao said a silent prayer, hauled back on the control arm, felt the cab mush out, touch ground, skidding and slewing across the savannah. He kicked the canopy release before the cab stopped, broke the seal on his safety harness and launched himself up and out to land sprawling in grass.

He rolled through the grass, feeling the insect bites like fire over every exposed part of his body. Hands grabbed him and he felt a jelly hood splash across his face to protect it. A voice he recognized as Thome of his own band said: 'This way, Johnny! Run!' They ran.

He heard a spraygun fire: 'Whooosh!'

And again.

And again.

Arms lifted him and he felt a leap.

They landed in a heap and a voice said: 'Mother of God! Would you look at that!'

Joao clawed the jelly hood from his face, sat up to stare across the savannah. The grass seethed and boiled with insects around the uptilted cab and the airtruck that had landed beside it.

Joao looked around him, counted seven of his Irmaos with Thome, his chief sprayman, in command.

Beyond them clustered five other people, a redhaired woman slightly in front, half turned to look at the savannah and at him. He recognized the woman immediately: Dr. Rhin Kelly of the IEO. When they had met in the A' Chigua nightclub in Bahia, she had seemed exotic and desirable to Joao. Now, she wore a field uniform instead of gown and jewels, and her eyes held no invitation at all.

'I see a certain poetic justice in this ... traitors,' she said.

Joao lifted himself to his feet, took a cloth proffered by one of his men, and wiped off the last of the jelly. He felt hands brushing him, clearing dead insects off his coveralls. The pain of his skin was receding under the medicant jelly, and now he found himself dominated by puzzled questioning as he recognized the mood of the IEO personnel.

They were furious and it was directed at him ... and at his fellow Irmandades.

Joao studied the woman, noting how her green eyes glared at him, the pink flush to her skin.

'Dr. Kelly?' Joao said.

'If it isn't Joao Martinho, jefe of the Irmandades,' she said, 'the traitor of the Piratininga.'

'They are crazy, that is the only thing, I think,' said Thorne.

'Your pets turned on you, didn't they?' she demanded. 'And wasn't that inevitable?'

'Would you be so kind as to explain,' Joao said.

'I don't need to explain,' she said. 'Let your friends out there explain.' She pointed toward the rim of jungle beyond the savannah.

Joao looked where she pointed, saw a line of men in bandeirante white standing untouched amidst the leaping, boiling insects of the jungle shadow. He took a pair of binoculars from around the neck of one of his men, focused on the figures. Knowing what to look for made the identification easy.

'Tommy,' Joao said.

His chief sprayman, Thome, bent close, rubbing at an insect sting on his swarthy cheek.

In a low voice, Joao explained what the figures at the jungle edge were.

'Aieeee,' Thome said.

An Irmandade on Joao's left crossed himself.

'What was it we leaped across coming in here?' Joao asked.

'A ditch,' Thome said. 'It seems to be filled with couroq jelly ... an insect barrier of some kind.'

Joao nodded. He began to have unpleasant suspicions about

211

their position here. He looked at Rhin Kelly. 'Dr. Kelly, where are the rest of your people? Surely there are more than five in an IEO field crew.'

Her lips compressed, but she remained silent.

'So?' Jao glanced around at the tents, seeing their weathered condition. 'And where is your equipment, your trucks and lab huts and jitneys?'

'Funny thing you should ask,' she said, but there was uncertainty atop the sneering quality of her voice. 'About a kilometer into the trees over there...' She nodded to her left. '...is a wrecked jungle truck containing most of our ... equipment, as you call it. The track spools of our truck were eaten away by acid.'

'Acid?'

'It smelled like oxalic,' said one of her companions, a blond Nordic with a scar beneath his right eye.

'Start from the beginning,' Joao said.

'We were cut off here almost six weeks ago,' said the blond man. 'Something got our radio, our truck – they looked like giant chiggers and they can shoot an acid spray about fifteen meters.'

'There's a glass case containing three dead specimens in my lab tent,' said Dr. Kelly.

Joao pursed his lips, thinking. 'So?'

'I heard part of what you were telling your men there,' she said. 'Do you expect us to believe that?'

'It is of no importance to me what you believe,' Joao said. 'How did you get here?'

'We fought our way in here from the truck using *caramuru* cold-fire spray,' said the blond man. 'We dragged along what supplies we could, dug a trench around our perimeter, poured in the couroq powder, added the jell compound and topped it off with our *copahu* oil ... and here we sat.'

'How many of you?' Joao asked.

'There were fourteen of us,' said the man.

Joao rubbed the back of his neck where the insect stings were again beginning to burn. He glanced around at his men, assessing their condition and equipment, counted four spray rifles, saw the men carried spare charge cylinders on slings around their necks.

'The airtruck will take us,' he said. 'We had better get out of here.'

212

Dr. Kelly looked out to the savannah, said: 'I think it has been too late for that since a few seconds after you landed, bandeirante. I think in a day or so there'll be a few less traitors around. You're caught in your own trap.'

Joao whirled to stare at the airtruck, barked: 'Tommy! Vince! Get...' He broke off as the airtruck sagged to its left.

'It's only fair to warn you,' said Dr. Kelly, 'to stay away from the edge of the ditch unless you first spray the opposite side. They can shoot a stream of acid at least fifteen meters ... and as you can see ...' She nodded toward the airtruck. '... the acid eats metal.'

'You're insane,' Joao said. 'Why didn't you warn us immediately?'

'Warn you?'

Her blond companion said: 'Rhin, perhaps we...'

'Be quiet, Hogar,' she said, and turned back to Joao. 'We lost nine men to your playmates.' She looked at the small band of Irmandades. 'Our lives are little enough to pay now for the extinction of eight of you ... traitors.'

'You *are* insane,' Joao said.

'Stop playing innocent, bandeirante,' she said. 'We have seen your companions out there. We have seen the new playmates you bred ... and we understand that you were too greedy; now your game has gotten out of hand.'

'You've not seen my Irmaos doing these things,' Joao said. He looked at Thome. 'Tommy, keep an eye on these insane ones.' He lifted the spray rifle from one of his men, took the man's spare charges, indicated the other three armed men. 'You – come with me.'

'Johnny, what do you do?' Thome asked.

'Salvage the supplies from the truck,' Joao said. He walked toward the ditch nearest the airtruck, laid down a hard mist of foamal beyond the ditch, beckoned the others to follow and leaped the ditch.

Little more than an hour later, with all of them acid burned – two seriously – the Irmandades retreated back across the ditch. They had salvaged less than a fourth of the equipment in the truck, and this did not include a transmitter.

'It is evident the little devils went first for the communications equipment,' Thome said. 'How could they tell?'

Joao said: 'I do not want to guess.' He broke open a first aid box, began treating his men. One had a cheek and shoulder

213

badly splashed with acid. Another was losing flesh off his back.

Dr. Kelly came up, helped him treat the men, but refused to speak, even to answering the simplest question.

Finally, Joao touched up a spot on his own arm, neutralizing the acid and covering the burn with fleshtape. He gritted his teeth against the pain, stared at Rhin Kelly. 'Where are these chigua you found?'

'Go find them yourself!' she snapped.

'You are a blind, unprincipled megalomaniac,' Joao said, speaking in an even voice. 'Do not push me too far.'

Her face went pale and the green eyes blazed.

Joao grabbed her arm, hauled her roughly toward the tents. 'Show me these chigua!'

She jerked free of him, threw back her red hair, stared at him defiantly. Joao faced her, looked her up and down with a calculating slowness.

'Go ahead, do violence to me,' she said, 'I'm sure I couldn't stop you.'

'You act like a woman who wants ... needs violence,' Joao said. 'Would you like me to turn you over to my men? They're a little tired of your raving.'

Her face flamed. 'You would not dare!'

'Don't be so melodramatic,' he said, 'I wouldn't give you the pleasure.'

'You insolent ... you ...'

Joao showed her a wolfish grin, said: 'Nothing you say will make me turn you over to my men!'

'Johnny.'

It was Thome calling.

Joao turned, saw Thome talking to the Nordic IEO man who had volunteered information. What had she called him? Hogar.

Thome beckoned.

Joao crossed to the pair, bent close as Thome signaled secrecy.

'The gentleman here says the female doctor was bitten by an insect that got past their barrier's fumes.'

'Two weeks ago,' Hogar whispered.

'She has not been the same since,' Thome said. 'We humor her, jefe, no?'

Joao wet his lips with his tongue. He felt suddenly dizzy and too warm.

'The insect that bit her was similar to the ones that were on you,' Hogar said, and his voice sounded apologetic.

They are making fun of me! Joao thought.

'I give the orders here!' he snapped.

'Yes, jefe,' Thome said. 'But you . . .'

'What difference does it make who gives the orders?'

It was Dr. Kelly close behind him.

Joao turned, glared at her. How hateful she looked . . . in spite of her beauty.

'What's the difference?' she demanded. 'We'll all be dead in a few days anyway.' She stared out across the savannah. 'More of your friends have arrived.'

Joao looked to the forest shadow, saw more humanlike figures arriving. They appeared familiar and he wondered what it was – something at the edge of his mind, but his head hurt. Then he realized they looked like sertao Indians, like the pair who had lured him here. There were at least a hundred of them, apparently identical in every visible respect.

More were arriving by the second.

Each of them carried a quena flute.

There was something about the flutes that Joao felt he should remember.

Another figure came advancing through the *Indians*, a thin man in a black suit, his hair shiny silver in the sunlight.

'Father!' Joao gasped.

I'm sick, he thought. *I must be delirious.*

'That looks like the Prefect,' Thome said. 'Is it not so, Ramon?'

The Irmandade he addressed said: 'If it is not the Prefect, it is his twin. Here, Johnny. Look with the glasses.'

Joao took the glasses, focused on the figure advancing toward them through the grass. The glasses felt so heavy. They trembled in his hands and the figure coming toward them was blurred.

'I cannot see!' Joao muttered and he almost dropped the glasses.

A hand steadied him, and he realized he was reeling.

In an instant of clarity, he saw that the line of Indians had raised their flutes, pointing to the IEO camp. That buzzing-rasping that had shaken his bones in the airtruck cab filled the universe around him. He saw his companions begin to fall.

In the instant before his world went blank, Joao heard his father's voice calling strongly: 'Joao! Do not resist! Put down your weapons!'

The trampled grassy earth of the campsite, Joao saw, was coming up to meet his face.

It cannot by my father, Joao thought. *My father is dead and they've copied him ... mimicry, nothing more.*

Darkness.

There was a dream of being carried, a dream of tears and shouting, a dream of violent protests and defiance and rejection.

He awoke to yellow-orange light and the figure who could not be his father bending over him, thrusting a hand out, saying: 'Then examine my hand if you don't believe!'

But Joao's attention was on the face behind his father. It was a giant face, baleful in the strange light, its eyes brilliant and glaring with pupils within pupils. The face turned, and Joao saw it was no more than two centimeters thick. Again, it turned, and the eyes focused on Joao's feet.

Joao forced himself to look down, began trembling violently as he saw he was half enveloped in a foaming green cocoon, that his skin shared some of the same tone.

'Examine my hand!' ordered the old-man figure beside him.

'He has been dreaming.' It was a resonant voice that boomed all around him, seemingly coming from beneath the giant face. 'He has been dreaming,' the voice repeated. 'He is not quite awake.'

With an abrupt, violent motion, Joao reached out, clutched the proffered hand.

It felt warm ... human.

For no reason he could explain, tears came to Joao's eyes.

'Am I dreaming?' he whispered. He shook his head to clear away the tears.

'Joao, my son,' said his father's voice.

Joao looked up at the familiar face. It *was* his father and no mistake. 'But ... your heart,' Joao said.

'My pump,' the old man said. 'Look.' And he pulled his hand away, turned to display where the back of his black suit had been cut away, its edges held by some gummy substance, and a pulsing surface of oily yellow between those cut edges.

Joao saw the hair-fine scale lines, the multiple shapes, and he recoiled.

So it was a copy, another of their tricks.

The old man turned back to face him. 'The old pump failed and they gave me a new one,' he said. 'It shares my blood and lives off me and it'll give me a few more years. What do you think our bright IEO specialists will say about the *usefulness* of that?'

'Is it really you?' Joao demanded.

'All except the pump,' said the old man. 'They had to give you and some of the others a whole new blood system because of all the corrosive poison that got into you.'

Joao lifted his hands, stared at them.

'They know medical tricks we haven't even dreamed about,' the old man said. 'I haven't been this excited since I was a boy. I can hardly wait to get back and ... Joao! What is it?'

Joao was thrusting himself up, glaring at the old man. 'We're not human any more if ... We're not human!'

'Be still, son!' the old man ordered.

'If this is true,' Joao protested, 'they're in control.' He nodded toward the giant face behind his father. 'They'll *rule* us!'

He sank back, gasping. 'We'll be their slaves.'

'Foolishness,' rumbled the drum voice.

Joao looked at the giant face, growing aware of the fluorescent insects above it, seeing that the insects clung to the ceiling of a cave, noting finally a patch of night sky and stars where the fluorescent insects ended.

'What is a slave?' rumbled the voice.

Joao looked beneath the face where the voice originated, saw a white mass about four meters across, a pulsing yellow sac protruding from it, insects crawling over it into fissures along its surface, back to the ground beneath. The face appeared to be held up from that white mass by dozens of round stalks, their scaled surfaces betraying their nature.

'Your attention is drawn to our way of answering your threat to us,' rumbled the voice, and Joao saw that the sound issued from the pulsing yellow sac. 'This is our brain. It is vulnerable, very vulnerable, weak, yet strong ... just as your brain. Now, tell me what is a slave?'

Joao fought down a shiver of revulsion, said: 'I'm a slave now; I'm in bondage to you.'

'Not true,' rumbled the voice. 'A slave is one who must

produce wealth for another, and there is only one true wealth in all the universe – living time. Are we slaves because we have given your father more time to live?'

Joao looked up to the giant, glittering eyes, thought he detected amusement there.

'The lives of all those with you have been spared or extended as well,' drummed the voice. 'That makes us your slaves, does it not?'

'What do you take in return?'

'Ah, hah!' the voice fairly barked. 'Quid pro quo! You are, indeed, our slaves as well. We are tied to each other by a bond of mutual slavery that cannot be broken – never could be'

'It is very simple once you understand it,' Joao's father said.

'Understand what?'

'Some of our kind once lived in greenhouses and their cells remembered the experience,' rumbled the voice. 'You know about greenhouses, of course?' It turned to look out at the cave mouth where dawn was beginning to touch the world with gray. 'That out there, that is a greenhouse, too.' Again, it looked down at Joao, the giant eyes glaring. 'To sustain life, a greenhouse must achieve a delicate balance – enough of this chemical, enough of that one, another substance available when needed. What is poison one day can be sweet food the next.'

'What's all this to do with slavery?' Joao demanded.

'Life has developed over millions of years in this greenhouse we call Earth,' the voice rumbled. 'Sometimes it developed in the poison excrement of other life ... and then that poison became necessary to it. Without a substance produced by the wire worm, that savannah grass out there would die ... in time. Without substances produced by ... insects, your kind of life would die. Sometimes, just a faint trace of the substance is needed, such as the special copper compound produced by the arachnids. Sometimes, the substance must subtly change each time before it can be used by a life form at the end of the chain. The more different forms of life there are, the more life the greenhouse can support. This is the lesson of the greenhouse. The successful greenhouse must grow many times many forms of life. The more forms of life it has, the healthier it is.'

'You're saying we have to stop killing insects,' Joao said. 'You're saying we have to let you take over.'

'We say you must stop killing yourselves,' rumbled the voice. 'Already, the Chinese are ... I believe you would call it: *re-infesting* their land. Perhaps they will be in time, perhaps not. Here, it is not too late. There ... they were fast and thorough ... and they may need help.'

'You ... give us no proof,' Joao said.

'There will be time for proof, later,' said the voice. 'Now, join your woman friend outside; let the sun work on your skin and the chlorophyll in your blood, and when you come back, tell me if the sun is your slave.'

Balanced Ecology
by James H. Schmitz

The diamondwood tree farm was restless this morning. Ilf Cholm had been aware of it for about and hour but had said nothing to Auris, thinking he might be getting a summer fever or a stomach upset and imagining things and that Auris would decide they should go back to the house so Ilf's grandmother could dose him. But the feeling continued to grow, and by now Ilf knew it was the farm.

Outwardly, everyone in the forest appeared to be going about their usual business. There had been a rainfall earlier in the day; and the tumbleweeds had uprooted themselves and were moving about in the bushes, lapping water off the leaves. Ilf had noticed a small one rolling straight toward a waiting slurp and stopped for a moment to watch the slurp catch it. The slurp was of average size, which gave it a tongue-reach of between twelve and fourteen feet, and the tumbleweed was already within range.

The tongue shot out suddenly, a thin, yellow flash. Its tip flicked twice around the tumbleweed, jerked it off the ground and back to the feed opening in the imitation tree stump within which the rest of the slurp was concealed. The tumbleweed said 'Oof!' in the surprised way they always did when something caught them, and went in through the opening. After a moment, the slurp's tongue tip appeared in the opening again and waved gently around, ready for somebody else of the right size to come within reach.

Ilf, just turned eleven and rather small for his age, was the right size for this slurp, though barely. But, being a human boy, he was in no danger. The slurps of the diamondwood farms on Wrake didn't attack humans. For a moment, he was tempted to tease the creature into a brief fencing match. If he picked up a stick and banged on the stump with it a few times, the slurp would become annoyed and dart its tongue out and try to knock the stick from his hand.

But it wasn't the day for entertainment of that kind. Ilf couldn't shake off his crawly, uncomfortable feeling, and while he had been standing there, Auris and Sam had moved a couple of hundred feet farther uphill, in the direction of the

221

Queen Grove, and home. He turned and sprinted after them, caught up with them as they came out into one of the stretches of grassland which lay between the individual groves of diamond-wood trees.

Auris, who was two years, two months, and two days older than Ilf, stood on top of Sam's semiglobular shell, looking off to the right toward the valley where the diamondwood factory was. Most of the world of Wrake was on the hot side, either rather dry or rather steamy; but this was cool mountain country. Far to the south, below the valley and the foothills behind it, lay the continental plain, shimmering like a flat, green-brown sea. To the north and east were higher plateaus, above the level where the diamondwood liked to grow. Ilf ran past Sam's steadily moving bulk to the point where the forward rim of the shell made a flat upward curve, close enough to the ground so he could reach it.

Sam rolled a somber brown eye back for an instant as Ilf caught the shell and swung up on it, but his huge beaked head didn't turn. He was a mossback, Wrake's version of the turtle pattern, and, except for the full-grown trees and perhaps some members of the clean-up squad, the biggest thing on the farm. His corrugated shell was overgrown with a plant which had the appearance of long green fur; and occasionally when Sam fed, he would extend and use a pair of heavy arms with three-fingered hands, normally held folded up against the lower rim of the shell.

Auris had paid no attention to Ilf's arrival. She still seemed to be watching the factory in the valley. She and Ilf were cousins but didn't resemble each other. Ilf was small and wiry, with tight-curled red hair. Auris was slim and blond, and stood a good head taller than he did. He thought she looked as if she owned everything she could see from the top of Sam's shell; and she did, as a matter of fact, own a good deal of it – nine tenths of the diamondwood farm and nine tenths of the factory. Ilf owned the remaining tenth of both.

He scrambled up the shell, grabbing the moss-fur to haul himself along, until he stood beside her. Sam, awkward as he looked when walking, was moving at a good ten miles an hour, clearly headed for the Queen Grove. Ilf didn't know whether it was Sam or Auris who had decided to go back to the house. Whichever it had been, he could feel the purpose of going there.

'They're nervous about something,' he told Auris, meaning the whole farm. 'Think there's a big storm coming?'

'Doesn't look like a storm,' Auris said.

Ilf glanced about the sky, agreed silently. 'Earthquake, maybe?'

Auris shook her head. 'It doesn't feel like earthquake.'

She hadn't turned her gaze from the factory. Ilf asked. 'Something going on down there?'

Auris shrugged. 'They're cutting a lot today,' she said. 'They got in a limit order.'

Sam swayed on into the next grove while Ilf considered the information. Limit orders were fairly unusual; but it hardly explained the general uneasiness. He sighed, sat down, crossed his legs, and looked about. This was a grove of young trees, fifteen years and less. There was plenty of open space left between them. Ahead, a huge tumbleweed was dying, making happy, chuckling sounds as it pitched its scarlet seed pellets far out from its slowly unfolding leaves. The pellets rolled hurriedly farther away from the old weed as soon as they touched the ground. In a twelve-foot circle about their parent, the earth was being disturbed, churned, shifted steadily about. The clean-up squad had arrived to dispose of the dying tumbleweed; as Ilf looked, it suddenly settled six or seven inches deeper into the softened dirt. The pellets were hurrying to get beyond the reach of the clean-up squad so they wouldn't get hauled down, too. But half-grown tumbleweeds, speckled yellow-green and ready to start their rooted period, were rolling through the grove toward the disturbed area. They would wait around the edge of the circle until the clean-up squad finished, then move in and put down their roots. The ground where the squad had worked recently was always richer than any other spot in the forest.

Ilf wondered, as he had many times before, what the clean-up squad looked like. Nobody ever caught so much as a glimpse of them. Riquol Cholm, his grandfather, had told him of attempts made by scientists to catch a member of the squad with digging machines. Even the smaller ones could dig much faster than the machines could dig after them, so the scientists always gave up finally and went away.

'Ilf, come in for lunch!' called Ilf's grandmother's voice.

Ilf filled his lungs, shouted. 'Coming, grand —'

He broke off, looked up at Auris. She was smirking.

'Caught me again,' Ilf admitted. 'Dumb humbugs!' He yelled, 'Come out, Lying Lou! I know who it was.'

Meldy Cholm laughed her low, sweet laugh, a silverbell called the giant greenweb of the Queen Grove sounded its deep harp note, more or less all together. Then Lying Lou and Gabby darted into sight, leaped up on the mossback's hump. The humbugs were small, brown, bobtailed animals, built with spider leanness and very quick. They had round skulls, monkey faces, and the pointed teeth of animals who lived by catching and killing other animals. Gabby sat down beside Ilf, inflating and deflating his voice pouch, while Lou burst into a series of rattling, clicking, spitting sounds.

'They've been down at the factory?' Ilf asked.

'Yes,' Auris said. 'Hush now. I'm listening.'

Lou was jabbering along at the rate at which the humbugs chattered among themselves, but this sounded like, and was, a recording of human voices played back at high speed. When Auris wanted to know what people somewhere were talking about, she sent the humbugs off to listen. They remembered everything they heard, came back and repeated it to her at their own speed, which saved time. Ilf, if he tried hard, could understand scraps of it. Auris understood it all. She was hearing now what the people at the factory had been saying during the morning.

Gabby inflated his voice pouch part way, remarked in Grandfather Riquol's strong, rich voice, 'My, my! We're not being quite on our best behavior today, are we, Ilf?'

'Shut up,' said Ilf.

'Hush now,' Gabby said in Auris' voice. 'I'm listening.' He added in Ilf's voice, sounding crestfallen, 'Caught me again!' then chuckled nastily.

Ilf made a fist of his left hand and swung fast. Gabby became a momentary brown blur, and was sitting again on Ilf's other side. He looked at Ilf with round, innocent eyes, said in a solemn tone. 'We must pay more attention to details, men. Mistakes can be expensive!'

He'd probably picked that up at the factory. Ilf ignored him. Trying to hit a humbug was a waste of effort. So was talking back to them. He shifted his attention to catching what Lou was saying; but Lou had finished up at that moment. She and Gabby took off instantly in a leap from Sam's back and were gone in the bushes. Ilf thought they were a little jittery and erratic in their motions today, as if they, too, were keyed up even more than usual. Auris walked down to the front lip of the shell and sat on it, dangling her legs. Ilf joined her there.

'What were they talking about at the factory?' he asked.

'They did get in a limit order yesterday,' Auris said. 'And another one this morning. They're not taking any more orders until they've filled those two.'

'That's good, isn't it?' Ilf asked.

'I guess so.'

After a moment, Ilf asked, 'Is that what *they're* worrying about?'

'I don't know,' Auris said. But she frowned.

Sam came lumbering up to another stretch of open ground, stopped while he was still well back among the trees. Auris slipped down from the shell, said, 'Come on but don't let them see you,' and moved ahead through the trees until she could look into the open. Ilf followed her as quietly as he could.

'What's the matter?' he inquired. A hundred and fifty yards away, on the other side of the open area, towered the Queen Grove, its tops dancing gently like armies of slender green spears against the blue sky. The house wasn't visible from here; it was a big one-story bungalow built around the trunks of a number of trees within the grove. Ahead of them lay the road which came up from the valley and wound on through the mountains to the west.

Auris said, 'An aircar came down here a while ago . . . There it is!'

They looked at the aircar parked at the side of the road on their left, a little distance away. Opposite the car was an opening in the Queen Grove where a path led to the house. Ilf couldn't see anything very interesting about the car. It was neither new nor old, looked like any ordinary aircar. The man sitting inside it was nobody they knew.

'Somebody's here on a visit,' Ilf said.

'Yes,' Auris said. 'Uncle Kugus has come back.'

Ilf had to reflect an instant to remember who Uncle Kugus was. Then it came to his mind in a flash. It had been some while ago, a year or so. Uncle Kugus was a big, handsome man with thick, black eyebrows, who always smiled. He wasn't Ilf's uncle but Auris'; but he'd had presents for both of them when he arrived. He had told Ilf a great many jokes. He and Grandfather Riquol had argued on one occasion for almost two hours about something or other; Ilf couldn't remember now what it had been. Uncle Kugus had come and gone in a tiny, beautiful, bright yellow aircar, had taken Ilf for a couple of rides in it, and told him about winning races with it. Ilf hadn't had too bad an impression of him.

'That isn't him,' he said, 'and that isn't his car.'

'I know. He's in the house,' Auris said. 'He's got a couple of people with him. They're talking with Riquol and Meldy.'

A sound rose slowly from the Queen Grove as she spoke, deep and resonant, like the stroke of a big, old clock or the hum of a harp. The man in the aircar turned his head towards the grove to listen. The sound was repeated twice. It came from the giant greenweb at the far end of the grove and could be heard all over the farm, even, faintly, down in the valley when the wind was favorable. Ilf said, 'Lying Lou and Gabby were up here?'

'Yes. They went down to the factory first, then up to the house.'

'What are they talking about in the house?' Ilf inquired.

'Oh, a lot of things.' Auris frowned again. 'We'll go and find out, but we won't let them see us right away.'

Something stirred beside Ilf. He looked down and saw Lying Lou and Gabby had joined them again. The humbugs peered for a moment at the man in the aircar, then flicked out into the open, on across the road, and into the Queen Grove, like small, flying shadows, almost impossible to keep in sight. The man in the aircar looked about in a puzzled way, apparently uncertain whether he'd seen something move or not.

'Come on,' Auris said.

Ilf followed her back to Sam. Sam lifted his head and extended his neck. Auris swung herself upon the edge of the undershell beside the neck, crept on hands and knees into the hollow between the upper and lower shells. Ilf climbed in after her. The shell-cave was a familiar place. He'd scuttled in there many times when they'd been caught outdoors in one of the violent electric storms which came down through the mountains from the north or when the ground began to shudder in an earthquake's first rumbling. With the massive curved shell above him and the equally massive flat shell below, the angle formed by the cool, leathery wall which was the side of Sam's neck and the front of his shoulder seemed like the safest place in the world to be on such occasions.

The undershell tilted and swayed beneath Ilf now as the mossback started forward. He squirmed around and looked out through the opening between the shells. They moved out of the grove, headed toward the road at Sam's steady walking pace. Ilf couldn't see the aircar and wondered why Auris didn't want the man in the car to see them. He wriggled uncomfortably. It was a strange, uneasy-making morning in every way.

They crossed the road, went swishing through high grass with Sam's ponderous side-to-side sway like a big ship sailing over dry land, and came to the Queen Grove. Sam moved on into the green-tinted shade under the Queen Trees. The air grew cooler. Presently he turned to the right, and Ilf saw a flash of blue ahead. That was the great thicket of flower bushes, in the center of which was Sam's sleeping pit.

Sam pushed through the thicket, stopped when he reached the open space in the center to let Ilf and Auris climb out of the shell-cave. Sam then lowered his forelegs, one after the other, into the pit, which was lined so solidly with tree roots that almost no earth showed between them, shaped like a mold to fit the lower half of his body, tilted forward, drawing neck and head back under his shell, slid slowly into the pit, straightened out and settled down. The edge of his upper shell was now level with the edge of the pit, and what still could be seen of him looked simply like a big, moss-grown boulder. If nobody came to disturb him, he might stay there unmoving the rest of the year. There were mossbacks in other groves of the farm which had never come out of their sleeping pits or given any indication of being awake since Ilf could remember. They lived an enormous length of time and a nap of half a dozen years apparently meant nothing to them.

Ilf looked questioningly at Auris. She said, 'We'll go up to the house and listen to what Uncle Kugus is talking about.'

They turned into a path which led from Sam's place to the house. It had been made by six generations of human children, all of whom had used Sam for transportation about the diamondwood farm. He was half again as big as any other mossback around and the only one whose sleeping pit was in the Queen Grove. Everything about the Queen Grove was special, from the trees themselves, which were never cut and twice as thick and almost twice as tall as the trees of other groves, to Sam and his blue flower thicket, the huge stump of the Grandfather Slurp not far away, and the giant greenweb at the other end of the grove. It was quieter here; there were fewer of the other animals. The Queen Grove, from what Riquol Cholm had told Ilf, was the point from which the whole diamond-wood forest had started a long time ago.

Auris said, 'We'll go around and come in from the back. They don't have to know right away that we're here ...'

'Mr. Terokaw,' said Riquol Cholm, 'I'm sorry Kugus Ovin persuaded you and Mr. Bliman to accompany him to Wrake on this business. You've simply wasted your time. Kugus should have known better. I've discussed the situation quite thoroughly with him on other occasions.'

'I'm afraid I don't follow you, Mr. Cholm,' Mr. Terokaw said stiffly. 'I'm making you a businesslike proposition in re-gard to this farm of diamondwood trees – a proposition which will be very much to your advantage as well as to that of the children whose property the Diamondwood is. Certainly you should at least be willing to listen to my terms!'

Riquol shook his head. It was clear that he was angry with Kugus but attempting to control his anger.

'Your terms, whatever they may be, are not a factor in this,' he said. 'The maintenance of a diamondwood forest is not entirely a business proposition. Let me explain that to you – as Kugus should have done.

'No doubt you're aware that there are less than forty such forests on the world of Wrake and that attempts to grow the trees elsewhere have been uniformly unsuccessful. That and the unique beauty of diamondwood products, which has never been duplicated by artificial means, is, of course, the reason that such products command a price which compares with that of precious stones and similar items.'

Mr. Terokaw regarded Riquol with a bleak blue eye, nodded briefly. 'Please continue, Mr. Cholm.'

'A diamondwood forest,' said Riquol, 'is a great deal more than an assemblage of trees. The trees are a basic factor, but still only a factor, of a closely integrated, balanced natural ecology. The manner of independence of the plants and ani-mals that make up a diamondwood forest is not clear in all details, but the interdependence is a very pronounced one. None of the involved species seem able to survive in any other environment. On the other hand, plants and animals not naturally a part of this ecology will not thrive if brought into it. They move out or vanish quickly. Human beings appear to be the only exception to that rule.'

'Very interesting,' Mr. Terokaw said dryly.

'It is,' said Riquol. 'It is a very interesting natural situation and many people, including Mrs. Cholm and myself, feel it should be preserved. The studied, limited cutting practiced on the diamondwood farms at present acts toward its preservation. That degree of harvesting actually is beneficial to the forests, keeps them moving through an optimum cycle of growth and maturity. They are flourishing under the hand of man to an extent which was not usually attained in their natural, untouched state. The people who are at present responsible for them – the farm owners and their associates – have been working for some time to have all diamondwood forests turned into Federation preserves, with the right to harvest them retained by the present owners and their heirs under the same carefully supervised conditions. When Auris and Ilf come of age and can sign an agreement to that effect, the farms will in fact become Federation preserves. All other steps to that end have been taken by now.

'That, Mr. Terokaw, is why we're not interested in your business proposition. You'll discover, if you wish to sound them out on it, that the other diamondwood farmers are not interested in it either. We are all of one mind in that matter. If we weren't, we would long since have accepted propositions essentially similar to yours.'

There was silence for a moment. Then Kugus Ovin said pleasantly, 'I know you're annoyed with me, Riquol, but I'm thinking of Auris and Ilf in this. Perhaps in your concern for the preservation of a natural phenomenon, you aren't sufficiently considering their interests.'

Riquol looked at him, said, 'When Auris reaches maturity, she'll be an extremely wealthy young woman, even if this farm never sells another cubic foot of diamondwood from this day on. Ilf would be sufficiently well-to-do to make it unnecessary for him ever to work a stroke in his life – though I doubt very much he would make such a choice.'

Kugus smiled. 'There are degrees even to the state of being extremely wealthy,' he remarked. 'What my niece can expect to gain in her lifetime from this careful harvesting you talk about can't begin to compare with what she would get at one stroke through Mr. Terokaw's offer. The same, of course, holds true of Ilf.'

'Quite right,' Mr. Terokaw said heavily. 'I'm generous in my business dealing, Mr. Cholm. I have a reputation for it. And I can afford to be generous because I profit well from my investments. Let me bring another point to your attention. Interest in diamondwood products throughout the Federation waxes and wanes, as you must be aware. It rises and falls. There are fashions and fads. At present, we are approaching the crest of a new wave of interest in these products. This interest can be properly stimulated and exploited, but in any event we must expect it will have passed its peak in another few months. The next interest peak might develop six years from now, or twelve years from now. Or it might never develop since there are very few natural products which cannot eventually be duplicated and usually surpassed by artificial methods, and there is no good reason to assume that diamondwood will remain an exception indefinitely.

'We should be prepared, therefore, to make the fullest use of this bonanza while it lasts. I am prepared to do just that, Mr. Cholm. A cargo ship full of cutting equipment is at present stationed a few hours' flight from Wrake. This machinery can be landed in and operation here within a day after the contract I am offering you is signed. Within a week, the forest can be leveled. We shall make no use of your factory here, which would be entirely inadequate for my purpose. The diamondwood will be shipped at express speeds to another world where I have adequate processing facilities set up. And we can hit the Federation's main markets with the finished products the following month.'

Riquol Cholm said, icily polite now, 'And what would be the reason for all that haste, Mr. Terokaw?'

Mr. Terokaw looked surprised. 'To insure that we have no competition, Mr. Cholm. What else? When the other diamondwood farmers here discover what has happened, they may be tempted to follow our example. But we'll be so far ahead of them that the diamondwood boom will be almost entirely to our exclusive advantage. We have taken every precaution to see to that. Mr. Bliman, Mr. Ovin and I arrived here in the utmost secrecy today. No one so much as suspects that we are on Wrake, much less what our purpose is. I make no mistakes in such matters, Mr. Cholm!'

He broke off and looked around as Meldy Cholm said in a troubled voice, 'Come in, children. Sit down over there. We're discussing a matter which concerns you.'

'Hello, Auris!' Kugus said heartily. 'Hello, Ilf. Remember old Uncle Kugus?'

'Yes,' Ilf said. He sat down on the bench by the wall beside Auris, feeling scared.

'Auris,' Riquol Cholm said, 'did you happen to overhear anything of what was being said before you came into the room?'

Auris nodded. 'Yes.' She glanced at Mr. Terokaw, looked at Riquol again. 'He wants to cut down the forest.'

'It's your forest and Ilf's, you know. Do you want him to do it?'

'Mr. Cholm, please!' Mr. Terokaw protested. 'We must approach this properly. Kugus, show Mr. Cholm what I'm offering.'

Riquol took the document Kugus held out to him, looked over it. After a moment, he gave it back to Kugus. 'Auris,' he said, 'Mr. Terokaw, as he's indicated, is offering you more money than you would ever be able to spend in your life for the right to cut down your share of the forest. Now ... do you want him to do it?'

'No,' Auris said.

Riquol glanced at Ilf who shook his head. Riquol turned back to Mr. Terokaw.

'Well, Mr. Terokaw,' he said, 'there's your answer. My wife and I don't want you to do it, and Auris and Ilf don't want you to do it. Now ...'

'Oh, come now, Riquol!' Kugus said, smiling. 'No one can expect either Auris or Ilf to really understand what's involved here. When they come of age —'

'When they come of age,' Riquol said. 'they'll again have the opportunity to decide what they wish to do.' He made a gesture of distaste. 'Gentlemen, let's conclude this discussion. Mr. Terokaw, we thank you for your offer, but it's been rejected.'

Mr. Terokaw frowned, pursed his lips.

'Well, not so fast, Mr. Cholm,' he said. 'As I told you, I make no mistakes in business matters. You suggested a few minutes ago that I might contact the other diamondwood farmers on the planet on the subject but predicted that I would have no better luck with them.'

'So I did,' Riquol agreed. He looked puzzled.

'As a matter of fact,' Mr. Terokaw went on, 'I already have contacted a number of these people. Not in person, you understand, since I did not want to tip off certain possible competitors that I was interested in diamondwood at present. The offer was rejected, as you indicated it would be. In fact, I learned that the owners of the Wrake diamondwood farms are so involved in legally binding agreements with one another that it would be very difficult for them to accept such an offer even if they wished to do it.'

Riquol nodded, smiled briefly. 'We realized that the temptation to sell out to commercial interests who would not be willing to act in accordance with our accepted policies could be made very strong,' he said. 'So we've made it as nearly impossible as we could for any of us to yield to temptation.'

'Well,' Mr. Terokaw continued, 'I am not a man who is easily put off. I ascertained that you and Mrs. Cholm are also bound by such an agreement to the other diamondwood owners of Wrake not to be the first to sell either the farm or its cutting rights to outside interests, or to exceed the established limits of cutting. But you are not the owners of this farm. These two children own it between them.'

Riquol frowned. 'What differences does that make?' he demanded. 'Ilf is our grandson. Auris is related to us and our adopted daughter.'

Mr. Terokaw rubbed his chin.

'Mr. Bliman,' he said, 'please explain to these people what the legal situation is.'

Mr. Bliman cleared his throat. He was a tall, thin man with fierce dark eyes, like a bird of prey. 'Mr. and Mrs. Cholm,' he began, 'I work for the Federation Government and am a specialist in adoptive procedures. I will make this short. Some months ago, Mr. Kugus Ovin filed the necessary papers to adopt his niece, Auris Luteel, citizen of Wrake. I conducted the investigation which is standard in such cases and can assure you that no official record exists that you have at any time gone through the steps of adopting Auris.'

'*What?*' Riquol came half to his feet. Then he froze in position for a moment, settled slowly back in his chair. 'What is this? Just what kind of trick are you trying to play?' he said.

His face had gone white.

Ilf had lost sight of Mr. Terokaw for a few seconds, because Uncle Kugus had suddenly moved over in front of the bench on which he and Auris were sitting. But now he saw him again and he had a jolt of fright. There was a large blue and silver gun in Mr. Terokaw's hand, and the muzzle of it was pointed very steadily at Riquol Cholm.

'Mr. Cholm,' Mr. Terokaw said, 'before Mr. Bliman concludes his explanation, allow me to caution you! I do not wish to kill you. This gun, in fact, is not designed to kill. But if I pull the trigger, you will be in excruciating pain for some minutes. You are an elderly man and it is possible that you would not survive the experience. This would not inconvenience us very seriously. Therefore, stay seated and give up any thoughts of summoning help ... Kugus, watch the children. Mr. Bliman, let me speak to Mr. Het before you resume.'

He put his left hand up to his face, and Ilf saw he was wearing a wrist-talker. 'Het,' Mr. Terokaw said to the talker without taking his eyes off Riquol Cholm, 'you are aware, I believe, that the children are with us in the house?'

The wrist-talker made murmuring sounds for a few seconds, then stopped.

'Yes,' Mr. Terokaw said. 'There should be no problem about it. But let me know if you see somebody approaching the area ...' He put his hand back down on the table. 'Mr. Bliman, please continue.'

Mr. Bliman cleared his throat again.

'Mr. Kugus Ovin,' he said, 'is now officially recorded as the parent by adoption of his niece, Auris Luteel. Since Auris has not yet reached the age where her formal consent to this action would be required, the matter is settled.'

'Meaning,' Mr. Terokaw added, 'that Kugus can act for Auris in such affairs as selling the cutting rights on this tree farm. Mr. Cholm, if you are thinking of taking legal action against us, forget it. You may have had certain papers purporting to show that the girl was your adopted child filed away in the deposit vault of a bank. If so, those papers have been destroyed. With enough money, many things become possible. Neither you nor Mrs. Cholm nor the two children will do or say anything that might cause trouble to me. Since you have made no rash moves, Mr. Bliman will now use an instrument to put you and Mrs. Cholm painlessly to sleep for the few hours required to get you off this planet. Later, if you should be questioned in connection with this situation, you will say about it only what certain psychological experts will have impressed on you to say, and within a few months, nobody will be taking any further interest whatever in what is happening here today.

'Please do not think that I am a cruel man. I am not. I merely take what steps are required to carry out my purpose. Mr. Bliman, please proceed!'

Ilf felt a quiver of terror. Uncle Kugus was holding his wrist with one hand and Auris' wrist with the other, smiling reassuringly down at them. Ilf darted a glance over to Auris' face. She looked as white as his grandparents but she was making no attempt to squirm away from Kugus, so Ilf stayed quiet, too. Mr. Bliman stood up, looking more like a fierce bird of prey than ever, and stalked over to Riquol Cholm, holding something in his hand that looked unpleasantly like another gun. Ilf shut his eyes. There was a moment of silence, then Mr. Terokaw said, 'Catch him before he falls out of the chair. Mrs. Cholm, if you will just settle back comfortably...'

There was another moment of silence. Then, from beside him, Ilf heard Auris speak.

It wasn't regular speech but a quick burst of thin, rattling gabble, like human speech speeded up twenty times or so. It ended almost immediately.

'What's that? What's that?' Mr. Terokaw said, surprised.

Ilf's eyes flew open as something came in through the window with a whistling shriek. The two humbugs were in the room, brown blurs flicking here and there, screeching like demons. Mr. Terokaw exclaimed something in a loud voice and jumped up from the chair, his gun swinging this way and that. Something scuttled up Mr. Bliman's back like a big spider, and he yelled and spun away from Meldy Cholm lying slumped back in her chair. Something ran up Uncle Kugus' back. He yelled, letting go of Ilf and Auris, and pulled out a gun of his own. 'Wide aperture!' roared Mr. Terokaw, whose gun was making loud, thumping noises. A brown shadow swirled suddenly about his knees. Uncle Kugus cursed, took aim at the shadow and fired.

'Stop that, you fool!' Mr. Terokaw shouted. 'You nearly hit me.'

'Come,' whispered Auris, grabbing Ilf's arm. They sprang up

from the bench and darted out the door behind Uncle Kugus' broad back.

'Het!' Mr. Terokaw's voice came bellowing down the hall behind them. 'Up in the air and look out for those children! They're trying to get away. If you see them start to cross the road, knock 'em out. Kugus – after them! They may try to hide in the house.'

Then he yowled angrily, and his gun began making the thumping noises again. The humbugs were too small to harm people, but their sharp little teeth could hurt and they seemed to be using them now.

'In here,' Auris whispered, opening a door. Ilf ducked into the room with her, and she closed the door softly behind them. Ilf looked at her, his heart pounding wildly.

Auris nodded at the barred window. 'Through there! Run and hide in the grove. I'll be right behind you . . .'

'Auris! Ilf!' Uncle Kugus called in the hall. 'Wait – don't be afraid. Where are you?' His voice still seemed to be smiling. Ilf heard his footsteps hurrying along the hall as he squirmed quickly sideways between two of the thick wooden bars over the window, dropped to the ground. He turned, darted off towards the nearest bushes. He heard Auris gabble something to the humbugs again, high and shrill, looked back as he reached the bushes and saw her already outside, running toward the shrubbery on his right. There was a shout from the window. Uncle Kugus was peering out from behind the bars, pointing a gun at Auris. He fired. Auris swerved to the side, was gone among the shrubs. Ilf didn't think she had been hit.

'They're outside!' Uncle Kugus yelled. He was too big to get through the bars himself.

Mr. Terokaw and Mr. Bliman were also shouting within the house. Uncle Kugus turned around, disappeared from the window.

'Auris!' Ilf called, his voice shaking with fright.

'Run and hide, Ilf!' Auris seemed to be on the far side of the shrubbery, deeper in the Queen Grove.

Ilf hesitated, started running along the path that led to Sam's sleeping pit, glancing up at the open patches of sky among the treetops. He didn't see the aircar with the man Het in it. He would be circling around the Queen Grove now, waiting for the other men to chase them into sight so he could knock them out with something. But they could hide inside Sam's shell and Sam would get them across the road. 'Auris, where are you?' Ilf cried.

Her voice came low and clear from behind him. 'Run and hide, Ilf!'

Ilf looked back. Auris wasn't there but the two humbugs were loping up the path a dozen feet away. They darted past Ilf without stopping, disappeared around the turn ahead. He could hear the three men yelling for him and Auris to come back. They were outside, looking around for them now, and they seemed to be coming closer.

Ilf ran on, reached Sam's sleeping place. Sam lay there unmoving, like a great mossy boulder filling the pit. Ilf picked up a stone and pounded on the front part of the shell.

'Wake up!' he said desperately. 'Sam, wake up!'

Sam didn't stir. And the men were getting closer. Ilf looked this way and that, trying to decide what to do.

'Don't let them see you,' Auris called suddenly.

'That was the girl over there,' Mr. Terokaw's voice shouted. 'Go after her, Bliman!'

'Auris, watch out!' Ilf screamed, terrified.

'Aha! And here's the boy, Kugus. This way! Het,' Mr. Terokaw yelled triumphantly, 'come down and help us catch them! We've got them spotted . . .'

Ilf dropped to hands and knees, crawled away quickly under the branches of the blue flower thicket and waited, crouched low. He heard Mr. Terokaw crashing through the bushes towards him and Mr. Bliman braying, 'Hurry up, Het! Hurry up!' Then he heard something else. It was the sound the giant greenweb sometimes made to trick a flock of silverbells into fluttering straight toward it, a deep drone which suddenly seemed to be pouring down from the trees and rising up from the ground.

Ilf shook his head dizzily. The drone faded, grew up again. For a moment, he thought he heard his own voice call 'Auris, where are you?' from the other side of the blue flower thicket. Mr. Terokaw veered off in that direction, yelling something to Mr. Bliman and Kugus. Ilf backed farther away through the thicket, came out on the other side, climbed to his feet and turned.

He stopped. For a stretch of twenty feet ahead of him, the forest floor was moving, shifting and churning with a slow, circular motion, turning lumps of deep brown mold over and over.

Mr. Terokaw came panting into Sam's sleeping place, red-faced, glaring about, the blue and silver gun in his hand. He shook his head to clear the resonance of the humming air from his brain. He saw a huge, moss-covered boulder tilted at a slant away from him but no sign of Ilf.

Then something shook the branches of the thicket behind the boulder. 'Auris!' Ilf's frightened voice called.

Mr. Terokaw ran around the boulder, leveling the gun. The droning in the air suddenly swelled to a roar. Two big gray, three-fingered hands came out from the boulder on either side of Mr. Terokaw and picked him up.

'Awk!' he gasped, then dropped the gun as the hands folded him, once, twice, and lifted him towards Sam's descending head. Sam opened his large mouth, closed it, swallowed. His neck and head drew back under his shell and he settled slowly into the sleeping pit again.

The greenweb's roar ebbed and rose continuously now, like a thousand harps being struck together in a bewildering, quickening beat. Human voices danced and swirled through the din, crying, wailing, screeching. Ilf stood at the edge of the twenty-foot circle of churning earth outside the blue flower thicket, half stunned by it all. He heard Mr. Terokaw bellow to Mr. Bliman to go after Auris, and Mr. Bliman squalling to Het to hurry. He heard his own voice nearby call Auris frantically and then Mr. Terokaw's triumphant yell: 'This way! Here's the boy, Kugus!'

Uncle Kugus bounded out of some bushes thirty feet away, eyes staring, mouth stretched in a wide grin. He saw Ilf, shouted excitedly and ran toward him. Ilf watched, suddenly unable to move. Uncle Kugus took four long steps out over the shifting loam between them, sank ankle-deep, knee-deep. Then the brown earth leaped in cascades about him, and he went sliding straight down into it as if it were water, still grinning, and disappeared. In the distance, Mr. Terokaw roared, 'This way!' and Mr. Bliman yelled to Het to hurry up. A loud, slapping sound came from the direction of the stump of the Grandfather Slurp. It was followed by a great commotion in the bushes around there; but that only lasted a moment. Then, a few seconds later, the greenweb's drone rose and thinned to the wild shriek it made when it had caught something big and faded slowly away...

Ilf came walking shakily through the opening in the thickets to Sam's sleeping place. His head still seemed to hum inside with the greenweb's drone but the Queen Grove was quiet again; no voices called anywhere. Sam was settled into his pit. Ilf saw something gleam on the ground near the front end of the pit. He went over and looked at it, then at the big, moss-grown dome of Sam's shell.

'Oh, Sam,' he whispered, 'I'm not sure we should have done it...'

Sam didn't stir. Ilf picked up Mr. Terokaw's blue and silver gun gingerly by the barrel and went off with it to look for Auris. He found her at the edge of the grove, watching Het's aircar on the other side of the road. The aircar was turned on its side and about a third of it was sunk in the ground. At work around and below it was the biggest member of the clean-up squad Ilf had ever seen in action.

They went up to the side of the road together and looked on while the aircar continued to shudder and turn and sink deeper into the earth. Ilf suddenly remembered the gun he was holding and threw it over on the ground next to the aircar. It was swallowed up instantly there. Tumbleweeds came rolling up to join them and clustered around the edge of the circle, waiting. With a final jerk, the aircar disappeared. The disturbed section of earth began to smooth over. The tumbleweeds moved out into it.

There was a soft whistling in the air, and from a Queen Tree at the edge of the grove a hundred and fifty feet away, a diamondwood seedling came lancing down, struck at a slant into the center of the circle where the aircar had vanished, stood trembling a moment, then straightened up. The tumbleweeds nearest it moved respectfully aside to give it room. The seedling shuddered and unfolded its first five-fingered cluster of silver-green leaves. Then it stood still.

Ilf looked over at Auris. 'Auris,' he said, 'should we have done it?'

Auris was silent a moment.

'Nobody did anything,' she said then. 'They've just gone away again.' She took Ilf's hand. 'Let's go back to the house and wait for Riquol and Meldy to wake up.'

The organism that was the diamondwood forest grew quiet

again. The quiet spread back to its central mind unit in the Queen Grove, and the unit began to relax towards somnolence. A crisis had been passed – perhaps the last of the many it had foreseen when human beings first arrived on the world of Wrake.

The only defense against Man was Man. Understanding that, it had laid its plans. On a world now owned by Man, it adopted Man, brought him into its ecology, and its ecology into a new and again successful balance.

This had been a final flurry. A dangerous attack by dangerous humans. But the period of danger was nearly over, would soon be for good a thing of the past.

It had planned well, the central mind unit told itself drowsily. But now, since there was no further need to think today, it would stop thinking . . .

Sam the mossback fell gratefully asleep.

The Dance of the Changer and the Three
by Terry Carr

This all happened ages ago, out in the depths of space beyond
Darkedge, where galaxies lumber ponderously through the
black like so many silent bright rhinoceroses. It was so long
ago that when the light from Loarr's galaxy finally reached
Earth, after millions of light-years, there was no one here to
see it except a few things in the oceans that were too mindlessly busy with their monotonous single-celled reactions to
notice.

Yet, as long ago as it was, the present-day Loarra still remember this story and retell it in complex, shifting wavedances
every time one of the newly-changed asks for it. The wave-
dances wouldn't mean much to you if you saw them, nor I
suppose would the story itself if I were to tell it just as it
happened. So consider this a translation, and don't bother
yourself that when I say 'water' I don't mean our hydrogen-
oxygen compound, or that there's no 'sky' as such on Loarr, or
for that matter that the Loarra weren't – aren't – creatures that
'think' or 'feel' in quite the way we understand. In fact, you
could take this as a piece of pure fiction, because there are
damned few real facts in it – but I know better (or worse),
because I know how true it is. And that has a lot to do with
why I'm back here on Earth, with forty-two friends and co-
workers left dead on Loarr. They never had a chance.

There was a Changer who had spent three life cycles plan-
ning a particular cycleclimax and who had come to the moment of action. He wasn't really named Minnearo, but I'll call
him that because it's the closest thing I can write to approxi-
mate the tone, emotional matrix, and association that were all
wrapped up in his designation.

When he came to his decision, he turned away from the crag
on which he'd been standing overlooking the Loarran ocean,
and went quickly to the personality-homes of three of his best
friends. To the first friend, Asterrea, he said, 'I am going to
commit suicide,' wave-dancing this message in his best festive
tone.

His friend laughed, as Minnearo had hoped, but only for a

241

short time. Then he turned away and left Minnearo alone, because there had already been several suicides lately and it was wearing a little thin.

To his second friend, Minnearo gave a pledge-salute, going through all sixty sequences with exaggerated care, and wavedanced, 'Tomorrow I shall immerse my body in the ocean, if anyone will watch.'

His second friend, Fless, smiled tolerantly and told him he would come and see the performance.

To his third friend, with many excited leapings and boundings, Minnearo described what he imagined would happen to him after he had gone under the lapping waters of the ocean. The dance he went through to give this description was intricate and even imaginative, because Minnearo had spent most of that third life cycle working it out in his mind. It used motion and colour and sound and another sense something like smell, all to communicate descriptions of falling, impact with the water, and then the quick dissolution and blending in the currents of the ocean, the dimming and loss of awareness, then darkness, and finally the awakening, the completion of the change. Minnearo had a rather romantic turn of mind, so he imagined himself recoalescing around the life-mote of one of Loarr's greatest heroes, Krollim, and forming on Krollim's old pattern. And he even ended the dance with suggestions of glory and imitation of himself by others, which was definitely presumptuous. But the friend for whom the dance was given did nod approvingly at several points.

'If it turns out to be half what you anticipate,' said this friend, Pur, 'then I envy you. But you never know.'

'I guess not,' Minnearo said, rather morosely. And he hesitated before leaving, for Pur was what I suppose I'd better call female, and Minnearo had rather hoped that she would join him in the ocean jump. But if she thought of it she gave no sign, merely gazing at Minnearo calmly, waiting for him to go; so finally he did.

And at the appropriate time, with his friend Fless watching him from the edge of the cliff, Minnearo did his final wavedance as Minnearo – rather excited and ill-coordinated, but that was understandable in the circumstances – and then performed his approach to the edge, leaped and tumbled downward through the air, making fully two dozen turns this way and that before he hit the water.

Fless hurried back and described the suicide to Asterrea and Pur, who laughed and applauded in most of the right places, so on the whole it was a success. Then the three of them sat down and began plotting Minnearo's revenge.

– All right, I *know* a lot of this doesn't make sense. Maybe that's because I'm trying to tell you about the Loarra in human terms, which is a mistake with creatures as alien as they are. Actually, the Loarra are almost wholly an energy life-form, their consciousnesses coalescing in each life cycle around a spatial centre which they call a 'life-mote', so that, if you could see the patterns of energy they form (as I have, using a sense filter our expedition developed for that purpose), they'd look rather like a spiral nebula sometimes, or other times like iron filings gathering around a magnet, or maybe like a half-melted snowflake. (That's probably what Minnearo looked like on that day, because it's the suicides and the aged who look like that.) Their forms keep shifting, of course, but each individual usually keeps close to one pattern.

Loarr itself is a gigantic gaseous planet with an orbit so close to its primary that its year has to be only about thirty-seven Earthstandard Days long. (In Earthsystem, the orbit would be considerably inside that of Venus.) There's a solid core to the planet, and a lot of hard outcroppings like islands, but most of the surface is in a molten or gaseous state, swirling and bubbling and howling with winds and storms. It's not a very inviting planet if you're anything like a human being, but it does have one thing that brought it to Unicentral's attention: mining.

Do you have any idea what mining is like on a planet where most metals are fluid from the heat and/or pressure? Most people haven't heard much about this because it isn't a situation we encounter often, but it was there on Loarr, and it was very, very interesting. Because our analyses showed some elements that had been until then only computer-theory – elements that were supposed to exist only in the hearts of suns, for one thing. And if we could get hold of some of them ... Well, you see what I mean. The mining possibilities were very interesting indeed.

Of course, it would take half the wealth of Earthsystem to outfit a full-scale expedition there. But Unicentral hummed for two-point-eight seconds and then issued detailed instructions on just how it was all to be arranged. So there we went.

And there I was, a Standard Year later (five Standard Years ago), sitting inside a mountain of artificial Earth welded on to one of Loarr's 'islands' and wondering what the hell I was doing there. Because I'm not a mining engineer, not a physicist or comp-technician or, in fact, much of anything that requires technical training. I'm a public-relations man; and there was just no reason for me to have been assigned to such a hellish, impossible, god-forsaken, inconceivable, and plain damned *unlivable* planet as Loarr.

But there was a reason, and it was the Loarra, of course. They lived ('lived') there, and they were intelligent, so we had to negotiate with them. Ergo: me.

So in the next several years, while I negotiated and we set up operations and I acted as a go-between, I learned a lot about them. Just enough to translate, however clumsily, the wave-dance of the Changer and the Three, which is their equivalent of a classic folk-hero myth (or would be if they had anything honestly equivalent to anything of ours).

To continue:

Fless was in favour of building a pact among the Three by which they would, each in turn and each with deliberate lack of the appropriate salutes, commit suicide in exactly the same way Minearo had. 'Thus we can kill this suicide,' Fless explained in excited waves through the air.

But Pur was more practical. 'Thus,' she corrected him, 'we would kill *only* this suicide. It is unimaginative, a thing to be done by rote, and Minnearo deserves more.'

Asterrea seemed undecided; he hopped about, sparking and disappearing and reappearing inches away in another colour. They waited for him to comment, and finally he stabilized, stood still in the air, settled to the ground, and held himself firmly there. Then he said, in slow, careful movements, 'I'm not sure he deserves an original revenge. It wasn't a new suicide, after all. And who is to avenge us?' A single spark leaped from him. 'Who is to avenge us?' he repeated, this time with more pronounced motions.

'Perhaps,' said Pur slowly, 'we will need no revenge – if our act is great enough.'

The other two paused in their random wave-motions, considering this. Fless shifted from blue to green to a bright red which dimmed to yellow; Asterrea pulsed a deep ultra-violet.

'Everyone has always been avenged,' Fless said at last. 'What you suggest is meaningless.'

'But if we do something *great* enough,' Pur said; and now she began to radiate heat which drew the other two reluctantly toward her. 'Something which has never been done before, in *any* form. Something for which there can be no revenge, for it will be a *positive* thing – not a death-change, not a destruction or a disappearance or a forgetting, even a great one. A *positive* thing.'

Asterrea's ultra-violet grew darker, darker, until he seemed to be nothing more than a hole in the air. 'Dangerous, dangerous, dangerous,' he droned, moving torpidly back and forth. 'You know it's impossible to ask – we'd have to give up all our life cycles to come. Because a positive in the world...' He blinked into darkness, and did not reappear for long seconds. When he did he was perfectly still, pulsing weakly but gradually regaining strength.

Pur waited till his colour and tone showed that consciousness had returned, then moved in a light wave-motion calculated to draw the other two back into calm, reasonable discourse. 'I've thought about this for six life cycles already,' she danced. 'I must be right – *no* one has worked on a problem for so long. A positive would *not* be dangerous, no matter what the three and four-cycle theories say. It would be beneficial.' She paused, hanging orange in midair. 'And it would be *new*,' she said with a quick spiral. 'Oh, how *new*!'

And so, at length, they agreed to follow her plan. And it was briefly this: On a far island outcropping set in the deepest part of the Loarran ocean, where crashing, tearing storms whipped molten metal-compounds into blinding spray, there was a vortex of forces that was avoided by every Loarra on pain of inescapable and final death-change. The most ancient wave-dances of that ancient time said that the vortex had always been there, that the Loarra themselves had been born there or had escaped from there or had in some way cheated the laws that ruled there. Whatever the truth about that was, the vortex was an eater of energy, calling and catching from afar any Loarra or other beings who strayed within its influence. (For all the life on Loarr is energy-based, even the mindless, drifting foodbeasts – creatures of uniform dull colour, no internal motion, no scent or tone, and absolutely no self-volition. Their

245

place in the Loarran scheme of things is and was literally nothing more than that of food; even though there were countless foodbeasts drifting in the air in most areas of the planet, the Loarra hardly ever noticed them. They ate them when they were hungry, and looked around them at any other time.)

'Then you want us to destroy the *vortex*?' cried Fless, dancing and dodging to right and left in agitation.

'Not *destroy*,' Pur said calmly. 'It will be a *life*-change, not a destruction.'

'Life-change?' said Asterrea faintly, wavering in the air.

And she said it again: '*Life*-change.' For the vortex had once created, or somehow allowed to be created, the Oldest of the Loarra, those many-cycles-ago beings who had combined and split, reacted and changed countless times to become the Loarra of this day. And if creation could happen at the vortex once, then it could happen again.

'But how?' asked Fless, trying now to be reasonable, dancing the question with precision and holding a steady green colour as he did so.

'We will need help,' Pur said, and went on to explain that she had heard – from a windbird, a creature with little intelligence but perfect memory – that there was one of the Oldest still living his first life cycle in a personality-home somewhere near the vortex. In that most ancient time of the race, when suicide had been considered extreme as a means of cycle-change, this Oldest had made his change by a sort of negative suicide – he had frozen his cycle, so that his consciousness and form continued in a never-ending repetition of themselves, on and on while his friends changed and grew and learned as they ran through life-cycle after life-cycle, becoming different people with common memories, moving forward into the future by this method while he, the last Oldest, remained fixed at the beginning. He saw only the beginning, remembered only the beginning, understood only the beginning.

And for that reason his had been the most tragic of all Loarran changes (and the windbird had heard it rumoured, in eight different ways, each of which it repeated word-for-word to Pur, that in the ages since that change more than a hundred hundred Loarra had attempted revenge for the Oldest, but always without success) and it had never been repeated, so that this Oldest was the only Oldest. And for that reason he was important to their quest, Pur explained.

With a perplexed growing and shrinking, brightening and dimming, Asterrea asked, 'But how can he live anywhere near the vortex and not be consumed by it?'

'That is a crucial part of what we must find out,' Pur said. And after the proper salutes and rituals, the Three set out to find the Oldest.

The wavedance of the Changer and the Three traditionally at this point spends a great deal of time, in great splashes of colour and bursts of light and subtly contrived clouds of darkness all interplaying with hops and swoops and blinking and dodging back and forth, to describe the scene as Pur, Fless and Asterrea set off across that ancient molten sea. I've seen the dance countless times, and each viewing has seemed to bring me maddeningly closer to understanding the meaning that this has for the Loarra themselves. Lowering clouds flashing bursts of aimless, lifeless energy, a rumbling sea below, whose swirling depth pulled and tugged at the Three as they swept overhead, darting around each other in complex patterns like electrons playing cat's-cradle around an invisible nucleus. A droning of lamentation from the changers left behind on their rugged home island, and giggles from those who had recently changed. And the colours of the Three themselves: burning red Asterrea and glowing green Fless and steady, steady golden Pur. I see and hear them all, but I feel only a weird kind of alien beauty, not the grandeur, excitement and awesomeness they have for the Loarra.

When the Three felt the vibrations and swirlings in the air that told them they were coming near to the vortex, they paused in their flight and hung in an interpatterned motion-sequence above the dark, rolling sea, conversing only in short flickerings of colour because they had to hold the pattern tightly in order to withstand the already-strong attraction of the vortex.

'Somewhere near?' asked Asterrea, pulsing a quick green. 'Closer to the vortex, I think,' Pur said, chancing a sequence of reds and violets.

'Can we be sure?' asked Fless; but there was no answer from Pur and he had expected none from Asterrea.

The ocean crashed and leaped; the air howled around them. And the vortex pulled at them.

Suddenly they felt their motion-sequence changing, against their wills, and for long moments all three were afraid that it was the vortex's attraction that was doing it. They moved in closer to each other, and whirled more quickly in a still more intricate pattern, but it did no good. Irresistibly they were drawn apart again, and at the same time the three of them were moved toward the vortex.

And then they felt the Oldest among them.

He had joined the motion-sequence; this must have been why they had felt the sequence changed and loosened – to make room for him. Whirling and blinking, the Oldest led them inward over the frightening sea, radiating warmth through the storm and, as they followed, or were pulled along, they studied him in wonder.

He was hardly recognizable as one of them, this ancient Oldest. He was ... not quite energy any longer. He was half matter, carrying the strange mass with awkward, aged grace, his outer edges almost rigid as they held the burden of his congealed centre and carried it through the air. (Looking rather like a half-dissolved snowflake, yes, only dark and dismal, a snowflake weighted with coal-dust.) And, for now at least, he was completely silent.

Only when he had brought the Three safely into the calm of his barren personality-home on a tiny rock jutting at an angle from the wash of the sea did he speak. There, inside a cone of quiet against which the ocean raged and fell back, the winds faltered and even the vortex's power was nullified, the Oldest said wearily, 'So you have come.' He spoke with a slow waving back and forth, augmented by only a dull red colour.

To this the Three did not know what to say; but Pur finally hazarded, 'Have you been waiting for us?'

The Oldest pulsed a somewhat brighter red, once, twice. He paused. Then he said, 'I do not *wait* – there is nothing to wait *for*.' Again the pulse of a brighter red. 'One waits for the future. But there is no future, you know.'

'Not for him,' Pur said softly to her companions, and Fless and Asterrea sank wavering to the stone floor of the Oldest's home, where they rocked back and forth.

The Oldest sank with them, and when he touched down he remained motionless. Pur drifted over the others, maintaining movement but unable to raise her colour above a steady blue-green. She said to the Oldest, 'But you knew we would come.'

'Would come? *Would* come? Yes, and *did* come, and *have* come, and *are* come. It is today only, you know, for me. I will be the Oldest, when the others pass me by. I will never change, nor will my world.'

'But the others have already passed you by,' Fless said. 'We are many life-cycles after you, Oldest – so many it is beyond the count of windbirds.'

The Oldest seemed to draw his material self into a more upright posture, forming his energy-flow carefully around it. To the red of his colour he added a low hum with only the slightest quaver as he said. '*Nothing* is after me, here on Rock. When you come here, you come out of time, just as I have. So now you have always been here and will always be here, for as long as you are here.'

Asterrea sparked yellow suddenly, and danced upwards into the becalmed air. As Fless stared and Pur moved quickly to calm him, he drove himself again and again at the edge of the cone of quiet that was the Oldest's refuge. Each time he was thrown back and each time he returned to dash himself once more against the edge of the storm, trying to penetrate back into it. He flashed and burned countless colours, and strange sound-frequencies filled the quiet, until at last, with Pur's stern direction and Fless's blank gaze upon him, he sank back wearily to the stone floor. 'A trap, a trap,' he pulsed. 'This is it, this is the vortex itself, we should have known, and we'll never get away.'

The Oldest had paid no attention to Asterrea's display. He said slowly, 'And it is because I am not in time that the vortex cannot touch me. And it is because I am out of time that I know what the vortex is, for I can remember myself born in it.'

Pur left Asterrea then, and came close to the Oldest. She hung above him, thinking with blue vibrations, then asked, 'Can you tell us how you were born? – what is creation? – how new things are made?' She paused a moment, and added, 'And what *is* the vortex?'

The Oldest seemed to lean forward, seemed tired. His colour had deepened again to the darkest red, and the Three could clearly see every atom of matter within his energy-field, stark and hard. He said, 'So many questions to ask one question. And he told them the answer to that question.

– And I can't tell you that answer, because I don't know it. No one knows it now, not even the present-day Loarra who are the Three after a thousand million billion life-cycles. Because the Loarra really do become different ... different 'persons', when they pass from one cycle to another, and after that many changes, memory becomes meaningless. ('Try it sometime,' one of the Loarra once wave-danced to me, and there was no indication that he thought this was a joke.)

Today, for instance, the Three themselves, a thousand million billion times removed from themselves but still, they maintain, *themselves*, often come to watch the Dance of the Changer and the Three, and even though it is about them they are still excited and moved by it as though it were a tale never even heard before, let alone lived through. Yet let a dancer miss a movement or colour or sound by even the slightest nuance, and the Three will correct him. (And yes, many times the legended Changer himself, Minnearo, he who started the story, has attended these dances – though often he leaves after the re-creation of his suicide dance.)

It's sometimes difficult to tell one given Loarra from all the others, by the way, despite the complex and subtle technologies of Unicentral, which have provided me with sense filters of all sorts, plus frequency simulators, pattern scopes, special gravity inducers, and a minicomp that takes up more than half of my very tight little island of Earth pasted on to the surface of Loarr and which can do more thinking and analysing in two seconds than I can do in fifty years. During my four years of Loarr, I got to 'know' several of the Loarra, yet even at the end of my stay I was still never sure just who I was 'talking' with at any time. I could run through about seventeen or eighteen tests, linking the sense-filters with the minicomp, and get a definite answer that way. But the Loarra are a bit short of patience and by the time I'd get done with all that whoever it was would usually be off bouncing and sparking into the hellish vapours they call air. So usually I just conducted my researches or negotiations or idle queries, whichever they were that day, with whoever would pay attention to my antigrav 'eyes', and I discovered that it didn't matter much just who I was talking with: none of them made any more sense than the others. They were all, as far as I was and am concerned, totally crazy, incomprehensible, stupid, silly, and plain damn no good.

If that sounds like I'm bitter it's because I am. I've got forty-two murdered men to be bitter about. But back to the unfolding of the greatest legend of an ancient and venerable alien race:

When the Oldest had told them what they wanted to know, the Three came alive with popping and flashing and dancing in the air, Pur just as much as the others. It was all that they had hoped for and more; it was the entire answer to their quest and their problem. It would enable them to create, to transcend any negative cycle-climax they could have devised.

After a time the Three came to themselves and remembered the rituals.

'We offer thanks in the name of Minnearo, whose suicide we are avenging,' Fless said gravely, waving his message in respectful deep-blue spirals.

'We thank you in our own names as well,' said Asterrea.

'And we thank you in the name of no one and nothing,' said Pur, 'for that is the greatest thanks conceivable.'

But the Oldest merely sat there, pulsing his dull red, and the Three wondered among themselves. At last the Oldest said, 'To accept thanks is to accept responsibility, and in only-today, as I am, there can be none of that because there can be no new act. I am outside time, you know, which is almost outside life. All this I have told you is something told to you before, many times, and it will be again.'

Nonetheless, the Three went through all the rituals of thanksgiving, performing them with flawless grace and care – colour-and-sound demonstrations, dances, offerings of their own energy, and all the rest. And Pur said, 'It is possible to give thanks for a long-past act or even a mindless reflex, and we do so in the highest.'

The Oldest pulsed dull red and did not answer, and after a time the Three took leave of him.

Armed with the knowledge he had given them, they had no trouble penetrating the barrier protecting Rock, the Oldest's personality-home, and in moments were once again alone with themselves in the raging storm that encircled the vortex. For long minutes they hung in midair, whirling and darting in their most tightly linked patterns while the storm whipped them and the vortex pulled them. Then abruptly they broke their patterns and hurled themselves deliberately into the heart of the vortex itself. In a moment they had disappeared.

They seemed to feel neither motion nor lapse of time as they fell into the vortex. It was a change that came without perception or thought – a change from self to unself, from existence to void. They knew only that they had given themselves up to the vortex, that they were suddenly lost in darkness and a sense of surrounding emptiness which had no dimension. They knew without thinking that if they could have sent forth sound there would have been no echo, that a spark or even a bright flare would have brought no reflection from anywhere. For this was the place of the origin of life, and it was empty. It was up to them to fill it, if it was to be filled.

So they used the secret the Oldest had given them, the secret those at the Beginning had discovered by accident and which only one of the Oldest could have remembered. Having set themselves for this before entering the vortex, they played their individual parts automatically – selfless, unconscious, almost random acts such as even non-living energy can perform. And when all parts had been completed precisely, correctly, and at just the right time and in just the right sequence, the creating took place.

It was a foodbeast. It formed and took shape before them in the void, and grew and glowed its dull, drab glow until it was whole. For a moment it drifted there, then suddenly it was expelled from the vortex, thrown out violently as though from an explosion – away from the nothingness within – away from darkness and silence into the crashing whipping violence of the storm outside. And with it went the Three, vomited forth with the primitive bit of life they had made.

Outside, in the storm, the Three went automatically into their tightest motion sequence, whirling and blinking around each other in desperate striving to maintain themselves amid the savagery that roiled around them. And once again they felt the powerful pull of the vortex behind them, gripping them anew now that they were outside, and they knew that the vortex would draw them in again, this time forever, unless they were able to resist it. But they found that they were nearly spent; they had lost more of themselves in the vortex than they had ever imagined possible. They hardly felt alive now, and somehow they had to withstand the crushing powers of both the storm and the vortex, and had to forge such a strongly interlinked motion-pattern that they would be able to make their way out of this place, back to calm and safety.

And there was only one way they could restore themselves

enough for that.

Moving almost as one, they converged upon the mindless foodbeast they had just created and they ate it.

That's not precisely the end of the Dance of the Changer and the Three – it does go on for a while, telling of the honours given the Three when they returned, and of Minnearo's reaction when he completed his change by reappearing around the life-mote left by a dying windbird, and of how all of the Three turned away from their honours and made their next changes almost immediately – but my own attention never quite follows the rest of it. I always get stuck at that one point in the story, that supremely contradictory moment when the Three destroyed what they had made, when they came away with no more than they had brought with them. It doesn't even achieve irony, and yet it is the emotional highpoint of the Dance as far as the Loarra are concerned. In fact, it's the *whole* point of the Dance, as they've told me with brighter sparkings and flashes than they ever use when talking about anything else, and if the Three had been able to come away from there *without* eating their foodbeast, then their achievement would have been duly noted, applauded, giggled at by the newly-changed, and forgotten within two life cycles.

And these are the creatures with whom I had to deal and whose rights I was charged to protect. I was ambassador to a planetful of things that would tell me with a straight face that two and two are orange. And yes, that's why I'm back on Earth now – and why the rest of the expedition, those who are left alive from it, are back here too.

If you could read the fifteen-microtape report I filed with Unicentral (which you can't, by the way: Unicentral always Classifies its failures), it wouldn't tell you anything more about the Loarra than I've just told you in the story of the Dance. In fact, it might tell you less, because although the report contained masses of hard data on the Loarra, plus every theory I could come up with or coax out of the minicomp, it didn't have much about the Dance. And it's only in things like that, attitude-data rather than I.Q. indices, psych reports and so on, that you can really get the full impact of what we were dealing with on Loarr.

After we'd been on the planet for four Standard Years, after we'd established contact and exchanged gifts and favours and information with the Loarra, after we'd set up our entire mining operation and had had it running without hindrance for over three years – after all that, the raid came. One day a sheet of dull purple light swept in from the horizon, and as it got closer I could see that it was a whole colony of the Loarra, their individual colours and fluctuations blending into that single purple mass. I was in the mountain, not outside with the mining extensors, so I saw all of it, and I lived through it.

They flashed in over us like locusts descending, and they hit the crawlers and dredges first. The metal glowed red, then white, then it melted. Then it was just gas that formed billowing clouds rising to the sky. Somewhere inside those clouds was what was left of the elements which had comprised seventeen human beings, who were also vapour now.

I hit the alarm and called everyone in, but only a few made it. The rest were caught in the tunnels when the Loarra swarmed over them, and they went up in smoke too. Then the automatic locks shut, and the mountain was sealed off. And six of us sat there, watching on the screen as the Loarra swept back and forth outside, cleaning up the bits and pieces they'd missed.

I sent out three of my 'eyes', but they too were promptly vapourised.

Then we waited for them to hit the mountain itself ... half a dozen frightened men huddled in the comp-room, none of us saying anything. Just sweating.

But they didn't come. They swarmed together in a tight spiral, went three times around the mountain, made one final salute-dip and then whirled straight up and out of sight. Only a handful of them were left behind out there.

After a while I sent out a fourth 'eye'. One of the Loarra came over, flitted around it like a firefly, blinked through the spectrum, and settled down to hover in front for talking. It was Pur – a Pur who was a thousand million billion life cycles removed from the Pur we know and love, of course, but nonetheless still pretty much Pur.

I sent out a sequence of lights and movements that translated, roughly, as 'What the hell did you do that for?'

And Pur glowed pale yellow for several seconds, then gave me an answer that doesn't translate. Or, if it does, the translation is just, 'Because.'

Then I asked the question again, in different terms, and she gave me the same answer in different terms. I asked a third time, and a fourth, and she came back with the same thing. She seemed to be enjoying the variations on the dance; maybe she thought we were playing.

Well ... We'd already sent our distress call by then, so all we could do was wait for a relief ship and hope they wouldn't attack again before the ship came, because we didn't have a chance of fighting them – we were miners, not a military expedition. God knows what any military expedition could have done against energy things, anyway. While we were waiting, I kept sending out the 'eyes', and I kept talking to one Loarra after another. It took three weeks for the ship to get there, and I must have talked to over a hundred of them in that time, and the sum total of what I was told was this:

Their reason for wiping out the mining operation was untranslatable. No, they weren't mad. No, they didn't want us to go away. Yes, we were welcome to the stuff we were taking out of the depths of the Loarran ocean.

And, most importantly: No, they couldn't tell me whether or not they were likely ever to repeat their attack.

So we went away, limped back to Earth, and we all made our reports to Unicentral. We included, as I said, every bit of data we could think of, including an estimate of the value of the new elements on Loarr – which was something on the order of six times the wealth of Earthsystem. And we put it up to Unicentral as to whether or not we should go back.

Unicentral has been humming and clicking for ten months now, but it hasn't made a decision.